THIS
IS
GOMORRAH

THIS IS GOMORRAH

TOM CHATFIELD

HODDER &
STOUGHTON

First published in Great Britain in 2019 by Hodder & Stoughton
An Hachette UK company

1

A CIP catalogue record for this title is available from the British Library

Hardback ISBN 978 1 473 68137 8
Trade Paperback ISBN 978 1 473 68138 5
eBook ISBN 978 1 473 68140 8

Typeset in Plantin Light by Palimpsest Book Production Limited,
Falkirk, Stirlingshire

Printed and bound in Great Britain by Clays Ltd, Elcograf S.p.A.

Hodder & Stoughton policy is to use papers that are natural, renewable
and recyclable products and made from wood grown in sustainable forests.
The logging and manufacturing processes are expected to conform
to the environmental regulations of the country of origin.

Hodder & Stoughton Ltd
Carmelite House
50 Victoria Embankment
London EC4Y 0DZ

www.hodder.co.uk

For my wife, always

Before, they were cousins. Now, they are brothers – bonded in this moment of terror and hope. Nineteen years old, a month between them, yet they are men bestriding the world.

Hamid watches his breath hang in the air. It is cold here, something he once thought impossible. Back home, he assumed Syria was like Egypt in the Indiana Jones movies – hot sand, bright desert light, gratefully grinning locals. Now, this is his icebreaker with the Islamic Republic's more terrified citizenry: pointing to his gloves, miming surprise and saying the word for cold, *barid*, with raised eyebrows. Once they are sure he's not blaming them for the temperature, they always laugh. Nervously.

His unit is fighting to consolidate control of the city. They are winning. Heavy weapons – their side's heavy weapons, brought from Iraq, manned by real soldiers who fought under Saddam – periodically shake the air and then the earth. Hamid has grown up fast. He closes his eyes, and there they are: the limbs lodged in rubble, the blood, the detonated mess of taken life. None of it is as much like a movie as he had hoped.

Yet his own life, much of the time, is good. Violence and comradeship suit him. There are rewards, both expected and unexpected. Drugs and women are plentiful, within sanctioned bounds: narcotics within houses used by troops working the trafficking routes, sex within houses holding women enslaved for the purpose. After some encouragement from more hardened recruits, he has got into both. Hamid, unlike his cousin, is a fighter. Kabir is more accustomed to keyboards than guns.

Then again, the internet is both a priority and a blessing in their war. For Hamid and the other foreigners, there are social media and online gaming sessions, chocolate spread, good winter clothes. They are the special ones: walking adverts for the global groundswell. Before long, he and his brothers from a hundred nations will eat fast food and drive fast cars and pray and shoot well-oiled Kalashnikovs together. They will grow old and honoured in the glow of their victories. Just as soon as they finish capturing this cold, dirty city, blow the shit out of the remaining rebel forces, and sweep across the region.

Today there was a crucifixion. It was his first. Hamid probes his conscience for shock – and his stomach for the sickness he struggled to master at his first beheading – but there is nothing. This may be because the victim's head wasn't mounted on a spike afterwards, but he feels he is making progress. As promised, experience has begun to bring wisdom. If only he could reach the same accommodation with his craving for cigarettes, which are outlawed. Actual tears have filled his eyes only once since his arrival in November, when a young man was given twenty lashes on the street for possessing a pack of Akhtamar Classic. It was unbearable to watch the precious tobacco ground into dust.

Right now, Hamid is on edge, hefting his weapon from hand to hand without being sure where to point it. They are waiting for the signal to advance from their current cover behind a half-destroyed apartment complex on the city's outskirts. Its breeze blocks gape like rotten teeth. In his mind, he enacts a routine that brings comfort at such moments of boredom and fear. He visualizes lighting a Lucky Strike, breathing it in, then cycling the smoke out through his nose to mask the burned and bloodied smell of this place.

Then, suddenly, he is dead.

Hamid's forehead caves in, puckered around a raw hole as the sniper's bullet exits the back of his skull. His body takes a curiously long time to collapse sideways, sprawled like a drunk's onto building dust and asphalt.

Cursing and throwing themselves to the ground, the men beside him try and fail to return fire. Only Kabir doesn't move, staring at the unmoving chest and limbs, the surprised face and weeping skull. This wasn't supposed to happen, a childlike voice in his head whispers. Don't the enemy know what spoil-sports they're being?

More high velocity rounds punch the nearby ground and masonry. Men are screaming. Kabir finally tears his eyes away and squirms towards deeper cover, brandishing his iPhone as he does – capturing a burst of photos of his cousin's corpse. With luck, the right angle will flatter the scene into something enduring.

His training was very clear about this. Every life, every death, is now a message. Just add social media and wait for the shares to begin.

CHAPTER 1

Pro tip: in life as in software, always start with the Frequently Asked Questions. It will stop you looking stupid later.

Here are the top three questions for getting to know Azi Bello. Who the hell is he? What's a darknet? What is wrong with the modern world?

We'll take them in reverse order.

There is little inherently wrong with the planet in this year of our Lord two thousand and fourteen that a medieval peasant wouldn't recognize from the wrong end of famine, rape and pillage. Thanks to a few centuries of unparalleled human ingenuity, everyone now gets to spend their time doing what only a few people used to do: reading, writing, trading, bitching about celebrities. The real novelty, however, resides in the fact that everything from child pornography and drugs to deadly weapons and even deadlier ideologies can be accessed on demand from several billion desks and pockets.

This is what darknets are all about. They're the places you go to get whatever society doesn't want you to get: the internet's midnight zones, hidden in plain sight, accessed through tools that, if you're doing it right, conveniently conceal your identity and location, alongside whoever you're sharing alt-right hard-core Nazi Islamist disinformation porn with. Bad people, good times.

Naturally, the most popular software for doing all this was developed by the US Navy. As some hackers like to mutter, there is nothing the United States government likes more than fucking with global rivals to their industrial military-surveillance complex. What do Chinese dissidents, Iranian freedom-lovers, New Zealand geeks shifting soft drugs across oceans and the North Korean government's discretionary procurement arm have in common? They all use The Onion Router, also known as Tor: an easily downloaded piece of software that will bury every click under dozens of digital relays between anonymous servers. It's like an onion, if onions were world-spanning networks: layer after layer of packed concealment. It has also been known to induce tears.

Anonymity is the theory. In practice, unless a user knows their stuff, they might as well launch a website featuring full name, home address and a flashing GIF reading *NSA please target me!* Being anonymous doesn't make you safe. On the internet, nobody knows you're a dog – but the trail of bone-shaped biscuits leading to your front door permits an educated guess.

Just ask Azi. Despite being a member of the hacking fraternity (very few ladies, rampant and rancid trolling by gender, toilet seats left permanently up) he goes under a version of his own name. AZ. People think it's a pseudonym, because no security-conscious specialist in their right mind would ever, *ever* use anything linked to any aspect of their actual identity online, but it's in fact just two-thirds of the name he got thirty-four years ago, south of south London, in the architectural equivalent of an arsehole, East Croydon.

Depending on what mood you catch Azi/AZ in, sticking so close to his real name is either a double bluff of rare cunning, a badge of pride, a mark of stupidity, or a mixture of all three. A high-functioning fuckup is how Azi usually describes himself. Good with big ideas, bad with little ones.

Today is a good day, because Azi is sitting at his desk eating Nando's finest – half a chicken with chips, dowsed in his own Sriracha hot sauce to the point where he can no longer feel his face – sipping a mug of cold coffee, and pretending to be a neo-Nazi.

Specifically, he is chatting away in a members-only social media group, pretending to be a recent but impressively active member of a global political movement called Defiance. The group is pledged to protect the Western way of life from the mounting threat of Islam, while maybe, just maybe, beating up people of the non-white persuasion and blaming societal ills upon the Transnational Conspiracy of Persecuted Minorities.

Defiance-baiting is a side-project which Azi has been working on for some time now. If pushed, he would describe it as an obsession, but nobody is pushing him, so he pretends it's a hobby. Nazis in general are bad news in good clothes. Smart neo-Nazis, with long-term ambitions involving the ballot box and a charismatic German figurehead affectionately known as Tomi, are a special class of trouble.

A political figure described in chummy abbreviation even by his enemies is worth fearing, Azi reckons – and this one is worse than any posh Brit. There's a serious chance Tomi could play a leading role in the next German government. Unless, of course, someone were anonymously to release detailed and incredibly compromising information about him during the next two months. And wouldn't that be a shame?

As Azi would be the first to admit, his base of operations is not your typical mastermind's lair. From the outside, it looks like an ordinary garden shed. From the inside, it looks like a crummy, cramped garden shed, into which someone long ago wedged an oversized IKEA desk and a pair of folding chairs, followed by the contents of several second-hand computer stores – because this is exactly what Azi did. Van Halen splutters through a pair of hidden speakers. Dismembered laptops, PCs and external hard drives sprawl around three large monitors, garlanded by cables. The only concession to comfort is coffee: a Hario V60 Dripper brewing Union's Revelation Blend on a tiny corner table, its wafting aroma Azi's antidote to the dust-and-ozone fug of constantly running hardware.

Azi himself is sporting an oversized hoody, trainers, jeans distressed by time rather than designer intent, and half a week's worth of stubble. He might pass for a decade younger, borderline handsome, if he shaved and disarrayed his hair more artfully. But that isn't going to happen any time soon. So far as he's concerned, the material world is a largely regrettable series of coincidences. It's what's onscreen that matters.

Exhibit A in this lifestyle philosophy is the standard lamp Azi has been expertly unseeing for over fifteen years, its ragged chintz drooped above his coffee station. Exhibit B is the fact that two of the people he feels closest to – fellow hackers with the handles Milhon and Sigma – might be male or female, cynical teenagers or bored Gen Xers, and located anywhere on Earth that English-speakers and the internet are found together. He has a hunch that they're both female, and a further hunch that Sigma has a soft spot for the enigmatic AZ, but he's savvy enough to know that this says a lot about him and little about reality.

Overall, life is good, even if his alleged career in penetration testing has taken an increasingly distant back seat to neo-Nazi enticement. Three thousand unread emails lurk in Azi's professional ProtonMail inbox, an impatient series of subject lines from his principal employer woven through them. Azi has started to regard these with abstract interest – as if they were a natural phenomenon whose accretion it would be a shame to disturb.

Because this is 2014, and zealots of all flavours have been using the internet since before web browsers were a thing, it is impressively difficult to get the members of groups like Defiance to admit that they would like to see brown, black and – oh why not – Jewish people repatriated with extreme prejudice, and that anyone who disagrees with them is equally expendable. Instead, they spend most of their time reminding each other to look reasonable, to make a strident public case that the elite have lost touch with ordinary decent people's justifiable economic anxieties, and to avoid violence unless they're certain it will be both discreet and decisive.

Azi has thus spent many months befriending some useful idiots who seem likely to tell him what is going on and to initiate him to higher levels within their hierarchy, so long as he, too, comes across as the kind of hearty ideologue who can't help speaking his mind among friends. And he has a sweetener to drop into the mix – a guarantee that he is the real deal. Guns, drugs and darknet contacts. Or, to be precise, the expertly prolonged promise of all of the above – because there are some lines which aren't prudent to cross, let alone turn into a profitable side hustle.

Between bites of wince-inducing chicken, Azi is busy showcasing a cornucopia of banned goods to one of the more evangelical young men of his online acquaintance, a recent British recruit from Blackpool called Gareth. Gareth claims to work in a betting shop and to spend all day watching Zionist front organizations buy up and then sell off assorted properties along his high street. Gareth also talks about international paedophile conspirators taking over children's computers and using their webcams to watch them at home – but, because Azi knows of at least one occasion on which this has actually happened, he has chosen to file that particular concern in a part of his brain marked 'worry about horrible shit like this another time'. It's a compartment that has become alarmingly full in recent months.

So far as Gareth from Blackpool is concerned, Azi isn't Azi. He's a white, strikingly handsome man called Jim. And the story of how Jim came into being spells out the two most important considerations in Azi's philosophy of hacking. First, you need to be so many steps ahead of your opponents that you've basically won before they even notice a battle has started. Second, whatever assumptions or expectations are out there, it's your job to break them. You lie, you cheat, you beg, you borrow, you distract and deceive.

This is the hacker's ethos: taking things apart and then putting them back together your way. You do it for the lulz, the naked curiosity, the chance to make other people look stupid and yourself feel clever. Plus, a bunch of neo-Nazis busy making the world a worse place deserves the mother of all hacks. A dose of righteous truth so vast and compromising that even their mothers will disown them.

CHAPTER 2

Here is how Azi laid his plans.

Eighteen months ago, at the start of 2013, Azi found a dead child. As a rule, the best untruths begin with a truth, which, in this case, meant the name of someone very young, their dates cribbed from a Tooting headstone.

James Denison died on 8 July 1982, at the age of two years and two days. *Dearly loved, forever missed, he sleeps with the angels now.* He was born again on 27 January 2013, in time for his thirty-third birthday, with a new face and a new story told backwards through time.

How is a thirty-two-year-old man called up out of the air? First, Azi sent off for the death and birth certificates. A bit of research – sifting the debris of his mother's life, her maiden name – a few very polite emails and letters, and the Register Office provided the lot. Azi had got his hands on some powerful paper, and so the real work began.

Let's tell a story. It's April 1982, and war is kicking off on a South Atlantic island nobody in Britain had heard about a few weeks earlier. The Argentine invasion of the Falklands is met by a force cobbled together from desperate pride and political expediency, eventually amounting to one hundred and twenty-seven ships. Somehow, by 14 June, the Brits have prevailed, and the Prime Minister is counting her patriotic blessings. These details are important. Accuracy matters with lies you'll be telling for years.

It's late June 1982. A little boy in Streatham, South London, is sick – very sick – and nobody thinks he is getting better. His dad is off somewhere, gone for over a year. His mum is wrecked by work and stress, cleaning in St George's Hospital, her mum helping out when she can, but nothing will rescue this situation, because little boys don't recover from this kind of cancer.

Except, in Azi's new story, this one does. A small box is buried under a stone in Tooting, joined nine years later by mum in a bigger box beside it, but this can safely be ignored. Life goes on.

The 1980s are now in full swing, greed is good, and James Denison is going to school. He moves around a lot, attending places that have since closed, or that have changed beyond recognition. An account registered to James's shiny new Gmail address populates websites and forms with a path winding through primary school, eight GCSEs, A-levels in art, French and maths – and then, to everyone's surprise, a degree from the University of Birmingham. Psychology, lower second class, documented by a certificate purchased online from a service that makes it look better than the real thing.

After his father's death in 1999 – the father who never got in touch, who drank himself into a carefully researched grave in Coventry – James is an orphan, on the cusp of adulthood. His student life makes no ripples. Time passes. The millennial wave breaks and subsides, the world's disquiet turns digital, terrorist-haunted, muttering its fear on loop. James is now going by Jim, and Jim is starting to show a denser data trail: past employers, residences, a stalled career in office accessory sales. He travels a lot, but only in the UK: major cities, big enough for anonymity. He is nobody, but he's a nobody you can look up.

It takes Jim a long time to get into the social media revolution, but once he does he is like a new man. He has a face that's made for media, his thinning hair bleached blonde, his angular cheeks and chin lovingly blended from stock images by Azi. Jim looks good for his age. If you squint – and if you grew up watching television in the late 1990s – he looks a bit like Spike from 'Buffy'. Handsome people attract more attention, but they also command trust and respect, and Azi is only too glad to cash in some of that white male currency for his own purposes.

11

On Facebook, Jim has one hundred and twenty-three friends who also don't exist. They talk about politics, football, food, music. They're bots: algorithms shouting at algorithms, following, liking, regurgitating borrowed words. Azi reckons there's only one way to tell bots and people apart online, and that's that robots actually pay attention to what other robots are saying. In fact, the bots' appetite for relentlessly targeted banter is a winning strategy all round – responses without learning, repetition without understanding, the perfection of an echo chamber in which everything is said, and nothing is heard.

As for Jim, his politics have turned a nationalistic flavour of libertarian. He hates outsiders meddling in this country that hasn't cherished him. His attitude to women can be divided into three categories: those he wants to protect, those he wants to teach a lesson, and those who need a good seeing to. The boundaries between these categories are not strictly patrolled. Jim is angry about almost everyone it is possible to refer to as 'them'. He is tailor-made for Defiance.

Actual people start following Jim, start getting in touch: kindred spirits. On 6 July 2013, over sixty people wish him happy birthday – and a quarter of these people actually exist. Behind the scenes, Azi is busily crafting details beyond expectation. Content flows across Facebook, Twitter, Instagram, Reddit, LinkedIn. Less is farmed out to bots, more is written by Azi himself as he steps into this second skin, tightening it across his own.

In August 2013, Jim starts to buy bitcoins with a credit card that can't be tracked. He runs an old laptop with the hacker's operating system of choice, Kali Linux, on it. He has a fake postal address in an empty building, where mail is collected irregularly from an empty hall. He uses the Silk Road marketplace on the Tor darknet to procure the final pieces in his personal puzzle: a driving licence and passport, faked to a good enough standard to fool expert eyes (fooling expert machines is another matter).

Jim exists. The world looks, and there he is. Weapons, drugs, they're all his for the asking. An intimate knowledge of these things is necessary for Jim to become who Azi needs him to be. It's easy if you know where to look in the darkness, in the place that understands you have a right to obtain whatever you can afford. One ounce of marijuana, Caramello: $215. One gram of cocaine, Colombian fishscale: $97. One gram of MDMA, white Mitsubishi: $37. OxyContin by the ten-pack: $248. One pack of Adderall: a wallet-friendly $6. All prices clearly stated alongside today's bitcoin conversion rates, seller ratings, user reviews and feedback. Capitalism loves an honest marketplace, and this is one of the few places Amazon won't be disrupting any time soon.

Other people behind false faces chat with Jim for hours about weapons, hacks, movies, politics, who they would most like to fuck, for how long, and with what tools. Jim and Azi play their parts, and it's amazing to Azi what you can say when it comes out of somebody else's mouth. Whores and faggots and buttholes, fucking and fisting and murder and suicide; wanking and weeping; tits and arses. Memes involving cartoon characters cracking Holocaust gags, pulling in a younger crowd. Azi thought he was a pretty cynical guy, but with every conversation, he is learning new things he doesn't much like about other people, and himself.

Some days, it feels like the filth has lodged behind Azi's eyeballs, tainting him with stains no shower can shift. On other days, worse days, he barely notices the friction between life and screen.

It's September 2013. Jim now claims to sell a few items as well as buying. His reputation is becoming solid, backed by carefully choreographed actions and evidence. He's becoming trustworthy – and trust is the killer app when it comes to twenty-first-century tech. Any script kiddie can hack machines. You can download ransomware and set it running armed with little more than a search engine and contempt for humanity. What Azi does is hack minds, faith, belief. He fools the world into whispering him its secrets.

October, November, December, a new year is born. The

face on the fake passport and driving licence, handsome with its perfect jawline, is easier to find and to believe in than Azi's own. Jim has friends on Facebook, likes on Instagram, endorsements on LinkedIn: places Azi doesn't exist in. He is a shadow, distant behind the noise.

The world trusts few things more deeply than appearances. And this is just as well – because Azi is counting upon its ignorance. Jim is tall, white and drunk on the superiority of his race. Azi is light brown, lean, running a pavement circuit most nights, until his mind has settled enough for sleep. When Azi hits the 2 a.m. streets, people either step fast to avoid him or ask if they can buy drugs. When Jim struts his stuff on social media, ordinary decent citizens line up to applaud. Jim and him, they're a perfect twenty-first-century team.

What I want, types Gareth from Blackpool, movingly, *is a fat Asian chick to let me cum on her face.* Jim commiserates. Azi swears under his breath, chews a last cooling mouthful of chicken, and tries to turn the conversation towards more practical matters. *U see that thing I wrote?*

Azi knows that Gareth saw it. Everyone saw it, because by the standards of the group it was a masterwork to stand alongside *Don Quixote*, *War and Peace* and *The Da Vinci Code*: a rhapsody to the white, bright future coming their way once Defiance makes its strength felt.

Gareth turns serious for a moment. *Your the man Jim gonna stand up for whats right.* Azi can almost see the tears of patriotic pride streaking Gareth's cheeks, and reaches for a matching solemnity. *Someone got to say it right lol, someone got to tell truth about kike fags.* Azi stares at the screen and, nauseatingly, catches himself feeling pretty proud of his composition. He came up with four hundred words of barely coded fascist invective, drawing inspiration from a noted white supremacist style guide that included such gems as 'multiple enemies can be confusing, so always keep it simple and blame the Jews' and 'it's okay to say that Jew feminist bitches need raping as long as you don't threaten to do it yourself.' Jim's final few reflections on traditional Christian values resonated especially well with Britain's core Defiance outposts.

Azi draws breath, types a fond farewell – *later u wanker lol* – and logs off. It's almost time. Gareth and others have made introductions, discreet recommendations. Jim checks out on paper, and the organization's more senior members have become aware that he has some tech skills, ways to get hold of things, a lot of issues he doesn't want amicably resolved. He's sent them scans of his documents, his history, doctored images of his attendance at rallies. He's legit.

Another few weeks. That's all Azi needs. That's how long he has to keep going.

CHAPTER 3

Like mountaineers, hackers take on challenges simply because they're there. The more precipitous the target, the better, with added kudos if you're the first person to plant your flag. Azi has pulled off several firsts in his time, but a personal favourite remains the casino he and Milhon cracked wide open via a fish tank.

Milhon has a special interest in gambling tech: she's told Azi more than even he cares to know about the industry's inner vicissitudes, and she was the one who suggested the target. But it was he who zeroed in on the vulnerability: one born not from the usual vectors of outdated software, disgruntled staff or sloppy networking, but from the casino's hunger for shiny new toys.

The fish tank in question was extremely shiny. Its fifty thousand litres of water were home to five hundred tropical fish, including two hammerhead sharks, plus a great deal of painstakingly grown coral and one sunken pirate ship. It girdled the casino's entrance in living blue, inducing the kind of child-like wonder designed to make losing lots of money feel fun. The fish tank also employed the very latest in water-monitoring sensors – which, Azi delightedly discovered, were about ten years behind the very latest of everything else in security terms.

It had evidently never occurred to either the people making or purchasing a really big, incredibly gaudy fish tank that someone might assault their system – or that it might be a bad idea to operate its sensors via a computer connected to the casino's main network. It was an open door, just waiting to be pushed.

From the comfort of his shed, Azi crept into the sensors' tiny minds in the guise of a water oxygenation crisis – and from there into everything else. He and Milhon worked through the night, debating the casino's comeuppance, steering clear of anything as crude as criminality. By the next morning, every screen in the building was advising visitors that today's gambling came with a money-back guarantee and two free fish. Forums and message boards across the world were alight for weeks with talk of AZ's latest triumph.

This was back in 2012: the early days of the Internet of Things, before scammers started to hijack vulnerable devices in their hundreds of thousands. These days, thanks to the assumption that connecting everything and anything to the internet is a Good Idea, the world is a wasteland of under-secured 'smart' devices, including televisions, showers, fridges, washing machines, printers, plug sockets and children's toys. Azi has a rule of thumb when it comes to this particular vision of the future. If someone describes an internet-connected fridge as anything other than a futile blot on the technological landscape, they're talking out of their arse.

Azi isn't sure if he has become more cynical in the last few years, or just clearer about the stuff that makes him angry: strong people kicking the metaphorical shit out of weak people, big companies exploiting the metaphorical shit out of everything they get their hands on, London's wallet-warping gentrification failing in any way to enhance Croydon's town centre beyond a choice of Starbucks or Costa. What Azi does know is that he loves a challenge – and that a challenge with the fringe benefit of disrupting racist pricks is almost impossible to resist.

The neo-Nazis remain poised to give him admin privileges but, until they do, all is quiet on the white Western front – except for the banter his alter ego needs to post several times a week.

Then, out of the blue, a new request arrives. And it comes from a familiar source.

Hey AZ u up for a challenge? Help me out?

Azi grins. Sigma is welcome to distract him any time.

Always for u, Sigma. Time to put on our capes, DDoS against injustice?

Not this time. Looking for a serious favour. Fair warning: it's dark in there. Fine by me if you run a mile.

AZ and Sigma have been hanging out for a year, give or take, but it feels longer. Time is different, online. Intensity matters more than duration – and they've been through a lot. Distributed Denial-of-Service attacks, conducted and defended against. Spammers and bot-herders brought to their knees. Civil unrest facilitated. Child pornographers exposed. Pop cultural references traded at whim. In as much as he trusts anyone, Azi trusts Sigma to be what her actions suggest – skilled, reliable, idealistic on the near side of fanatical. She's also unlikely to say she's in trouble unless she really, really means it. He hesitates only long enough to seem serious.

For u, sure. I'm going nowhere. Send and share. How bad can it be?

This last question is bravado, because they both know it has only one honest answer. No matter how bad you can imagine it being, there's already something worse out there. When people think they can get away with anything, they try to get away with everything. That's the rule.

You asked for it. This one's bad news for the world, and worse news for me. Don't take too long.

Azi takes a deep breath, pours himself a fresh coffee and positions his cursor over the link Sigma has just sent. Outside his shed's one window, unwatched, the last twilight sinks towards darkness.

Investigating Sigma's research safely means hopping into a virtual machine – a simulated computer running inside the real one, identical so far as software is concerned, but without access to anything that could be assaulted or subverted. It's like, Azi always thinks, putting someone inside a prison that looks the same as their house while they're sleeping: until they start rattling the windows, there's no way to tell the difference.

A dozen files unzip: far fewer than he expected. At the top is a text file created by Sigma, presumably containing her conclusions. Azi leaves it for last. He wants to form his own first impressions.

The next file turns out to be a PDF of the special Ramadan edition of a propaganda magazine from the Islamic Republic. It's shockingly inoffensive, given its subject matter: the format bland and glossy, the tone relentlessly proselytizing. Articles alternate between scriptural justifications for jihad, heroic depictions of warriors, and idyllic images of daily life in the Republic itself. It's almost dull, if you ignore the incitements to murder.

Much more entertaining are the next five files: email and message logs containing frustrated exchanges between the magazine's editors and their superiors. Halfway through an especially irate multilingual debate about their audience's level of education (*make it simpler*, seems to be the basic message, *because many foreign brothers are idiots*), Azi realizes what he's dealing with.

The files belong to a famous dump of documents released in mid-2013 from inside the Islamic Republic. The assumption at the time was that they came from a disaffected insider. Various security services (alongside every curious freelancer in the business) extensively probed them for revelations before deeming them minor news: useful only for sarcastic meme-making about a terrorist state's internal wrangles. Azi went through a few himself, fascinated by the details it was possible to infer from Microsoft Word version histories. Then he moved on to Jim, neo-Nazis and the incremental abandonment of paid work.

The last few files in Sigma's collection, however, are different. At first, Azi can't see why anyone would be interested. All his screen shows is some incomprehensible junk, presumably encrypted, followed by a brief comma-separated list of names and numbers. Sardar Kerr, 475000. Mahmud Harrison, 850000. Ziad Hussein, 1255000. And so on. Why do some of them feel familiar?

A minute, then he figures it out. They were all featured in the magazine he's just been scrolling through: dead soldiers, snipers, suicide bombers singled out for praise. In total, the comma-separated document lists fifty names. He double checks, dashing between search boxes. Each of them died at some point in the previous year, and each of them is accompanied by a six- or seven-figure number.

Picking up speed, conscious that time may be short, Azi opens the final few files. These are different again. They look official, gathered and combined from a variety of sources: electoral roles, telephone directories, public record offices. This must be something Sigma has put together herself, over many weeks. Why?

On impulse, Azi brings up another search box and starts typing. Sardar Kerr. Mahmud Harrison. There are multiple hits for each name, appended to page after page of official documentation: images, contact details, up-to-date links. Sigma has got hold of scans of things that you don't just find lying around, and meticulously cross-referenced them with her earlier research. French and German passports, names, addresses. The names are different on the official documents, but the faces are the same – and, as Azi keeps looking, the connection finally becomes clear.

Fifty Islamic martyrs have returned from the grave. Their deaths were widely publicized. Yet the conclusion her research asks him to believe is that this was nothing but cover – and that they have been quietly embedded in the heart of Europe. It's absurd. Yet she has provided the links, connections to her evidence in government databases, electoral roles – the stuff that even his own expertly crafted alter-ego, Jim, doesn't have. Azi types some of the new names into a variety of official websites, one at a time. They're real.

He pauses. It's possible she has somehow faked what he's seeing. But what purpose would that serve? And what about the six-figure numbers beside each name? They can only mean one thing. Money. Yet even top-quality fake passports and identities are purchased for tens rather than hundreds of thousands of dollars. What kind of facility would a terrorist state be prepared to pay over a million dollars per person for – and how could even the best fakes match the biometrics now linked as standard to genuine identities?

If everything Sigma has sent is what it seems, the fifty fake identities are effectively genuine – indistinguishable from the real deal. The Islamic Republic shouldn't have access to this kind of expertise. Nobody should – because it means some of the world's secure and sensitive systems have been compromised, and the results sold on the blackest of black markets. And nobody has noticed a thing.

Finally, Azi opens the file Sigma herself created. It's only a few lines long, but it jolts him back in his seat.

The names, the money, the cause. Do you see what I see? They're onto me. I don't know who to trust, AZ. They're close. This is Gomorrah, I'm sure of it.

Gomorrah. A name rumoured at the edges of the most twisted forums: a place the worst people dream of visiting. A punchline to jokes about the stuff no darknet will sell you. Everyone knows what they got up to in Sodom, but what happened in Gomorrah? *Brimstone and fire. The smoke of the country went up as the smoke of a furnace.* Those are the Bible's last words on the matter, but out there in the darkness there's much more to be said. A marketplace for martyred souls, for life and death. The only place either of them knows that might have sold what she's found to a terrorist state.

It's an hour since Azi opened Sigma's files. His coffee is cold, the city night is a faint din of cars, trains, voices, sirens. The screen waits for Azi's reply.

Okay, I see it. I see where you're coming from. How can you be sure? Where did the list come from – the link that holds it all together? Who says this isn't fiction, disinformation, someone else's idea of a joke?

Sigma replies instantly, at the speed of speech.

I don't know if I should tell you. Not yet, not until you know what you're dealing with. I'm on the run.

Oh shit. For real?

Exposed. Cover blown. Taking a free Wi-Fi ride as I type.

How bad is it?

I'm alive, so they can't know where I am yet. I wanted you to see it, AZ. Question is, can I trust you?

You know I'm good.

I know AZ. But this is my life, this is *me* we're talking about. So I'm asking – can I trust *you*? Because pretty soon I think I'll need a real friend. Offscreen. I want to meet.

Azi doesn't reply. This isn't the kind of chat he should be having – not if he values the breath in his body. Past a certain point, there's no such thing as trust. This is that point. He has a notion that Sigma is a British woman, much as she seems to believe he's a British man. But he's equally aware that 'she' could be a sweaty bloke eating Doritos in his underwear trying to mess with AZ's mind – and that is just one among ten thousand possibilities, none of which he can rule out. Real life is off the table.

He looks down at his hands, taking a moment to type and retype his reply. He tries not to imagine whatever might be about to happen to her.

If I can help, I will. But no names, no details. No meetings. Once you take it offscreen, I'm no hero.

A pause at her end.

Cheers, AZ. Can't expect more. Stay safe. Drop me a line if you change your mind. Gotta run. Literally.

Azi exhales. He could start digging. He's itching to stick his nose where it doesn't belong. Sigma has earned his help and he wants to trust her – to follow their connection where it leads. But he has rules and following them is the only way to stay safe. Hedge everything, trust no-one. If necessary, watch a few old episodes of 'The X-Files' to get in the mood.

Whether true, untrue or somewhere in between, this has peril written all over it – not to mention the serious prospect of physical harm. Azi Bello hovers a last finger over the keyboard, pauses, then clicks. The messages vanish.

Five minutes pass. He douses a new filter of ground coffee with freshly-boiled water, logs in as Jim and contemplates a last update for the day – a homophobic rant, perhaps, for variety.

Then someone raps three times on the door of Azi's shed.

CHAPTER 4

Azi slams shut one of several open laptops that are running in parallel to his other systems. This is one of the kill switches he has engineered to lock and encrypt every device on his networks. The screens on his desk turn blank. A scattered selection of phones and tablets buzz then fall silent. Even the music stops.

At the same time, significantly less efficaciously, he swivels in his seat with enough force to hurtle cold coffee across the shed in a centrifugal wave. The shed is just ten by six feet and every non-coffee-making surface is choked with digital detritus, so this move wrecks several hundred pounds' worth of exposed circuitry. This doesn't immediately bother Azi, however, because he's too busy staring at the smartly dressed woman who has appeared in his now-open doorway and is regarding him, her arms folded, as if he's a specimen in a petting zoo.

'I told them you'd spill your coffee, Azi. But this really is quite a mess.'

She has the sort of clipped English accent and sleekly bobbed hair that Azi associates with news anchors – if news anchors also conveyed an effortless impression of don't-even-think-about-messing-with-me menace. Clearly, what's called for is an assertion of his preparedness and general adequacy to this situation. Equally clearly, he has neither the means nor the will to achieve this.

'Who are you? What are you doing in my house? I mean, my shed. I mean—'

Azi starts to stand up, reaches for a handful of additional words that his throat mangles into grunts, then takes the executive decision to sit down again and close his eyes in the hope that things will go back to normal if he can't see the world for a while. Unfortunately, he can still hear.

'Azi Bello, it's a pleasure to meet you at last. Honestly, we love your work. The thing with the fish tank, your recent infiltrations among small-fry neo-Nazis. But now you've reached the point of intervention, because the request that just landed on your desk is of very particular interest to myself and my colleagues.'

Azi pushes one hand through his hair and swallows. Hard.

'And what jurisdiction are you working in, exactly?'

Even as he says the words, he thinks he knows. There aren't many things that earn a hacker this level of attention – and he's not into any of them. Except, since about an hour ago, for the big 'T'.

His system is secure, he's sure. Which means they must have been watching him some other way. And they must have been watching for a while. Yet the first he heard about anything terrorism-related was from Sigma, just now, so they must have been watching *him* because of *her*. And this suggests that several of his worst-case scenarios are playing out in parallel.

By now, Azi's mind and pulse are racing. Didn't Sigma's message suggest that she was on the run from a bunch of people with violence in mind? So mightn't this assault upon his Fortress of Solitude be nothing whatsoever to do with officialdom, and everything to do with some well-spoken professionals in the interrogation, torture and body-disposal business? On which note, a few measured words seem anxious to emerge from his mouth . . .

'Oh fuck oh fuck oh fuck please don't kill me. I don't know anything, I swear! I mean, I'll tell you everything I know. Which isn't much. Oh shit. I'm about to die, aren't I? In my own shed!'

'No, not quite.'

'But you'd say that even if you were going to kill me, wouldn't you?'

The woman sighs, pulls in a short breath, then deftly unfolds Azi's spare chair and sits in front of him, legs crossed at the ankles like she's the Duchess of Cambridge watching a parade of veterans and schoolchildren. Her face is very close to his but, given the space, that could be as much by necessity as by design.

'Azi Bello, you need to stop talking and start listening. You fucked up, and I'm here to tell you what is going to happen next. Don't even think about arguing, trying to leave, or doing anything other than offering your conspicuously docile participation in this conversation.'

In the absence of alternatives, Azi does as he is told. The woman smiles. It's not a nice smile, but neither is it obviously homicidal. He smiles back. He can smell coffee drying on his clothes. *Why does coffee smell so good when you're brewing it, then so repellent later on? Is she as repulsed by the smell as him? Should he offer her a cup of coffee?* Perhaps he's just trying very, very hard not to think about what is happening.

'My name is Anna. Now that we're sitting down calmly, the people watching us from inside a van not far from here are going to be a little bit happier. They will stay that way for as long as you sit, nod and listen. Do you understand?'

Azi sits, nods and listens. *Think*, his brain mutters. *Think. Think. You're in shock, you're panicking. Don't do that. Breathe, pause. Make eye contact. Say something.* He moves to sip his coffee, then remembers he recently threw it across the room. So he sips the rim of his empty mug instead. *Smooth.*

'I get it,' Anna says. 'You're wondering what I know, why I'm here. What you can say without digging an even deeper grave for yourself.'

He winces, and she sighs again.

'Poor choice of phrase. Nobody is going to kill anyone – not if I can help it, anyway. You have no idea how lucky you are that this meeting is happening in such a congenial setting. I'm not even here to arrest you. I'm here because you are going to do something for me.'

'Okay. Sure. Do you want some coffee? I was just making some when you . . . knocked.'

'How kind. Don't get up, I'll pour it myself.'

She does so, turning without rising from her seat. Her movements are smooth and effortless – as if she knows the interior of the shed intimately. As she probably does. His voice catching, Azi skirts towards whatever life-dismantling revelations have just walked into his shed.

'How did you find me?'

'That's what everyone asks first. The answer is always the same. There's no way in hell I'm telling you. We've known about AZ for years but finding the connections was what mattered. Between AZ and Sigma. Between AZ and Azi Bello. I will say that part wasn't easy, thanks to your admirable professionalism. But—'

'But?'

'Clever people are always stupid, in their own way. Your sentimental attachment to this place let you down. The house, the garden, the shed. We've been indulging in a little old-fashioned surveillance. Given that you're as amateurish at physical security as you are good at the digital stuff, we opted for a couple of high-res pinhole cameras in your roof. It worked a treat.' That smile again.

'In my roof.' Azi looks up, as if correctly identifying the roof might win him some brownie points.

'Yes, in your roof. Directly above your desk. Why bother assaulting a well-defended information system if you can record the operator's every click and keystroke?' She shrugs.

'Well, I wish I'd thought of that.'

'Quite. We have everything, logged, registered, reproduced. All your little secrets.'

There is a barely suppressed laugh in Anna's voice and Azi's brain dives to the pit of his stomach, pausing to whisper *you are so fucked right now but don't worry, I'll be back with a cunning plan just as soon as I've dealt with the very serious business of ensuring you don't shit your pants.*

'We know everything about you, Azi, or at least everything we need to know. Most of it is good, much of it is a little worrying. And a few bits, I'm sure you know which, are so impressive that we couldn't afford to throw you into the warm embrace of the legal system even if we wanted to. Even though certain friends of ours would be delighted to see that happen, on both sides of the Atlantic.'

Sooner than expected, his brain returns with some coherent sentences.

'Okay. Let me see if I get this. You're not going to lock me up. You're sitting here drinking coffee when you could be bundling me into the back of a windowless van. So this must be a pretty big deal.'

Azi tails off. It turns out that knowing what people won't do is not a good guide to what is actually going to happen.

'What do you need from me? Why do you care about Sigma so much?'

'There are things I can tell you, and others I cannot. Please don't waste my time trying to find out about the second category. Yes, we are very interested in the person calling herself Sigma. We have been waiting months in the hope that she would, eventually, come to you – that she would do what she has just done, and ask for your help. Unfortunately, you have told her that you're not willing to get out from behind your keyboard. But don't worry, we're going to change that.'

'Excuse me?'

'You're going to send Sigma a message. Right now. Saying that you want to meet.'

This is so far from anything Azi expected that he momentarily forgets to be terrified.

'Why would I do that? Why would you want me to do that?'

'Remember what I just told you about questions? I'm going to make this nice and simple, Azi. This young woman – and yes, she is a woman – is extremely important to us, and it is our intention to use you to get to know her a little bit better. You're a valuable asset. How does that feel?'

'Gomorrah. That's what this is all about.'

'I don't want to hear you say that out loud again. Ever. You have no idea what you're dealing with. If they were sitting here instead of me, you would have minutes to live. And trust me, they wouldn't be happy ones. Munira Khan. That's her name. She'll tell you, I'm sure. She's getting desperate – and you are about to be the only good thing that has happened to her in a long time. That is all you need to know, for now.'

'No. No way. I don't do entrapment.' Until the words come out of his mouth, Azi hasn't realized he feels strongly about this. Whoever Sigma is, she deserves a better friend than him – even if his claim to the moral high ground is pretty tenuous. Anna looks at him steadily, then shifts her tone towards something almost conspiratorial.

'Azi, we are on the same side. The people we are attempting to stop are worse than the infants you've been baiting, the ones playing at white supremacy from their bedrooms. These are the people your kindergarten Nazis dream about going to for lessons. We are trying to save Munira – and I'll be able to tell you more about who "we" are later. Frankly, I'm making quite a show of faith by asking you to help us like this. I know you like to think of yourself as a good guy. This is your chance to make a difference. Here.'

Without fanfare, Anna reaches into her jacket pocket and hands him a pack of papers. There's one line typed on the first page. *Victoria Station, tomorrow, 10 a.m.* Azi opens his mouth, then closes it. Nothing he says will make things better, but he has a feeling they can still get considerably worse. Anna taps the desk.

'That's where and when you will set up the meeting. We don't know where she is, exactly, but we're confident she'll come to you. We fight faith with faith, these days. The most precious information lives inside people's heads. And, as you know all too well, the most secure message is the one that passes through no technology at all. Voices and faces, handshakes and crowded public spaces.'

With a last suck on his mug, Azi summons his strength.

'So, what? You've got enough on your surveillance system to send me to prison if I don't help you out. And you're sitting there, drinking my coffee, expecting me to nod and say thank you for the opportunity to join Her Majesty's secret service, or whoever you are, instead of serving at her pleasure? How do I know you're not going to kill Sigma on sight? How do I know we're not both dead the moment we meet?'

Anna shrugs. 'You don't. It doesn't matter, because I'm not

offering you a choice. You are going to pay attention to everything we tell you and do everything in your power to help us out. You saw what Sigma sent. It's real, and we are the people trying to stop it. All things considered, you should be thanking me. Not least because I told them to leave you a little something in your bank accounts.'

Azi's head shoots up in alarm. 'Excuse me?'

'They wanted to empty them out – but I said you could be trusted enough to be left with a little something. You'll be reimbursed in due course and, in the meantime, we don't want you too well-resourced. Consider it non-invasive proof of how serious we are. Then consider all the other ways we could have proved this.'

A silence falls as Azi looks around at the place that's been the heart of his life for over two decades. The peeling band posters. The ancient memes he made into postcards. Lego Gandalf, guarding the server rack. To a stranger's eyes, it must all look pretty pathetic. That's the trouble with getting out of the habit of seeing things: it doesn't stop the world looking back.

'And if I do say no?' he asks. 'What if I suggest to Munira, if she does agree to meet me and that's who she really is, that we're both in a shitload of trouble and the best thing we can do is run for our lives?'

The woman whose name might be anything but Anna gives him a lovely smile and reaches out across the table to shake his hand.

'We both know you won't do that. It's been such a pleasure to meet you, Azi. My colleague will join you shortly, and then I'd suggest taking a shower. The smell of coffee is really quite unpleasant.'

And with that, she walks out.

CHAPTER 5

It's as though Kabir's mind took a video of the moment and can't stop showing it. His personal YouTube channel, playing on loop: the collapse of his cousin's face into something else, the body falling, and then falling again, and then falling again into the dirt. Waking and sleeping, Kabir imagines a sniper's eye picking him out through its scope, tracking his head in close-up as one finger hovers over the trigger. An itch travels between his forehead and the nape of his neck, the presentiment of a bullet. His cousin's face flips from life to death, and round they go again. His boss gave him some pills to help him sleep, which make things a little better, although he sometimes struggles to rise for dawn prayers.

They had done everything together, up until that point. From Britain to Syria via Turkey, pretending they were just package holidaymakers until a bus, then taxis, then local handlers brought them into border territory and across. Recruitment was everything they had hoped, as well as some things they hadn't thought to fear: the soul-sapping exhaustion of boot camp, the pedantry of doctrines whose defiance meant death, the fear etched into everyday life. In the face of this, they made each other brave, relished the privileges of power and hatched plans involving marriage permits and fair-skinned virgins.

Then one of them lived and one of them died, and everything was different.

Yet his cousin's death was also the making of him. With no camera to hand, Kabir had had the presence of mind to capture everything on his iPhone – and the people in charge like that kind of thinking. It looked authentic, gritty, personal. It made the BBC news. Martyrdom plus going viral is almost as good as living. Sometimes it's better, if it brings more recruits in the battle for hearts and minds.

Back in England, Kabir had vaguely considered becoming an audio-visual support tech, and had done lights and sounds for friends' club nights. Out here, he is now a confirmed and startlingly well-paid member of a mobile media unit, whose job description bears little resemblance to the classic jihadi role. With Raqqa secure, he traverses the Islamic Republic's local environs, looking for human interest and struggling to meet his Key Performance Indicators.

Each day, the autonomous production unit within which Kabir is a junior producer – the Islamic Republic is remarkably pedantic about job titles – is expected to generate between thirty and fifty pieces of content, ranging from films to social media updates to pamphlets to podcasts. Glorious deaths and gory executions are all very well, but it's not enough to wave guns and denounce apostasy. The whole point is that the state is Remaining and Expanding, albeit funded in substantial part by kidnappings, lootings, slavery, drug deals and extortion.

Kabir is unworried by such economic necessities. The young Muslims whose minds he is reaching for appreciate military triumphs and training montages but, he has learned, there's also a considerable audience for footage of infrastructure repairs, entrepreneurial initiatives, moments of pious domestic bliss, and passionate guilt-tripping in the service of saving Sunnis from slaughter. Anything and everything that suggests an empire risen from the ashes of Western hypocrisy.

What most impresses Kabir is the sophistication of the ecosystem he's feeding into (his vocabulary is laced with words like this now: *media ecosystems, cyber jihad, platform agnosticism*). His small team's content will be repackaged by an ever-shifting swarm of loyal supporters across the world, distributed where its effects are likely to be the greatest – a cocktail of clear, strong emotion mixed to order, like the words that brought him here. *Your life can have meaning, your faith can bring glory.* Who needs Hollywood? He has cash in his pocket, the fear and respect of Raqqa's conquered citizens, and a cushy requisitioned apartment near the market – in the company of several cooperative comrades willing to translate his shopping lists.

Some things take getting used to, but Kabir takes comfort from the fact that the city is only gradually coming to terms with its new status. Public piety is on the rise, with scores of citizens kneeling spontaneously in the streets when the call to prayer sounds out. Women are increasingly seen only in the company of men. They use the loudspeakers in the streets for announcing executions, and it has taken him a while to perfect his facial response: something between enthusiasm and battle-hardened indifference, accompanied by a resolute silence. Public speech is strictly monitored, and swearing is forbidden. The last Brit to mutter *holy fucking shit* while watching an apostate's head being ineptly hacked from its body was lucky to get away with twenty lashes.

Other forbidden things include, in no particular order: un-authorized gatherings; listening to recorded music; teaching or learning anything aligned with the Western worldview; shaving; and breeding pigeons. Kabir has never liked pigeons, and his beard provides luxuriant proof of his manhood, but the paranoia that attends listening to Pharrell Williams in his flat is starting to get old. At some point, he assumes, things will get easier – and his rise through the ranks of the chosen will bring its rewards. At some point, his talent will be fully recognized. If he's lucky, that point may be tomorrow.

Tomorrow, Kabir will be helping to shoot an action movie unfolding in real life: the latest instalment of the mega-hit *Clanging of the Swords* series. He'll be embedded with fighters for the first time since his cousin's death, this time as part of a full film crew, closely overseen by the Al-Itisam Establishment for Media Production. It's his chance to get noticed by the great and the good of high-production-values propaganda – the people who came up with *Windows on the Land of Epic Battles* – and he's determined to wow them, even if it means setting aside the subtleties he usually prefers.

If Kabir doesn't make a good impression, they might decide

he's better off sitting at a desk uploading interminable religious speeches – which is why he's currently alternating between press-ups and squats on his living room's tiled floor. After two sets of ten, the burning in his chest and thighs becomes unbearable, so instead he practises picking up and putting down his heavy new Sony camera. This lasts for twelve repetitions, by which time his shoulders and arms are trembling and his grip keeps sliding off the handle. It has been a while since Kabir's initial training and, even then, his pre-jihadi special interest in media made it possible to avoid the tormenting extremes Hamid thrived upon. Sports were never his thing at school.

Heavy with sweat, Kabir eases onto his sofa and starts flicking through a selection of officially sanctioned social media accounts: always good for inspirational distraction. There's very little to do in the evenings, now Hamid is gone, beyond attempting not to commit transgressions punishable by dismemberment. His eyes flicker around the room. All of the apartment's books, magazines, newspapers, pictures and wooden chairs were incinerated in the shared courtyard at the back, before his arrival, but the walls boast several cross-shaped patches of unfaded paint, leading him to suspect its occupants were Christians. With an effort of considerable will, Kabir manages not to visualize any of the things that may have happened to them.

He'll be right there tomorrow, beside the warriors every step of the way. He can't hesitate, stumble or fall under the sentence of a sniper's eye. He shivers. A few more moments of recuperation, a few more pills to hurry the night away, and then nothing will be able to stop him.

CHAPTER 6

Azi is staring at his trainers. It's 9:55 a.m. and the station is crowded with commuters and tourists. Trying to track even a fraction of these striding strangers makes his head spin. He has a backpack and a hoody, he has been loitering for fifteen excruciating minutes beside the spot arranged with Sigma/Munira, and he gives it a maximum of another ten before a security guard starts loitering near him in turn. Hands shoved in pockets, his mind racing through possible scenarios, he fails to notice the young woman with the quiet tread until she's beside him.

'AZ?' she says cautiously, like someone meeting a man from a dating app for the first time. 'You're here. You actually came.'

'Yeah, I came.' He smiles at her. He can't remember the last time he smiled spontaneously at someone, but she's got one of those faces. And she looks so apprehensive, so young. Suddenly, he's no longer the victim. He's the one with the power – and he needs to reassure her. 'Don't worry, I'm not about to kidnap you and harvest your organs. I promise.'

Shit. Where did that come from? But she returns his smile.

'Good to know. Awesome. Thank you so much for coming, I'm so grateful. I'm Munira. Hi.' Azi blinks, trying to compose his expression into something confidence-inspiring. This is way too much like a date. He's got to get better at this, fast, before he accidentally invites the woman he's meant to be entrapping to lunch and a matinee.

It doesn't help that she is much prettier than he is comfortable with.

'I'm Azi. Hi. Let's walk and talk, keep your eyes down as much as possible.'

They set off across the concourse, matching the pace of a

large group of tourists. The tourists are slow, earning them the undying hate of a succession of commuters, but Azi figures it's a bad idea for them to look like they're in a hurry. Munira is watching him closely.

'I'd always wondered how you pronounce it. Not A-Z. Azzi. And what's your real name? Or do you not want to tell me?'

'Er, it's Azi. AZ, Azi? Kind of a double bluff?' Why do things that seem clever as hell on the internet always sound so stupid when you have to explain them in real life?

'That is unbelievably bold. Call me Munira, please. Sigma is for the forums.'

'Oh sure, of course. Munira. Suits you.' She looks up at him, eyebrows raised, before looking back down.

'You're not what I expected,' she says. 'Not at all. I thought you'd be, you know?'

'A crusty white guy working the grunge Assange look?'

'Or maybe a bit Snowden, with the glasses and the jumpers. Anyway. I'm just glad you're here. So glad.'

And then she bursts into tears in the middle of Victoria Station.

Azi has no idea what to do with a stranger's tears, let alone the tears trickling down the cheeks of a mysterious woman he's just met.

Apart from the tears, Munira looks exactly like the photograph she attached to their second exchange of messages: the one he conducted under the firm tutelage of Anna's colleague. She is slim, modestly dressed in jeans, a jumper and the red headscarf she suggested for unambiguous identification. A bulky bag is slung across one shoulder, but she hefts it with ease. She is weeping, yet coiled with nervous energy, her feelings flashing across her face. Is she acting? Is he acting? He has certainly got a great deal of rehearsed persuasion to impart.

Uneasily, Azi hovers his arm an inch behind her back, maintaining their motion. She seems to swallow her tears back, brushing them away. He decides to ignore the crying. Dial the Britishness up to eleven.

'Hey. Look. Munira, let me cut to the chase.'

She smiles again and it reaches her eyes, now slightly red. Like him, it seems, her instinct is to dig herself out of panic with words.

'Cut to the chase? I don't think I've ever heard someone say that in real life before.'

'Get to the point, then. Cut me some slack, I've actually never done this before. I looked at your research, closely, and what you've found ties in with some things I've seen. Some really bad things.' He lowers his voice even more. 'Gomorrah, trafficking routes, the far right and the Islamic Republic, everything in between. It's big.'

Azi pauses to glance around at his surroundings. Are they being watched? Of course they're being watched. He presses on.

'You know that already – and I don't know what you've been through. But I'm here to tell you that it's not something we can face alone. We need reinforcements, and protection, and we're not going to find any answers until we get both.'

'Wait. Slow down, please. Are you saying that you believe me?'

'Yep, and then some. Munira, whoever is after you . . . neither of us is safe now. Not any more. I'm sorry.'

She stops walking and turns to look at him, her eyes narrowed in suspicion. He takes a deep breath, edging towards his gamble.

'They almost got me. Yesterday, within hours of your first contact. I've got the clothes on my back and a bag of kit. I almost didn't come . . . I'm sorry. I wanted to warn you, but I have to go, and soon.'

This is the moment. Azi has embarked upon his key untruth. He has a black rucksack on his back, and it's true that this contains everything he was allowed to pack. He's pretty sure he looks every bit as desperate and homeless as his story suggests – because he is, helpfully, both of these things.

It is twelve hours since Anna's visit. Immediately after she left, a middle-aged man appeared at the shed door. Brisk and unruffled, he looked like he had popped by to fix the central heating, armed only with a box of tools, an air of fatherly competence and the capacity to snap Azi's body like a twig if he even contemplated resistance.

First, Azi was instructed to undelete Sigma's messages, claim he'd had a change of heart and suggest a meeting. It was horribly easy to play the role, and she was horribly grateful. She told him her name, she provided her photo, she said it was no problem to get to London in time – then mentioned that two of her cousins had been recruited by the Islamic Republic, and that she was in possession of information its agents were desperate to obtain. Something about the access details for Gomorrah, carried only in the software between her ears. Sick with guilt, Azi sent reassurances.

With this out of the way, the man got Azi's signature on the bundle of papers Anna had left – about the only format secure enough for their purposes – and then, after requesting a cup of tea with three sugars, began drilling Azi through what was to come. Azi was permitted a shower and, after somehow falling asleep at 1 a.m., was woken six hours later, made to rehearse relentlessly over more cups of strong tea, then instructed to pack before being turfed out of his own home. His instructions would be issued via a nondescript new phone that he must keep about his person at all times. His own devices were all forfeit.

Now, while trying to hold Munira's gaze, Azi is conscious of the two things that matter most in any manipulation: urgency and constraint. Hence the story of his own crisis. By creating urgency and eliminating other options, you create opportunity – a context within which someone's only choice is to do what you want, even if they believe the decision is up to them.

'How did they find you?' Munira whispers, bringing him back to the crowded concourse. The air smells like disinfectant and coffee.

He almost breathes a sigh of relief, then catches himself and turns it into one of exhaustion. 'They didn't, not quite. It's obviously no coincidence that they came right after you made contact. They were monitoring AZ's activity somehow – they've probably been doing it for a while. If they'd found me at home, I can't imagine what would have happened. But I had everything on remote, spoofing my location: empty shed, dummy machines. They trashed the place, two of them. I saw it, before they took out my cameras. But it was me they were after, and that means they're close to finding you too. Very close.'

'Oh my God. Our communications, the last messages we sent. Please tell me they were secure. They're not watching us right now, are they?'

She looks into his face and now he sees terror in her eyes. He swallows a fresh mouthful of guilt. This is just a job. No different to lying online. He lies for a living: this is just an upgrade.

'God, no, honestly. Fully secure. All they saw was Sigma getting in touch with AZ. Whatever trace they ran took them to the wrong place: metadata only. This time.'

'I'm so sorry, Azi. If I'd known, if I had thought, I never would have dragged you into this. I can't believe they could touch you. It's because I asked around. About finding you. I thought you were the best – that you were a ghost! If they can get to you, if they're that good, I mean, we're done. We're as good as dead.'

They have been half-whispering, their words evaporating into a sea of footsteps, greetings, apologies, exclamations and loudly answered mobile phones.

Azi looks at Munira and starts to move with more purpose, indicating with a nod that she should follow. They reach some escalators and ride up, into the fluorescent bowels of a shopping arcade. Windowless and busy, its strapline promises *everything you could ever need in one central location*, presumably because fast food, greetings cards and high street fashion can slake any heart's desires.

Azi buys half a dozen miniature cupcakes from the first stall they pass, seduced by the heaped display. He needs something to do with his hands besides twisting and untwisting the straps of his rucksack. And, as all hackers and coders know, sugar is your friend – bad for the body, great for the brain.

He eats two cupcakes before he remembers to offer one to Munira. She's watching him with a compassion in her eyes that makes him want to confess. Can he trace a secret message in the pink icing and hand it over? *Run!* But there's not even space for three letters, let alone punctuation. The fact that he's thinking these things suggests he is in no state to be improvising. Stick to the plan.

'Look,' he says. 'I don't know what you thought I could do – what we could do together – but I need to get out of here. I'm sorry that all I've got is bad news. I know we don't know each other, not really, but . . . I'm glad we met. I wish I could have done more.'

'What am I supposed to do now? I'm running out of places to go. Fuck.' She's walking quickly now, towards the exit. Azi has very little time left for this to work.

'Do you have friends you can trust? People they can't have been watching?' This is his biggest gamble. *The idea needs to come from her, not you.*

'Not here. Not right now. Azi, wait. If you've got some plan that gets you out of the country, surely, maybe . . . you can take me? It wouldn't be for long, and I've got cash. I can pay my way.'

Azi can hear seconds passing as he stares at her, chewing his bottom lip like someone about to take a chance on a stranger.

'Do you have your passport?'

She nods, gesturing to her bag.

'And nobody knows you're in London?'

'They can't. The content of our messages was secure, right? If the people who got to you were watching me, I'd be long dead. I don't think they know my face or my real name. You?'

'Sensible to assume they know too much for comfort. But I've got nothing on me they can track, I left nothing behind they can use, and it's not easy to watch airports unless you're, you know, police or government. I'm going, right now. A favour, from a very old friend. If I vouch for you, if I say you're with me, he should be able to sort us both out . . . so you need to decide, fast.'

She nods quickly, looking into his eyes again as if she remembers losing something there. Until this point, Azi realizes, he hasn't genuinely believed in the sequence of events he went through again and again in his kitchen. This doesn't happen in real life, to two strangers, to smart people with homes and ideas and knowhow. Unless those same smart people discover that their choices have been outsourced.

'It's not just about my cousins, you know,' Munira continues after a pause. 'They were the reason I started to look into things. The two that flew off to Turkey, we're all better off without them. But what I found . . . you've seen a few of the files, but there's so much more. Whatever you think it is, it's worse.'

Azi stops outside a chemist.

'Do you want to go in there and grab a toothbrush or whatever? Meet out here in five minutes and then we need to get on a train. We'll have time to talk later.'

'I can come? Will that be okay with your friend?' She looks at him with wide eyes that make him even more determined to get it over with.

'Yeah. I figure I owe you, and at least this way we can pool resources. I can contact him, while we're on the train. Go. Hurry.'

As she walks away he pulls out the phone he was given before leaving home and types a message: *Done*.

They're going to Berlin.

CHAPTER 7

Since its birth on America's Western frontier, hacker culture has dreamed of gun-slingers and justice: of heroes and villains at war over manifest destiny. In other words, it has always been riddled with self-delusion.

White Hats are the goodies. They're career researchers in the security business, handsomely paid when they find vulnerabilities in software and let the vendors of said software know. Perhaps you've spotted a way to bypass the authentication process on an airline website? They'll offer you a few hundred thousand air miles for the info. Maybe you cracked a messaging app's allegedly impassable crypto? You need some serious skills to pull this off – but then you're closer to half a million dollars. Assuming, of course, you were officially authorized to conduct your hack in the first place – and that you tell the app's creators rather than seeing what the criminal fraternity can come up with.

If you head towards the criminal fraternity, that's when you need to put on your Black Hat. Selling what you know means you're a bad guy too, outside the law and likely to find a bounty on your head. If you're lucky, it'll be years before any evidence of your crimes comes to light. If you're careful, you'll already have half a dozen new exploits ready to roll. For every loophole that closes, another dozen open. Somewhere in the rear-view mirror, almost out of sight, governments legislate for the last decade's abuses, creating further opportunities as they do. It's almost as if they want everything that everyone does online to be insecure by design.

Then, like in all the best movies, there's the bit in between: the zone of human interest. People who don't fit into either camp are called Grey Hats, and they sell some of the twenty-first century's most powerful secrets to governments and corporations alike: one-time backdoors into systems the world thinks are secure; snooping techniques even the spooks haven't heard of; malware able to spread and lurk for years, waiting for the signal; vulnerabilities deep in the software of satellites.

Azi has spent the last decade on the pale side of this grey zone – but he has also become increasingly unhappy with the whole hackers and hats thing. The hacker vibe is so naff, so retro-cyberpunk, complete with 1990s movie references: Johnny Lee Miller hacking the Gibson and Angelina Jolie's pixie haircut. He has come to consider himself as something else: a connoisseur of biases, blind spots, delusions, illusions, confusions, bewilderments, aversions and longings; the moments of weakness and madness; the overlooked and the understudied; the groupthink and the solecism; the fact that very few people are still concentrating when they get to the end of lists like this.

That's what he thought yesterday, anyway: back when he was the one in control. Now, everything he thought he knew is gliding into memory. Hunched wordless opposite a beautiful stranger on the Gatwick Express, Azi can feel his past coming unanchored. Living a lie is one thing – but he has no idea what to do with his own sunken truths.

Once upon a time, Azi wanted to be a hacker with all the desperate energy in his teenage body, because that was what escaping his 1990s meant. Empty teenage years in London's hollow rim. East Croydon Station, a creeping blot of concrete and steel. Ducking past street corners where his peers gathered for aimless hours, eking out McDonald's meals, cheap booze and cigarettes. The cavernous IKEA where he worked warehouse shifts on weekends and holidays, which had opened to fanfare in 1994, looming like a yellow-blue demigod over the ugliest road in southern England.

This was where he began to build his elsewhere: a screen and a modem his route to somewhere apart, to a place his mother's questions about school couldn't reach. A copy of *Snow Crash* on the floor beside his bed, a photocopy of the

Hacker Bible in German, crudely translated using a stolen school dictionary. 'Chaos Computer Club,' it said on the cover. It became his motto, together with those opening lines that snaked through a maze of circuitry: 'A path can always be found out of even the most oppressive or addictive predicament.'

Azi remembers all this like it was yesterday because, until today, he still lived in the same house and worked from the same shed that, aged thirteen, he ineptly patched up, hammering roofing felt in bent layers while trying not to fall off a kitchen chair, not knowing he should have stripped the old roof's greasy remnants first.

It was dry inside – just – but a fungal smell clung to the chipboard for years. The interior was dimly lit and cramped, half-filled by an ex-display MALM desk on whose underside some bored child had scrawled a stick figure massacre. Azi squeezed two folding chairs, a side table and that ancient standard lamp into what remained of the floor area, then squeezed himself into two jumpers and a pair of fingerless gloves to keep the chill air at bay. Plus he felt more like a hacker in fingerless gloves.

None of it mattered. This was where it all began, with a white snake of telephone cable slung along the fence all the way from the kitchen socket to a hole in the shed wall, through which it slithered into the rear of a 14.4 kilobits US Robotics Sportster Faxmodem. Along that cable came the entire world – extremely slowly, when his mum wasn't using the phone. It was everything that his other (and more practical) early digital bible, *The UK Internet Book*, had promised – alongside the warning that, the internet being what it was, it wouldn't be long until he upset someone.

It took Azi just under a week.

'Mate? Did you hear about the American bloke who hacked his telephone by whistling at it?'

This was Azi's best friend, Ad, staying over after school one dismal Friday in December 1994 to behold The Shed for the first time. Ad – pale as paper, long limbs unblemished by fat or muscle – leant back as far as wooden walls and his IKEA chair would permit, striking a pose of studied indolence. Azi – brown-skinned, compact, fourteen years young and still awaiting his growth spurt – nodded and grinned.

Ad's dad was as enigmatically absent as Azi's, but his mum did something important with teams at Microsoft, meaning Ad had owned an IBM PC with a 486 processor while Azi was still making do with the school's battered BBC Micros. Now that Ad had a spanking new Pentium PC at home, his old 486 had taken pride of place in Azi's shed together with the all-important modem. It was a new beginning.

When it came to computers, Ad's status in Azi's life was close to divine: a creature touched by proximity to the future. Azi was his disciple, and this revelation about phreaking out telephones was the most important thing Azi had ever heard. As Azi finished nodding, he sensed that Ad's wisdom demanded a more formal verbal cue.

'How, Ad? What did he do?'

'You won't believe it, right, but he whistled down the phone line using some toy whistle he found in a packet of biscuits or something, and that note tripped the switches or something, right, and then he could make free calls, as many calls as he liked, to anywhere.'

'To anywhere?'

'Yeah. And this was ages ago, before we were born, but . . . you know those noises a modem makes, when it's dialling?'

'Yeah, mine is set to V.32bis modulation with the local echo on, keeping the serial port at fixed settings, sending CD on connection, variable link speed negotiation. The Demon package seems great, so I reckon I'll have enough bandwidth for the web and everything.'

Azi had been practising this in his head all day. It was important that Ad knew that he knew it – that Azi was more than a dumb apprentice. He always got better marks than Ad at school, and computers were surely the same. You put in enough hours and, eventually, you knew more than anyone else.

'Right, so it's talking to the computer at the other end, and just like people in America who worked out you could whistle the right noise and use it to fool the phone system, I have something that can kind of do something even better, like, you know, in *WarGames*?'

Azi knew. They both knew everything that happened in *WarGames*, because they had watched Ad's VHS copy of the classic 1983 movie about two dozen times in the last six months. Azi stayed at Ad's house at least once a week, and Ad's mum didn't care how late they went to sleep, or what they watched on the TV in his bedroom.

The luxury of this felt almost obscene to Azi, alongside Ad's unkempt long garden and brand-new kitchen-diner. Over and over, they watched Matthew Broderick hack his way into a video game called *Global Thermonuclear War*, discover that it was in fact a real military missile system and then save the world by teaching the system the concept of mutually assured destruction. It was glorious, even if his and Ad's gleeful count of technical errors had reached double figures (you would never be able to login to a system like NORAD without both a username and a password, they liked to mutter).

'So you know in *WarGames*, at the start, right,' Ad continued, 'when he's dialling up all those numbers looking for a machine to hack? Well, thing is, I've got something that can do that on this.' Ad let the magnitude of what he was saying sink in for a moment, then produced a floppy disk from deep in his khaki jacket's pockets with a flourish. TONELOC.EXE was written in extremely neat felt pen on its white label – because Ad's determined diffidence did not extend to his handwriting. He slipped the disk into the computer.

'No way.'

'Way. It's a war dialler, that's what you call it, after the movie, right . . . and we can use it to keep on dialling up other computers until we find something we can talk to, and try to break into.'

'Like Matthew Broderick.'

Ad nodded.

'And, but, are we allowed to do it? I mean, what if we get caught?'

'Azi, trust me. Only a lamer gets caught. Are we lamers?'

'Nah. No way.'

'So we're good, right, we're good. Let's play a game.'

'What's the primary goal?'

'Same as always, Professor Azi. To win.'

And it worked. One nervous installation later, the computer was dialling numbers in automated sequence, the modem's buzz and hum populating a log file of failed and promising attempts. They watched in awe. Azi had never experienced anything like it. He was in a tiny, filthy shed in Croydon, yet he was also reaching out to household after household, mapping the invisible lines that linked them all.

Like a spider at the heart of its web, he watched and waited while the machine worked through the local phones they had specified. Ad sipped Um Bongo and glossed the war dialler's findings in a whisper: dozens of dead ends in the form of lines with no modem, but also some systems that talked back, that could perhaps be fooled, hijacked, twitched into action.

This was interrupted when Azi's mum called them in for tea, serving the sausages and waffles that Azi insisted such an occasion demanded. She was just asking them what they had got up to at school when the phone calls began.

It was his mum who picked up the first call, told the caller it must be a mistake and put the phone down. The second call came a minute later and, bewildered, she went through the same operation. Two minutes later, the phone rang again – and this time Azi leapt to answer it. *You rang me*, an old man's voice bleated, *I rang back and there was just this noise – are you selling something? Are you recording this? Is it about my TV licence?*

'It's just a mistake,' Azi replied, a heavy mass lodged in his stomach as he realized the scale of their error.

They had made the calls from his mum's landline. They had told the computer to work through a block of local numbers, and to hang up if a human rather than a modem answered. Now, once the modem was offline, people were ringing back, because this was the 1990s in South London, not California in 1983. The war dialler had gone through over two hundred numbers in the last few hours. That was, what – twenty people if even one in ten knew how to call back?

Azi's mind reeled. Ad had become fascinated by his last sausage, transfixing it with a downturned gaze as he cut it into smaller and smaller pieces. The phone rang again, and Azi's mum gave them both a long look. The few members of his mum's family he had met went rapidly from loud to ear-splitting when they were angry – but not her. She became quieter, more intense, like she was folding in on her feelings. She got sad, and he hated that.

'You done this, Azi? You done something on that computer?'

'Yes, Mum. By accident though!'

'Something bad? Police?'

'No, Mum. We just tried something, it was stupid, we didn't even think it would work.'

'People going to be ringing my phone all night?'

'No. Or yes. Maybe?'

'I'm tired, Azi. I'm out of the house before you wake. You answer the phone, you fix things up. This never happens again. You slow down, you do things right. You're a good boy. Whatever you do, I never want people calling our house – never. Do you understand this?'

'This is it, I promise. I'll never do it again.'

At this, half a smile crept along her face.

'Never get caught again, you mean.'

'Okay, Mum.'

They ate their final sausages in silence, interrupted every five minutes by another call for Azi to field. It was his first taste of hacking and, he later realized, the best lesson he could have learned. Never leave a trail. You're not a predator reeling in prey. You're a nobody: a ghost in someone else's machine.

CHAPTER 8

Berlin swelters in its summer, the riverside a throng of young and old. Pedestrians snake in both directions, while others watch from deckchairs or scattered tables. It's a picture of plurality; of multiculturalism and democratic success. A post-card from a future inconceivable only half a century ago.

Deep inside his dark clothing Azi is sweating. He has spent too much life indoors for this kind of heat. Beside him, Munira walks with the efficiency of someone accustomed to heatwaves. Like the locals, she is dressed practically, which means as little clothing as possible: shorts, flip-flops, olive green vest, a tattoo in the shape of a small star winking from the inside of her left wrist. Without a headscarf – she claims only to wear them when placating family members or meeting secretive strangers – her dark hair tumbles past her shoulders, bouncingly immodest. It's a good look.

Azi squints into the sun and tries to go with the flow, admiring the endless procession of museums and concert halls, churches and government buildings, talking into the air.

'I'm not made for meatspace, Munira. The whole walking and talking in the sunshine thing. The sooner they put my brain in a jar and hook it up to a machine, the better.'

'Meatspace? Wow. You just went ahead and said that out loud, like it's a real thing that normal humans might say.'

'Ha. I regret to inform you that I know someone who says it regularly.'

She grins at him. 'Let me guess. Old friend? Sidekick? Nemesis?'

'Something like the first two. Maybe leaning more towards the latter these days. We haven't spoken in a while. We used to spend a lot of time on computers together, before it was cool.'

'You're so old. So pre-millennial! This off-grid low-tech thing we're doing, it's messing with my mind. But this is how you grew up, isn't it? Nothing but meatspace as far as the eye can see.'

Azi holds his hands up. 'You win, it's a terrible word. Fancy searching for an internet café?'

'Yeah, because those places still exist. With public computers and Windows 98.'

'I get it. I'm basically your grandfather.'

'Not mine, you're not. Horrible old man. Used to hit my dad with lengths of rubber pipe.'

So much of what Munira says – good or bad, bold or sad – is thrown out like a punchline. Azi has never met anyone else quite like her. She is lively and quick-witted: utterly transformed from the woman he met on that station concourse.

Skin-crawling paranoia and presentiments of unspecified disaster had pursued them through Gatwick. They shopped and drank coffee and smiled wildly at strangers, boarded their flight at the end of an overlit wasteland of corridors, read and reread in-flight magazines in silence, then queued for an hour so they might emerge into the ancient eyesore of Schönefeld Airport. They departed and they arrived. That in itself is a victory.

Now, Munira is glowing with unexpected hope. This is the first time in months, she tells him, that she hasn't been constantly looking over her shoulders: now it's just every ten minutes. Her happiness gnaws at his guts. Azi walks and awaits further instructions via the phone in his pocket. This is all he knows, because this is all he needs to know. Like Jim, he's merely the tool of someone else's deception. So he keeps talking.

'Tough childhood?'

'For my dad, yeah. Less so for me. He hated his old man, the way his mother was treated, everything. I guess he wanted it to be different for his kids. School, computers, wearing trousers and T-shirts – he wanted me to have that. Mum, not so much. Her family, not at all. You come from a big family, you know what it's like? Anyway, I was able to tell the rest of them to stick it, most of the time. I'd run away a lot. Sit with my third-hand laptop on a bench, stealing the Starbucks Wi-Fi. This was five or six years ago, when you were middle-aged.'

Azi nods, riding the wave of her conversation, content to listen.

'I was a good girl. But I was smart, and they didn't see that. Apart from Dad, they all just wanted me to meet a nice boy, make nice babies. He got me that old laptop – and then I decided to find out how things really worked. And there was a boy, of course. An unsuitable white boy with glasses and a *World of Warcraft* habit.'

'Lucky you.'

'He cheated on me, so I hacked his Battle.net, sold everything he had for cash and made him cry. Bet you've never done that to a girl. I'm sure you were a nice boy.'

'Yeah. Something like that.'

'I *knew* it. Let me guess. Did you make your mother proud? Photos on the stairs, your height marked on the doorframe with pencil. The apple of her eye.'

'Not to put a downer on things but . . . she's dead. My mum died. Before I got to make her something closer to proud.' Memories shift inside him, struggling towards the surface. He pushes them down. Munira is horrified.

'Shit. Shit, I'm sorry. I wasn't trying to, you know, take the piss out of your dead mother. I don't watch my mouth. I get carried away.' Her expression is a mix of mortification and pity.

'It's fine. Honestly. I love . . . I like that you're honest with me. I just think I need something to eat.'

'I saw a veggie place near here. It was rammed, which is good given our interest in privacy. Then again, nobody knows we're here apart from your mysterious friend, and you say he booked the flights through an equally mysterious agency, so what exactly is there to worry about?'

'You're asking me a question?'

'No. Yes. I think I'm asking you to explain one more time

what we are doing here. Because I'm happy to be here, sure. But . . . look at us. They almost got you. Because I was looking for you. How can you know they aren't watching now?'

Azi suddenly feels very old and very tired.

'Honestly? I don't know. This whole situation has been insane from the start.'

Munira shakes her head, pushing away whatever angst was building. 'Sorry, sorry. I know that. It's hot, my head hurts. Azi, I just want all of this to go away.'

Her tone is still light and fast. You wouldn't think from her expression that they were anything other than a couple of tourists deciding where to go for food. Azi has no idea which of her selves is more real – the fast-talking hacker, the hunted victim, the confident joker, the rebel daughter – and it seems she isn't sure either. Obviously, she ought to get away from him. Perhaps, if he makes a move on her, that will be a plausible means of getting her to vanish. Historically this has always proven to be pretty effective.

But the people sending him orders through his mobile phone would know, because they know everything. They have planned for every improvisation he might attempt. After years of thinking he was the smartest person in the room, it occurs to Azi that he has spent most of his life in rooms containing just one person. With an effort, he summons his best impression of reassurance.

'Look, look. This is not because of you. It's because of them, the people who are after you. Always, because of them. And I fucked up. That's on me. All you did was ask for help, from the person you felt was in the best position to provide that help. Not your fault he turned out to be, upon closer inspection, slightly shit. None of this is your fault.'

She snorts, looks around, then clasps his shoulder – as if touching another human were the easiest thing in the world. Their ensuing silence isn't quite companionable, but the tension has dissipated. It's too much, thinking one thing and saying another. Surely people normally get some government-sponsored training for their double life?

Joining a queue of preposterously attractive and under-clothed young people, feeling outmoded and unanchored, Azi nurses the hope that his day will improve on the far side of a falafel wrap.

Like everything else in the modern mobile workplace, the tradecraft imparted to today's intelligence assets revolves around apps. Also, like everything else in the modern mobile workplace, this allows for considerable economies when it comes to training budgets.

The mysterious new phone Azi was given in exchange for everything he used to own looks entirely ordinary, but is running a heavily modified version of Android from which every vulnerability has systematically been stripped (in tech as in warfare, the smaller the surface exposed to attack the better). Via this delectable device, he has, since their meeting at Victoria Station, been experiencing the solicitudes of an app named New Action Directives Issued Remotely, or NADIR for short.

Running this app is the only thing Azi's phone can do. It tells him what to do next, and then he does it. Essentially, NADIR is a satnav, and its psychological effects are dismayingly familiar. The more you encourage someone to rely upon step-by-step instructions, the more they behave like someone who requires step-by-step instructions to do anything: passive, unquestioning, liable to drive off the end of a pier if commanded. Azi is well aware of this effect – he has exploited it in others often enough – and is disturbed to find his own mind numbing in response to the app's not-so-gentle prompts.

Apart from using the phone to stay in touch with his 'friend', they are forbidden from undertaking any online activities. Azi has sold this to Munira as a security precaution – but it's also an effective isolation tactic. He hasn't been offline for this long since he was fourteen years old. It's like his mind has shrunk. Entire rooms full of knowhow are emptied and boarded up. Although, he would concede, the absence of constant interactions with neo-Nazis can only be good for his faith in humanity.

So far, their instructions have been to wander parkland, plazas and museums in a strange simulation of tourism. It's four hours since they landed in Berlin, and Azi is starting to feel stretched thin. To make matters worse, his falafel tasted like sawdust and he could kill for some fried chicken. When a new action directive arrives, he's so eager to read it he almost drops the phone.

Tell her you are leaving, to meet your friend. Walk three blocks east from the Brandenburg Gate, along Unter den Linden, and await further instructions. She is to meet you outside Checkpoint Charlie in two hours.

How can they be so sure she'll listen to him, he wonders? How do they know she won't run? Azi's heart sinks as he contemplates just how confident they must be – and just how complete their surveillance. What he needs to do, he tells himself, is stay calm. Eventually, there will be an opportunity to snatch some advantage. There's always something that hasn't been anticipated.

'Hey, Munira.'

'Yeah?'

'I've heard from my friend. He wants to meet, just me. We'll sort things out, then pick you up outside Checkpoint Charlie. In two hours.'

'Because if I'm living in a spy novel I might as well see the sights, right?'

'Something like that. Just a couple of hours, then you'll be safe.'

She gives him a hard look.

'Safe. That sounds good. Lucky for you that I'm not bothered about being abandoned in a strange city, trusting a man I just met. I'm not even slightly terrified, just so you know—'

'Munira. It will be okay, and I will be there. I promise.'

She laughs, as if not quite in control of her voice.

'That's good to know. That's great. I'm just . . . I don't want to be afraid any more. I've spent a long time being afraid. I really, really want to trust you, Azi. Can I ask you something?'

'Of course.'

'What happened to your mum?'

'Excuse me?'

'I want to know something real, about you. My dad is dead. I didn't tell you that. Heart attack, two years ago. I think, if he was still alive, none of this would have happened. He'd have kept an eye on my cousins, given them a good talking to. Or turned them in to MI5. Right. Your turn.'

Azi stares at her. Suddenly, only the truth will do.

'It was my second year at uni. Hit and run, completely random. Except she always crossed the road without looking, in the same spot, so I guess I could have said something. If she had ever listened to me about things like that. Which she didn't. I got a note in my pigeonhole. That's how long ago this was: a little piece of folded paper, with a university crest on it, telling me to see my tutor at once *about a serious personal matter*. I knew, right then. Because there was nothing else in my life that mattered. It was just me and her – then it was just me. I can't believe how long ago it all was.'

Azi and Munira look at each other. He has never said this much about his mum to a living soul. Munira pauses, unusually inscrutable. Then she reaches out with both arms and clasps him, drawing herself into his chest, lifting her lips in a whisper beside his face.

'Don't let me down, Azi. Please. Come find me.'

And before he can answer, she has gone.

CHAPTER 9

Azi picks his way along the street, buffeted by crowds, remembering the clean smell of Munira's hair, the clasp of her arms. He has no idea what to do with the echoes of these sensations, but nor can he stop his body remembering them.

The wide pavements around the Brandenburg Gate are clotted with tourists on walking tours: mostly young Americans, their eager caffeinated gazes sliding off Azi's face. Once he is in the right area – and certain Munira isn't following him – he pulls out the phone again. He has to admit, the app is an excellent form of cover. As a tourist, he'd look peculiar if he didn't spend most of his time staring fixedly at a digital device.

NADIR tells him to turn into a café on the main road's south side. It's the kind of place he hates: a coffee-shop-cum-makerspace-cum-advert-for-trans-national-tech-brands, mixing exposed brick, aspirational furniture, baked goods and inspirational verbs. Worst of all, there's free high-speed Wi-Fi that everyone apart from him can use.

Having sufficiently hated the space, Azi shifts to hating everyone inside it, and then on to hating himself. Finally, he surrenders to the app's latest command: buy a coffee and wait at a table for two. Is he allowed a toasted sandwich, he wonders? The fact that he is even asking this question is depressing. He adds one to his order – compared to London, it's astonishingly reasonable – then sits and waits for the bearded barista to bring it over. Immediately after it arrives, a tall blond man of about his own age sits down opposite him and begins to speak, his accent heavy but precise.

'Azi!' the stranger exclaims with alarming familiarity. 'It is good to see you, my friend! I am so glad you could make it.'

Silence doesn't seem to be an option. Azi clearly ought to

be accustomed to random people who know everything about him invading his space and launching into conversation as if they've been friends from birth.

'Yes. Er, how are you?'

At this point his sandwich arrives and he's grateful for something else to focus on. He picks it up and takes a quick bite, then coughs as scalding cheese removes a layer of skin from the roof of his mouth. The man carries on as if nothing has happened.

'You should check your messages. And then give me a hug, you rascal! A proper one, man to man, friend to friend.' The stranger's bonhomie is so convincing that Azi momentarily wonders if he does, in fact, know him.

He checks NADIR. The words *trust this man and do what he says* appear. Great. He rises and fumbles into a clumsy embrace. The blonde stranger is lean but roped with muscle, his limbs tight against the fabric of a skinny grey T-shirt. He looks like a climber, or an endurance athlete. Everything about him is pared down and action-ready. By comparison, between his several days of stubble and battered trainers, Azi feels like someone the master race wouldn't have much trouble mastering.

'Follow my lead, stay nice and calm,' the man whispers before sitting down fast and pulling out a tablet which he taps away on as he talks. 'We are all thrilled you could take the job. People like us – people like you and I – we're rare commodities. That must be why we are such good friends! But this is not a place for talking shop.'

'Right. So we are—' Azi's attempt to interrupt is politely but firmly halted by a raised finger, so he attempts another bite of the sandwich. It doesn't go much better than the first.

'We are two old friends at a rendezvous. A lovely French word, don't you think? Catching up for about five minutes, which is the typical length of time such things take, I am told. And then it will be time to depart for proper conversation in greater privacy.'

'Right. Remind me, how did we meet? Uni? Spy camp? A

bit odd that I'm not quite able to remember, but I'm sure you'll help me out.'

'Azi, Azi, you require no alibi, no lies, because who you are is known to nobody else here. How wonderful that your life-long discretion has done all the legwork for us! But for the sake of argument, let's say that we studied computer science together, got on like a burning house, generally had a marvellous time. There will be details at our destination.'

'And that is where, exactly?'

'Just follow my lead. You are an expert on this, I think: the memorable and the forgettable. We are a team, Azi Bello. Working together to rescue the lovely Munira Khan – who I think you are starting to like quite a bit, yes? Smile, relax and tell me a little about your trip.'

The lower half of Azi's face does something that couldn't, even generously, be called smiling. 'You'll have to forgive me, but today I have an app for a brain and no free will. I'm a bit short on improvisational banter.'

Already a vision of genial relaxation, the man seems somehow to turn this up a notch, reclining into his seat while tapping his tablet with disinterested dexterity. It's like sitting opposite a Vodafone commercial. Aren't InfoSec agents supposed to be nondescript, as opposed to chiselled extras from a lifestyle catalogue?

'Well, we have a minute, my friend. In my experience, the best thing is always to keep as close to the truth as possible. Let us try again, for the sake of practice. Tell me about your trip.'

Azi attempts a genial tone. 'Delightful, considering it was the most terrifying three hours of my life to date. Although there's a lot more competition for that now, after your girl Anna dropped in for coffee. Let me think. Rock, hard place.'

'Now, now. You're a smart guy, Azi. And doing well so far under all this pressure. Can I give you some advice?'

'Oh please do.' Azi has the sudden sensation that he's two people, and one of them is regretfully watching the other start to lose his shit. Ah well, one of him thinks, you were always going to fall apart at some point. It may as well be while you're sipping *Kaffee mit Milch* with a trained Teutonic killer.

'You have been under a great deal of pressure, of a kind you are unused to. It is tough. So you should relax, allow yourself to enjoy this. Think of it as a foreign vacation, with step-by-step instructions. Being looked after every step of the way – a friend such as I rolling out the red carpet! It is all so much better than the alternatives.'

'Okay. So . . .' With an effort of will, Azi makes the more measured version of himself take the reins. He can do this. Just a normal day, just a normal café. He can pull back from whatever brink he strayed towards. 'We met at university, in London. We stayed in touch, online, through work projects. We haven't seen each other in real life for years, but we must be close, because you're offering myself and Munira a place to stay. Given the way you look, I'd say we don't share too many hobbies.'

The man opposite him taps his palms in brief applause. 'Exactly! And my lack of knowledge of your personal life is easily explained due to you not existing on any form of social media. It's very good really, your absence of Facebook. There are some details that cannot be improvised, which I'll take you through. Including my name, which to you is Odi Wolff. And now it is time for us to depart. Companionably.'

'Can I finish my sandwich at least? All I've had today is bad falafel.'

'If you like. But you haven't had much luck eating it – and there's great food where we're going.'

The man calling himself Odi stands up and ushers Azi out of the coffee shop.

CHAPTER 10

Kabir feels he has finally experienced a revelation like those he dreamed of when he set off from home all those months ago – a fire in his heart that illuminates the world. Unfortunately, this revelation has taken the form of fear, self-loathing, nausea, sleeplessness and desperate guilt, all neatly swaddled in the fact that he will be executed if he reveals any of these feelings.

On the plus side, he hasn't yet been burned screaming inside a cage, which puts him several steps ahead of the subjects of his recent edit job: enemy fighters whose immolation it is his job to reconfigure in slow-motion replay in order to make the whole experience more filmic. On the minus side, he has begun to talk in his sleep, waking himself up with the muttering, and he's worried that a point will soon come at which he no longer controls what he says during the daytime either.

The fact that Kabir spent much of the filming for *Clanging of the Swords* curled up in a foetal position around his camera begging unseen snipers not to kill him means that he is temporarily working full-time from his cubicle on other people's propaganda – and it's what he has seen second-hand that has begun to crumble his faith in the Islamic Republic.

When you watch a stoning or a beheading in person, Kabir reflects, it's easy enough to stay in the right frame of mind – to think appropriate thoughts in the company of brothers, your blood pumping, comradeship thick in the air. When you repeatedly watch the same thing on a computer screen, however, as you edit and upload and append appropriate sentiments to someone else's capture of events, it suddenly starts to seem . . . what, exactly?

Kabir doesn't like to say. *Insane, psychopathic, deranged, bonkers, wrong*? Words like this creep dangerously towards the front of his brain and the tip of his tongue. He bites them back and keeps working. He has started grinding his teeth, which isn't ideal given that dentistry tends towards the basic here. A crown has dislodged from one at the back, and its exposed nerve jolts faintly with every breath. He still takes the same number of pills, but they no longer touch the whispering parts of his brain.

This – a voice mutters in his head, sounding more than a little like his late cousin – *isn't great or glorious or sacred or cool. It's a bunch of pricks boasting about how much they like killing people. It's basically your dad shouting at the telly. But with weaponry.* Kabir tells his dead cousin to shut up, tells himself he needs to stop talking to dead people, then hunches determinedly over his laptop and keeps fiddling with sliders and fade effects.

The scene onscreen runs forwards and backwards in time as he trails one finger across the trackpad, flicking between life and death. To his intended audience, it should bring fear and awe in various proportions, depending on whether they're viewing from inside the Islamic Republic (in which case, fear is the primary aim) or from among the diaspora of potential recruits (in which case the urge to inflict fear on others is preferable).

Kabir doesn't have a plan, yet, but he has become aware that some other foreigners have also begun covertly expressing an interest in not spending the rest of their lives here. This is another reason why there have been fewer video-game, whoring and recreation sessions. One of his closer comrades from Germany, an idealist with a clear preference for the 'helping fellow Sunnis' aspect of their mission over 'killing everyone else', has recently been in daily contact with his sister back in Berlin – but Kabir has a shrewd notion that this particular sister doesn't exist.

Muhammed the German, as he's known, exchanges detailed imprecations with her almost every day via Facebook, and claims he is close to recruiting her to the cause. But he's also careful to do all his typing discreetly, when their superiors aren't around. If it turns out that Muhammed's sister needs to be met on the Turkish border, and that Muhammed alone can be trusted to provide reassurance and bring her across, Kabir suspects this may be the last he sees of his friend – unless he can get involved in the escort gig.

Outside, in the conquered maze of Raqqa, winter days are a memory: desert heat sears off brick and concrete, driving children into the shade of courtyards to play in timid rabbles. Many of the schools have been shut down for being insufficiently Islamic, which creates a kind of holiday-meets-prison-camp feel. When he's not hunkered underground, Kabir has been told to hand out sweets and small change, the better to herd young volunteers towards training camps. He has edited videos shot inside these, too: one heart-warming scene of pre-teens executing sheep was especially memorable.

The state of its troops' training is just one of many sore spots Kabir wishes he hadn't identified within the Islamic Republic. For a start, there's an embarrassing skills shortage when it comes to the infrastructure of international jihad. Among those who wish to bring death and terror to the infidel in destinations such as London, Paris, New York and Berlin, there are far too many whose enthusiasm outweighs their precision: bomb-makers whose creations explode prematurely in pointless martyrdom; conspirators who fail to coordinate their timings, and turn up early and under-prepared; improvisers of explosive devices who only succeed in blowing off their own hands; drivers who don't know their way around the cities they're supposed to be terrorizing. Moreover, skilled trainers and practitioners are targeted and killed at a steady rate by enemy nations (which is basically everyone), putting a premium on those who have been around long enough to know what they are doing.

Kabir has also experienced particular unpleasantness around one message in his care. At the start of this month, Caliph Ibrahim gave a speech from the site of their most glorious conquest, Mosul, announcing a worldwide caliphate in which all humanity must come together – either as believers or subjugated others. Every devout Muslim male, assuming they wish to belong to the first of these categories, is thus instructed to begin unceasing conflict against the second.

Together with Muhammed the German, two surly Pakistanis and Google Translate, Kabir has helped transcribe, translate, reformat and distribute Caliph Ibrahim's inspirational message across the world. Unfortunately, it has also fallen to him to report back some of the less-than-enthused regional reactions it has received, and his superiors don't take these things well. The Army of Islam, a worthless rival group of Islamists, had the nerve to call Ibrahim 'delusional', while other Sunni insurgents have muttered unhelpful things about megalomania, self-deception and the sowing of divisions. Kabir couldn't possibly comment – at least, not without having his tongue ripped out of his living throat – but global unity doesn't seem to have got notably nearer.

Onscreen, he is watching footage of another senior Sunni cleric calling Caliph Ibrahim an overreaching idiot unworthy of his self-appointed titles. It's one among dozens of broadcasts from Qatar that he's obliged to check and is proving especially colourful in its commentary. Best not to flag up this one until he's certain the management are in a robust mood. He probes at his back tooth with his tongue. The rot is setting in.

CHAPTER 11

Odi turns out to be right about the food. Azi expected, at best, the German equivalent of his garden shed – and at worst, a blindfold and precautionary beating. Instead, he got five minutes of pointedly companionable walking, then the keys to a small apartment three blocks from the coffee shop.

They walk up to the top floor of a handsome building colonnaded over the pavement. Everything in it is new, every surface a clean line and pale shade. The fridge has been stocked in accordance with continental tastes: cold meats, eggs, salad, cheese, a bar of posh milk chocolate with a cow on it. There is a loaf of fresh bread, butter, coffee ready to brew. Even by the standards of the last week, it is not what he expected.

'This seems like a pretty comfy pad for city-centre enhanced interrogations.'

'Okay, Azi, we can cut the crap. You are working for us – by which I mean myself, Anna, and what you might call our back-office staff. I know that you have come here under duress, but I expect you to be professional. You may even enjoy it. On the table is your new laptop, and on it are files that will spell out most details in due course. You will depart to pick up Munira in just over an hour, leaving time for a shower, a change of clothes, some food and a preparatory briefing. In that order. Any urgent questions?'

Azi opens his mouth, closes it, and selects the most obvious inquiries from the dozen he could pose.

'What is this place? And who exactly are you working for?'

'For the purposes of our story, this is my flat. And you are my guest. Pretty cushy, no? There is a fine view of the Französischer Dom, the French cathedral. Although, actually, it has never been a cathedral.'

'And you are—?'

'Myself, I am your great mate Odi, aiding you in your hour of need. So far as Munira is concerned, I am affluent, discreet and loyal. So far as you are concerned, I am part of a taskforce interested in the intersection between technology and terrorism. We are small, independent, and we know what we are doing. Look around, my friend. I meant it when I said you should relax. Nobody knows you are here apart from us.'

Azi nods. 'And?'

'And nothing. We have considerable resources, but we face even more considerable challenges. You should be flattered to be joining our little organization. It is very well thought of.'

'Oh, I'm really honoured. So I should call you, collectively—?'

'There is no need to call us anything. Please, take a moment and focus. This is the truth you will live: my flat, our friendship. As you can see from these surroundings, I have done well since leaving London! I am making this accommodation available, you and Munira are going to work from here, and we will keep an extremely close eye on you. She must be put at ease, drawn into your confidence. Your exploits with the members of Defiance will also come in useful.'

Azi looks around. The comfort of the flat is almost narcotic after the last twenty-four hours. He wants to believe in it. Hot water, food, drink; stillness and silence; a desk with a view and an Ethernet port. More than anything, he realizes, he is hungry to touch the sleek new laptop lying unopened on the desk – to power it up and refill the blocked channels of his mind. It's a trap. It's an opportunity. It's achingly odd, because he is excluded from all the information that might turn this scenario into sense.

'Odi, I'm going to take a shower. Then I'm going to eat, then I'm going to drink a lot of coffee. Only then will I even attempt to get my head around all of this. Okay?'

'But of course, my friend. As long as you stick to our timings, please make yourself at home. There are clean clothes in the master bedroom, in the chest of drawers. They will fit.'

'Now that is just fucking sinister.'

'We aim to please.'

Ten minutes later, fresh from the shower and trying to choose between the crinkled sportswear in his rucksack and the crisp threads in his sinister chest of drawers, Azi finds himself thinking about magic.

Magic played a big part in Azi and his friend Ad's youthful imaginations, both because it was the only thing either of them ever did that impressed (some) girls – at least until Ad pushed his luck with the places the coins reappeared – and because it employed a similar artistry to hacking. Magic was what someone saw when you hijacked their assumptions, bypassing the bit of the brain that reasoned out explanations. Arthur C. Clarke had things exactly wrong. Advanced technology isn't indistinguishable from magic. There are just two kinds of person: those who understand how something is done, and those who don't.

Clearly there are many important things he doesn't yet know. But where are they to be found? How tightly locked down is his new life? Questions buzz like insects, ugly at the edge of vision. Somewhere, somehow, something will have been over-looked – an absence within which magic can be made. The only problem is, they have many months' head start on him, massive resources, a deep knowledge of his past and total control over his physical and economic wellbeing. Not to mention an inscru-tably dangerous German pretending to be his best mate.

As if on cue, Odi leans into the room, gazing with exagger-ated ease at Azi's fluster. 'Coffee is brewing, and you may help yourself to food. We have forty-five minutes to go through what is on the laptop, and to talk over a few things. Then you will get your friend. Then we will all have dinner.'

Azi nods, dresses in his own old clothes and heads into the living room. Odi is now seated at a spotless glass table, with the open laptop beside two cups of black coffee. Gesturing Azi to sit beside him, Odi turns the screen towards them.

'First things first. You will keep the NADIR phone on you

at all times. No other devices leave or come into this flat. I will take care of the machine Munira has brought with her. We have military-grade satellite and microwave-based networks, so please do not consider mucking around. Now, look at this.'

Odi hovers the mouse over a minimized browser, then clicks. A selection of open webpages leaps into view. To Azi's astonishment, they all show variations on the same thing: the Defiance forums frequented by Azi's alter ego, Jim. Jim is both logged in and looks to have been highly active during the last twenty-four hours, which can only mean one thing: someone else has been pulling the strings of Azi's puppet. And they've been doing an excellent job.

'That's my . . . that's the fake identity I've been working on. You've been logging in as him?'

Odi nods. 'Yes indeed. Munira knows how to access Gomorrah. We are sure of this, although the information lives only inside her head: why else would the jihadis be so very keen to kill her? She knows how to access the dark marketplace, but Gomorrah will never let someone like her in. They grant access only to very particular people. The verified agents of totalitarian governments, of well-funded and discreet criminal enterprises, of parties of a certain political persuasion. Do you see where this is going?'

Azi thinks he does, but he wants Odi to spell it out. He shrugs. Odi is unimpressed.

'Playing the fool does not suit you. Jim will be our way into Gomorrah. Munira will tell you the details, Defiance will provide Jim with the necessary legitimacy, then Jim will be our access. So long as she confides in you, all will be well.'

Put like this, it sounds beautifully simple – which means, Azi decides, that almost all of it is in fact horribly complex. 'And then?' he asks.

'Then nothing. It is only Munira who knows about you, besides us. So perhaps you would like to return home? She will need our protection, but you will be a free agent. Albeit one under close supervision.'

Azi sips his coffee, determined not to express his shock at

the thought of returning home – that this might even be an option. Once again, it's something he can't afford to start believing in. Pursing his lips, Odi taps the mouse a few more times, highlighting blocks of text.

'Here are the most recent messages I have sent, volunteering Jim for a prominent piece of online campaigning. He is an impressive piece of work, Azi, and every bit as much an asset as you are. Online anonymity is strictly for amateurs, these days. Arms dealing, terrorism, trafficking – all of it works on a first-name basis.' He pauses, looking wistful. 'It is really too bad. Unlike the Russians and Chinese, we do not have armies of fake citizens ready for service. You will need to convince her that breaking into Gomorrah is the only way she can learn about those tracking her – the only way to gain some kind of evidence, some bargaining chips.'

'So why didn't Munira go to the proper authorities already?' Azi asks. 'Why would she go on the run, and approach me, rather than just go direct to you guys—'

Odi raises a cautionary finger. 'It is very charming that you cannot answer those questions yourself. Why might the cousin of two known terrorists not wish to approach her government with vague evidence of a planned attack, gleaned through her own theft of data from a senior agent of the Islamic Republic? Why might she be fearful, desperate and distrustful of anyone other than a few fellow-hackers?' He gives Azi a careful, unkind look. 'Until we stepped in, the famous AZ was quite willing to abandon Sigma to her fate. The limits of trust, yes? This is why we play our games. This is why you will do what I tell you.'

Azi's chest tightens. He doesn't like being reminded that he was ready to walk away, or that all his caution failed to protect him. Then again, Odi has revealed far more than Munira has told him so far: that she stole information from a senior Islamic Republic agent, that she probably knows how to access Gomorrah. Gathering what courage he can, Azi decides to see how far Odi can be pushed.

'Munira isn't stupid, you know. She's going to think this is weird.'

'You do not trust me?'

'Why would I trust you? Fear, yes. Trust – that's a long way away. How did you find me in the first place?'

'I have told you what is happening. This is not a time for debate.'

'I see that, yeah. But I also see problems. There are some things I need to know.'

Odi stands up, the smile on his face becoming fixed. 'It is not your job to see problems. You do not know enough to see anything. It is your job to listen carefully and to play your part.'

Not knowing what else to do, unsure what he wishes to say, Azi also stands up. 'Come on, you can tell me something, can't you? I mean—'

With a gentle movement of his chin, Odi looks Azi up and down – then launches an open-handed blow into the centre of his chest.

Azi collapses backwards. It's as if someone is standing on his ribcage, stamping the air out of his lungs. He cramps into the carpet, his face pressed into its thick pile, twitching with useless adrenaline. It smells of chemicals, as if some deep stain has only recently been removed. Odi's voice has become even more precisely articulated, its edges sharp as knives.

'You have asked your questions. Here is your answer. You do what I tell you, because fuck you. You read your notes and you play your part, because fuck you. When I tell you to do things, you do them. Because, fuck you. Stand up.'

'C-can't. Can't.' Azi is spluttering. After years of living online, he had almost forgotten how excruciating real-world consequences can be.

'On your feet. Breathe in through the nose, out through the mouth.'

Odi hauls Azi to his feet, without effort, as if something tedious but useful has been got out of the way.

'Don't let this worry you, Azi. It is very important that you know I am serious. That is all. Drink some coffee, clear your head. Eat something. Then bring Munira here.'

CHAPTER 12

Munira was there: stood outside Checkpoint Charlie, looking unlike anyone Azi might walk up to and casually kiss upon one cheek. Yet it almost happened like that – apart from the kiss, which he fumbled into a handshake. Nevertheless, she was waiting, he was on time, and they left together.

Things have gone downhill ever since. Not just because Azi remains bruised and uselessly angry; and not just because what he has recently found out is taking a lot of processing; but also because, as he was told in no uncertain terms, his objective this evening is to escalate his intimacy with Munira. Not exactly his area of expertise.

Staring at the angular crockery and glasses Odi has set on the table, Azi allows Munira to fumble for conversation.

'So, Odi, you guys met at university?'

'Yes, yes. Student union, 1998. Although neither of us were there.'

'Excuse me?'

'Neither of us were there, because we were in the computer science lab. Working late, as we did most nights, until they threw us out at closing time.'

Odi muffles a snigger at his own wit. Now that Munira is here, his manner is more self-indulgent than businesslike – with hints of well-heeled smugness. The character Odi is playing has done much better than Azi since leaving university and isn't afraid to flaunt it. Perched towards the edge of an obviously expensive chair – like everything else in the flat, it seems never to have been used – she presses on.

'I should have known. You hit it off?'

'Eventually. Not to begin with.'

'Right. It takes a while.'

'To start with, he thought I was a bit of a prick. Many people do, I have noticed.'

Another snigger. Munira fails to look charmed.

'But you became friends anyway?'

'You could say so. Azi and I did not do many of the regular student things, but we both had a taste for computers and inexpensive alcohol.'

'And what are you up to these days?'

'I wrote a piece of software that someone paid a great deal of money for. It has paid for many other things in turn.'

Odi waves his hand in a casual encompassing gesture that makes Azi grit his teeth. Odi is remarkably convincing in the role of benefactor-cum-provocateur: supercilious, faintly debauched, accustomed to handling the human traffic of hangers-on. Munira, Azi realizes, is trying to compose her expression into something like gratitude – but it isn't really working. At best, she looks like she's fighting indigestion.

'So this place is—?'

'Somewhere I keep for special guests. It's discreet and serves a purpose. May I serve you some food?'

At last finding something to look genuine about, Munira nods. Odi has placed a heaped bowl of salad on the glass lounge table – leaves, grains, cheese, pomegranate seeds – alongside dark, dense bread and chilled white wine. Whoever the people behind Odi actually are – Azi feels torn between the account he's been offered, and visions of a cackling bald man running the show from inside a volcano – they clearly understand aspirational millennial cuisine. Odi serves himself after Munira, then Azi, then continues speaking through a mouthful of bread.

'Azi has told me a little of your story, Munira. I don't need to know more, and I don't want to know more, except for these two things. What do you need – and what will happen if you don't get it?'

Munira looks to Azi. His turn. Half a glass of wine has softened his focus, but he has rehearsed what needs to be said. He takes a last sip, for luck, and clears his throat. 'We need to find out as much as we can about who ripped our lives apart, what they are doing, and how we can stop them from finding us and . . . making trouble. Pretty clear-cut, I think. Safety, security and technology required. Dire consequences feared.'

Despite the wine, Azi feels shaky by the time he finishes. Saying things makes them real, even if they started out less than true. His home, his history: both of these have evaporated into abstraction. They are things that used to exist. How long has Munira felt like this, he wonders. How many other people are living like this, right now – running from something, the borders to their past suddenly closed?

Odi rolls some wine around his mouth in a magnificently irritating show of self-indulgence. 'Well. It seems to me that you two homeless Brits are in need of rest, recuperation and as much incidental pleasure as we can manage. Do you not drink, Munira?'

'No. Thank you.'

'Very sensible. The body is a temple!' To her arched eyebrows, he adds, 'I am not mocking you, no. You seem more sensible than Azi here, who I have seen in quite a state on multiple occasions. That pub, what was its name?'

'The Crown,' Azi improvises, thinking back to the days when he used to hang out in pubs with real people. There were never many but, once upon a time, there were some. Then, gradually, there weren't. 'Yes, the Crown. That's the one. I fell into the fruit machine. It kept sneaking up on me.' As the past decade yawns beneath him, he tries to look like he's recalling a hilarious incident.

Odi nods, as if fondly transported, then musters a more serious tone. 'Well, clearly you two have stumbled on something serious. And this is what we live for, you and I – lives at stake and freedom on the line. This is why people protest on the streets, hide in embassy cupboards, hack the Pentagon. The world is going to shit and it's all recorded, somewhere. If we don't fight for truth and justice, who will? Come on, both of you, I am being sincere. Let us toast your safety and your success.'

Odi brandishes his drink at them. As the glasses clink, Azi touches one hand lightly to his chest, remembering pain.

If there is any freedom to be won here, it won't be on Odi's watch.

Two hours later, Munira and Azi are still sitting beside one another at the glass table, the laptop and the remains of dinner in front of them. Odi stepped out five minutes ago, seemingly drunk – although Azi noticed that he didn't actually consume much of the alcohol he slopped into his own glass – leaving Azi to unveil his 'plan' to Munira in peace. And this means introducing her to Jim.

With a flourish, Azi begins: a synopsis of his own escapades, a few dropped hints around accessing Gomorrah, Jim's life story. The wine helps. Munira's eyes widen. For the first five minutes she simply listens, her face unreadable. Then she lets out a delighted cry.

'Azi, you cunning little catfish – wriggling around in a pond full of Nazis! This is too good, really. Total fascist ownage! How long have you been at this?'

He tries to look modest, not entirely successfully. 'A year, ish. Maybe eighteen months.'

'Wow. Wow! And what is Jim up to, these days? I get the feeling you've got another nice surprise for me.'

This time Azi doesn't even attempt modesty. Instead, glowing with Munira's praise, he outlines the nature of their opportunity: of Odi's plans as modified by, he would like to think, his own rather greater finesses when it comes to matters of deception.

As Azi sees it, the electronic activities practised by Defiance fall into three categories: mobilizing their base; forging fruitful connections with like-minded groups; and preparing themselves for political power. Underlying this is a simple proposition. A large number of upstanding citizens feel themselves threatened on all sides – by Islam, by self-serving elites, by unemployment and outsourcing, by the loss of certainties they've forgotten they were never sure about. Defiance believes that xenophobic ultra-nationalism is the long-awaited answer to their prayers.

The party doesn't put things quite like this, but then it doesn't need to. Given that the majority of the base they're aiming to rouse consists of angry white men, pricking their aggrieved pride is about as complex as toasting a slice of bread. You simply spread a story about someone who isn't like them (non-white, non-native, female) getting something that they feel entitled to (a job, a home, sympathy) and then wait. For older people, you do it with words and pictures. For younger people, you do it with video, memes and snark.

What Jim has recently volunteered to do is turn the latest barnstorming speech from the party's German leader, Tomi – fresh from a week of increasingly prominent appearances on network television – into a mailshot aimed at sympathetic audiences across the UK and America. Core party members handle the European operation, but Jim is now considered a foreign asset of impeccable enthusiasm. All of which has Munira, who has by now started flicking through the open tabs for herself, transported with delight.

'I love what you've done with those swastikas in that GIF! Very contemporary.' Intensely aware of her proximity, Azi gestures at the screen.

'They're not swastikas. Important distinction, especially in Germany. They're patriotic crosses, some kind of Teutonic thing. These people never call themselves neo-Nazis, remember, not a whisper of the N-word in public. They deploy only the most ancient of racially pure Christian imagery.'

She nods, scanning the highlights of Tomi's speech. 'Azi, this is amazing. I knew you were good but this is next level. You know what I find scariest, though?'

'Er, the fact that you're simultaneously being pursued by murderous Islamists while potentially pissing off neo-Nazis and the custodians of an ultra-secure darknet marketplace?'

'Apart from that.'

'Apart from that, no.'

'The fact that most of this guy's speech . . .'

'Tomi.'

'. . . that most of this guy's speech, Tomi, sounds kind of reasonable. Resistance against a totalitarian religion. Taking pride in your neighbourhood. A return to common sense in politics. He's funny, kind of a loudmouth uncle. It would be so much better if they were all racist idiots. But they're not.'

Azi takes a deep breath. Here is something, finally, that he can speak honestly about.

'People ask me where I'm from, sometimes, back home. And when I say I'm from Croydon, they then say—'

'Yes, but *where are you really from*. I've been there. What do you tell them?'

'East Croydon. Then I tell them to go fuck themselves.'

'No, you don't.'

'In my head, every time. Not so much with my mouth.'

'Because then they might kick your head in.'

'I keep my head down. Online, that's where I make a difference. Trouble is, it's the same for them. Nobody is ever alone, now, no matter what their flavour of crazy. Someone who agrees is only a click away. Someone who has been there before, got the T-shirt, built the bomb. I hate these people, Munira. I hate what they are, I hate what they do. But most of all, I hate what they pretend to be – how they persuade the world that they're right.'

They both pause – but not for long. Because Azi has something remarkable up his sleeve.

How will Jim sufficiently wow Defiance's senior management in as short a time as possible? This is a crucial question, because there's no point doing anything unless Jim can gain Defiance's blessing to make an approach to Gomorrah. Odi's team have thus provided something truly impressive: a video, allegedly obtained via Jim's existing darknet contacts, offering a taste of the riches available in exponentially more abundance via Gomorrah. It's a brilliant piece of work, and it goes something like this.

President Barack Obama looks directly into the camera from behind the desk of the Oval Office and, in measured and statesmanlike tones, declares that the United States is a nation

founded upon the principles of white, Christian exception-
alism, that it is the solemn duty of patriots to drive out those
who do not fit into this vision, and that they should do this
by any means possible. The speech lasts approximately ninety
seconds. After it has finished, he looks soberly into the camera
for a moment, gives a neat Nazi salute, then reaches below
the gleaming wood of the Resolute Desk and pulls out a
shotgun, the barrel of which he slots into the roof of his mouth.
Then he blows his own brains out.

It's a technological proof of concept, demonstrating the
algorithmic manipulation of high-definition video. It's also
extremely good. The software generating it has processed a
selection of existing recordings, then created an immaculately
convincing virtual being: one able to do and say anything its
controllers wish.

Azi has heard about similar tech under development, but
nothing approaching this level of accomplishment. Clearly,
they have enough under wraps to dangle some as bait, with a
concealed additional package – a few lines of malicious code
embedded in the subtitles, granting permanent access to
computer memory if anyone watches the video outside a secure
system. Given the appeal of its content, this is more than likely.
Azi himself once infected half the computers in an elite hacking
team by mocking up some grainy footage of the Bin Laden
raid, then sending it via a spoofed friendly email address. This
is phishing's golden rule: almost everyone is susceptible to
sufficiently expert enticement.

Munira stares at the screen, then at Azi, then back at the
screen again. 'This is unbelievable, Azi. Un-fucking-believable.'

He tries to turn on the modesty one last time. 'I've had it
around for a while. Custom job. For the enticement of neo-
Nazis . . . it's part of my old plan. I had the video specially
made to reel them in. And there's a special something extra
buried in the subtitles, for anyone stupid enough just to click
and play.'

'Nice. Friendly. So the plan is that Jim becomes our way
in, and then . . .'

Her words hang in the air. This is the crucial part. For all her openness, Munira has told Azi very little of what she does and doesn't actually know about Gomorrah – and about who is hunting her. But Odi and Anna were clear that she represents about their only hope of accessing it – and that her trust in her saviour, AZ/Azi, is their best hope of accessing her knowledge. Azi tries to radiate reassurance.

'Jim does the email campaign, shows this to senior Defiance types, boasts about his darknet contacts, does some cool tech stuff for them, then mentions Gomorrah. And they think, why not give it a try, let's see if he can deliver? That's where you come in – because the people behind Gomorrah would never in a million years let you, me or any random anywhere near it. But a known white supremacist with the backing of the world's most successful neo-Nazi movement . . . he'll be vouched for. They might even let him sell some warez.'

Munira pauses. 'And you're sure this will work?'

'Of course not. But I do know that it's custom-designed Nazi catnip: a black president removing the top of his own head in the name of white supremacy. And it's an advert for someone's very specialist services. You'd have to be a rubbish power-mad fascist not to want it.'

Munira smiles, letting her elbows drop forwards onto the table. 'Can I ask something?' Her tone is soft, uncertain. 'I mean, I know how it sounds but – that was a weird vibe, with you and Odi. Earlier. Were the two of you ever an item? You know, together . . . like, boyfriends? That kind of thing.'

Azi leaps back in his seat. 'What? God, no. Jesus. We were close, but he's not my type. I mean, he's a man, and that's not really my thing. I mean, there's nothing wrong with that kind of thing. I just don't, you know . . . What gave you that idea?'

'I don't know. Even though he's doing us this big favour, you just seem so . . . I wondered if you had a history.'

Azi snorts. 'No, that's just me and my non-existent people skills. I can barely handle talking to the postman. Not that people do that anyway, these days. I guess I feel bad that I haven't seen much of Odi, before all this. I've been shut away a long time.'

'I've noticed. I'd say you should get out more, but it's hardly the time. Unless, you know, you fancy a bit of dancing, a night on the town?'

'You're joking, right? I mean, if we could . . . but you're joking. Right? I mean, that's not exactly . . . Yes, you're joking. Of course.'

Munira stares at Azi for a beat. 'I don't do well with them either, relationships. Especially men. I guess you'd call it trust issues. There were a lot of traditional ideas in my family, a lot of expectations. I didn't fit many of them. Know what I mean?'

'Uh, I think so. It was just me and my mum, growing up. Not a lot of community: she'd burned whatever bridges she used to have. So I did my own thing. I had a friend. I had a modem.'

She flashes a grin. There's a steel to Munira, bright at moments like this. They're both leaning forwards, and Azi can feel the heat from her body – alongside something matching in his own. By some measure, she is the most physically attractive woman he has ever spoken to for longer than five minutes. When was the last time he got close to someone he liked, let alone loved?

With a shock, he realizes that it must have been his mother, in both life and death: when he embraced her to say goodbye at the start of term, then when he embraced her body in a windowless room after the identification process. Not a mark visible, yet all life gone. It made no sense. It still doesn't. At home, sometimes, he kept on speaking to her – asking the cramped rooms full of her things what they thought. The sofa proved a good listener.

Azi stares, blinks. Munira is speaking. 'Azi? Don't tell me you're dropping off. Focus. I need to know more about you, now we've started. I reckon I deserve a few details. Do you have a type? Do you have a track record?'

He blushes. 'No type, and not much of a record. I've always liked smart. That's it, really. Smart.'

'Smart. And sassy? Any other words beginning with S?'

'Sometimes.'

'Seriously?'

'Stop. I'm running out. Sleep, silence, I like those words too.'

'Hell, no! I've seen what you've seen. We need coffee and chocolate. Old-fashioned stimulants. The German is gone, the night is young. We're going to do what we do. We're going to work.'

She grins again. Maybe, just maybe, it's all going to be all right.

Then she leans forwards and kisses him on one cheek, the other cheek, and – fleetingly, impulsively – in-between. Stunned, Azi runs a fingertip across the heat her lips have left behind. He has just realized two things. His troubles have barely begun; and the point will soon come at which he can no longer lie to her.

CHAPTER 13

Azi wakes early the next morning, after troubled sleep and unremembered dreams. The flat is silent. The laptop and empty coffee mugs are angled on the table where he and Munira left them, before slipping exhausted into their respective rooms. Light streams through spotless windows. It's appallingly ordinary – and he wants as little as possible to do with it. Throwing on his running kit, he scrawls a quick note – *gone for a run, will be careful, back soon* – and descends through discreetly secured doors. He needs not to be in this place. He needs to reset his mind and shake himself free of the feelings last night set in motion.

Soon, his legs are taking him towards a massive needle that erupts into the skyline about a mile north-east of the flat. Without Google Maps to guide him or Wikipedia to inform him, it feels like an astonishing feat of exploration to run through an unfamiliar city. Did people really do this every day, once upon a century? Did he ever live his life this way?

Azi doesn't have a handle on Berlin. It's prosperous, the pavements packed with crowds ambling through rising heat, but it feels somehow looser than London – a little less shoving, a lot more public space unclaimed for anything other than existing. This needle, for example: there is nothing else like it. No other tall buildings. No other retro space-age architecture. Just a seemingly endless succession of institutional-looking colonnades, museums and churches, spotted with blank plots.

His lack of internet-on-demand is a nagging absence, but it also creates the welcome distraction of speculation. Perhaps the needle is a Cold War relic, built to assert the supremacy of the West – or the East. Perhaps it was a TV or radio tower, broadcasting capitalist or communist propaganda. Or perhaps it's more recent: a symbol of reunification, embodying nothing more than the excitement of getting together to build a really tall needle. It's certainly big. If there isn't a viewing platform, he's going to be disappointed.

Presumably, he is under constant monitoring from the single-purpose phone lurking in his pocket, not to mention a tail and whatever state-backed tech Odi can access. Odi left him a generous supply of euros and seems relaxed about expeditions, which depresses Azi more than if he'd been ordered to stay put. GCHQ and the NSA have long possessed the ability to turn every single phone, tablet and computer in every single pocket into a covert monitoring device, and once you cross-reference this with AI and facial recognition it's pretty much game over for public privacy. Who cares about mass surveillance when every twenty-first-century citizen has purchased their personal panopticon?

If Azi is to have any hope of taking control of his situation, he needs to get hold of something he can play with, technologically speaking. But how to obtain his own device, secret and secure? Something small, self-contained, easily rendered inert; internet-connected, yet able to survive the casual-yet-meticulous inspection of his person and belongings.

He has now been running for fifteen minutes and can feel his endorphins bringing some clarity – the comfort of a biochemical machine doing what evolution intended. Above the brick-and-metal spire of a pretty church, the needle looms just a block away, its slope broken by a sphere two-thirds of the way up. It looks like yesterday's vision of the future. A cheerful crush of summer bodies sweeps past. Crowds are good: both anonymous and opportune. He looks around, savours the pavement's tidal swell, then heads into the busiest venue he can find – a place called Balzac Coffee on the corner of a monolithic modern block.

Inside, across the generically coffee-shop-ish selection of tables and soft furnishings, mostly young people are doing what young people mostly do: basking in proximate mutual ignoring. Azi is a sucker for this sociable aloneness. On a normal day, he would contentedly spend hours not watching other people not watching him in a place like this. Nothing is normal about today, however, and in the spirit of over-compensation he strikes up a conversation with the pink-haired man serving at the counter.

'One iced coffee to drink in, *bitte*,' he says – and then, as the barista calls out the order and turns to accept his money, 'By the way, do you know what that tower is?'

'Berliner Fernsehturm. Television Tower. It is famous,' the barista says cheerfully, as if he isn't asked this question multiple times daily. 'You can go up, there is a nice view and a revolving restaurant.'

'Have you ever been up it?'

'I am from Berlin so, no.' He smiles and hands over a drink and Azi's change. 'Here, iced coffee, enjoy!'

I could get used to this, Azi thinks, sipping his drink while scanning the room. The last time someone smiled at him in a Croydon coffee shop, they were trying to distract him while their mate nicked his mobile phone. On which note – Azi looks around the tables and, sure enough, several people are sporting identical phones to his NADIR model. Here is his opportunity. A little sleight of hand, a little luck, and perhaps he can fool some very clever people with a very simple trick.

One of the phone-owners is a young mother. The baby on her lap is devotedly pummelling her face with a stuffed unicorn while she tries to sip some juice. She looks exhausted. Her phone is on the table in front of her, beside a half-empty pack of baby wipes. Grinning apologetically, Azi gestures towards her table's Wi-Fi password sign and then picks it up, waving at the baby. Shooting him a look of pure malevolence, it bursts out screaming. Quickly, he replaces the sign so that it's in front of her phone, sweeps the phone off one edge of the table and slips it into his pocket, then starts striding purposefully towards the exit.

He's almost there when something catches his eye. It's a woman, seated alone on a sofa. She's waving at him, smiling warmly in recognition. Lifting her arm high, like someone hailing an invisible taxi, she raises her voice and calls out.

'Azi, over here! Come and join me!'

Through the cascading shards of his plan, Azi does a double and then a triple take. It's the woman from his shed. Anna. Her hair is styled differently, her clothes less smart, but it's clearly her. With a dreadful weight growing in his chest, he picks his way across the café.

'Azi. Fancy meeting you here! The phone please, and be quick about it.' She holds out one hand. Azi hands over the stolen phone.

'Well done. Now wait here.'

He watches as she casually loops through the tables, heading towards the stand for sugar packets and napkins. She bumps into the side of the oblivious young mother's table and discreetly replaces the phone while smiling at the crying baby. She then picks up a handful of napkins and is back with Azi moments later.

'I wouldn't pull any further stunts like that if I were you. You're not the right kind of clever and I don't enjoy humiliating you. At least, not when you make it so easy.' She stands up. 'Walk with me to the Television Tower?'

'Do I have a choice?' Azi mutters, picking up his iced coffee. It's beaded with condensation and looks much less appealing than in the photo above the counter. He follows Anna out into the bright morning and they begin walking. Between the telling-off and the fact that he's wearing shorts, Azi feels about eight years old. Anna, on the other hand, seems genuinely cheerful.

'I'm pleased with the start you've made, pick-pocketing aside. You and Munira are getting along very well. It's all quite touching – and very much in line with our best-case scenario.' She glances at him, an eyebrow raised.

'I'd like to be direct with you, Azi. Assuming you can get over the manner of your arrival – which I suggest you do, fast – we have delivered on our promises. I'm happy for you to express any concerns you may have, so long as you pick a more productive manner than petty thievery. You know something about what we are up against, but it's reasonable that you wish to know more.' She pauses, as if admiring her surroundings. 'So. Here I am.'

Azi squints into the sun, shading his eyes with one hand. 'I guess Odi is a little . . . intense. Not big on discussions.'

'True enough. This is a beautiful city, isn't it? He grew up near here. He isn't called Odi, of course, but he is German – East German. Odi was born into things you grew up reading about in books, and he is extremely good at doing what needs to be done.'

Azi swallows. There's something there, he thinks – something between Anna and Odi that goes beyond business.

'I want to know how you found me.'

Anna starts walking again, forcing Azi to scamper in her wake.

'I'll make a deal with you. Get us into Gomorrah – you and Munira pull off access for Jim – and I'll consider sharing that information. They're not coming for you, if that's what you're worried about. They have no idea that you're here, or that you even exist. You are merely convenient. And now, just to prove what good hosts we are . . .'

They're almost at the base of the Television Tower, its bulk soaring out of what looks like a decrepit 1980s shopping centre. Anna brandishes an A4 printout, the words *Fast View Tickets* visible at its top.

'. . . I will show you the best view in town. After which you will be running directly home to the flat. Interesting conversations are happening in your absence.'

CHAPTER 14

By the time Azi returns to the flat, he no longer knows what to think about anything. Anna was charming, knowledgeable and not a little terrifying. The view was wonderful: the snaking river, green-speckled city, low grey tower blocks jostling with red tiles and domes; the white walls and grey roads, sprawling without a masterplan.

What Anna meant by 'interesting conversations' becomes clear as soon as he staggers through the door, panting from the pace at which he took the stairs. Munira is sitting at the living-room table surrounded by pens, scraps of paper and half-eaten pastries of some description. The laptop is open in front of her and she's flushed with excitement. She beckons Azi over as soon as he walks in, sending an involuntary shiver through him. Odi is sprawled on the sofa, sipping coffee and simulating a hangover, one arm rested across his eyes. He calls out without opening his eyes, prompting an equally involuntary wave of dislike.

'I came bearing *Berliner Pfannkuchen*. The good ones. In the kitchen there will soon be coffee. Great things have been achieved in your absence, but I feel like shit.'

Azi doesn't answer. He's too busy staring at what's onscreen: the forum where he and Munira posted the video last night. The threaded comments and responses below their post are now numbered at over two hundred, and counting: English, German, French, snatches of something like Polish or Czech. Senior members of Defiance and guests with advanced access privileges are falling over themselves to congratulate Jim, as well as to compete in a gaily informal festival of below-the-line racist fantasy. If even a tenth of them have viewed the video in a standard browser, their machines will have been hopelessly compromised by the code lurking in its subtitles.

That's not all. Switching to another tab, Munira brings up Jim's private messages. There are congratulations on his draft mailshot – the tone was just right, the click-throughs are expected to be excellent – followed by heartier congratulations on his video sourcing. These are followed by both enthused and aggressive inquiries as to what he knows, what he can get hold of, where he can get it, and whether there is anything they need to know about his bona fides, criminal record, public profiles or past history. Should he be hiding anything, the consequences will be dire. Otherwise, he's a hero – and they would like to follow up on his darknet hints in haste.

It's remarkable: a success beyond their wildest hopes. Only once Azi has taken in what he's looking at and turned to Munira does she speak. 'We're in, Azi! Well, basically. I've told Odi all about it. We've got a plan.'

Azi starts. 'You've told Odi, you've got a plan, you've . . . done *what?*'

Before Munira can answer, there's a voice from the sofa. 'She is clever, this one. She has not told me everything . . .' Munira nods at Azi encouragingly '. . . but she has suggested that you are on the cusp of something big. And that you may require a little German-language assistance in, how did you put it, my dear?'

'Fast-tracking an application process.' Munira follows her nod with a brief but reassuring squeeze of Azi's arm.

'Yes, precisely. A few carefully-worded notes to some neo-Nazis, from some fabricated folks of my own. Nothing like your creation, my friend, but good enough for what you require, I am told! After all, I am not in the business of knowing more than I need to know. Come, you must need coffee. I certainly do. Join me in the kitchen.'

Regretfully moving away from Munira, Azi edges into the spotless kitchen area around the corner. It's a symphony of stainless steel and discreet illumination. Odi staggers in, activates a bulky Miele bean-to-cup coffee machine, then places his face an inch from Azi's ear. His voice is a cut-glass whisper.

'Everything is progressing. I am fabricating a groundswell of German-language endorsements for Jim, in a manner Munira has specified most helpfully. There are other matters that I will be leaving to deal with. You will set as much as possible in motion, then you will take her out for a walk and await further instructions. We are far closer than I thought we would be. Get close, draw out the final method of approach to Gomorrah. Be as charming as you like, but stay professional. Do not get emotionally involved.'

Azi says nothing. The coffee machine works through its cycle, spitting out a strong brew that Odi slops into two clean cups before calling into the living room, his voice sing-song with self-satisfaction. 'I will drink this, I will eat a last pastry – for my health, you understand – and then I will go and do what you have asked me to do. It is a fine day. I know how to contact you both. Have fun.'

Half an hour later, having elaborately assured her that there's no risk involved, Azi and Munira venture out.

On the basis that it's a demonstrably normal thing to do, they end up wandering around a nearby museum dedicated to Germanic history. It features sections of the Berlin wall and recreations of political protests alongside accounts of Nazi Germany, before and after – including the free and fair elections that brought Hitler to power in 1933. Azi has never visited a museum before whose history feels quite so close, or so dangerous. There are also some magnificently appointed toilets.

After rushed sandwiches, they put the Television Tower directly behind them (Azi knowledgably points it out for Munira's benefit and is rewarded with an eye roll) and head through the Brandenburg Gate into the Tiergarten, a long, landscaped slice of parkland bisected by a four-lane road, densely wooded to the point of oppressive. There is an unspoken agreement that they should walk in as straight a line as possible: diametrically away from the flat, towards the distant protrusion of a column in the middle of a roundabout.

Every now and then, their hands touch. Azi finds himself focusing obsessively on this contact, trying to read its intimacy. His emotional involvement is fast approaching the point of non-containment. He can still feel where Munira's lips met his, last night; where she touched the bare skin of his arm, earlier in the flat; where her fingers have brushed his, just now. Eventually, he finds his way towards the questions that matter.

'Munira.'

'Azi.'

'Are you ready to tell me how this started? How they found you, how you found them?'

She widens her eyes. 'Uh, I guess. I mean . . . is this why you wanted to go for a walk?'

Azi shrugs. 'I find it easier to think when my body is doing something else. It can make things clearer.'

Munira takes a long breath. 'This has been nice, acting like we're normal people. But I guess we're not. It's ridiculous. I would never have known anything, except for what happened when my cousin was getting recruited. Someone special came for him. Some big deal with the outreach arm of the Islamic Republic – top secret, very professional. Only he made the mistake of using a thumb drive in a laptop that was on loan from me.'

Azi smiles appreciatively. 'I can imagine you'd set that up in a pretty non-standard way.'

'No shit. I'd been hacking from home for half a decade. It was logging everything: keystrokes, camera, the works. My cousin got up to some nasty shit, the sort of stuff you really don't want to know about your relatives. Then the recruiter plugged in a USB drive, tried to cover his tracks – badly – and when my cousin gave the machine back, I got a whole lot more than I expected.'

Azi prompts her gently. 'Everything you sent me, the names, the details?'

'And more. A few things I didn't send. It's so simple, that's what's crazy. That's why I asked Odi for help, because it's the last piece in the puzzle – the way I asked him to vouch for Jim, the locations, the words. I've been wanting to tell you everything. But I've seen what they can do, Azi. I've seen it, I've seen . . .'

Munira stops walking, runs both hands through her hair, then places her arms around him and her face tight against his chest, as if he's the only thing that can stop her being swept away. Softly, she keeps speaking.

'It's not just a marketplace. There's a dedicated darknet, custom software. But it's *personal*. You apply by name, they invite you in, and then you belong to them. This guy from the Islamic Republic, the big shot, he was a gold card member – only he isn't alive any more. I found him. They worked out what had happened, they came for me, I'm not even sure who they are, but . . .'

As the words catch in her throat Azi brings his arms around Munira, willing her to understand that they are in this together, that he is not going to let her down – desperately hoping that he can make these things stay true.

They're standing on the crowded pavement, a flood of strangers passing on either side, the flash and ripple of vehicles filling the road. It's ordinary and strange: as if the entire world is in motion except them. The NADIR phone in Azi's pocket feels huge. They're being listened to right now, he reminds himself. The only way to keep her safe is to press on.

'It's okay, Munira. It's okay. We're going to get them. We're going to break in, take what we need. We're going to be the ones in control. You said it's about an invitation, that Odi is providing evidence. What does that mean? What does Jim have to do?'

Her voice whispers against his chest, for his ears only. 'You know those stories when someone makes a bargain with the devil – when they say his name three times, and he comes? It's like that. There's a username for messages, on Signal. Gomorrah. So simple! You send a secure message, you offer the right evidence. Then they send a one-time link, just for you. Fully customized. Whatever your heart desires.'

Azi is filled by the sudden urge to confess – to blurt out

the truths and questions rattling inside his head. Instead, he reaches towards a different honesty.

'I . . . I remember after my mum died. There was this maze of bureaucracy, so much to do. A lot of people I didn't know were kind. Everyone was kind to me. They were determined to keep me, the university. And I hated them for it. A guy like me, a story like mine – they fell over themselves to help. Money to support me, time out if I needed, extra tuition to help me catch up. Grief and gratitude, that's all I was supposed to feel. It was like they owned me . . . but there's nothing worse than being owned.'

A pause. He was trying to say something true. Now that the words have left his mouth, however, he can't help thinking that there are many things worse than being owned – and that Munira is running from people who want to do several of them to her. After a moment, no longer whispering, she lifts her face and speaks.

'Did Odi help you?'

Azi has to swallow the urge to laugh. 'Yeah. I needed a friend. And the best friend I had, the only other friend I had, let me down. So there was just good old Odi.'

Munira squeezes him, hard. Then she takes his hand and starts walking again, a lightness in her step. 'It's okay, Azi. I honestly think it's going to be okay. We are going to get this done. Us and good old Odi, whatever the fuck he's up to right now.'

They walk in silence for another minute. As if on cue, an update buzzes onto Azi's phone. He pulls it out, glances at it, then stares. It's not what he expected. Nothing like it.

We have a situation. I am sending someone for you, right now. Stay calm and comply. Less than a minute.

Azi walks a few more paces and turns to Munira, something poised on his lips; a sentence, a warning, a kiss. He's not quite sure which, because before he can act, someone blocks their way. A casually dressed man of similar build to Odi, his hands held out in not-quite greeting. The man speaks, just loudly enough to be heard.

'Azi. Munira. Your ride will be here momentarily.'

His voice is warm, with a faint Atlantic twang. Before they can process what is happening, a red Prius pulls up beside them. They're almost at the roundabout, and cars behind honk merrily as they swerve to overtake. The man continues.

'It's okay, Odi arranged this. Munira, get into the car.'

With a gesture that looks like invitation but involves the application of knee-buckling pressure to Munira's back, he sweeps her into the front seat and closes the door. It's less than thirty seconds since he appeared. Azi blinks in astonishment, starts to move, but it's too late. The man slides into the rear seat and closes the door in a single motion.

Then, with a faint whirr, the car is gone.

Azi takes a few steps, gets out his NADIR phone, waits. After an agonizing few minutes, a second message appears.

Munira is being taken to a secure location. You will return to the flat. We will explain later. For now, do as you are told.

Then the screen turns blank. Azi has no plans, no ideas, no information. He doesn't know anything. He can't face the flat. So he walks, and then he runs, past the roundabout, scanning roads, cursing the endless trees. He walks and runs some more, without direction. The park ends, replaced by a broad bridge and a traffic-filled tree-lined avenue. He keeps walking, putting distance between himself and the place where Munira was taken, fear and guilt and something else he cannot name beating against the back of his skull – dead memories, trying to drown him.

Eventually, the long summer day starts to end. Azi has crossed rivers, parks, wide roads, passed buildings like stacked concrete Lego blocks. He is exhausted, yet not exhausted enough.

Then there is a buzz in his pocket. NADIR jolts into life, a single message onscreen.

If you want to see her alive again: tell no-one, come alone, now.

There is an address. Azi has money in his pocket so he hails a taxi, gives the details, then sits back and breathes deeply until he can hear something other than his own pulse.

Once again, his choices have been outsourced.

CHAPTER 15

Zealots in the Islamic Republic take many forms, but, in Kabir's experience, Dr Tal is one of a kind. For a start, there's his habit of dropping to the ground and doing sets of fifty press-ups in the middle of a conversation, invariably followed by careful inspection of the triceps bulging down the back of each arm. The baggy garb and directionless gun-waving that most warriors adopt for photographs isn't for him. No, Dr Tal is an Instagram male, attuned to the most flattering angle for every pose – and to the most body-hugging fit of robes or surgical scrubs, as the moment requires. His charm, when he chooses to unleash it, is as potent as his musky cologne.

They met a week ago, when Kabir made the mistake of showing some kindness towards one of the city's stray dogs – a beleaguered and diminishing band of creatures. Kabir dropped a scrap of meat in front of an especially melancholy three-legged Labrador, bending to place it near the dog's gasping tongue, and when he stood up, found Dr Tal gesturing to him from across the street.

They got talking. Dr Tal was British, intelligent, and was clearly permitted a great deal of latitude thanks to his medical training (trauma surgeon) and ironclad self-confidence. Dr Tal also loved animals, or at least felt a compassion towards them absent from his attitude towards humans. He could take or leave people, but animal suffering bothered him. It was one of just two things he appeared to care about beyond his own brilliance, the other being the unbelievably amateurish state of medical logistics in Raqqa.

Having brought his world-class training, contempt for lesser mortals and exquisitely symmetrical cheekbones to the Islamic Republic, Dr Tal was in a more or less permanent state of rage at its inadequacy to appreciate his talents. By the end of their conversation, it had become clear that he regarded Kabir as his newest friend, ally and handily expendable factotum.

Since then, things have gone from bad to worse. Because Dr Tal is literally unable to take no for an answer – it's as if he cannot even hear the word being spoken – he has now been introduced to Muhammed the German and decided that Muhammed and Kabir should together serve as a kind of honour guard to his ambitions.

The two men nominally remain attached to their media unit, and Kabir remains nominally confined to desk duty, but it took Dr Tal just five minutes of charismatic insistence to have them reallocated to the sacred task of recording his every photogenic exploit. These include both life-saving surgeries and life-ending masterclasses in methodical torture, each conducted with the same fascinated abstraction, as if he were performing a tricky piece of music from memory.

None of this, thankfully, will matter for much longer if Muhammed the German's plan comes off. Kabir and Muhammed share enough English – and have exchanged enough meaningful meditations upon the unholy, reprehensible, unthinkable evil of deserters – to establish that they both favour scarpering back across the Turkish border as soon as humanly possible. To this end, the recruitment of Muhammed's imaginary sister is developing well, with fabricated Facebook messages circulating successfully up the chain of command. Unburdened by reality, she has turned out to have a degree in chemical engineering, speaks four languages, and hates Western decadence with a deep and abiding passion.

As Kabir and Muhammed have also discerned, however, even the most liberal Western politician will be unlikely to welcome fighters from the Islamic Republic with open arms unless they come bearing a prize. Intelligence is the obvious route: the names of senior operatives, the locations of training camps and urban headquarters, vital elements of infrastructure and bureaucracy which they could obtain from the pre-propaganda flowing across their desks. Yet Kabir has something more special in mind: a compilation of the recruiters, fixers and middlemen most instrumental in bringing bodies to and fro across the border, together with the lucrative trafficking routes that sustain those parts of their economy not based on oil, tax or antiquities.

This, surely, will be worth some Western gratitude – even money, if they play their cards right. Kabir's access to computer systems makes it possible. He'll just need to be very, very careful – and turn Dr Tal's impositions to their advantage.

The fact that Dr Tal has been a massive recruiting hit makes this tricky. For a start, it has raised Kabir and Muhammed's visibility; and that's before Kabir considers the fact that Dr Tal would happily slice them into chunks and feed them to stray cats if he suspected their intentions. Even worse, he and Muhammed now spend much of the time competing for their master's affections.

This morning, after Muhammed picked up Dr Tal's shopping and Kabir tidied his villa, they presented him with the rough cuts of their latest masterpiece: a video of Dr Tal performing surgery on a six-year-old girl injured in an air strike. Kabir is out of favour today, making Muhammed the sole addressee of the verdict.

'Brother, I admire what you have achieved. The first and last sections will work, the middle can be cut. She is a beautiful thing. I assume we have footage of her returning home, embracing her family. Ah, septicaemia? What a waste. But we have enough. *Jazakallah khair*, brother.'

Kabir clenches his jaw, silently, then unclenches it somewhat less silently as his rotten tooth flares. Dr Tal hasn't even looked at him since he entered the room, and Kabir thinks he knows why. Muhammed's contact with his fictional sister recently reached the doctor's attention and, on the basis of her profile picture and attainments, Dr Tal has decided that she might be the only potential recruit in the entire Islamic Republic adequate to his exacting standards. Kabir's kindness to canines is yesterday's news.

On the plus side, the icy insanity of Dr Tal's patronage offers some hope when coupled to imaginary sisters. Given the doctor's clout, and his hunger to meet this vision of feminine fanaticism, obtaining permission and transport for a trip to the Turkish border will not be difficult. Having discussed the matter in ferocious whispers under cover of toilet visits – about the only time Kabir and Muhammed can be sure of privacy – they have determined that this is a chance they must take.

Kabir shuffles out of Dr Tal's gratuitously expansive living room, reviewing their prospects. He almost has his hands on some data that looks interesting (or at least that looks like he isn't meant to be able to get his hands on it), the Americans seem poised to deliver on the promise of death raining down from the heavens, and Dr Tal is positively frisky at the prospect of a world-class conquest. All the signs are good. Or, to be more precise, all the signs are awful if they remain.

Just before he reaches the door, Dr Tal's voice catches him, amplified by the floor and walls' exquisitely patterned tiles.

'Brother Kabir, you forgot my Red Bull. And the dogfood.'

And, of course, there's vengeance to be considered.

CHAPTER 16

The taxi drops Azi on a quiet, dark street. The screen is dazzling when he pulls the phone out of his pocket to read a new message. *Enter through the gate. Follow the drive.* There's only one gate, made of wrought metal, in front of a derelict expanse. With the sense that he's issuing his body instructions from a great distance, Azi slips through.

As his eyes become used to the darkness, Azi makes out two brick-built domestic buildings and, behind them, a large industrial-looking warehouse, also brick-built. Wild shrubs and weeds are thicketed everywhere except for the remains of a driveway. Azi walks along the broken concrete, his mind a mess of fractal memories: Munira, her body against his, the endless trees, the noise of tyres, the suddenness of her absence. The cool air feels good against his skin.

Ahead, beside the blocked-up outline of a large opening in the warehouse, a battered metal door is ajar. Azi looks for further commands onscreen, but there's nothing. Apart from his own breath and footsteps, he hasn't heard a sound since he left the taxi. Holding up the phone's faint screen-light, dislocated from the dark world, he walks in.

The corridor he enters is strange enough to end any sense of reverie. Its walls, floor and ceiling are perfectly smooth concrete, tapering to invisibility. It's as stark and pristine as the exterior is decrepit, and Azi has the sensation that he is standing still while the building glides past him. A muffled impact sounds in the distance, followed by echoes and faint scrabbling.

Azi freezes. Somewhere nearby a heavy door slams open and shuts, a white blaze dazzles and fades, then a pair of arms is pressing him against one wall, slamming his face against concrete and his wrists behind his back. The phone clatters to the floor. A voice sounds in his ear.

'What the hell are you doing here?'

It takes Azi a few seconds to recognize it as Odi. Or rather, as the person he has been calling Odi – but who is clearly something different at this point in time. Odi is breathing raggedly, his hands trembling as they grind Azi's wrists together. There's a stink like hot metal in the air.

'You lot told me to come!' Azi shouts, the wall cold and damp against his face. He can feel his neck muscles screaming.

Odi loosens his grip. 'Turn around, slowly.' More muffled noises are coming from closer than Azi is comfortable with. Odi's voice is a ferocious whisper. 'Why are you here? Who told you the location?'

Azi is somehow terrified and outraged at the same time. 'Look, mate, it was a message on the app, *your* app. It told me to come here, alone, if I ever wanted to see her again. After *you* took her! I assumed—' He breaks off. What did he assume? That someone was playing games, or that something had gone very wrong. Or both. With an effort, he pushes down the panic that has started to clot in his throat.

'We didn't send that message. We are under attack. You must leave, right now, and go straight to the flat. Where you will wait for me to come, in person.'

Odi is afraid, Azi realizes. The metallic smell is coming from him, layered over sweat. With a grunt, Odi releases him and staggers back, then pushes against one wall until a seemingly solid slab of concrete gives way. Before he enters, he meets Azi's gaze.

'I'm not your enemy, Azi. *We* are not your enemies. Go.'

Then he is gone, and Azi is in darkness.

He should run. Yet he can't. Whatever this is, it has something to do with her – and something to do with events beyond any anticipation.

Azi checks himself over. He's wearing his backpack, regular clothes and running shoes. Thanking God for his taste in nondescript black and grey sweatshirts, he pulls up his hood and wipes the sweat from his upper lip with the back of his sleeve. This is it: the moment he decides. He's just a guy from East Croydon; just another ghost in the machine. But he knows what opportunity looks like – and what it means to have made a promise. He can't go back to the apartment and hide.

Before he can change his mind, astonished by his own resolve, Azi makes his way to the part of the wall Odi disappeared through.

'All your base are belong to us,' he mutters, pushing hard.

It doesn't make him feel as cool as he hoped.

Once the door has cracked open an inch, Azi forces himself to wait and listen. Clearly, unarmed and untrained civilians are not going to be challenging Jack Bauer any time soon, but he's played enough *Metal Gear Solid* and *Splinter Cell* to know the value of stealth.

The sounds he heard earlier remain muffled – detonations mixed with banging – and neither Odi nor aggressive strangers rush out to confront him. He waits for a few more minutes, forces his body into an approximation of readiness, then opens the door wider and slips through.

Beyond is a huge room with stark concrete floors and strip lighting. It's almost empty, save for a few pieces of office furniture on one side. Around the desks, jagged shadows radiate from an expensive mess of computer equipment that seems to have been hurled onto the floor. At the far end is another door like the one he is peering through. Whatever is happening, it lies beyond.

Azi sprints across the echoing floor. Power and network cables run through hefty slots in the concrete. The equipment is stripped-down, serious gear; a couple of small server racks and workstations, laptops, tablets, smashed-up banks of identical monitors; physical firewalls and surge protectors; scattered boxes of portable tricks ranging from USB keyloggers to Wi-Fi Pineapples.

Crouching behind a desk that has flipped onto its side he begins rifling through the smaller items, sorting and inspecting them. What he needs is the kind of thing Anna stopped him stealing in the coffee shop: a phone, tablet, some device he can make his own. The desk is the same IKEA model he has at home in his shed, and it feels bizarrely familiar to be hunkered alongside it sifting gadgets and cables. At least, it feels familiar right up to the point at which two black-clad figures burst through the far door and start shooting at him.

Having never been shot at before, Azi's first reaction is to run. Suppressing this stupidity, he ducks and makes himself as small as possible against the top of the desk. He's surrounded by a technological arsenal worth thousands of dollars, capable of infiltrating government facilities at thousands of miles, yet the only object of any use right now is 140 by 65cm of veneered MALM plywood – and possibly the bent leg of a FLINTAN desk chair, if he can swing it with enough force. In other words, he's dead as soon as they start taking serious aim.

The seconds slow as Azi watches a bullet bounce off the concrete near his left leg. Then another one thuds forcefully into the table beside him, blasting a fist-sized chunk into sawdust. He tries to pull himself together, but there's not much to grasp. Blood is hammering in his throat and ears, and all he can hear apart from gunshots is his own soon-to-be-silenced heartbeat. It seems cruelly apt that cheap office furniture will mark his final resting place.

Then he spots something among the scattered tech: several small silver boxes that, if he's lucky, are the military cousins of a crowd-dispersal device he knows well. It's called the Mosquito, and can produce intense, high-pitched bursts of sound. Throw enough ultrasonic interference into the mix and the results can be disabling.

Azi fumbles several towards him, flips their rear switches to a range of different frequencies, then punches them into life before hurling them across the room and cramming his fingers into his ears.

Even at a distance and through covered ears, the result is remarkable: a burning sensation deep in his brain, as if someone is slowly peeling off the plates of his skull. The gunfire stops.

Fighting waves of nausea, Azi struggles into a crouch. The sonic burst will last around thirty seconds and, while he's not sure he'll be capable of running once it ends, he can at least die in the attempt.

Just as he's about to go, however, there's a burst of gunfire in a different key and direction, followed by silence. He freezes. Thirty seconds elapse, then a face caked in blood appears around the edge of his table. Azi stares. The face stares back. Then it speaks.

'Oh for fuck's sake.'

It's Odi, apparently both injured and incredibly pissed off. He slumps against the desk and gestures towards the far door. On the floor lie the two men who were, until recently, shooting at them. Azi lurches to his feet, and discovers that his legs don't work very well while his eyes are looking at dead bodies. A sour taste of bile rises in his mouth and, after fighting it for a moment, he vomits. It's almost a relief. Only once he's finished this and pushed his hood down does he notice quite how profusely Odi is bleeding.

'Odi! Shit, mate. I'll get help. This way is safe now, is it?' He spits the last vomit out of his mouth and nods to the far door.

Odi grunts through gritted teeth, attempting to staunch the bleeding with his hands. Moving as fast as he can, Azi dashes across the room and through the door. It opens into a corridor identical to the one he entered along, save for the detail that a massive hole has been blown through one of its walls from the overgrown grounds beyond.

Emergency lighting floods the scene in red. Three dead men in civilian clothes are lying face down near him in the corridor, neat holes in the back of their heads. Two more are sprawled nearby. One of them is the man from the Tiergarten pavement. Munira isn't there.

The scene and its body count are so extreme that Azi finds he has temporarily run out of reactions. Did Odi kill all these people? Did they kill each other? What is going on?

'Azi?' an incredulous voice calls out from behind him.

It's Anna, dressed in some serious-looking combat gear, holding a gun with businesslike ease. She walks towards him, a bowel-loosening parody of a smile on her face.

'How and why are you here?' Her gun, Azi notices, is pointing between his eyes.

'Don't shoot! After your people took Munira, I got a message on my app to come here. I walked into this. Odi's injured, through there. He needs help.'

'It's on the way. Jesus Christ, what a fucking mess.'

Anna walks over to the bodies, checking them one by one, never lowering her weapon. 'This was a raid,' she says, 'which shouldn't have been remotely possible. And I suspect that it has something to do with you.'

'They came for Munira?' he asks, already knowing the answer.

'They took her, which is different. They also took a lot of our gear. It's complete chaos and the last thing I need right now is a guy who has been living and working in a shed for the past decade following me around. You'll be dealt with later.' She starts to head to the door Azi came through, one hand still tracking him with the gun.

Azi is close behind.

'Wait . . .' He hesitates, gestures for her permission to take off his rucksack, then produces one of the smallest and strangest pieces of hardware he picked up. It's little bigger than a standard thumb drive but, he's pretty sure, a great deal more significant. For a start, it seems to have a GPS, microphone, camera and network capabilities, plus God knows what else lurking in its firmware. It's also markedly different in manufacture from everything else on the site. 'I found this.'

'What is it?'

'Exactly. It's not one of yours, right? Yet it was in the trashed computer gear. Which I think means it was active before all this kicked off. Which I think means you have even more problems than you thought.'

Anna's eyes widen. She snatches it from him. 'And you just happened to find this, did you?'

'Crawling on my hands and knees through computer crap is a speciality of mine.'

Her jaw clenched, she looks at him, at what she's just taken off him, then reaches a decision.

'None of what I'm about to say is happening. Do you understand? I am not telling you to make your own way out of this building and do whatever the fuck you need to do to get away from here and lie low. I am not telling you that we have been infiltrated, that some of my best people are dead, and this is the biggest fucking intelligence disaster since someone reckoned Saddam was stockpiling poison gas. I am not saying this, and you are not going to stay in touch via our mutual friend.' She pauses.

'I will, however, shoot you in the face, just for the hell of it, if you're still here in ten seconds. Are we clear, Azi Bello?'

He's already halfway out of the hole.

CHAPTER **17**

The best escape plans, Azi reckons, must look pretty similar to the best hacking assaults – because they both involve doing unexpected things quickly. Heavy with adrenaline, his feet pounding the tarmac, he puts block after block between himself and the warehouse, then hails a taxi and takes stock.

Time is already running out, for him and for Munira. He has a change of clothes, his passport, a heap of highly traceable electronics, several hundred euros in cash and no idea what just happened. But he also has his freedom, and a mandate to put as much distance as possible between himself and the warehouse of horrors.

First things first: appearances. Azi tells the driver to take him to a pharmacy and picks up razors, shaving cream, deodorant and plasters. Then he staggers back into the car.

Next is a chicken shop, grim and dank enough to be almost like home, its neon sign heralding flavours no salad can match. Azi pays off his cab, demolishes a bucket of wings big enough to offset his post-gunfight tremors, then orders several off-brand energy drinks and tries not to start screaming or weeping at strangers.

When the shaking in his hands has finally settled, Azi wedges himself behind a tiny table next to the toilet and tips out the most important electronic item in his stash: an Android burner phone which, with a little persuasion, picks up an open Wi-Fi network and comes online. It's late at night on Central European Time, which means it's early afternoon on the west coast, which means that – by his reckoning – there's a decent chance that his friend Milhon will be responding to messages.

Milhon is on Azi's mind both because he's pretty sure she's California-based, and because she is the one person in the world he believes can and will help him get what he needs within the next couple of hours: money, money and more money.

Specifically, as she spent several of their past exploits explaining in detail, Milhon is an expert in the realm of Pseudo-Random Numbers (PRNs to their friends): the strings of data that pass for unpredictable in the world of machines. Engineering a top-notch Pseudo-Random Number Generator is a complex art – and she was one of the best, right until she found out that the 'research institute' employing her was being paid by the Russian mafia to reverse-engineer stolen slot machines.

Being both an idealist and a hacker of considerable ability, she has been lying low ever since – except for sporadic infiltrations in AZ's company. Right now, Azi is after the same thing as Milhon's ex-employers: an app able to predict when any slot machine of the right type is about to pay out its jackpot. And, if Milhon is to be believed, this is exactly what she came up with.

All such an app needs is for you to feed the system enough information for it to assess a slot machine's PRNG state, then start playing it at precisely the right moment and – hey presto! – you're guaranteed a win. Which is about the only edge currently adequate to Azi's requirements. The only hard part is that you remain at the mercy of randomness: the payouts come when they come, or don't, and there's nothing you can change about that.

Azi is certain she will have kept a copy, largely because nobody sensible discards software that smart. The question is whether there are any circumstances under which a sensible person might share it. Licking his lips one last time, he logs into one of his secure accounts and sends juice-stained finger-tips flying over the burner phone.

Milhon! AZ here. Emergency favour: real deal, can't explain now. As big as it gets.

Mercifully, he has to wait just five minutes for an answer. *I'm listening.*

This is it. Willing himself to stay calm, Azi thinks back to when Sigma's first plea arrived: a lifetime ago, when his world was still a shed and a screen. He refused to meet her, then dragged her into a trap. Praying that this hasn't set some kind of karmic precedent, he keeps typing.

Download of your casino app, latest version, for me to run on Android. Urgent.

Can Milhon see the panic behind his words? Are any of the things he believes about the person on the other side of the screen true? It's another five minutes before the answer comes.

You'll owe me. And then some. And then some more.

I will. Life or death, no joke. Hoping to save a friend.

Then she asks what he was afraid she would ask.

Got something to give?

Azi winces. He could lie or offer empty promises. Or – worse – he could inflict the truth on her. But some knowledge shouldn't be shared. The app will give him a chance, if he moves fast enough. If he's lucky.

Cover blown, no tech. But if I make it, whatever you want.

A last, agonizing pause.

Deal. Only for you, AZ. Only for you. Be seeing you.

Azi almost punches the air with joy, thudding both knees into the table's cracked underside.

AZ is back.

With chicken in his stomach and Milhon's app downloading onto his Android burner, Azi packs up and locks himself in the chicken shop bathroom for long enough to shave and fasten a fragment of plaster across each fingertip, masking his fingerprints. By the end of the process he almost looks respectable – at least by his own recent standards – and should be slightly harder to track.

As fast as he can in the cramped space, he then strips to his underwear and runs two of the pocket-sized devices that he picked up in the warehouse carefully across his body. After five minutes, he has found one tiny tracker on each forearm that Odi presumably sneaked beneath his sleeves under the cover of his initial assault: ultra-adhesive slices of silicone so finely crafted that they're almost indistinguishable from freckles. With luck, Munira will be sporting several of the same.

Finally, Azi dresses in the cleanish clothes in his rucksack, counts his cash, hails a cab on the street outside and heads for the nearest casino.

The Spielbank casino at Potsdamer Platz is a modern enough Berlin institution to care more about Azi's cash and passport than his general appearance. At the entrance stands a statue of a bear with a fruit machine in its stomach, the creature's paw raised in a mix of triumph and greeting. Inside, the sprawling space is clean and softly lit, the 2 a.m. crowd composed of young tourists and local regulars drifting across four floors of escalating appetite for risk – slots at the bottom; poker, blackjack and roulette up top. The regulars are easy to spot, their glazed eyes and slumped shoulders uniform as they chase the next dopamine hit.

Azi walks among the slots, conscious that he needs to look like a harmless tourist to avoid being trailed by security staff. The giant neon figure of a blonde in cowboy hat and boots is sprawled along one wall, the roof is a brushed steel arch, and the air conditioning is excellent. To Azi's relief, a young American near him is filming her winning combination and its payout on her phone – meaning there's no etiquette against mobiles on this floor. He gets his Android burner out, loads Milhon's app and starts to wander in search of the right kind of machine.

There are over three hundred machines in total, most of them brand new. Azi almost despairs at finding a model with a predictable PRNG until he reaches a cluster underneath the giant blonde's head. Beside her on the wall is an aggressively phallic neon cactus, and between this and her torso is a cluster of eight slots of a type Milhon has listed – WinBig. Four of them are in play, their gamblers' faces glowing in the lurid neon. Trying to look as gormlessly touristic as possible, Azi sets about registering the state of each active machine.

As he soon realizes, it could be a long haul. The problem

is that big wins don't come along very often – and it takes quite a few observations to calibrate the app for each machine. This means that the odds of him finding a sure winner before the casino closes at 5 a.m. are not as good as he had hoped. The process also requires him to spend a great deal of time looking harmless – and lose just enough money to look profitable – while fiddling with his phone. *Come on*, Azi mutters to himself. *You've been preparing for something like this for most of your adult life.*

By 3 a.m. he is nervous. There are six further suitable machines on the other side of the slot floor, and Azi has managed to assess four of them in addition to the initial eight. None is anywhere near a big enough payout. Security guards pass by frequently and, given the contents of his rucksack, he doesn't fancy a pat down.

To allay further suspicion, he heads up one floor to the bar – mirrors, glass, rich reds and reflective metal; a hygienic version of fin-de-siècle decadence – and orders an espresso which he proceeds to load with brown sugar. By the time he has finished ripping open sachets he is essentially drinking a coffee-flavoured heap of sugar, but he doesn't care. The edges of his vision are beginning to wobble with fatigue.

Then he sees it: another WinBig machine, nestled near the entrance to this floor. It's being played by an angry-looking business type. Azi pours himself a glass of iced water from the jug on the bar and sidles over until he's close enough to start entering combinations in his phone. One spin, two, three, four, five, six – Milhon's app completes its calibration and Azi almost drops off his stool in shock. The highest jackpot is due in ten spins. Twenty thousand euros.

He pauses, his mind racing. Will the business type play for ten more spins? Almost certainly: he seems to be in it for the duration and has already shot several hostile glances in Azi's direction. What then? Azi gets to his feet and begins to make his way out of the bar. As he passes by the machine, he stumbles and not-very-accidentally launches his entire glass of iced water into the man's considerable midriff.

As Azi suspected it would be, the reaction is ferocious. The business type splutters, swears and unleashes a burst of insults into Azi's face. With the appalled manner of the habitually inept, Azi grabs a napkin and begins to dab limply at the man's cheeks and sodden crotch, only to find his wrists grasped in two hairy hands. Looking bewildered, Azi falls backwards onto the floor, shouting for help. The man pushes him down, shouts a few times and manages to get one vicious kick into Azi's ribs before security arrives: two huge men, restraining the German and shepherding him out of the door.

At once, Azi leaps to his feet and starts gesturing that there's no problem at all, that these things always seem to happen to him, that he's fine. He waits, twenty seconds, thirty, sipping the solid sugar dregs of his espresso. Then he eases himself into the padded chair at the slot machine, loads it up with all his remaining credit, and starts to play. With any luck, Milhon is as good as he has spent the last year believing.

A few minutes later, digital bells and whistles indiscreetly announce that he has won the jackpot. Five minutes after that, he is cashing out at the nearest booth, accepting his winnings in the form of four hundred neatly bound fifty-euro notes.

Ten minutes later, he is on the street contemplating the worst-case scenario he is about to embrace: making Gomorrah his exit strategy.

CHAPTER 18

Given the carnage unleashed earlier, going anywhere near Gomorrah itself is what Azi would usually deem One of the Worst Ideas in History. On the other hand, precisely because of this fact, it's about the only option he reckons nobody will anticipate. Trying to summon his last conversation with Munira, Azi runs through her words about obtaining the darknet client.

There's a username for messages, on Signal. Gomorrah. So simple! You send a secure message, you offer your evidence . . .

As soon as Azi has logged into the necessary Signal account on the stolen burner phone, Jim Denison asks Gomorrah to add him as a contact.

Azi holds his breath in the darkness, gingerly touching the swollen upper lip and aching jawbone given to him by the German. For ten minutes, he waits on a quiet backstreet, close to the main drag on which the casino stands. Street cleaners and delivery vans bustle through the first of the morning light. Everything is taking too long. Even if he can make use of the cash, even if his desperate hopes are answered, it may already be too late. Helplessly, he paces.

Then, a miracle: his request is accepted. A few moments later, there's a message.

Please send required verification.

Of course: evidence. If he's very lucky, whatever instructions Munira gave Odi will have ticked the remaining boxes in Jim's profile. Azi fires off links to Jim's profiles, the Defiance forums, everything he can find. Then he waits.

The minutes slouch past with agonizing slowness until, at last, a new message arrives.

Please send required verification.

The same again. It's all automated, of course. No people, no risk, no mistakes. And Azi has failed to send what's needed. Desperately, he browses everything he can access about Jim, numb fingers moving as fast as he can make them across the phone's slipping screen. It's too busy here for him to stay much longer – too ordinary. The night's secrecy is evaporating. What will he do if this doesn't work?

Then he finds it, on the forums: a public exchange between some of the most senior members of Defiance and several new names, repeating what appear to be stock phrases in English and German. A stilted conversation about Jim: a code, hidden in plain sight. Azi double checks, copies the link, pastes it into the email and waits, praying he has found the necessary form of words.

A minute, then a new message appears. Azi has to read it five times before he can believe what he is seeing.

Welcome Jim Denison. Please specify client OS.

This is it: access. After taking another long breath and peering over both shoulders in turn at the street's gathering light, Azi types a single word in response.

Android.

A further few minutes, then a link appears. He clicks, downloads, installs, and waits for a secure connection to the darknet's private servers. Everything is bespoke. Only a named and verified user of the client software can even detect Gomorrah's existence.

Achieving a secure connection seems to take for ever. Azi blinks, frets, paces, passing the phone from hand to hand. Then, the next time he looks at the screen, a single phrase is hovering in crisp white letters against the darkness.

This is Gomorrah.

He's in.

Hardly daring to breathe, he taps the screen. There's a pause, then a cloud of smaller type appears. It's some kind of user agreement.

I, Jim Denison, endorsed by the Defiance party, currently based in Berlin and resident of Thrale Road, South London, agree to abide by this service's code of conduct: to accept supervision and monitoring via this device, to deliver all goods and services as promised, to pay in advance in entirety, to maintain absolute discretion, and to obey all of the above upon pain of death. I submit to these terms in perpetuity.

And people complain about Facebook, Azi thinks, tapping to agree. At least the phone hasn't asked for a drop of his blood. One more tap, and the marketplace opens.

As with almost every darknet destination Azi has frequented over the years, what appears next on his screen is disturbingly ordinary. Gomorrah closely resembles a spreadsheet: heavy with text and selectable columns, awkward to scroll on a mobile device. It's like an old-school eBay for evil.

Azi starts to browse. If you're buying, you either bid on predetermined offerings with countdown timers or enter a special request together with timescale and budget. If you're selling, you specify a service and a reserve price. The interface is impressively uncluttered, and the existence of an Android client is an unusual touch, but otherwise it has the counter-intuitive dullness that marks a genuine illicit marketplace.

There are also, however, some major differences from the marketplaces Azi is accustomed to researching on Tor. For a start, there are no drugs. In general, drugs are far and away the most popular darknet products, thanks equally to the level of demand, profit and ease of transportation. On Gomorrah, everything on offer appears either to be a service, a software exploit or some hard-to-obtain hardware – and the pricing levels are stratospheric.

Bidding on ownership of a five-hundred-thousand-machine botnet is at three million dollars. A set of next-generation NSA microwave listening devices is a few hundred thousand. Remote exploits for the latest Predator drone firmware are at ten million, and climbing fast. Almost nothing is off limits, up to and including the most closely guarded data and software of several intelligence services. If even half of this is real, the world at large needs to rethink the meaning of cybersecurity.

What shocks Azi even more than this, however, is the

handling of payments, complaints and disagreements. Profound paranoia is a required state of mind for conducting any darknet business. Encryption keys are ubiquitous, as are cryptocurrencies; false identities are created and abolished according to regular schedules; it's assumed that law enforcement will at some point shut down almost every site that's out there.

Here, however, there are indications of what he can only call a quiet, service-orientated confidence. Payments are accepted in a wide variety of currencies. Real names are known to the system. As he had hoped – but hardly dared to believe until now – cash is readily accepted by couriers and fixers, with all kinds of real-world encounters easy to facilitate (payments, trafficking, murders). It all feels extremely convenient, even civilized; a far cry from those darknet forums where nine out of ten assassins-for-hire are either FBI agents, blackmailers, or both. Enforcement and reliability are guaranteed, because the people behind this most discreet of marketplaces have their gaze fixed upon every single user – and an ability to punish failure in the most absolute terms.

In his two decades of peering through the holes in the modern world, Azi has never seen something that makes the unthinkable feel this mundane; a purchasable compendium of hacks, vulnerabilities and manipulations that would ordinarily take lifetimes to locate. It's as if someone announced an auction expressly designed to hasten the collapse of civilization. Which, now that he thinks about it, couldn't be more perfect for his purposes.

Opening a sub-section devoted to urgent local cash services, Azi outlines Jim Denison's immediate need.

Berlin-based transportation urgently required. Fifteen thousand euros cash, departure in one hour, discreet central location. Sealed package to be taken cross-continent.

Triumph and fear boil in Azi's chest, alongside incipient exhaustion. He's on the run, he's on his own and he has no idea what the hell is going to happen next.

It's time to hit the road.

CHAPTER 19

Dr Tal does not have a high opinion of dentists. Kabir discovered this when the agony of his rotting molar finally prompted him to ask the doctor for help. Dentists, Kabir has learned, are little better than glorified nurses. Dental nurses are worse even than regular nurses. Then, somewhere beneath even these half-humans in the chain of being, there are the kind of people who expect world-class trauma surgeons to peer into their stinking mouths.

They're on the road. Muhammed the German is driving their requisitioned off-roader, Dr Tal is seated in the front passenger seat, Kabir is crammed in the back alongside sundry medical supplies and firearms. Since the Caliphate was declared, fighters have continued to flood into the Islamic Republic – the new Minister of Education in Mosul is himself a German ex-trafficker – and this means Muhammed's sister is travelling a well-trodden route. This in turn means that they may be up a shitty creek with no means of propulsion if too many recruiters or recruitees profess ignorance of her existence.

To make matters worse, Kabir has a USB key stuffed up his arse, delicately wrapped in a surgical plastic bag that previously contained one of Dr Tal's facemasks. In a metaphorical sense, at least, Dr Tal is sniffing his rear end, and this brings Kabir some comfort as he bounces from side to side, watching dust rise in torrents behind them.

He's not quite sure what data the USB key contains, but some of it must be good. It took him barely an hour to Google and download the necessary exploits, using a borrowed admin account whose details he has watched one of his superiors type out with a single slow finger every day for the last month. In what he hopes is an effective insurance policy, he also downloaded a lavish selection of malware and then activated the lot. With luck, they'll put it down to a foreign cyberattack.

Dr Tal and Muhammed look pretty chummy, as they have for much of the last week, but this doesn't mean much. Kabir's experience out here suggests that people like Dr Tal don't have friends, only acquaintances who are more or less convenient; and Muhammed is currently a great deal more convenient than Kabir. Up front, Dr Tal heartily slaps Muhammed across the shoulder, joking about today's trafficking traffic. They have passed some military and civilian four-by-fours, but the bulk of the other road users are a motley succession of independent traders hauling oil across the Republic in the biggest tankers they can get hold of.

The traders buy their oil, under licence, directly at the fields in crude form. It's a strategy that transfers most of the risks and costs away from the authorities, but that produces infamous traffic jams. Once the Americans begin their air strikes in earnest, Kabir thinks, there will be a great deal of burning.

As they ride out an especially aggressive bump, swerving simultaneously to avoid being overturned by a tanker, Kabir watches Dr Tal clench and unclench his fists against the dashboard. The man is formidable, his lazily sprung physical strength always on the edge of violence. No wonder he fits in so well. Dr Tal is perhaps the sanest man Kabir has ever met, because his obsessions only make him more effective. There's no pity or hesitation in him. At this point, bouncing like a sack of rice in the dusty and overheated air, Kabir reaches a decision. He needs to start thinking like Dr Tal if he wants to make it out alive.

Out of the blue, Dr Tal announces that it's time to stop. Through his window Kabir can see the slender white-and-red chimneys of a power station, shivering in the heat. It's elegant, almost like a mosque, the light glancing off the unrippled water in what he assumes is a cooling pool. Kabir imagines bombs falling from the sky, the towers tumbling, the shockwaves snapping every bone in his body. He has got to get out of this place. He has got to get into a town with dentists.

They pull over, onto scrubby grass beside the shade of a lone rocky outcrop. Kabir snaps a few shots for the greater glory of Dr Tal's social media presence, and stares into as much of the light as he can bear. The sky is vast, the land is flat, the sun is merciless. Muhammed the German and Dr Tal drink deeply from their water bottles. Kabir waits before being given permission – a contemptuous nod – to do the same, weighing the moment. He has so many questions to answer.

How soon can he kill them both?

CHAPTER 20

Having expected the unexpected, Azi is disappointed to discover that being covertly transported across Europe in the back of a truck is just as unpleasant, disorientating, frightening, claustrophobic, disempowering, dull and constipation-inducing as he would have guessed.

He is seated inside a wooden crate of modest proportions, having specified his needs with paranoid precision: leave a receptacle just large enough to fit one person at a quiet location, leave inside it a day's worth of food and water (and a bucket, which was the service provider's one suggestion during their terse exchange), then collect said crate and convey it by road to an isolated spot on the outskirts of Athens.

He has five thousand euros left after paying for his passage. He left the rest of the cash outside the crate, crammed into a plastic bag: an inflated fee for a transfer entailing no false documents, but, he knows, worth every cent if it can guarantee discretion.

Azi is taking Anna's instruction to lie low extremely seriously. To prevent tracking, he dispatched his NADIR phone into the back of a long-haul lorry with one well-aimed throw, before relinquishing the comforts of Berlin's Wi-Fi networks and removing the batteries from every scrap of stolen hardware on his person. Now that he's helplessly confined, the merits of all of this have begun to feel less clear. Is Odi still alive? Should Azi have stayed closer to Berlin? Shivering at the memory of bullets gouging through chipboard, Azi suppresses his doubts.

Going unrecorded, Azi reflects, is becoming one of the twenty-first century's priciest privileges. Hence the twin (and sporadically overlapping) classes of people who get to indulge in luxuries such as privacy, silence, clean air and sound sleep: the very rich and the very bad. Poverty may guarantee irrelevance, but it no longer keeps you off the grid.

Then again, nobody is doing much effective surveilling of anyone in Greece these days, which is one of the reasons – Azi tells himself – it makes perfect sense for him to head there. It's a nation wobbling in geopolitical earthquakes: unemployment, asylum, immigration; the aftershocks of financial crisis, building their resonance into new disaster. It's the badly latched gate into and out of Europe – its loans and politics curdling, its police armed and dangerously underpaid. Even the refugees are desperate to move on.

If Munira is still alive – and he is currently trying to keep all other possibilities far from his mind – then the Greek capital's semi-functioning underside should be an ideal place for picking up intel, asking questions and seeking discreet assistance. It's also much too late for him to change his strategy; although not for him to endlessly re-analyse his choices and fears.

Above all, it's the dead bodies that keep coming back to Azi. Locked in sweating darkness, he sees himself stepping again and again over corpses in the warehouse. Sometimes, a bullet topples him to join them. Sometimes, one of them has Munira's face.

There are approximately twenty hours left of this bumping, agonizing, uncertain journey – assuming he isn't simply pulled out of his crate and executed – and, desperate to put some distance between his thoughts and present reality, Azi finds himself tumbling into the past.

July 1998. With school behind them, Azi and Ad had stabilized the routines of their friendship into something almost perfect: hours of companionable silence devoted to hacking, Internet Relay Chat and forum banter; multiplayer games of *Doom II* and *Diablo*; research into the intricacies of all the above; and as much tepid lager as they could bear to drink, neither being prepared to confess that they didn't like the taste.

They had also fallen into two complementary roles. Azi provided the strategy, the meticulous preparation and the paranoia necessary for self-preservation, while Ad provided the swaggering ambition and contempt for lesser mortals. They had a good thing going and, like all good things involving teenage boys, it was fraught with bravado and self-sabotage.

Backed by Azi's research, Ad's favourite trick was to ring up a blameless mid-size company, open with some confident-sounding questions about their IT, then ask to be put through to the computer room. At this point, he would pretend to be an administrator from whoever supplied their software. *I'm sorry to say that we are ringing round to report an urgent bug. The current version of your software is compromised. You may already have lost data. But I can patch everything up remotely if you just provide a few details . . .*

It never failed to astonish Azi what could be achieved through the correct combination of fear and hope. After some token queries, which Ad met with a mix of jargon and amicable contempt, the sysadmin on the other end of the line would grant them access to a systems manager account. The same sysadmin would then gratefully stay on the line while Ad and Azi introduced a remote patch permitting backdoor access to the entire database. After this, unless the company was unusually adept at monitoring network traffic, they wouldn't notice anything amiss until their email system began spontaneously inviting clients to perform sexual acts with one another.

Over time, Azi began working on pre-scripted lines for Ad to deliver during calls, in search of ever more effective social engineering techniques – as the manipulation of others' trust and expectations was known. Azi liked knowing the proper name for things. If the scam didn't work, hanging up immediately would arouse suspicion. Instead, Ad should cheerily promise to send a patch by disk in the post before ringing off. If the scam did work, he should stay on the line for a few extra minutes, exchanging pleasantries and asking if there was anything else he could do.

Over the years of their collaboration, Azi-the-apprentice had started to feel like Azi-the-brains-of-the-operation – but Ad had subtle ways of pushing back. Sometimes, Ad played dumb then showed his hand: things he knew that Azi hadn't got around to reading. Sometimes, Ad acted like mere details were beneath him. Sometimes – and these were the best times – they both got lost in the moment, barely able to contain their excitement when they found a new approach.

Then there were the worst times, when Ad went on the offensive.

'Mate, your research is fucking shoddy. I'm doing my thing, chatting my tits off. Only you've got the wrong name for their IT supplier, the wrong guy as head of department . . . this isn't amateur hour.'

Azi had learned the hard way that arguing with Ad was never a good idea. Yet he could never help defending himself.

'It's not my fault their website is out of date! I don't even know why they bother having one. And there's no way you should have told that guy to go and play hide-and-go-fuck-yourself.'

Ad grinned in a manner calculated to drive Azi crazy. 'It was good for him. A . . .' unforgivably, Ad supplies air quotes '. . . "valuable learning experience". I thought he was going to cry.'

Sighing, Azi attempted to leverage the gravitas of his just-turned-eighteen years. 'Seriously, Ad, we cannot afford to piss people off. It's too dangerous. What does your sticker say?'

Ad's sticker said FREE KEVIN in black block capitals on a yellow background and was affixed to his pride and joy: an IBM ThinkPad 770 laptop with integrated DVD-ROM drive, handed down as a gift from his mother. Azi would have needed to work non-stop in IKEA for a decade to afford something like it.

The sticker was part of a campaign run by the American magazine *2600: The Hacker Quarterly* – Ad was one of the few people in the UK to have persuaded his mum to arrange a subscription for him – and referred to the American hacker Kevin Mitnick, aka the World's Most Notorious Hacker, aka the Person Ad Most Wants to Be and Sometimes Thinks He Already Is.

Having finally been tracked down by the FBI, Mitnick was being detained without bail under threat of hundreds of years of prison time. So far as Azi was concerned, this made him an example of what his and Ad's future would look like if they weren't careful. So far as Ad was concerned, this made him an example of why as many websites as possible needed to be taken down and turned into FREE KEVIN banners, and why the world's entire non-techy population deserved to be punished for their ignorance. Adopting one of his more artfully innocent looks, Ad fixed Azi with a grin.

'The sticker is just flagging the freebie you get when you buy the laptop. Personally, I keep my Kevin in a cupboard under the stairs.'

'You didn't buy that laptop. And stop being a dick. That sticker says that you can't be too careful. It says you can't trust anyone, that if you don't take things seriously, you'll get caught.'

'You need glasses, mate. They're not going to get us. We're good. Some of the stuff I've got on here, some of the things you haven't seen, they're going to blow your mind. SQL injection, you see that in *Phrack*? I'm ahead of the game.'

Azi nodded, trying not to choke on a sudden burst of conscience. He already knew what was on Ad's laptop. He knew because he had hacked it, last week, while Ad was doing a beer run to the nearest corner shop.

Azi had committed this ultimate betrayal via a program called Back Orifice, developed by the fine hackers at Cult of the Dead Cow, which granted total control of any Windows system. He had also more or less managed to convince himself that he was doing this for Ad's own protection. The very fact that Ad was running Windows was a sign he wasn't taking things seriously. Not every sysadmin was an idiot. Not every hacker was an ally. You couldn't trust anyone, that was the rule.

'Are you all right there, mate? Is there something you want to tell me?' Ad sounded horribly solicitous.

'No! I mean, yeah. Kind of. Look, mate, I'd just like you to be more careful. And I'd like to see the new stuff you've got. SQL injection sounds pretty cool.'

'Yeah. But you've seen it already.'

'What?'

There was a hardness in Ad's face that Azi had never seen before.

'I said, you've seen it already. Unless you think my own mum is spying on me? I mean, I basically have to help her find spellcheck but, you know what, maybe she's undercover? Maybe she's an even bigger two-faced fucking liar than you. Otherwise, the number of people who could install Back Orifice on my computer is basically one.'

'Jesus. Look.' A sickening heat spread across Azi's body. 'Look. Mate. I was worried, that was all. You've got to believe me, all this Mitnick stuff, the whole world is going crazy about hackers . . . I just wanted to keep you safe.'

'Ask me how I knew.'

Azi looked around his shed wildly. Nothing in it suggested any escape from this conversation. 'How did you know?'

'I have remote access to your PC. From my desktop box. Your PC used to be mine. Remember? I thought I'd keep an eye on *you*, mate. Added a little something to your Linux OS when you weren't looking. Now who's running a lame box? How does it feel, you smug prick?'

Azi, usually the reserved one, usually the one to keep his temper, lunged ineffectually towards Ad with something between a slap and a blow – a move that, thanks to the lack of any space between their folding chairs, saw him collapse across his friend's lap, banging his head on the desk in the process. Ad contemplated him in disgust.

'I've watched you, getting cocky. Taking my stuff, thinking you know it all. Appointing yourself boss. And yeah, I saw you downloading my porn too. How was that for you, by the way?'

Humiliated and glowing with shame, Azi scrabbled back into his seat.

'Ad! I was worried about you. About us getting caught. What you did was . . . cheating.' Azi sounded pathetic even to his own ears.

'I did it because it's what needs to be done. Listen to yourself. Cheating? There's no such thing as cheating. Anything goes, everything goes. I was doing you a favour. Think about it. I'm your best mate. I'm the only one who would take this kind of shit from you, who would do it back, who would tell you everything. We're not kids any more. The end of the summer, one month away – what's happening? I'll tell you what's happening. You're making a mistake if you do anything other than come with me to America.'

So that was what this was about. An old argument in new clothes.

'Jesus.' Azi tried a mollifying laugh. 'Dream on. You might have the money, but all I've got is a couple of uni offers and a lot of application forms for financial aid and a fucking shed. I can barely afford a travelcard to Zone One.'

Ad was implacable.

'Uni? Waste of time and money. *We* should be telling *them* what to do! America, it's the land of opportunity, mate, and you've got everything you need to make it. Fuck your offer from, what is it, the University of Outdated Bollocks. The internet, all of this, it's going to take over the world. We are the future. We *own* the future. I'm your best mate, and I want you to come with me. You know I'm right. You *owe* me.'

Azi sighed.

'Look. I'm sorry I hacked your machine. I'm sorry about everything, Ad, I'm so sorry . . . but I'm staying here.'

The next month, Ad was on a flight to San Francisco – and Azi was accepting an offer to study computer science in London.

They stayed in touch, online, but it wasn't the same. Ad seemed to expect an apology: for Azi to turn around and admit he was wrong about everything. Azi didn't know what he expected, but he was pretty sure that Ad was a shitty friend.

Azi followed his friend's exploits online, as best he could, aware that their worlds were overlapping less and less. Ad had talent, dedication and imagination. But he also had an unlovely contempt for anyone and anything he considered beneath him – a category that seemed to include the senior management of every start-up he worked for.

Ad worked brilliantly but erratically. He won a scholarship to Stanford, then dropped out. He sent Azi angry, pleading, unapologetic messages in the middle of the night. Why the fuck was Azi wasting his time in Olde England when San Francisco beckoned? Why did nobody have a sense of humour about the mysterious replacement of every image on their Friendster profile with anthropomorphic genitals?

Now, at a distance of sixteen years, sitting inside a pitch-black box beside a bucket of his own urine, the whole thing seems ridiculous to Azi: that the most important friendship in his life fell away so fast. Then again, it turns out most things are like that. They're there, they're a part of who you are – and then they're gone, never to return.

Azi thinks about Munira, then about his mother, then about the fact that he must stop thinking about Munira and his mother in such close proximity. Not least because he needs, more than anything, to believe that only one of them is dead.

Finally, without noticing any transition, Azi falls into a dead sleep. Through the day and then the night, the truck rolls along progressively worse roads, rocking his wedged limbs.

An hour before dawn, the engine stops and the quality of air and light shifts. A series of shudders and blows jolt him awake into a body so stiff he can barely turn his head. There is a sense of movement, a bump and a more distant engine roar. Then silence.

CHAPTER 21

Once Azi is fully awake, his most unpleasant surprise is that the agonizing discomfort of being trapped in a crate for twenty-four hours turns out to be no big deal when compared to the yet-more-agonizing discomfort of departing said crate.

As he starts to stretch out and return some sensation to his numbed nerve endings, it feels as if his arms and legs have been doused in molten metal. Azi bites his cheeks, chokes back involuntary tears, massages his screaming muscles and tries not to descend into hysteria. Eventually, he's ready to kick against the sealed side of the crate. After five blows, it yields, collapsing with a thud and shudder.

He blinks. The pain is receding, but there's plenty of fear waiting to replace it. Has he been betrayed? Is he anywhere near the destination he specified? It's night-time and there is little more light outside than in, but there is space – vast, needless space.

Avoiding the bucket of urine, Azi hunches into a crawl and exits into warm dry air with a smell of pine and exhaust fumes. Car lights sketch sporadic arcs in the distance. He seems to be at the bottom of a wooded slope near a road. He seems to be thirsty, hungry and sobbing, although that comes under control as he consumes the last of his food and water (crisps, cheese sandwich, soft drink, apple – the kind of lunchbox his mum used to pack for school trips to the Science Museum).

If this is Athens, Azi has a lot of walking to do, although he's not sure in which direction. He is carrying a small heap of stolen government electronics and one worse-for-wear change of clothes, and doesn't speak or read a word of Greek. On the plus side, he has his freedom, five thousand euros cash and a destination in mind.

With a shrug, he stumbles towards the night sky's brightest edge.

Four hours and eleven miles later, Azi is starting to doubt the wisdom of embarking on post-incarceration hikes through dustily huge cities on summer mornings.

To put it mildly, he does not feel perky. Through a combination of luck and monoglot direction-begging, he has managed to trudge his way almost to his desired destination. But he is out of food and water, and hasn't yet felt brave enough to restock.

The result is almost hallucinogenic: a light-headedness that makes his aching body feel far away and the increasingly bright streetscape jerk like a stop-motion animation. Then again, the area he has recently entered is itself hallucinatory.

Every exposed surface and accessible inch of plaster is a psychodrama of slogans and graffiti; a stew of ferocious public utterance and private grievance. There are images of protest, demon-headed men wielding fire, Nazis crushed by booted anti-fascists, politicians as cartoon animals and ancient philosophers in gasmasks. *Welcome to Athens* reads a small, flaming scrawl, next to a cursively rendered *Fuck the Police*. Beside these, blood-red stencils in Greek and English spell out the name of the district. *ΕΞΑΡΧΕΙΑ. EXARCHIA.* The last resort of those who give a fuck. Azi's target zone.

According to most tourist guides, Exarchia is a crime-infested hellhole packed with more or less interchangeable anarchists and addicts. According to locals, it's an international beacon of free-thinking resistance to the debaucheries of capitalism and the rising threat of fascism. According to *Vice* magazine, you should check out a new place called Warehouse, which is the sort of place you'll enjoy if you hate the word 'mixologist' but enjoy getting pissed and talking shit about Marx with some guys in leather jackets.

Most importantly, Exarchia is a place of refuge from almost everything that makes technological modernity quite so good at keeping people under control: surveillance, consumerism, social media analytics. Numbed by heat and exhaustion, Azi contemplates the streets, the nearby smell of cooking, and with famished eagerness steps towards the aroma.

Unfortunately, Azi manages to misjudge the height difference between the kerb and the road in front of him and, after attempting to balance upon several inches of empty air, crashes forehead-first into the tarmac.

Everything goes very bright, then very dark, then somewhere in between. At some point there are friendly – or, at least, not overtly hostile – hands around his shoulders and waist. Then there is a smell he associates with hospitals and doctor's waiting rooms. Gradually, it becomes clear to Azi that he is indeed seated in a waiting room. He is offered water, after which he feels a great deal better.

The room he's sitting in is small and crowded, but also cool and clean, with a tiled pale floor and animal pictures on the walls, presumably for the benefit of children. He likes it. He is being looked after. Following a considerable wait, during which the tiles and animals intermittently swim out of focus, he is ushered into a tiny back room in which a dark-haired woman sits behind a desk.

Her fierce competence reminds him of Anna, although, once she speaks, there's several degrees more warmth in her tone. The sounds coming out of her mouth are incomprehensible. Azi stares at her blankly, then mutters one word.

'English?'

She nods, shifting languages effortlessly.

'You are lucky I studied in London. I am Dr Eleni. Welcome. And your name and your nationality are—'

Azi vaguely prepared for this during his wait. 'Er, Ad. Adam. British.'

'Mr Adam British?'

He gets the feeling that this doctor finds him amusing. 'No, sorry. My name is Adam, and I am British. I'm Mr Adam Walker.'

'And do you have any identification?'

To Azi's relief, his unopened rucksack was still attached to his back when he returned to consciousness, but he has no intention of producing anything from it. So he shakes his head, after which the room takes a while to stop moving.

'Okay. No problem, Adam, I will still examine you. Please, follow the light. With your eyes, not your head! Better. You don't speak any Greek? Do not worry, nobody speaks Greek. I believe that you have a concussion, as well as that nasty gash. You fell over?'

Azi tries to make his response as dignified as possible. 'Off a pavement, yes. Onto a road.'

Dr Eleni nods in energetic sympathy, her latex-gloved fingers pursuing each other across his skull as she completes her examination. 'It happens. Please try to stay still while I clean you up and ask a few questions.'

She rattles through a list of inquiries about the date, time, identity of the US president, and how exactly Azi botched stepping off a pavement. He gets through it, earning himself some bandaging around his head and a cheerful discourse on remuneration.

'There we are, that is better. Now, this is my clinic, and it is free for those who cannot afford it. But I would rather see a European health card and charge the government. I don't suppose you have anything that shows your citizenship? The government cannot afford it either, but I care less about them.'

She is, Azi reckons, a little older than him – and a great deal more grown up. Her hair is tightly curled, her skin dark under a blue cotton T-shirt. She deserves as much honesty as he can muster, but he's not about to start unrolling grubby fifty-euro notes.

'I'm very sorry but I really haven't got anything.'

Her attention intensifies. 'You are not a tourist, then?'

'Er. No . . . Not really. I don't like sightseeing.'

'You should see the Acropolis. Everyone should see the Acropolis.'

'Right. Apart from that. I'd love to see the Acropolis, obviously.'

With a sympathetic smile, Dr Eleni opens a slim laptop and

starts typing. At the same time, as if the two activities inexorably accompanied one another, she embarks upon a well-rehearsed monologue.

'Only you can't see it unless you pay twelve euros. Everyone should see the Acropolis, but this country won't let them. It's a crime. The streets near here used to be full of markets, full of people. But they taxed and fined and drove them out of business, to punish them. Because nobody who has real money pays anything in this country! Only the poor. I have no problem taking money from the government, despite the difficulties they are in, for this reason. So, what are you doing here?'

Azi ventures the near-truth he has been preparing.

'I work with computers. Web design. Bit of activism. I'm working on something, and now some people are looking for me. I came here because—'

Dr Eleni needs no further prompting. 'Ah! Because you read about it online. I understand. I know people like you. Computer people, sitting behind your desks, changing the world on email. Until someone comes knocking at the door. Then you wake up in the real world. That is your story, yes? Well, now I will tell you about the real things you need. Food, water, rest. You are dehydrated. I assume you know nobody, that you have no resources?'

'Yes and no,' Azi mutters with the growing sense that the more clueless he seems, the more likely it is that Dr Eleni will make things happen.

'I thought as much! So, I can give you a chance. If you really know computers, you may be useful. If you make yourself useful, you can find a place to stay. That is how it works, around here.' She finishes typing with a flourish. 'I will make an introduction, for accommodation. They will feed you in the park if you say that Eleni sent you. You will get soft drinks. If you ask nicely.'

Azi smiles what he hopes is his best and most British smile.

'I always ask nicely. It's kind of my thing.'

CHAPTER 22

By the next morning, Azi has officially become a squatter.

At least, he has become the most recent participant in an ongoing attempt to seek collective autonomy from dominant social structures, which – he is told – entails the rejection of all forms of state power and provision. This suits him fine. Since the financial crisis, almost a third of the housing in Athens has stood vacant, and some of the apartments and shops that haven't turned into hipster hangouts have become a kind of anarchist-operated safety net for those at society's sharp end. Someone wishing to avoid both official surveillance and unofficial inquisitiveness couldn't wish for a better base.

While 'organized by anarchists' sounds like a contradiction in terms, Azi has rarely met a more disciplined bunch of people, nor a more devotedly process-driven administration. Everyone has an equal voice, everyone has a vote, and everything gets collectively debated, although woe betide the debater who hasn't read at least one shockingly dense FAQ outlining the Anarchist Library's international protocols for Collective Decision Making. The online resources section alone contains a giddy selection of flowcharts, and takes forty thousand words to address knotty questions like 'what do anarchists think causes ecological problems?' After the two hours of debate it took yesterday to admit him on probationary terms to the building, Azi has already started thinking of ways to improve their taxonomy.

As he wakes, Azi takes stock of the communal dorm into which he collapsed last night. The high shuttered windows admit slivers of light onto a dozen mattresses and blanketed bodies. A few sticks of furniture and personal possessions demarcate what was once a living room into personal zones that are largely respected. One Afghan and two Syrian refugees, each around twenty years old, sprawl next to eight Greeks who range from eighteen to a well-weathered sixty. Azi was the first to sleep, last night, and is the first to rise today – but the family rooms above them are already radiating shrill cries.

Having tiptoed with his rucksack towards the shared bathroom, Azi tries not to look too hard at the decayed tiling while completing the physical transformation programme he began in the Berlin chicken shop. First, he dons the vaguely anarchistic clothes he bought at a stall yesterday evening: black, capacious and spattered with Greek slogans. Second, there's a similarly mirthless pair of boots. Third, with a wince, he pierces each ear with a needle and inserts a hooped silver earring. Fourth and finally, he cuts off all his hair.

In the movies, shaving your head invariably entails a photogenic montage, with clumps of suspiciously clean hair dropping to the floor in time with motivational drumbeats. In real life – at least, in the all-too-real life that Azi is currently living – it turns out the process is more like hacking apart a patch of brambles with a butter knife. He swears and cuts his fingers and gouges his scalp as, with exhausting tardiness, clumps of knotted hair come away under his razor's scything.

On the plus side, all this self-mutilation should only serve to increase his anonymity. Less cheeringly, the reflection watching Azi through the cracked mirror resembles a hip-hop backing dancer fallen on hard times, perhaps having absconded from an especially gritty video shoot. It's not a strong look. But it may keep him safe.

By the time Azi has finished, he's half-crazed with discomfort and hunger, the latter thanks to the smell of grilled vegetables, sweet chai and strong coffee rising to fill the stairwell. It's almost homely. The old apartment building is crumbling but sound. Graffiti spatters its exterior, alongside two large cloth banners spelling out *home* and *welcome* in English; inside there are posters, a few pictures, and schedules for cleaning, cooking and security volunteering.

Notwithstanding his exhaustion and his appearance, Azi likes it. As part of yesterday's probationary proof of usefulness, he improved residents' internet access by several orders of magnitude and network security by another few on top of that – and he has tentatively volunteered to give a talk in the 'events' room this morning under the title 'Er Hello Nice To Meet You All Maybe I Can Give You A Few Tech Tips'.

As long as he remembers to drop phrases like 'cultural hegemony' and 'intersectionality' every few minutes, he's sure everything will be fine.

To Azi's surprise, his talk is well-attended. By the time it ends, several simultaneous translations are being provided – and one of the translators, a young Syrian who speaks chasteningly comprehensible English, is quick to explain why.

For those fleeing violence or trying to survive with few resources, Azi learns, maintaining internet access is more important than almost any other consideration. This is where their community of knowledge resides: updates on safe routes, available transport, bribable officials, hazards and betrayals, sustenance and shelter. Simply helping people to maximize the battery life of their phones while reducing their chances of being tracked can be lifesaving. Almost everything Azi says is instantly distributed along the digital grapevine. Tomorrow, perhaps, he'll start to put together a wiki.

As Azi also learns, Exarchia is going through a quiet patch, at least by its own historical standards. So far as his new friends are concerned – some of whom, he has to admit, do wear leather jackets and talk shit about Marx – the local life he has staggered into is tranquil almost to the point of boredom. Having been a hotbed of radicalism for over half a century, today's best riots have a hard job living up to yesteryear's. Local anarchists can sometimes be seen running either towards or away from bunched police in riot gear, depending on the strength of feelings on each side. But most of the time the authorities stay away, although there are rumours that they are herding drug dealers into the area to drive down property prices. Judging by the number of trendy tourists seeking out haunts extolled by *Vice*, they're failing.

Azi passes the next few hours in semi-tranquillity, inspecting sundry mobile phones, tablets and jury-rigged electrical supplies – including a solar-powered charging station set up by one enterprising Greek. Finally, feeling altogether saner and better fed, he takes his leave and makes his way towards a patch of wall on the corner of Tzavella and Mesologgiou Streets that he's been told, in no uncertain terms, to visit. On it is an incongruously spotless black-and-white plaque, one by two feet, featuring an image of a fifteen-year-old boy. *There but for the grace of God*, Azi thinks, Munira's face shivering in his mind.

As Azi learned over breakfast, the boy on the plaque was a student called Alexandros Grigoropoulos, shot during an altercation with two policemen in December 2008. He was unarmed. The killing triggered protests and riots across the country, but its greatest impact was here. Six years later, the rage and sadness are still raw. Sprawled around the plaque are stencilled letters and washes of colour, slogans on filthy pebble-dash, wreaths of yellow flowers wedged into nooks, peeling posters stretched around the street corner. More flowers rot in baskets on the tiled heat of the pavement.

Between heavy breaths, Azi gathers his strength – because he can't put off the next stage of his plan any longer. He needs to get online, securely. He needs to start doing some good. And this means something he has been dreading since the moment he crawled out of the crate: Stournari Street, Big Sur and begged favours.

CHAPTER 23

Stournari Street slices west from Exarchia Square for a tree-lined half mile of shuttered shop windows, its walls webbed with slogans to the height of a scrawling hand. Despite appearances, this has been the premier place in Greece to buy tech of all types for at least two decades, and is jokingly called the Greek Silicon Valley by almost everyone Azi has met – although he's not sure whether the joke is on Silicon Valley, Greece, or just reflects the fact that most people can only name one place associated with computers. It's a few hundred yards from the Grigoropoulos shrine, and Azi jogs towards it through the alternating shade and dazzle of gridded streets, practising the words that he hopes will open both literal and metaphorical doors.

Stournari Street was already sufficiently renowned in hacker lore to feature in the magazines of Azi's youth, back when sharing code meant copying it line by line from printed paper, and it's partly this history that drew him to Athens. In that pre-web era, while Exarchia's bars heaved with Marxists saying the kind of things that Marxists have been saying in bars since at least 1917, tech-savvy students were on Stournari Street, scheduling appointments to sell cracked commercial software. Local hackers would hand out business cards and then meet for coffee above computer shops, advertising their skills as a way of launching mainstream careers. In those days, everyone's hat was a shade of grey. The dark side of computational creativity hadn't gone global.

Azi sincerely hopes that some of that idealism still lingers in one of the street's more infamously independent electronics boutiques: an outfit called Kremvax, whose proprietor is known as Mr Fuck the Government after his role in a notably profane online campaign, or Mr Government for short. Azi has never met Mr Government, but he has corresponded and collaborated with his hacker alter ego for six years under the pseudonym Big Sur – as in the famously rugged stretch of Californian coast, as in a nickname with no connection whatsoever to a middle-aged Athenian with a tangled greying beard and penchant for 1980s band T-shirts.

The fact that Azi long ago traced Big Sur to this particular shop will, together with his knowledge of their shared exploits, hopefully serve to verify his identity. Although it will be entirely understandable if Azi is instead assaulted for the crime of appearing on a fellow practitioner's doorstep. You can never tell with old-school geeks – especially when their reputation includes spectacularly vindictive acts of sabotage.

From the outside, the shop looks not so much closed as reinforced against military intervention. Two layers of metal shutters crisscross the window, the door is similarly barred, and no lights are visible inside. Undeterred, Azi presses an intercom button three times and waits, then waits some more. Eventually a voice rattles through.

'*Ya su?*'

'*Ya su.* Er, English? I'm an old friend, I believe? We met on the Conficker botnet. All hands on deck.'

'*Fiye!*'

Azi hesitates. 'Can I come in, please? AZ, that's me. You're Big Sur.'

'*Fiye!*'

Azi is already getting desperate. For a start, he has no idea whether he's even speaking to the right person. Then there's the fact that, even if he is, they may decide to ignore him – or drop a pre-owned PC on his head. But this doesn't mean he can't take a chance.

'My mum, your mum, nobody else knows that. You should never have told me. But you did.'

Like Azi, Mr Government lost his mother at a youngish age. Azi has no idea how, why or when it happened – even in their most eloquent moments of bonding over IRC they were never that indiscreet – but he knows that this conjunction of knowledge is almost unfakeable. The tone of the intercom voice rises several dozen decibels.

'*Malakas! Gamisou!*'

'Excuse me?'

'Seriously, you need a translation, no one here has told you to fuck off? *Edakrysen o Iesous*! Jesus wept. Come in, come in. If you're lying, I'm screwed anyway.'

The shutters lift with a wheeze that sounds almost human, then the door opens to display one of the most magnificent stomachs Azi has ever seen – a rotund expanse straining the words 'Bob Seger & the Silver Bullet Band Against the Wind' almost into illegibility on a faded black T-shirt. Mr Government stares at Azi, then beckons him through the door and closes it behind them.

He really is, Azi thinks to himself, an extremely big man – perhaps six and a half feet tall, and close to the same around the middle. Tattoos girdle each of his forearms. Mr Government looks like a child's drawing of a pirate, if that child had been told to draw a pirate who ate everyone else on his ship. His voice is a roll of slow thunder.

'So, you're AZ. Wow, you look . . . I don't even know what you look like, friend. Not something good.'

'Yup. And I'm sorry, I'm sorry. Nobody knows I'm here. I need a favour.'

The front of Mr Government's shop is expertly cluttered, like a 1930s hardware store. A staggering quantity of components are arrayed from floor to ceiling on each wall, rendering the whole incomprehensible to anyone but its owner. Without changing his expression, Mr Government beckons Azi into a back room that makes the front look positively minimalist: boxes upon crates upon packets upon cables, archaeologically layered through the last few decades of computing history.

Azi could spend all day rummaging in a place like this. In fact, that's more or less his plan, although the bearded giant filling the doorway may have other ideas. Mr Government fondles his beard thoughtfully with one massive hand – the tattoos, Azi realizes, are circuit boards – then reaches towards Azi and crushes him into a heartfelt embrace.

'My little friend. God himself knows how fucked you must be, to come like this. Don't tell me. Seriously, tell me nothing, keep it between yourself and the man upstairs. You start dropping hints, I'll be forced to eat you. Ha!' A laugh ripples seismically through Mr Government's torso. 'No need to look like that, I'm living the vegan dream. It's an ancient Greek thing: the triangle man, Pythagoras. What do you need?'

Azi shudders, swallows and coughs before finding his voice. His brain doesn't seem to be able to stop noticing the sheer *scale* on which Mr Government is built. 'Gear, some good stuff. A place to keep it that's more than discreet. A few days. I have cash, I can pay my way.'

The mighty head nods. 'Heavy wizardry, deep magic – whoever they are, I feel sorry for them already. A thousand euros for the gear, and my lifelong silence is complementary. Unless they turn this into a movie, in which case I must insist I am played by Dwayne Johnson. The Rock! Now there's a big man with heart. Please take what you need, and I'll show you a place. I love what you do, AZ. Sorry I can't be there with you but—'

'Too close to home, I know. I owe you. I won't forget.'

'Make somebody wish they'd never been born. For old times' sake.'

Half an hour later, Azi leaves bearing a code for a recessed metal-and-glass door leading off the street into some apartments near the back of the shop. The door opens into a tiled stairwell, from whose first-floor landing a second code grants access to what was once a cupboard but will soon become Azi's windowless temple to heaped electronics.

Over the next few hours, Azi's gleeful rummaging yields a rig that, when combined with a few lovingly dismantled and reassembled devices from Berlin, should equip him to do most things short of starting a nuclear war. If he's patient. Speed is the one thing he can't afford – because everything rests upon invisibility, which in this case means tethering his new Linux laptop to an untraceable selection of burner phones whose identifying MAC codes he'll change several times a day. So far as anyone monitoring local networks is concerned, he's changing to a new device every six hours.

In addition to the laptop, Azi perches two monitors on a narrow perimeter of metal shelving, while hardware and software firewalls girdle his virtual machines like Russian dolls. Unless the laptop is opened and unlocked by him, everything stays encrypted. The room's outside wall has a large metal vent, and he has taken two desk fans to shift the air, but it must still be close to thirty Celsius inside by the time Azi's work is done and the machinery has begun to crank up its own cooling.

The space is approximately half the size of his beloved shed, and his metal chair has to remain folded for him to open or close the door. Yet between this and the squat, Azi has never been more grateful for the freedom of uncomfortable spaces.

To Azi's surprise, the first thing he does after testing his privacy and security measures is to send Ad a message. It only takes a moment, but it's still something he thought he would never do.

Back when they were still hatching plans for world domination – via East Croydon, circa 1997 – they agreed that anonymously posting a very particular message on the Alt. Folklore.Urban news group would indicate that one of them was in life-threatening danger. They called it the bat signal, both because a Batman reference was the height of 1990s cool and because the idea was for something easily, anonymously viewable from anywhere – a silhouette in the digital sky. By mutual agreement, the message was to read:

Hey, does anyone remember that episode of Batman set in a shed in Croydon?

Astonishingly, the news group still exists – and Azi has never managed to forget that line. So he posts the message, winces at his own hopeless nostalgia and turns his mind to more important matters.

Anna told him to stay in touch via their mutual friend, which can only mean Jim. He doesn't want to start populating Jim's feeds with fresh activity but, as soon as he has logged in, notices with relief that either Odi or Anna has done something extremely sensible – namely, getting Jim to send a private message to himself containing an alphanumeric key for encrypted communications plus a ProtonMail address.

In other words, they can start exchanging secure emails as soon as they've swapped keys. Azi sets himself up a brand new ProtonMail account, then sends a message containing just two words in addition to his key.

Hi, Jim.

A reply bounces back in the style of Jim within the hour. *Who the fuck is this do I know u? What's that pub where my old mate got pissed and fell into the fruit machine?*

It's a good test. Somebody else could, theoretically, have hacked into Jim's identity by now. Azi replies with the name that he improvised during dinner in Berlin.

The Crown.

Within five minutes, there's another message.

Update us on your status. We have no news about the girl.

Azi's heart tries to escape from his chest. Munira's not dead, he tells himself. If she was, they would surely have found her body by now – because her death would have been a warning, an example. Which means that whoever took her has a use for her. Which means that they're doing something right now that can be traced. There's hope.

Azi sends a selective account of his actions since Berlin: just enough to let them know that he has left the city and is in possession of technical resources; that he is not (so far as he can tell) in immediate danger; and that he will do everything he can to help while remaining in full control of his own circumstances. There's no way he's going back, not now he's free. Not while everything that happened in Berlin remains unexplained. The reply takes fifteen minutes.

Although this channel is secure, we will send limited information while we continue internal security audits. The compromise of our location and systems remains unexplained. Our own autonomy as an organization is being severely curtailed. Do what you can

*to find her, but do not lose sight of the big picture – the names
on the list, the power behind it. Many, many more lives will be
lost if we cannot bring down Gomorrah. Send further information
as soon as you have it. Look after yourself.*

It's about what he expected, although the news of 'compromised autonomy' is intriguing, suggesting the presence of other major players in the intelligence space. Then again, given the scale of what's unfolding, this must always have been a great deal more than Anna and Odi's hobby.

Gomorrah is the key – and it seems that nobody knows he was able to use it except, of course, for the people behind Gomorrah themselves. Now that he has his new hacking rig, Azi has destroyed the burner phone he used in Berlin, but even so he reckons the time he can safely stay in Athens is measured in days. He needs to act fast.

His working theory is that it was the Islamists and their agents who tracked down Munira, hoping to clean up the appalling error of allowing her to escape with access details. After all, they must have men in Europe and a great deal of terrified respect for whoever is behind Gomorrah. Munira doesn't seem to have been killed, which means they want information more than they wish to exact vengeance. What he needs to do is stay calm, think clearly and work through his options in order.

He turns to his monitor and, surprised, registers the arrival of one last message from Anna and Odi.

Thought you'd like to know: we found you thanks to this.

Azi cautiously investigates the attachment, which turns out to be a cached social media profile: an internet archive record of a Friends Reunited page for Azi Bello that existed, briefly, in the early 2000s. There's almost nothing on it. A uni freshers' photo, a few lines about computer science, a bad joke, a contact email. Almost nothing – but just enough to lead a sufficiently dedicated, well-resourced investigator to the back garden of a terraced house where the man who created the profile still lived. A horribly easy mistake to make.

The only problem is, Azi is certain he has never seen it before.

CHAPTER 24

Azi reads and rereads the information Odi and Anna have sent about how they found him: the social media profile he's never seen before, the implications. It's an expert stitch-up but, beyond that, the possibilities are boundless and bewildering.

Are they trying to test or manipulate him? Did someone set him up, or want to send him a warning? Is the entire thing an elaborate ruse? Safe inside his virtual machines and a stack of proxies, he probes the cached page, but there's no malicious code there. Just old, accurate information that nobody should ever have got hold of, let alone compiled into something so brilliantly compromising.

For now, he needs to move on. He's here and he's free and Munira needs him. What matters is the future, not the past. Azi tries to gather his focus. But every avenue he investigates seems to have been bricked up – and there's a nervous chill at the base of his spine that won't stop tingling.

In Berlin, the post-massacre cover-up operation must have been immensely well-resourced: it's shrouded in absolute informational silence, and the warehouse's location lacks both CCTV coverage and nearby residents whose social media might be trawled for news.

Hunting for any recent hints of Sigma and Munira also proves fruitless, as do Azi's explorations of some authentically unpleasant forums that might hold insights into Gomorrah. Azi even stalks Ad online – his old friend appears to have an enviably clean-living Californian lifestyle, although he wouldn't put it past Ad to have fabricated the entire thing.

Eventually, despondency and exhaustion drive him back to the squat just inside its curfew. Low voices speaking in many languages loop through the air, sharing God knows what horrors. The day has been an intensifying series of disappointments, and sleep doesn't come easily.

The next morning, Azi decides to follow much the same routine as on the previous day in the hope that it will bring better luck: sustenance in the form of porridge, caffeine in the form of tooth-clenchingly sweet coffee, comradeship in the form of a lecture on the art of digital discretion. As he descends towards the kitchen, however, he freezes. Someone is bellowing his old friend's name across the bottom of the stairwell.

'Adam. Adam Walker!'

Azi is halfway through wondering whether he can hurl himself out of a window when he remembers who he's pretending to be. He *is* Adam Walker. And his interlocutor is the redoubtable Dr Eleni, half-hidden behind two immense plastic bags full of clothes.

'Hello, Adam Walker! *Kalimera*, good morning, over here. Mr Adam, at last! Are you making yourself useful? My goodness, you look different. Here, you can be useful to me – these are clothes for the little ones, upstairs. You will carry the bags, I will keep an eye on my more precious burden, here, and we will go together.'

Azi affects even more bewilderment than he feels.

'Er, sure. What's that about a burden?'

Bundling the bags into his grasp – they contain enough second-hand clothing to last a bevy of babies into adulthood – Dr Eleni exhales theatrically and steps aside to reveal a small, staring boy, clinging to the back of her legs. She lifts him into her arms.

'This is my child, the smaller one. You have seen a child before? Nikasios, after his father's father. Cypriots. This little man is helping *mama* at work, because big *papakis* forgot that this is what *mama* has done twice a week for the last month. I am visiting my ladies – upstairs, the ones who cannot easily come to see me.' With her free arm she makes a curving gesture that, eventually, Azi identifies as indicating pregnancy. 'The boy has been eating off my ears.'

'Excuse me?'

'Shouting, begging for sweets. As men do. Now he is quiet, which is why I will keep him close. You carry the bags, and all this will happen fast.' She points to the stairwell. 'Come on, up, up! *Viasou*, let's go!'

Nikasios doesn't stay quiet for long. Once the delivery is finished – Azi hovers outside the door of the family dormitory while an epically rapid Greek monologue echoes within – Eleni seems unfazed by the sight of her offspring hurtling down the stairs and into the packed kitchen. Taking up a bowl of porridge, she dispenses words of hygiene-related wisdom to those on cooking duty ('no meat, none, not in this heat; that is not hand-washing, that is giving your germs a shower') while using her free arm to shepherd the little boy towards a bench.

Azi queues for a shot of frothing coffee, then watches as Eleni sits down and Nikasios hurls himself onto the floor at her feet. Adjusting the now-filthy bandage circling his head, Azi tries for a casual tone.

'Are you going to listen to my talk?'

'One of us, perhaps. Or we may both become preoccupied by *kaka*. Who can tell?'

The boy is clasping her legs and burbling joyously. Azi, who has very little first-hand experience of children, estimates his age at somewhere between one and four – pending further investigation. He offers what he hopes is a blameless smile in the child's direction, and Nikasios dissolves into sobs. Without looking down, Eleni hefts the boy into her lap.

'He loves people. This is just the nap he wishes he did not need. They fight sleep. Because life would be too easy if we did what is good for us! Does this sound familiar? Time for your *pipila*, my little golden one?'

She produces a pacifier which, on the third attempt, Nikasios accepts and begins to suck while watching Azi with care, as if this unclean stranger might turn into somebody interesting. For once, Azi is lost for words. Gradually, the little boy's eyes roll backwards in their sockets, flicker, then shut. Eleni looks up.

'You have just witnessed a miracle. *Thauma*, a wonder! Do not for a moment think it is always like this. Perhaps your face has worked magic upon him. Your dressing, it is disgusting, let me have a look . . . You are due to speak? You should get on with it. His sleep cycle is thirty minutes.'

Azi nods. There's something about watching a small child fall asleep that requires no comment or reason. It takes him several minutes, and one more shot of coffee, to summon the weary hypervigilance his topic demands.

Azi's theme for today is surveillance, and how best to avoid it. Most demonstrators have been aware for some time that the police use devices with a variety of badass names – StingRay, Wolfpack, Gossamer, swamp boxes – to imitate the radio towers that mobile phones connect to in order to function. This allows them to hoover up the international mobile subscriber identities of every single phone user in the vicinity and then match these to other records, keeping everything in their secret surveillance data dungeons for ever. This is why anonymous burner phones are a great idea.

Unfortunately, spoofing mobile phone towers is now amateur hour when it comes to protests. What worries Azi is the stuff you can't turn off: your face, the way you walk, the speed at which you type, the personal email account you checked just once five years ago from a supposedly secure location. For most people, these vulnerabilities are their unknown unknowns: the things they don't even know that they don't know about. All of them can be redressed, but only as long as you're prepared to take drastic measures. Hence his opening theme: how to stop machines from matching you to a recognizable pattern. He doesn't get far.

'Why is it that you wish us to tattoo our faces?'

As one of the best English-speakers in the room, Eleni has assumed the honour of expressing incredulity to Azi on the behalf of every other sentient being present – a tone she has no trouble striking over the slump of her slumbering son. Azi tries to look pleased by the chance to explain himself.

'Temporary tattoos. It's for facial recognition. The police, government, their systems can get your faces from photographs, right?'

'This is why people wear hoods, masks.'

'But you can't do that all the time. And they can take those off. Markings like this can stop a machine being able to recognize you. I've sketched a sample, here . . .' Azi brandishes a piece of paper that is not, he would admit, much of an advert for his craft skills '. . . and you can find better stuff online. The point is, it works. Mostly. So, look at me. You may have noticed my new look since arriving . . . shoes and clothes nothing like I wore before. Less hair. You're trying to fool machines, so you need to change your outline, your proportions, the patterns made by everything you do.'

Azi touches one hand self-consciously to his scalp. What matters, he tells himself, is that he doesn't much resemble the man who left Berlin. The fact that almost every part of him either itches or seems afflicted by horrible stiffness, or both, is beside the point. Before he can continue, another interjection comes from the back of the room.

'Do we believe that the future of action lies behind masks, that this is how we undermine the legitimacy of oppression? We are not ashamed. Politicians are corrupted, the government is corrupted! To educate the crowd, you cannot hide behind a mask. The icons of history, to make the people think, they did not hide their faces—'

The speaker is a ferociously bearded young man wearing what look like hemp pyjamas, and his tone suggests that he long ago confirmed the absolute correctness of his view. This is the trouble with addressing assemblies of anarchists, Azi thinks, let alone Greek anarchists – there's no such thing as a proposition they won't dispute. But before he can reply he is cut off by Eleni.

'Be quiet, Kostas! We all know what you think, you have told us often enough. I do not hide my face, I am not a criminal. I am a doctor. But I have seen what happens, the way protest is treated. Perhaps we should let Mr Walker tell us how to avoid trouble and stay safe. Otherwise, people are going to eat wood. That is a Greek expression—'

Azi winces, trying to get things back on track.

'I get it. People are going to get hurt. With wood.'

As Azi has already gathered, Athenian anarchists come in many flavours – but all of them concur that sticks as well as flowers are needed to defend a revolution, to say nothing of motorcycle helmets, 'borrowed' police batons and riot shields. Arrests and beatings are a weekly routine for those towards the militant end of the spectrum, where throwing rocks at officialdom is considered an eloquent mode of political expression. As for those who don't agree, the trouble with self-organizing assemblies is that nobody speaks for everyone, and it's hard to maintain the non-violent high ground when representatives of the state are bludgeoning you in the face. Backtracking, he attempts another approach.

'Look, let's think about masks as an idea. Please? Whether you want to avoid being recognized, or just avoid trouble, in either case you're trying to conceal a pattern. But doing this means you need to understand what kind of patterns machines can spot. How you type, that's a pattern. They can track it. But I can show you a plugin that evens out the rate at which you press keys. Devices . . . first, you need an operating system that doesn't leave a trace. Something called Tails is a good start. I'll put some of this on a wiki. Money . . . every time you touch it, you become part of a pattern—'

'You don't need to tell us that, we're anarchists!'

This, shouted by the bearded one from the back of the room, qualifies as a joke. As translations ripple through the thirty or so people now gathered, laugher follows. Azi, trying to ride the mood, keeps going.

'Right, but you still need something for purchases, sometimes, and anonymous browsing and cryptocurrencies don't keep you safe . . . unless you mix them up and know how to hide the nodes you access them through. Really, it's all much easier if you just want to steal things and break them . . .'

He sighs, contemplating a parallel world in which he has

spent the last decade stealing stuff, cackling and buying Ferraris.

'. . . but building systems, fixing faults, keeping people safe: it's tough. A lot of the time, it sucks. The odds aren't good, which is why, actually, assaults and constant stress are the only way to keep things safe. I'm getting off track, er . . . constant stress. Otherwise, they'll get you. Somebody will. Whatever you think happens in the darkness, think again. It's worse.'

Eleni raises her eyebrows as if to say, *try being a doctor for a day, chum.* Azi risks a grin. Then a new voice sounds from the very back of the room.

'Someone has been asking around – about a man like you. Tell us, what are *you* running from? What are you bringing into our home?'

For a moment, Azi's mouth hangs open. He closes it and, leaning against a nearby table for support, manages to croak out one syllable.

'Who?'

But the room has no answers. Before he can find out who spoke – before he can say another word – Nikasios's full-throated wails turn the air into their echoes. Eleni stands to soothe her son, several simultaneous debates break out in the middle rows, and half a dozen people decide it's time to get tea.

Not knowing what else to do, Azi mutters inaudibly and slips onto the street as fast as he can.

CHAPTER 25

Once upon a time, Kabir learns from their talkative hotel manager over dinner on the evening of their arrival, foreigners wishing to come and fight for the Islamic Republic were welcomed with open arms on both sides of the border. It was a fine business. A dozen or so recruits would gather in the hotels on the Turkish side, equip themselves with weapons and black bandanas from obliging local entrepreneurs, then relax for a few days while the fixers did their thing.

This more or less corresponds to Kabir and his cousin's experience last November, and he had assumed things remained much the same. After a few days of waiting on the Turkish side, a discreet message arrived late at night indicating that fixers had finished their fixing. There followed a taxi ride to the border, a stroll around inconvenient landmines, then the comforts of another taxi and hotel ahead of official recruitment. The route was well-trodden, everyone either took their cut or kept tactfully silent – and safe passage in the opposite direction could be arranged through the same channels.

Today, things are different. Recruits are still arriving, but the Turkish government has started to take a more active interest in regional peacekeeping – perhaps because the momentum from this summer's campaigns has begun to alarm those in distant as well as nearby lands. Kabir is vaguely aware that opposition to the Islamic Republic may coalesce into something effective if the country stops ripping itself apart with civil war. With hundreds of thousands of people continuing to flee both the civil war's chaos and the Republic's mercy, it's a less than auspicious time for him to become one among numberless refugees.

What he needs is some well-connected people with a sincere

interest in the information residing in his rear end. And this has suggested a plan to him. If Muhammed and Dr Tal were to go ahead without him – and if something were to go wrong with their border crossing, meaning that neither of them ever returned – Kabir would be free to negotiate his own fate at his own pace. What's more, he would be free to move his bowels without engaging in the frankly horrific process of removal and reinsertion that occupied him soon after their arrival, and that on its own makes the entire betrayal seem worthwhile.

Having finished his opening lament, the hotel manager is now regaling Kabir and his companions with praise for Muhammed's fictional sister and her bravery, while discreetly suggesting that all things remain possible so long as enough cash is involved. Dr Tal has no doubt the state will pay what is reasonable, or that helping in this holy task is preferable to the lingering death prone to be experienced by those lacking faith. The hotel manager, it turns out, couldn't agree more.

After an unpleasant cup of coffee – all the coffee in the Islamic Republic is bad, but this hotel seems to have pulled out all the stops in creating a simultaneously bland and acrid anti-flavour – they retire into three adjoining rooms with a fine view of a fading sunset above rooftops.

The occasional gash of rubble among houses and the sounds of distant heavy vehicles are all that suggest they aren't on holiday, but Kabir knows he has no margin for error in his machinations. His actions must be decisive and entirely convincing. The border town they're in, Jarablus, is a vital supply line for the Republic, and the prison in the basement of its recruitment centre is notorious even by local standards, where execution is considered preferable to incarceration. Fortunately, using his phone via a VPN on the Wi-Fi network, he should be able to conduct some discreet online research – once he has pretended to conspire for one last time with Muhammed in their shared bathroom. Unfortunately, Muhammed is both terrified and desperate for reassurances Kabir has no desire to give.

'Brother, you are sure your information is good, what you have on USB? That we will be well met?'

'*Inshallah*, yes. But that is for later. Your story, your sister, the meeting place – you are confident? You won't go crying to your friend the doctor?'

'Brother! I wish to return to my family, to my country. And I know that we are dead men if he suspects. I have prayed, I have tried to make my peace. But I am afraid. It is as if he sees everything. It is as if, in his eyes, I am already dead . . .'

And so on. Kabir lets him talk, less than half-listening as Muhammed mutters pieties, sweats and trembles, talks about the people he loves. On cue, Kabir reassures him that they will all cross the border together, engineer a meeting with his supposed sister in the town square on the other side, then jump in a taxi and get far away from Dr Tal. It's a plan that might even work, but Kabir has no interest in finding out. They flush the toilet twice and run the taps, then clasp hands in farewell.

Back in his room, Kabir gets out his trusty iPhone. It doesn't seem to be working, so he turns it on and off again. Still nothing. He plugs it in to charge, waits, then tries to launch Safari. Nothing. Swearing under his breath, he waves it around, hoping a stronger signal might shake the system into life. Nothing. Kabir swears again, more loudly, but there's nothing to be done. It will have to wait until morning.

He will have to engineer some delay.

CHAPTER 26

All at once, Azi's timetable has shortened to nothing. He can't go back to the squat. He can't find out who has been asking around. He can't show his face or ask questions. The only safe place he knows is the tiny computer room – and so he spends the best part of an hour approaching it by the most circuitous route conceivable, dodging into and out of shops, looking over his shoulder, trying not to freeze in panic or lie down despairing on the pavement.

He could be mistaken, a part of him mutters. It could all be nothing more than a false alarm, an idle comment. The thought is a comfort and so he avoids it, focusing instead on the next twenty-four hours. Bottled water, crisps and fruit and snacks, purchased in cash from a few small shops. A bucket. It's like the back of the lorry all over again – only, he tells himself, this time he is the one in the driving seat. He has a machine, an internet connection; he has his freedom; he has hope. Despair is not an option.

For the first hour in the room he simply sits, sweating, running scenarios and willing his mind to still itself – to come out of the world and into the task in front of him. Gradually, a familiar focus creeps through him; an absorption in the flow of information; the testing and probing of the world's weaknesses beyond his monitor's bright window.

There's no data trail in Berlin. Azi hasn't heard anything more from Odi and Anna – and he's happy to stay well away from whatever betrayals and internal convulsions they're wrestling with. Gomorrah and Sigma are also shrouded in silence, and he's pretty sure that logging into the dark marketplace from Athens would bring nothing but pain. But, he realizes, he does have another link to Munira: something that binds her directly to the people that took her. Family.

Azi knows that Munira's cousin, Mohammed Hamid Husam, was born in Bradford and died at the start of this year fighting for the Islamic Republic in Raqqa. It's one of the first things she told him. But he also knows this because someone took a photo of Mohammed Hamid Husam's dead body just after a sniper drilled a hole in his forehead, and this image was widely shared online alongside the metadata embedded in the image file by the iPhone 5 on which it was taken.

Metadata is a snooper's best friend. It's a layer of information *about* information, recorded by default during the file creation process – and, in the case of the Exchangeable Image Format file generated every time an iPhone takes a picture, this metadata includes latitude, longitude, phone model, operating system, time and date of image. The owner of the phone that captured Husam's death never thought to turn off this feature, and for some reason the Islamic Republic allowed him to hang on to it. So there it all was: a map in miniature.

The iPhone's owner was, Azi soon comes to suspect, Munira's other cousin, Kabir Asim Kamal: both because the two men are known to have travelled together, and because one of the first captions associated with the image reads *until we meet in paradise cuz*. To Azi's delight, cousin Kabir appears to be as prolific with this phone as he is unaware of its privacy settings. And this spells opportunity.

Azi sets up an image trawl: a piece of code designed to crawl across the web looking for image files matching the precise metadata for Kabir's phone, OS and camera software within a fixed geographic area and set of dates (northern Syria during the course of this year). This should turn up any publicly accessible images Kabir might have taken plus, with a bit of clever coding, many of the traces of their surreptitious circulation elsewhere. Because not many people in northern Syria have been taking and sharing photos on an iPhone 5 that hasn't had a software update in almost two years, Azi reasons, there shouldn't be too many false positives. Assuming Kabir has kept using the same phone. Assuming he isn't dead in a ditch by now.

Gradually, trying to contain his excitement, Azi gathers dozens of shots, many of which are associated with the social media accounts of a minor jihadi celebrity – a doctor whose feed bizarrely mixes look-at-me posing with stray-dog portraiture. Plotting the most recent images over time puts Kabir and the doctor close to the border, west of Aleppo, in the company of at least one other man. The captions and hashtags are largely unhelpful, but it's significant that Azi has even managed to find so many files. Clearly, these people are involved in propaganda and publicity. Clearly, Kabir is a bit too fond of this phone for his own good.

Once the trawl has done its work, Azi inspects the gathered mosaic of images: the shops, faces and signs behind their subjects, the gates and barbed wire fences. How many air strikes have resulted from some idiot jihadi sharing a selfie, complete with GPS coordinates, featuring a secret facility in the background? Kabir Asim Kamal barely features in any photos himself, but there is one in which he looks down his own lens from arm's length while gesturing towards what looks like a community project. *Another triumph*, the caption notes, *for the great and glorious Republic.*

Everyone in the image looks miserable and terrified, and none more so than Kabir: gaunt and sunburned under a wispy beard, eyes sunk sleeplessly into his face. This particular self-exiled Brit doesn't seem to be having a lot of fun. And his iPhone appears to have direct access to his photogenic doctor mate's social media accounts.

Azi rubs his hands. The afternoon is starting to slip away, and he can feel fear creeping around the edges of his concentration – the animal urge to cover his tracks and flee. Forcing this aside, he peers into Kabir's pixelated gaze; at his tired young face, blinking into the light. Kabir's most recent image, posted just a couple of hours ago, was taken near the border town where, Azi assumes, he and his companions will stay the night. This suits Azi perfectly. As all self-respecting police states know, the hours of early morning are ideal for psychologically impactful interventions – and Azi has no intention of resting until he has seen this through.

He starts selecting his tools. It's time to get in touch.

CHAPTER 27

A couple of hours after Kabir finally slips into sleep, tangled in sweat and cheap hotel sheets, something unexpected wakes him: the arrival of an iMessage on his phone's lockscreen, loudly and repeatedly marked by an alert he thought he had set to silent.

Kabir fumbles towards it, caught between relief that it's not broken and anger at being awakened through the haze of his last few pills. He clicks the home button, but the message just sits there. He rubs his eyes, he reads it, then reads it again, then reads it a third time. Nothing he does seems to have any effect on the phone or the words filling its screen.

Hi Kabir. Hope you're enjoying Jarablus. I know who you are. I know where you are. I know what you are doing. I need you to do exactly what I say, starting now. Reply to tell me you understand. Do nothing else. If you don't reply within an hour, you will be dead before the morning.

After the longest fifty-nine minutes of his life – during most of which time his iPhone has been shut inside a bedside chest of drawers, lurking like a reptile while he paces the room in escalating ecstasies of panic – Kabir sends a two-word reply to his unseen tormentor.

I understand.

What else can he do? If eight months living in an authoritarian fundamentalist state have taught Kabir anything aside from how to judge jump cuts in jihadi propaganda, it's that everything you say and do may eventually be used against you. This means you should always say as little as possible. Within minutes, a reply has popped up on the hijacked phone.

Good. I'm going to show you what I can do. Leave your room and head to the reception area in your hotel. Behave as though everything that happens is exactly what you expected. You will not be hurt if you do this.

It's a demon, Kabir finds himself thinking. It's a *shaitan* whispering unseen evil into the machine, coming to torment him. Or it's a hacker, another part of Kabir thinks simultaneously, someone working either for or against the Caliphate who has decided, for inscrutably evil reasons, to torment him. There isn't as much of a distinction between these possibilities as he would like.

Kabir heads downstairs. It's after midnight, and only the night manager is in the reception area. He gestures a greeting to Kabir, who hunches on a worse-for-wear leather banquette near the entrance, trying to look like he isn't clutching a demonically possessed iPhone in one hand. Ten minutes pass, then four armed men walk quietly in from the street and gesture at the night manager, who passes them a handwritten note. Still soundless, two of them enter the hotel's lone elevator and two head into the stairwell.

Five minutes later, there's a muffled burst of banging and screaming from the upper floors, then two of the armed men descend the stairwell with their victims hooded and cuffed in front of them: Muhammed the German, stooped and bleeding through the front of his hood; and Dr Tal, apparently untouched. They leave as silently as they arrived. The night manager gestures to Kabir once again, as if to apologize for the interruption. Soon after, another message appears on the phone.

I hope you enjoyed the demonstration. Those men were traitors. But you knew that already. It is you who reported them – you who drew attention to the secrets they have been sharing online, the way they have been contacting your enemies. You're a hero. Reply to say that you understand, then return to your room and await my instructions.

Kabir types out two words once again, then takes the lift back to his room. The two doors next to it are in fragments. One armed man is at work inside each room, ripping the contents methodically to pieces. Kabir's room is untouched, but through the thin walls he can hear steady crashing, tearing sounds. His iPhone is greased with sweat, but he doesn't let go. Devoid of ideas, he sits on the edge of the bed and stares into its screen until, after half an hour, another message appears.

What I did to them, I can do to you. You are under suspicion. You may be arrested tomorrow, depending upon what the others say. If you want me to help, you will need to do everything that I tell you. You will need to do it exactly as I specify, without questions. Reply to say that you understand.

Kabir replies. Another five minutes pass.

Good. We need to speak. You will receive a call from me within the next ten minutes. Answer me honestly. I will know if you are lying. If you lie, I will send these men to your room. You will not be treated as gently as your friends. Reply to confirm your full name, your date of birth, your home address in England, your parents and your siblings.

This box of a room, still resonating with next door's sounds of splintering wood and ripped fabric, is a private hell. This is the ending his journey has earned. Kabir opens a bottle of water from the minibar, sips, then grinds his jaws until the rotting pain of his teeth blots out every other sensation and the world is no larger than a few screaming nerves. Then, he does exactly what he has just been told.

Against his clenched left hand, the iPhone vibrates. A call from an unknown number. Kabir waits until the bright lights clear from his vision, sips his water again, and answers.

CHAPTER 28

It wasn't difficult for Azi to take control of Kabir Asim Kamal's phone, once he'd put together the data. It's all about the pattern: those mistakes we repeatedly, unwittingly make. Kabir was posting to a selection of social media accounts, none under his own name, but all associated with the same email address. This turned out to be the same email address he had posted on a Craigslist ad, two years ago, offering his services as an AV support tech for musicians. It took Azi less than half an hour to paste together a phishing scam: an email informing Kabir that someone had attempted to compromise his accounts, and that he needed to confirm his identity and change his password by clicking on the link.

The link led to a perfect replica of the appropriate website, but Azi didn't even need Kabir to enter his details. The instant Kabir clicked on the link it let loose a lean malware package expressly designed to compromise an iPhone 5 that its owner hasn't kept updated. Laughably simple. The malware even came with a handy drop-down menu, including variably priced ransomware options and a cheerful 'brick it' button.

The first thing Azi did was turn the iPhone into a fully functioning audio and video surveillance device, while leaving its performance unaltered. For as long as it remained charged, he could listen in to anything within range of its microphone. And Kabir was a sufficiently obsessional owner that his phone was never out of sight.

Azi's hunch about their destination proved correct. He started his surveillance soon after his targets checked into a hotel near the border, rapidly fixing their location to the nearest few metres. Then, pushing fantasies of vengeance and justice to the edge of his mind, he sat back in his tiny seat to soak up the three men's conversation.

They were mostly speaking English, which helped – even the hotel manager was fairly fluent – and it didn't take long for Azi to finalize his plan of attack. Apparently, the men had come here to meet the one called Muhammed's sister across the border. This was planned for tomorrow, if they could find suitable fixers, which meant that Azi needed to strike tonight. Isolate, terrify, extort: that was the order of play.

The first thing Azi did was to populate Dr Tal's widely followed feed with a day's worth of backdated and as yet unpublished rage against the Islamic Republic – to make it look as if he was poised to enact a publicly disillusioned desertion. *I came for holy war but all I have found are holy fools #ScrewTheCaliphate* was one of Azi's favourite lines – especially because it allowed him to repurpose a leering image of the doctor and his mate Muhammed striking a pose in front of a power station. *Mo and me are outta here and there's nothing you can do to stop us #CatchMeIfYouCan* was another nice touch.

Azi followed this up by sending a series of urgent, horrified emails and texts from Kabir's hijacked accounts to the most senior contacts Azi could dig out of his address book, using the arse-kissing style favoured for all official communications.

> *Most revered commanders, I am writing to tell you of a most urgent attempted desertion; a betrayal of the holy Republic by men I had trusted, but now know have nothing but evil in their hearts. I enclose details of unpublished media and messages, which you may verify for yourself. Please, I beg you to act fast. I attach the details of their rooms, together with my most humble prayers for your wisdom and judgement.*

And so on, and so on. Once you've searched a thousand or so of their past emails for convincing details and tone, it's remarkably easy to sound like someone else. Machine learning could probably accomplish a pretty good impression, but Azi has always valued the personal touch.

With all this done, Azi paralysed the iPhone, made his preparations and put the final piece into place. In the guise of Kabir, he liaised with the now-awakened local authorities, agreeing to a plan in which Kabir would appear at reception at a set time while his treacherous companions were captured. Azi looped in the hotel management just to be sure, then sent Kabir a text message with his initial instructions.

It worked like a charm. Now, with the witching hour upon them, all that remains is a friendly phone call with a jihadi so terrified and bewildered he is barely able to speak.

'Kabir. Kabir Asim Kamal.'

'Yh—'

'Kabir Asim Kamal. Confirm your name.' Azi's voice is cold with fury. 'Or this conversation will end, and you will die.'

'That is . . . I am him.'

'You work for me, now. Do exactly as I say.'

Kabir's voice trembles through the phone's static. 'Yes. Sir.'

'I'm going to ask you some questions. Answer me honestly. You have a cousin?'

'He . . . I had, but he died. He was killed.'

'You have other cousins?'

'At home, two.'

'Ten and fifteen, two boys. I know this. I am testing you. When did you travel to the Islamic Republic?'

There's a pause, then a high, panicked tone. 'I don't know, please, I don't remember . . . Last year, after the fireworks, November . . . with my cousin.'

'What was his full name? When did he die?'

'January . . . the middle of January. Hamid, Mohammed Hamid Husam. I was there. Please.'

'Good. You have one more cousin.'

'No. No, only them, I swear it.'

'Liar. I will know when you are lying, always.' Azi is speaking faster, now, intensifying the interrogation as he approaches the only question he cares about.

'No! I swear.'

'Munira Khan. The only daughter of your father's brother. She is also your cousin.'

'I don't understand. Please—'

'She is your cousin.'

'She is. She was, I mean. I think. Please—'

This is wrong, Azi thinks. But he keeps his voice flat, implacable. 'Explain.'

'She. There was a girl, a little girl. They were very poor.'

'Explain.'

'She died.'

This is far beyond wrong. Azi's reply is barely a whisper. 'Impossible.'

'She died, I swear it. Before she was one year old.' Kabir's voice is trembling with so much fear that Azi finds it hard to understand him. Yet there's no deception in his words – only the desperate desire to please.

'You're mistaken. You're lying.'

'No. Please, no. That was her name. She is dead.'

Azi tenses, twitches and then grinds his free hand into his forehead. It's impossible. What can it mean? He thinks back, to Sigma's messages, to their meeting. To what it means to steal a life, step by step, starting with a dead child. A single sentence starts to run through his mind on repeat. *There is no such person as Munira Khan. There is no such person as Munira Khan.* Silently, sickened, he realizes his bandage is slick with blood. He needs to maintain control. But it's a battle to find his voice.

'I believe you.'

Kabir explodes with gratitude. 'Thank you! In the name of God, the most gracious, the most—'

'Enough.' More than anything, Azi realizes, he wants the man on the other end of this phone to be hurt. To be hurt, terribly, as Azi has just been hurt. 'You told me the truth. This means you may be useful.'

'Yes. Of course, anything. Who are you? What do you want?'

'I want information. I am not a friend of the Islamic Republic.'

As if he has been waiting all his life to hear this phrase, Kabir starts to gush with more words. 'I am not their friend either! This was my plan, to bring information out of the country. I hate them, I want to help the West. I only ever came because I wanted to find out their secrets, to bring them back. I have secrets! I can send them! My cousin, I hated him. I have secrets with me, now! I promise you, I have been working against—'

Azi can't bear to listen. *There is no such person as Munira Khan.* Savagely, he cuts Kabir off.

'For as long as you are useful to me, I will keep you alive. I will send instructions. You will obey them. That is all. Do not leave your room, do not move until I tell you.'

'Yes, of course. Thank you, brother. Thank you!'

'I'll be in touch.'

Azi spits out these last words, ends the call and slams the phone against his metal desk. Pain shoots up his arm, the impact resounds through the tiny room, but he's already deafened by whispers that won't be silenced.

There is no such person as Munira Khan.

She has been dead for two decades.

You have given your heart to a corpse.

CHAPTER 29

Hardly knowing where he is going, Azi exits the tiny room into the night's last darkness. Summer days begin fast here, sketching the sky first in grey and then a succession of blues, as if the dark is defrosting. He gulps street air and sprints through block after block before, finally, allowing himself to lean against a wall and slide onto the pavement.

Once again, his world is falling apart. Munira's cousin, a coward who would say anything to save his skin, has hollowed out its foundations.

The dead baby, the home address, the data he traced afterwards from Kabir's details. Taken together, it is too much to be lies or coincidence. The person he met, the woman he thought he was trying to save, was a fiction: a plotline put together piece by piece to deceive him. And he believed every word.

The pavement is cold under his thin clothing, its slabs crisscrossed with cracks. He trails his fingers along one, then notices his hand is bloody, then remembers why. The filthy bandage is hanging off his head but there's no pain. Just emptiness and the stink of unclean streets against his own unwashed skin. All his hopes are lies.

Were Anna, Odi and Munira conspiring together? Given the events of Berlin – the deaths, the destruction, the look on their faces – he is sure they were not. So Munira must have been a trap that they walked right into. Which makes him an ignorant piece of bait. How could he have failed to notice?

Resting his head on his knees, Azi already knows the answer to that question. Urgency and constraint have done their thing. By creating urgency and eliminating other options, you create opportunity – a context within which someone's only choice is to do what you want, even if they believe the decision is up to them. Even his feelings have been someone else's choices – a romance just good enough for a fool.

It's been seventy-two hours since Azi crawled out of a box past a bucket of his own urine into the outskirts of this city. It's past time for leaving. Whoever Munira was – whoever she is – she must know that he didn't die in Berlin. She may know that he is here, as may others. She may have delivered the tracking device he found in the warehouse; she may have created Azi's cached profile, set him up in the first place, hand-picked him for heartbreak. He has trusted too many people. He has put too many people in danger. He has failed.

Trying to force his mind into motion, Azi staggers up and makes his way through the still-dark streets, not thinking about where he is going. Movement itself is a comfort. *Perhaps you can run*, a voice whispers between his ears, *and never stop running – swallow up the miles beneath your feet until there are fields around you, drop everything, become nobody, hide from the world.* His body aches for an open space. But nothing is good and there are no good options.

Then an answer comes, quickly, with a kind of recognition: as if it has been waiting all along for him to see it. Turning around, muttering silent curses against the woman who betrayed him, he dashes back through the last of the night to Stournari Street, through the metal-and-glass door, up the echoing stairwell, into a windowless room from which he can send a message to a secure email address still waiting for his response.

I have information you need, urgently. I am in Athens and can meet you at midday today, local time. You need to trust me. Meet . . .

Azi stops typing. He's asking for trust – but can he trust anyone? Not as such. Yet he does know that what he's doing is better than the emptiness Kabir's words have opened – better than the city stretching away with nothing but flight and fear to offer.

He has knowledge, he has leverage, he has value. Amid the snarl of falsehoods and bad options, he has something they desperately need: a truth about Munira.

Where and how can he meet them? What he needs is the opposite of everything he came to find: public space, surveillance, security; the safety of a thousand phone-wielding strangers; a place where no surprises can be sprung, where everything is dazzling in the light of day.

> . . . *on the Acropolis, at the front steps of the Parthenon. Greet me by name, from a distance. One person, unarmed. Reply to this message to confirm. I will be there. Bring snacks.*

Azi Bello is going to bring whatever palace of lies his enemies have built crashing down around their ears.

CHAPTER **30**

'Twenty euros. Twenty euros!'

Eleni is obviously delighted at how appalled she is. She's also, Azi suspects, eager to commence a long exposition – so he tries to deflect her with a nod.

'I'm afraid so. But I'm paying.'

'This is not the point. Twenty euros! Robbery. It is even more than I thought.' She looks Azi up and down with more than her usual briskness. 'You can afford forty euros, fine. Even though this makes the free food and bed you have been enjoying a betrayal. But your crime is nothing compared to the mendacity of the state.'

'Well, nothing compares to that.'

Azi and Eleni are savouring the delights of queuing in baking heat and barely adequate shade, which is what it takes to enter the Acropolis on a fine summer's day. The quality of Azi's banter may be sub-par, but he has decided that mock-levity is a better approach than begging Eleni on hands and knees to get away from him if she values her life. She's not someone who likes being told what to do.

Azi's troubles began when he called into the squat at high speed to pick up his stuff. Once again, Eleni was paying an early-morning visit to her less mobile patients. Once again, she was taking a lively interest in pretty much everything being done by pretty much everyone – and, with Nikasios in his father's care, latched herself onto Azi the moment he mentioned he was visiting the Acropolis.

He tried to prevaricate, put her off and generally change her mind without making a scene. Yet here she is. Pushing away a memory of Nikasios asleep in her arms, he tries to look and sound whatever passes for normal these days.

'So, Eleni, can you tell me a little about the history of all this?'

'No.'

'Excuse me?'

'I am not your Google. Look it up. You didn't bring me here to talk about history.'

Azi tries to turn up his charm another notch.

'No, but . . . you said I should visit. And I figured I owe you.'

'I came because I worry.'

He smiles, charmingly. 'That's very kind. Thank you.'

'You don't understand. I came because I worry you are not who you say you are – that you are not even the kind of person you say you are. You ran away very fast yesterday, you were moving even faster today. Perhaps I am a fool to take an interest, but I feel responsible. Are you spying on the people who are looking after you, Mr Adam Walker?'

'Jesus. No. No! I swear it.'

Azi is authentically appalled. Eleni stiffens all of her five and a half feet and looks him in the eye.

'So, who *are* you spying for?'

'Nobody. Nothing. Honest.'

'They tried to get to me, a while ago. Very friendly. Because of my work, because of my status, some police in suits – they wanted me to keep track of things. In the interest of safety. They are afraid, of violence, of terrorists, of the people. Soon we will have very different men in power.'

Azi hasn't yet abandoned all hope of ingratiation. 'And women?'

'Mostly men, this is still Greece. I told them I would share no information, I would do what I do and treat every person I see with respect, patch them up, share some hope. As I did for you. Yet I think you have not earned what was given.'

They are at the front of the queue now, ready for the bag search. It's a glorious day: the finest since Azi arrived, the bright blue sky shivering with light, the land carved up by clean shadows. Comparing the exquisite rubble of the hillside in front of them with the streets below, jostling their way towards the horizon, Azi wonders whether the last two thousand years have really represented much progress. Although at least they're no longer fans of the using-slaves-to-build-everything approach to civil engineering. Trying to strike a note of wounded conciliation, he looks directly at Eleni.

'I'm sorry. I have kept some things hidden, yes. But I'm on the same side as the people I've met in Exarchia. I love that place. I mean what I say about privacy, freedom. I just need my secrets.'

'Very well, let us say I believe you. Yet this is not the problem. You're not a very good spy, are you?'

'What are you talking about? I'm not a spy.'

Eleni deploys what must be her approximation of a whisper. 'Clearly. You see that man behind us in the queue, with the hat. Don't look! How likely do you think it is that he has a cochlear implant?' Azi looks blank.

'A what?'

'As a doctor, you notice these things. It's a device implanted in the ear that allows you to hear, if you are deaf or hear very badly. Anyone can be deaf, of course. But I do not think he is.' A pause, then Azi's bewildered expression entices Eleni into further speech. 'The worst deaf person is the one who does not wish to hear! That's you, by the way: this is how we talk about a stubborn fool. I think this man is wearing an earpiece. I think he is following us, although I may be wrong.'

Azi has had enough. 'Right. Right. You should go, Eleni. Right now, just in case.'

'I should, yes. But I think I will stay here. I would like a few answers. And you have picked a good place to meet. We have gone through security, and I think nobody will try anything in this location.'

'Great.' Once again, Azi gives up on imposing his will anywhere near Eleni. Then he has an idea. 'Hey, can deaf people with implants hear? I mean, could we make a loud noise and see if he reacts – like throwing a ball at a blind person, to test them?'

'The implants allow them to hear. This is the entire point of the implants.'

'Oh.'

'And what kind of idiot throws a ball at blind people? You have been watching too many movies.'

Amid a sea of hats, shorts, selfies and sandals, Azi and Eleni trudge across baked uneven rock through the pillared remnants of a civilization that was, according to Eleni, *basically fascist but had some good ideas*. The man in the hat is sporadically visible at a distance but, after about five minutes, he is absorbed into the throng. Even the weight of tourists can't touch the geometry of this place, its dominance of the landscape, the insistence that this plateau is not so much part of the city as kin to sky and mountains. Not knowing what else to say, Azi decides to share his one interesting mathematical insight into its architecture.

'They're not actually straight, you know. The pillars. They deliberately built them at a slight angle, different distances apart.'

'And you wish me to ask why they did this?'

'I'm going to tell you whether you ask or not. They did it because perfectly straight, perfectly evenly spaced pillars don't look straight or even. When people look at them, they get distorted by perspective. The ancient Athenians knew you have to build something that isn't perfect to create the appearance of perfection.'

'I admit, that is an interesting fact. Which is why all of us learn it in primary school. But thank you for explaining my own culture to me.'

Azi doesn't say much more after that, although he can't help looking around with mounting wonder. They have arrived at the front of the Parthenon, alongside several hundred other people. The sun is directly overhead, and the floppy hat he rammed onto his shaven head this morning – two euros from a street stall – doesn't seem to be stopping much of its heat. Three broad, broken steps lead up to eight pillars and the remnants of a vast façade. Up close, everything feels outsize, built for giants; the vertiginous light and the heat and the crowds are a kind of compression in Azi's head and, struggling to catch his breath, he stops walking, listens, then turns to Eleni.

'Can you hear that?'

They both stop for a moment. Sure enough, a voice is calling his name, away to the far side of the steps. 'Eleni. There's a signal, and I think I've heard it. I'm going to meet someone now, over there. Stay here.'

'This time, and only this time, I will listen to you. But I will be watching.'

Azi sidles through tourists towards the voice – a man's voice, casually loud, as if he doesn't care whether whoever he is looking for answers or not. It is the man in the hat, leaning patiently on a stone block twice the size of Azi's torso, right at the edge of the public access. He spots Azi and waves.

'Azi.'

'And you are?'

'Odi and Anna send their apologies. They say hi. Time to go.' Azi pauses, noticing that the man is much closer to him than he was five seconds ago.

'Right, er. About that. A little show and tell, maybe, before we rush into anything?'

The man seems amused. 'Of course. Snacks. You like baklava?'

'Hate it. But thanks.'

Shifting his weight, Azi steps back, but even as he does this he feels an arm on his elbow and a cool gentle pressure on his side. *That's strange*, he thinks, *I don't remember having a drink in my pocket.* Yet, a warm liquid seems to be spilling into his clothing. He looks down. Where the man touched him there is blood, wet and hot and thick in the loose fabric of his top. For a moment he feels nothing. Then there is pain – awful, paralysing pain that stops his movement and starts to collapse his legs towards the ground. The man is moving again towards him with a careful, fixed expression of concern for an acquaintance struggling in the heat.

Somewhere behind Azi, a woman's voice begins to scream, her swearing assaulting the air around them. The crowd ripples and then fractures in panic. Azi doesn't know the Greek word for 'terrorist' but he's pretty sure it's being echoed in a cacophony of languages as tourists rush away from this summit in a gathering tide.

Next to Azi, the man hesitates – only briefly, but enough for Azi to stagger a few steps towards the screaming woman. It's Eleni, he realizes, seeing her now. She is looking at him, pointing, her face a grimace not of panic but determination. Beside him, the man has returned, slipping around a mother and two clasped children. Movement is getting more difficult for Azi, but he would be too slow even if his life wasn't leaking out of his side.

Frustratingly, instead of a last few moments of clarity, time has started to become incoherent for Azi, jerking like a badly buffered video clip. Behind the man, a tourist with wild dreadlocks has appeared. The tourist is holding something that Azi cannot quite focus on, but that looks like a lump of the Parthenon steps. The tourist is lifting it up, high above his halo of hair, then bringing it down. It hits the man on the back of the head. He is on top of Azi, twitching and then limp. There are two voices above him, calm amid mayhem.

'I screamed. It was the only thing I could think of to stop this idiot from dying.' Eleni extends her hand to the tourist. 'I am Eleni.'

'I also was forced to improvise. Pleased to meet you, Eleni. My name is Odi.'

Finally, darkness.

CHAPTER 31

After almost two days of silence, Kabir is falling to pieces. Having held out for the first twenty-four hours, he has since sent a dozen messages from his hijacked iPhone, seeking some response from the demon on the other end, the all-seeing entity that has become a blend of man, machine and hacker clichés in his mind. Kabir's messages started off short, but the latest was an entire paragraph of begging and promises. His hands sweated and slipped as he typed and retyped, trying to find the magic words that might bring answers. None came.

Having been warned not to leave his room, Kabir dashed downstairs this morning, trying not to look at the wreckage of the two empty rooms beside his. He went to the nearest market for more bottled water and food supplies, briefly considered making a run across the border, then headed back to the hotel. His behaviour is suspicious, but he doesn't care. Nothing matters apart from keeping his phone charged and receiving. Everywhere he goes and everything he does is surely being recorded, so he doesn't read or reply to emails, doesn't check social media. It's a test, or a punishment, or a game. He is not only crazed with fear but also crazily bored. Every minute is longer than the last.

Finally, he cannot bear it any more. Avoiding the hotel lift, which is too claustrophobic, he clatters down the stairs and finds the hotel manager sitting in the small office behind reception, his garrulousness deflated into misery. Midnight arrests are not good for business. Conjuring an approximation of authority, Kabir instructs the manager to leave his computer logged into an admin account and then to make himself scarce.

With the door shut and locked, Kabir takes a deep breath and heads into the tiny private bathroom adjoining the office for a routine he has practised more times than he likes to remember since Raqqa – the defecation of his USB key. Digging it out of his shit, while disgusting, isn't the worst bit. That would be the care with which it has had to be rebagged, fastened, lubricated and reinserted each time. Today, at least, something new is in order. Kabir recovers, debags and inspects the key, washes and dries his hands with care, then plugs it into the ancient Windows PC sitting on the manager's desk. While the computer opens the thumb drive for browsing, he composes a message to the demon in his phone.

I'm emailing some files to my own account, the best I can find! I know you can access them. I've encrypted them: Kabir123456. Please, I'm begging, get in touch. I'll do anything. More files, names, anything you want. Please, please.

Calming his shaking hands, breathing slowly, Kabir picks twenty megabytes' worth of the most hard to obtain files from his digital excavations, copies them into a new folder, then logs into his webmail. Within ten minutes, he has sent the email to his own account. Within another five minutes, he has rolled back the manager's computer to its previous state. Mission accomplished. Kabir watches his phone, waiting, testing out a tiny sense of hope. He has done something quite clever, he thinks. And it feels so good to have done something, if only because anything is better than waiting.

Then there is a burst of noise. There are men outside, in the lobby, shouting at the manager, asking questions too fast for Kabir to understand. Kabir retreats into the toilet, and in the thirty seconds available to him puts his mobile phone into the same bag as the USB key, seals it tightly and thrusts the package around the U-bend. He finishes just before two black-clad men crash into the office. Behind them, Kabir can make out the figure of Dr Tal.

'That's him,' Dr Tal says, quietly.

Before Kabir can dispute this, one of the men punches him in the bridge of his nose, rocking his head backwards. A second punch finds his stomach, bending Kabir into a crouch before the other man starts kicking him. His body blossoms into pain.

'Stop. Please.'

This is Dr Tal again, and Kabir somehow manages to lift his head as the doctor approaches. Surely, even now, there is something he can say. *This was a terrible mistake. We are all victims.* Surely there is hope.

Dr Tal nods and the two men step back respectfully, conceding a favour. With economical grace, Dr Tal produces a pair of surgical gloves, stretches one onto each hand in turn and kneels beside Kabir on the floor. His tone is solicitous.

'How is your tooth?'

'Dr Tal, I can expl—'

'You should let me take a look.'

Dr Tal takes the bottom of Kabir's jaw in one hand, lowering it carefully. The latex of his glove is warm and dry. It brings back memories from childhood: of a dentist's white room, Kabir's mother sitting outside. At the end of each appointment, Kabir rinsed and then spat pink liquid into a tiny basin. He promised to be a good boy. He starts to cry.

'I see it.' The calm strength of Dr Tal's hands is far worse than being kicked. Unhurried, careful, his fingertips test each tooth in turn. 'Second upper right molar, number seven. It's very bad.'

Kabir can taste the salt of his tears now, as they flow from both eyes into his open mouth. The gloved hand is methodical, unhesitating.

'I will tell you why I hate dentists. They are merely . . . technicians. I have always had a calling. Do you understand?'

Kabir nods.

'Good. It is important to me that you understand.' The hand withdraws from his mouth, closes his jaw, rests lightly on his cheek. 'I persuaded them not to interrogate you. You may think this is a kindness . . .'

Without breaking the flow of his words, Dr Tal slams his free fist into the hinge of Kabir's jaw, precisely where the rotten tooth is festering. Kabir almost passes out from the pain, jerking his neck in an attempt to avoid a second blow. Dr Tal doesn't seem to notice.

' . . . but I simply do not wish you to be alive any more.'

Without shifting his gaze, Dr Tal sweeps aside Kabir's arms and starts to land further blows, now using both hands. Bone breaks. Blood and tears mix with fragments of tooth. Kabir gurgles through the agony, desperately seeking words. None come.

After some time, Dr Tal pauses to inspect his work. Maxillary, mandibular, zygomatic arch and orbital fractures. A broken nose, both eyes leaking fluid. He nods, then shifts astride Kabir and begins to throttle him, leaning his weight into the ineffectually thrashing body. He maintains this position until he is satisfied no life remains. It takes several minutes, but the doctor is in no hurry.

When he is satisfied it is done, he stands up, strips off his gloves and drops them beside the corpse.

'Search the body and the room. Then string it up. This one deserves an audience.'

The men set to work. Thoughtfully, Dr Tal gets out his phone and starts taking photos.

CHAPTER 32

The young woman is drinking premium whisky on someone else's tab, relishing the burn as she watches the hotel bar fill with businessmen, some hungry-eyed, some lonely, some neutered by laptops and phones and tablets.

She grew up between spaces like this: the lightly perfumed and perpetually clean enclosures of hotel foyers, diplomatic residences, ambassador's receptions, privately hired restaurants. Beyond the triple-glazing, poor people lived and died vividly in humid air, scrabbling for purchase on capitalism's flawless skin. She lived inside the belly of the beautiful beast, schooled alongside premiers' and dictators' sons, heiresses to industrial fortunes, clusters of minor royals. It was fun. Then she found something in herself that didn't fit, and life became much more interesting.

Her employers have a saying: *there is no such thing as somebody else's problem.* Professionalism means taking ownership of everything you encounter. If you create more problems than you solve, someone else will step up to solve the problem you have become. A silenced gun to the back of the head, or a long-distance shot, or fast-acting toxins, or a carefully angled knife. Or the right word, spoken in the right tone in the right place.

It would be ironic if words ended her career, because stories are her preferred weapon. It's amazing what a well-worn narrative arc can do. It's amazing what a name and a claim will cause people to believe. Or how profoundly people will fool themselves in the effort to avoid unhappy endings. Like five-year-olds, they join the dots.

Yet something has gone wrong with the story of Azi Bello. He was supposed to die in Berlin. Then he was supposed to die in Athens. Now he's busy not dying in a heavily guarded hospital suite while comparing notes with the intelligence community's best and brightest, which isn't saying much, but may be enough to make things awkward. It's a shame. If she hadn't decided that unfulfilled desire was very much his thing, he might have turned out to be good in bed. That and the whole good Muslim girl charade.

Fortunately, Azi and his keepers are more alike than they realize, because they're both desperate to rescue the future from the past: to mount an all-out assault against yesterday's bogeymen. Terrorists, fanatics, master criminals: the zealots most recognizable to voters. Also, like any boy with a big brain and a dead mother, Azi wants to save the girl and prove himself a hero – and that makes him as predictable as a bad novel.

What she needs to do is clear. It's time for spunky little Munira Khan to pop up, desperate and distracting, leading her erstwhile protectors towards something authentically awful. A few messages and they'll be back chasing shadows. And she only needs to make it last a couple of days.

The whisky glass is empty and the man who paid for it is asking if she wants another. She does. It passes the time and helps bury the recent past. Whatever information Azi thinks he has found – whatever news his Athenian escapade unearthed – none of it will matter soon.

She almost wishes she could be there to watch.

CHAPTER 33

Azi has been meandering through the margins of consciousness for an unknowable length of time. Now he seems to be heading back towards reality, shedding layers of dream and paranoia as he goes. *It's a shame*, he finds himself thinking, watching a softly lit white ceiling resolve into clarity. There was something lovely about not knowing what the hell was going on. As he awakes, he knows the world will expect him to start paying attention.

For a moment, he wonders whether he's back in Eleni's clinic. Then he realizes he's lying down, his mouth thick with sleep. He tries to look around, fails, and briefly panics before registering the pillows heaped around his head. *I ought to be in pain*, he thinks. All he can find is a heavy warmth. *I'm on some good drugs.* He remembers how he broke his arm when he was nine years old, tumbling off his bike onto pavement. After the panic and the agony, the hospital made everything go away, leaving him dazed in a room like this. *Is my mum here yet?* Then he remembers that she is dead, that this is something broken deep in his life he often needs to remember upon waking.

'Azi. I'm going to move your pillows and sit you up.'

It's Anna, her tone unexpectedly solicitous. He manages a grunt in response.

'Uh—'

The bed underneath Azi's shoulders tilts with an effortful whine. The room is bright but windowless, the bulky equipment arrayed along one wall surely too futuristic for any public hospital. Anna is raising his bed with a remote control on the end of a thick grey wire. Having angled Azi to her satisfaction and beaten a last pillow into submission, she leans back in a wooden chair and continues.

'I don't have much time. Can you understand me? Can you speak?'

Azi tests his way towards words. His lips feel desiccated, his tongue alien and huge in his mouth. With effort, he makes them work.

'Just about.'

'You've been here for two days, which is a very long time in our world. Now, I believe you have something to tell me.'

Perhaps it's the bed rest, or the drugs, or the seemingly regular presence of near-death experiences in Azi's life these days, but he has woken into an unfamiliar clarity. The words are lined up in his mind, waiting to be spoken. Gesturing for her to pass the cup of water that's beside his bed, Azi drinks deeply, waits for Anna's face to swim into steady focus, then starts to speak.

'So . . . I got hold of Munira's cousin in Syria. The one who didn't die. I verified everything, tracked him down and scared the shit out of him, until I was certain he would tell the truth. Then I questioned him. He had never heard of Munira. I mean, he had a cousin called Munira, but she died when she was a baby.'

'Go on.' Her face is a mask.

'I double checked, and . . . it was all a setup. Munira Khan was a false identity. I'm certain. She took someone's life, just like I did with Jim. The woman you were following, the person you brought to Berlin, she planned it all. It's on my laptop, in a room in Exarchia. I can show you. Oh shit!' Azi's mind leaps to Kabir.

'Oh shit?' Anna is still expressionless but she's now leaning forwards, inspecting him minutely. Presumably he's being recorded and monitored and guarded, and quite possibly prepared for extraordinary rendition. But none of that bothers Azi, at least for now.

'I never got back to Kabir in Syria. Munira's cousin, the one who didn't get killed. Now he's probably dead, or going crazy with fear in a hotel room, or confessing his sins under torture.'

Anna inspects him for another moment, then leans back again and folds her arms.

'Either way, he can wait. Keep going. Convince me.'

Azi takes another long drink of water.

'I didn't create that cached social media page you sent. I've never seen it before, which means someone else wanted you to find me. But they had to make sure you were looking, so they dropped my name, pretended to be a desperate hacker on the run. It's a huge amount of effort, planning. They must have wanted something from you, badly. So, they came up with an irresistible prize . . .'

Azi stops to sip some more water, his mind racing to stay ahead of his words.

' . . . and gave you a chance to access the world's most dangerous darknet, dressed up like your own brilliant idea.'

Anna doesn't move. 'What did they want?'

This is where Azi's clarity starts to run out. But he has no reason to hold back.

'My guess is, they wanted to get inside your operation. They persuaded you to take them there. When you snatched Munira in Berlin, why was that?' Anna says nothing. 'An alert, I'm guessing. Hostiles in the area. So, you swooped down and took her right where she wanted to be. And she led her people there, bugged the place, took your tech apart while your eyes were on the explosions. She found out everything you knew, then vanished. Leaving you compromised, discredited, desperately trying—'

'That's quite enough for now, Azi.'

For a moment, Azi thinks Anna is going to hit him. Then he realizes that what's on her face isn't anger. It's closer to shame. She looks away from him, composes herself, then starts speaking as if nothing has happened.

'What you're talking about is the result of a years-long intelligence operation which involved us identifying you and leveraging your status as an asset. There are things that don't add up. For a start, the terrorists' identities: the information Munira sent at the start. Gomorrah would never expose either itself or its clients like that. Every piece of that information is real. There's a small army watching the jihadis who got those European identities right now. Every day we wait is a risk.'

Azi doesn't have an answer for this. But he's not letting go of what he knows.

'Look at the facts. Munira Khan is a fake identity, and a good one. She is the reason you found me, which makes me . . . just another part of the story. How do you think that guy found me, at the Acropolis? He knew everything you knew, everything that was in my message. You've been hacked.' He pauses, then barks out a laugh that is more bitterness than mirth. 'You've been owned.'

Despite himself, despite everything, Azi feels a faint glow of satisfaction at saying this to her. Anna doesn't rise to the bait.

'We've been hacked, yes. But that could have happened when they took Munira. The destruction, the killing, perhaps it was all a diversion. She didn't have to be a part of it.'

Through the haze of anaesthesia, Azi is starting to lose his temper.

'How could they have known where she was? Don't you get it, there's no way they could have known anything unless she had a way to get messages out, to communicate her location, to broadcast it all back. She was running rings around all of us! And then . . .'

The one thing Azi hasn't yet told them, he realizes, is that he accessed Gomorrah in Berlin. But before he can speak again, Anna reaches a decision.

'I didn't want to tell you this yet, Azi, but we've heard from her. From Munira.'

The news drives everything else out of Azi's head. This bed, this bright room, the whole setup – he can't bear that her lies have followed him here. Or that he might be wrong.

'What have you heard? How? Actually, you know what, I don't care. She's a liar, a fake. She's working for them and the whole thing is a con.' His fists are clenched, his nails pressing into his palms. They've been cut, he notices. He has been washed, cleaned, tidied up – packed away in a place where he can no longer cause trouble. Desperate, he looks to Anna.

'Please. Please, believe me. What I'm telling you is the only thing that makes sense. I have a computer, in a room in Athens. There's a code. You can see what I found for yourself.'

Anna looks at him for a long time. Unable to hold her gaze, heavy with exhaustion, Azi glances around the room and then across his own slumped body. There's an IV drip in his arm. There's a large man sitting next to his door, his back to Azi, his wide neck vanishing into a dark suit. Finally, Anna leans towards him and lowers her voice.

'Perhaps I do believe you, Azi. But others will not. And that means we have a problem.'

Leaning back, she raises her voice to issue a command and the large man stands up and comes over to them. Anna produces a pen and paper notepad from her pocket, passes them to Azi and tells him to write down the exact access details for his machine in Athens. Then she hands these to the man and dismisses him.

Azi slumps back in the bed, then blinks. Unless he's imagining things, Anna has just given him her version of a reassuring smile. It's still borderline terrifying – but it suggests a solidarity he badly needs. Unsure what to say or do, for the first time since waking he starts to inspect his body. His chest and side are a tight-fitting mass of straps and bandages. He runs both hands across them, across his forehead – now bandage-free – then turns to Anna.

'Am I, you know, badly damaged? Am I going to be okay?'

She nods. 'Astonishingly, yes. You were stabbed with a non-metallic blade. A second strike would have sliced your carotid, but the first was intended only to disable. Your doctor friend and Odi saved your life.'

Azi jolts up again.

'Shit. Is Eleni okay? Where is she?'

'There are a lot of things you don't need to know about, Azi, and this is one of them. She's fine. Like you, she has been taking a short break from everyday life while signing several confidentiality agreements. Unlike you, she will soon be home.'

Anna looks at her watch, taps it and stands up.

'You would do well to remember that none of us are the masters of our fate, not any more. We will be out of here shortly.'

Offering him a thin smile, she leaves the room.

Azi shifts his weight and notices, for the first time, that he's not only been washed, shaved and tidied into something approaching decency, but that a fresh bandage has appeared on his left arm at some distance from any injury he can remember. A small, hard lump beneath the bandage suggests the reason: a subdermal tracker with, judging by its size, extremely high specifications.

Somebody is very keen to ensure he can't go walkabout again.

CHAPTER 34

They depart an hour later, escorted by the suited large man from the room and another who might be his twin. The elasticated bandages that are strapped and swaddled around Azi's midriff allow him to walk easily enough, but he's not looking forward to the next time he has to run.

Whatever kind of medical facility they're leaving, it's not open to the general public. After winding through a tangle of bright corridors, a battered people carrier collects them at speed from a street-level parking bay before lurching onto bustling streets. They drive fast through progressively more dilapidated suburban sprawl until arriving at a glass-fronted office wedged between apartments.

It is, Azi decides, crummy enough to have a kind of character – albeit one distant from the luxury of the Berlin flat and the warehouse's vast vacancy. Beyond a reception desk that looks precisely like the downmarket front end of several generically downmarket local firms, they enter an office that is also almost offensively generic: cheap furniture, tiled carpets, fluorescent lighting. The musty air suggests somewhere unused: a place of refuge and contingency.

Azi looks for glimmers of badass tech, but all he can see is an aged photocopier and a drip coffee machine. Surely no self-respecting ultra-secretive intelligence division should be making use of digs like this? He contemplates expressing an opinion along these lines until Anna intervenes with a special glare she seems to have been working on just for him.

Apart from the silence and speed with which everything is happening, it feels almost mundane. Their two escorts take up positions just outside the door, and Anna gestures Azi to sit opposite her at a chipped wooden table that isn't – for once

– from IKEA. From her pocket, she produces a Samsung phone, unlocks it and places it on the table. Azi isn't sure what this signifies, so he decides to ignore it.

'Nice phone. Is Odi here? I mean, he saved my life . . . again. I'd like to thank him.'

Anna looks pained.

'He's unavoidably detained elsewhere. As we may all be, soon. Look at the phone, Azi. Look who's logged in.'

Azi picks it up. It's a similar setup to his NADIR phone, but with more functionality – a selection of secure apps including a bespoke web browser. He clicks, and Jim's face looks up at him out of the depths of the Defiance forums. This is one of the devices Odi and Anna have been using to keep Jim operational. Azi isn't sure what it signifies.

'You're logged in as Jim. Why?'

Anna gestures with one finger. 'Go to his private messages, the most recent one. I want you to see it.'

Azi does what he's told. A new message arrived ten hours ago, while he was still unconscious: one line from an anonymous new forum member sent directly to Jim.

Help please have got out am alive hiding in dark help come please near instanbul i think

Azi's voice sticks in his throat.

'This is what you meant . . . it's from her.'

Anna nods. 'We found the physical tracking devices we planted on her, discarded outside Berlin. But we've been able to track the IP address this message was posted from, to the Turkish border. Clearly, it is supposed to be her. Clearly, we are supposed to believe she has innovated a means of contacting us. Typing in the darkness, on a stolen or borrowed machine. Something like that. A heroic and desperate effort.'

Her voice drips with contempt. Azi is still having trouble speaking.

'Why?'

'Because we are supposed to chase after her, like useful idiots.' She stands up abruptly and starts pacing the room. Azi is reminded of a caged animal, hunting shadows. If Munira were to walk in, one look would melt the flesh off her face. Anna keeps speaking. 'It is very important that Munira believes we are doing exactly this – that we are idiots. But . . . most things are now well beyond our control. Our colleagues across Europe; the Americans: they are trying to decide what to do with you. And me. They have made it very clear that anything you have touched, that everything we have done, is suspect.'

Azi watches her, thinking of the gaping hole in the warehouse wall, the sprawled bodies, the emergency lights painting the scene blood-red. Anna has lost a great deal more than him. With a quick breath, he pulls himself to attention.

'Her message . . . it's a good thing. In a way. This wasn't part of her plan – Berlin should have been the end of it. So she's trying to cover up, keep us distracted. She can't know what I've found out, and that means she's vulnerable.'

Anna stops pacing. 'I like your thinking, Azi. But don't make the mistake of focusing on her. It's what's behind that matters. Gomorrah, the links to the Islamic Republic. Remember – whatever she hoped to accomplish, it worked. She's tidying up loose ends.'

They look at each other for a moment, something like respect hanging in the air. Then one of the suited men raps on the door, strides in and passes Anna a dark plastic bag. She hands it to Azi. Inside is the computer from his den in Exarchia, delivered with unearthly speed. Flexing the fingers of each hand in turn, he places it on the table and turns to Anna.

'Okay. Down to business. There're things I need to show you on this: messages, my research, a man in Syria who may not be dead yet. Just wait, I promise . . .'

Suddenly, there's a commotion at the door. Both suited men simultaneously produce guns from inside their well-cut clothing, meeting Anna's gaze before moving to investigate. By the time Azi has blinked and turned his head, there is also a gun in Anna's hand and she is gesturing him up from the desk, towards the back of the room. She puts her hand in her pocket, clenches a concealed object, and a section of the wall behind them glides open to reveal what looks like a concrete cupboard.

'I knew it!' He gives the cupboard an appraising glance. Pretty badass. 'I knew this place came equipped!'

'Azi,' she hisses. 'If there's anything important you've forgotten to tell me, now is very much the time.'

He thinks.

'There is no way on earth that whatever this is has anything to do with me. I mean . . . I did manage to access Gomorrah in Berlin, really briefly, in order to get to Athens. But I disposed of everything, covered my tracks, never went near it again . . .'

Azi is backing into the concrete space as he says this, trying to muster a response adequate to the appalled sequence of expressions playing across Anna's face. Before he can say another word, however, the door into the room reopens and the fractionally smaller of the two men appears, breathing heavily, clutching a mobile phone.

'A telephone call, ma'am. A guy in the street brought a message to reception. We're holding him, but he looks like a nobody – paid anonymously to deliver a message. He said it was urgent. I gave him the number for my burner and there's a man on the other end, right now. He's asking for Azi.'

Anna's face is an escalating mix of astonishment and anger. She speaks fast, never taking her gaze off Azi.

'Speakerphone, now. Trace it. I want everything about the messenger and everything about how someone could find us here. I want that computer shut in the fridge, now. I want answers. And most of all, Azi—'

'Er, yes?'

'I want you to do exactly what I tell you while not failing to mention any incredibly fucking important information until the last minute. Do you understand? Whoever this is, tell him nothing. Just keep talking.'

'Will do. Yes, ma'am.'

So much for mutual respect.

CHAPTER 35

The voice on the other end of the line is crackling, faint and clearly being relayed between a succession of servers. But it's also unmistakable.

'I'm on speakerphone?'

'Yeah. Yes.'

'I'm speaking to Azi?'

'Yes.'

'Is that really you, mate? Do you know who this is?'

'Er.'

Azi pauses. Obviously, there is only one person this can be. Obviously, there is no way whatsoever that this person can be calling him, here, now.

'Ad?'

'The same. How've you been, you tosser?'

'Not bad. You know.'

'I expect you can't talk right now. Bet they want to know how I found you, though . . . Hesitate once for yes, twice for no. Nah, I'm just messing with you. You're all over the news. Mainstream media, conspiracy nuts, social networks, you name it. You're a trending topic. Not that anyone knows it's you. Just a bit of murder at the Acropolis, some maniac bashing in a man's head with a relic. Terrorism, fear stalks the land, blah blah blah. But I saw you. And after the bat signal, I put two and two together. I figured it was time to save your ass . . . You're quiet, Azi.'

With her free hand, Anna has by now gestured for the man who carried in the laptop to bring her a pad and pen, and is scribbling in block capitals WHO IS HE? WHAT IS THE BAT SIGNAL? IS HE A THREAT? Azi shakes his head vigorously while pointing at this last question, then takes a deep breath and starts to speak.

'Well, um, it's certainly been a long time since we grew up together in East Croydon and discussed the whole bat signal secret message thing, that one of us could send when we were in trouble although . . . . obviously there's no way I could have told you where I am because I sent that when I arrived in Athens, and that's pretty much all the contact we've had since, er, you moved to California and started working with people like, whatsit, that Institute—'

'Azi, mate. Breathe. You're going to pass out. You can't see me, but I'm waving to the people in the room.' He raises his voice. 'Hi, people in the room! Yes, I am an old friend, calling in Azi's hour of need.'

For a moment, Azi feels like one of the victims of Ad's hacking phone calls fifteen years ago: an unwitting volunteer in someone else's magic trick. Then something inside him shifts. He's not a teenager, and his oldest friend has blundered into something he can't possibly understand. He raises his voice.

'Ad, you have no idea what's going on here. How did you find me?'

Ad sounds nonplussed.

'I got your message – nicely done – then silence, and then all this kicked off in Athens. Almost didn't recognize you given your new look, but someone put a video on Facebook that's basically ten seconds of you bleeding. I checked out hospitals in Athens, found out you weren't in any; checked out private clinics, unlisted facilities, paid a few people to watch doors, analysed street camera footage. Then, for the grand finale, I had a lot of people on the street running options. Nothing's too good for an old mate. Presto!'

The words *WHAT DOES HE MEAN?* have appeared on Anna's paper, but Azi knows what Ad is talking about. When it comes to the climax of a big magic trick, it pays to have options. The magician produces your card from inside the sealed envelope he gave to an audience member beforehand. What he doesn't tell you is that there was also another envelope in his own pocket, another one hidden under your seat, another one ready to palm into your jacket pocket, another one poised to be dropped from the ceiling, and so on. Each envelope has a different card in it, so the magician has as many chances to be right as he can set up in advance. It's a numbers game.

Similarly, Ad must have anonymously paid dozens of people to lurk outside private clinics in the Athens area, watching for the appearance of any vehicle that might be transporting him – and then paid many more people to knock on the doors of wherever these transports ended up. It must have cost a small fortune, but then Ad never seems to have had a problem getting his hands on money. It's like a bad dream, thinks Azi, wondering for a moment whether he should pinch himself.

Anna swears under her breath, then speaks.

'You can talk to me now. I'm looking after Azi. He's fine.'

Ad now sounds less sure of himself.

'Look, Azi has told you who I am. I can't believe I'm doing this, but he needs me, and I owe him. Some shit has hit the fan, right? You think you can't tell me anything, but now I'm going to tell you something that'll change your mind. You all right there, mate? It's about this girl.'

'We're listening.'

'So, until about a year ago I was working at this place, the Existential Institute, and the usual thing happened, they decided they didn't want me working there any more. Mutual disagreement. But while I was there, I met this girl, and she was amazing. I mean, I really opened up to this woman. Things I'd never told anyone. Intense, emotional shit. And I mentioned your name a few times, Azi. Shared a few things.'

Azi can't stop himself from interrupting.

'Jesus, Ad! What did you tell her? What did she look like . . . Wait, were you guys, you know, together?'

'Straight in there, eh? No, we weren't, you know, *together*. We never met IRL. There's this app for people who work in Bay Area tech, Geek Elite, so you don't waste your time with normals. We met on there, we talked, we talked some more. Chatted on the phone, you know how these things go. She was amazing. And legit – mutual acquaintances, knew the scene. Then something came up and she had to leave. I wouldn't have suspected, except she made a mistake. I worked it out when I, er, spied on a colleague who was using the same app. There was a line of text from a different girl that looked familiar. I got this feeling, so I checked it out – and there it was. A top-notch phishing expedition. She was looking through the company for geeks who hung out with British hackers. And she was using multiple identities, rehearsed scripts . . . social engineering and then some. Took me about two hundred fucking hours going through messages to work it all out. I had to automate it in the end, set up a semantic—'

Anna cuts him off. 'We get the idea. What we need to know is *why* we are having this conversation.'

'It goes like this. Distress call from Azi. Crazy assault in Athens. Blatant disinformation fed to the public about what happened. Me spending the last eighteen months wondering why anyone cared so much about what I got up to in East Croydon. Answer: it's all about whatever the fuck is happening to you right now. Which you really ought to tell me about. By the way—'

'*What?*'

'I expect to get paid for this. I can send over my details. There's a few more things I know. The name Rachel ring any bells?'

Both Azi and Anna answer that it does not. There's a pause on the other end of the line.

'Well I guess . . . she obviously used a whole bunch of fucking pseudonyms, didn't she? But still. I know stuff.'

Azi rolls his eyes.

Via a secure and blisteringly fast internet connection Azi has by now established that Kabir's phone is no longer online, that one of Kabir's last acts was to give him access to twenty miscellaneous megabytes of data from the Islamic Republic, and that Ad wishes to continue chatting with them via an increasingly irritating series of secure messages.

You're really not going to tell me anything, mate? After all the work I put in? Surely your comrades are willing to show a little gratitude. I mean, it's not as if I've told anybody else what I've put together. Although I could.

Anna seems violently unamused by pretty much everything that has happened in the last half hour, but she has at least continued to listen to Azi.

'Is your friend threatening us? Is he capable of going public with whatever he thinks he knows?'

Having done a lot of communicating via a secure line in a room beyond Azi's earshot, she is seated back at the table. On his laptop, Azi sifts through the files Kabir sent, scrolling through screen after screen of data while trying to work out what on earth Ad's dating entanglements signify. He replies warily, not sure how well he can be said to know whoever his friend has become.

'Well, he's kind of a dick, but in a good way. Mostly. He's just stubborn, you know? I think he's feeling guilty. We were close a long time ago. Then he buggered off to California. Honestly, I never thought he'd remember the bat signal.'

'Very moving. But what I need to know is, how seriously should I take him?'

'I wouldn't normally take anything Ad says seriously. But this dating app, the connections there – it's all pretty strange. Look, in these files that Kabir sent, right before whatever happened to him. They're mixed, but this is interesting. Trafficking stuff, routing information, logs. There's some overlap with the Gomorrah operation – it must have been a huge thing, faking all those deaths and then sending the jihadis to Europe. Notice anything weird?'

Anna waves her hand impatiently. 'Just tell me.'

'The IP addresses. A lot of this is darknet stuff, but the exit nodes aren't all masked. This is sloppy, they shouldn't have hung on to it. Maybe they were using an earlier version of the Gomorrah client? Anyway, the locations don't make sense. There are nodes in Syria, the Middle East. But then there are a ton on the other side of the world. In California.'

Azi points to a browser tab in which he has marked all the exposed nodes on a map. Syria and California are lit up like twin constellations, a scattered few bright dots between them. Anna looks at him sharply.

'What does this mean, Azi?'

'I don't know. I'd need more data, more time. But I think Ad must be the missing link. Between me, Munira, all of it.'

'Or he's just a meddling idiot.'

Azi pauses, tries to reason things through.

'I don't think so. You found me because of a cached social media page that someone created with old, accurate information. How did they get it? Ad is the only way. I've been thinking about it, and I reckon he's the only possible source. But he would never have created the page itself. So someone phished the information out of him. Someone good enough to target him and fool him – which isn't as easy as you might think. Someone like Munira.'

Anna looks thoughtful.

'Would you say your friend's the meticulous type? Or prone to overconfidence?'

'Definitely not meticulous. Obsessive, brilliant, yes. But he wouldn't know meticulous if it wrote a detailed paper for him.'

'I thought so. I've had a word with some American friends – those that are still prepared to listen to me. He's about to get a nasty surprise.' She raises one eyebrow.

'What are you talking about?'

'You'll see. He's not spoofing his location half as well as he thinks he is.'

Azi waits, wondering wistfully how long it is since he had a decent cup of coffee – and whether he'll ever drink something sufficiently caffeinated to dispel the chaos brewing in his head. Anna sits back. The suited men appear, then disappear again. Then a new message from Ad appears.

There's a man here watching me type this, another man in the back seat of the car I've just been escorted into, and two more that I can see outside. They say it's all going to be okay so long as I send you a message saying just how keen I am to help. Which I am, obviously.

Azi moves to speak, but Anna gestures him into silence. A few minutes pass, then a final message comes through.

Er, mate, what the fuck have you got me into?

Anna gives Azi a careful look.

'Azi, have you ever been to California?'

CHAPTER 36

She scrolls through the briefing file on her screen, only half-reading it, focusing on her own slow breath as she steadies her pulse. Her colleague's voice crackles through the laptop's speakers – envious, probing for weaknesses, testing her will.

'Are you still there, Amira? Have you considered my proposal?'

He is pathetic, she thinks: obsessed with winning a game she has no interest in playing. Using her real name is a sign of desperation on his part – a last provocation. It means he has no cards left to play. She takes a careful sip of tea before answering.

'You are too kind, Michael. I do not want or need your help. As you know, I pride myself on cleaning up my own messes. Besides, it would be a long way for you to come from Dresden.'

There's a spluttering sound from the other end of the line. He really must have thought that she did not know his location – that she wasn't privy to this level of information. Just another idiot, like the would-be assassin in Athens, like the American agents running around with their guns and their gear and their crumbling ambitions. She's glad that Odi's intervention at the Parthenon proved fatal, even if it has led to inconvenience. Death is the most elegant riposte to failure. She allows faint concern into her voice.

'Michael? You're very quiet. Rest assured, I know where to find you, should I require assistance. In the meantime, you have plenty to do. I will send the German file after this call. I expect you to go through it carefully.'

'Of course.'

He's trying to sound impassive, but he doesn't have the knack. After another mouthful of tea, she shuts down the conversation and gives the file her full attention.

There's a name at the top – Tomi Christian – followed by a biographical outline. Tomi Christian, founder and leader of Germany's Defiance party, born in 1969 in the city of Görlitz, clasped against the Polish border. Tomi Christian, tipped as a future leader of Europe's most populous and wealthiest nation. Riding a groundswell of expertly massaged loathing all the way to the top.

Things were very different in 1969. Tomi was born into the miasma of East Germany, trudging a history his government was too poor to dismantle: cobbled streets and neglected churches, Gothic and Baroque façades. The border that split Görlitz in two was younger than the city, drawn along the river in 1945 after what the Russians called the Great Patriotic War. Its legacy defined his early life. Partition, poverty, guilt, humiliation. A dismembered city in exile from its past.

Tomi lived to see a new unification. Not for Görlitz, but for Germany itself. He lived to see power and pride restored, history polished to a Hollywood shine, wealth and travel raising up a new Europe. For a while, he dared to hope. Yet he also lived to see these promises betrayed: his people ignored by their leaders, their values and way of life abandoned, a new invasion of immigrants and alien ideologies welcomed into their land.

Tomi saw his country win and squander its freedom. So he began a movement of his own. A message of hope for the true German people. A promise to take back control, delivered with easy grace. This lightness of touch was among his greatest assets: the approachable manner, the media-friendly grin, the amused contempt for those in Berlin and Brussels who underestimated him again and again.

Now, Amira knows, Tomi is posed to return in glory to the place of his birth – to stand in the Untermarkt at the heart of the old town, addressing a throng of media and believers. They will press into the cobbled square to hear his gags and sincerities: to witness his apotheosis. The old East, not Berlin, will drive the nation's rebirth: ten thousand activists sharing his words as he speaks, crafting content for a million more, fanning the pyre of mainstream politics.

And so long as everything in this file is successfully executed, they'll be part of a spectacle none have anticipated: the show Gomorrah wants the world to watch. A massacre – although not of innocents. A night of shattered glass and long knives.

She takes a last sip of tea, studying the leaves in the bottom of her cup, savouring the dregs' tannic bite. Munira Khan's first message has received a reply – a promise of help at all costs, of a dragon-slaying expedition into the lair of the beast. Carefully, she starts to consider the next phase of her entrapment.

Amira always cleans up her messes. Strictly speaking, Azi Bello doesn't need to die. But it's too satisfying an opportunity to turn down.

CHAPTER 37

For reasons that Azi is confident will become clear at some future point – albeit a distant one – he is sitting in a large and impressively uncomfortable chair in the living room of a sprawling apartment on the second floor of a seemingly deserted building somewhere in the San Francisco Bay area.

It's decorated in either a Spanish or Mexican style, or perhaps an ill-advised mix of both: patterned tiles, whitewashed rough walls, heavy furniture hewn from dark wood edged with ornate metal. Ad is sitting opposite him, on a smaller but presumably equally uncomfortable chair, kicking his legs absent-mindedly as he taps at a tablet. They haven't yet said a word.

Azi has been in California for four hours. Chaperoned by a near-monosyllabic Odi, he flew from Athens via London on a pair of commercial flights that – Anna assured him – represented a deep and barely deserved expression of courtesy by their American hosts. During twenty hours of travel, Azi managed to watch five movies, read two airport thrillers, eat three meals from tiny trays, drink countless tiny cans of ginger ale, and generally wallow in denial. Reality reintroduced itself in the form of a hulking black SUV full of suited, silent men on the far side of Arrivals. He and Odi were delivered to this apartment. Ad was already there. Odi wordlessly headed into the kitchen. Nothing has been explained.

Azi has been sitting opposite Ad for three or four minutes when, finally, Ad looks up and speaks, his tone somewhere between insolence and hysteria.

'I reckon they buy these places at auction. Failed hotels,

apartment complexes. Cheap and totally tasteless. Like budget dungeons.'

Azi tries to smile, but his face has misplaced the expression. Ad keeps speaking.

'I've been making myself at home, best I can. Given I'm a prisoner. Total surveillance, tech lockdown, I can't even watch fucking iPlayer on this thing.' Ad waves the tablet, then tosses it onto a tiled side table with a crash. 'And of course there are guys outside, very discreet. Not that anyone has told me anything, except that I fucked up. But you, you were the man who never got into trouble, who wanted to live in a shed – and look at you now! I mean, look at you.'

Ad tails off, prompting Azi to consider his own appearance. His head is shaven, his ears still pierced, his body clean but battered. Dark loose clothes bulge around his bandages. Azi looks like he feels: harder and more brittle than the person plucked out of his old life.

As the silence between them grows, Azi looks closely at Ad. Perhaps the most shocking thing is just how good Ad looks. The teenager who left for California at the end of the 1990s was a mess of knees and elbows in ill-fitting clothes. The man in front of him is a triumph of American dentistry, high-protein diets and personal training, with artfully unstyled hair and a skinny jeans and T-shirt combo that probably cost more than every single item of clothing Azi owns.

Azi composes himself before speaking.

'It's good to see you, Ad. Really. You look good.'

Ad seems taken aback by the genuine feeling in Azi's tone.

'It's good to see you too, mate. I mean, you've bolloxed up my entire life and you look like shit, but still . . . it's good to see you.'

Azi manages a grin. 'Well, I have nearly died twice in the last week. I got stabbed and everything.'

Standing up, he raises his top to reveal the extensive strapping holding him together – alongside, he notices, an emerging geography of scrapes and bruises, black and yellow against his skin. Ad whistles at the sight.

'Shit, what have they done to you? How much trouble *are* we in?'

He still sounds the same, thinks Azi – the troublemaker who doesn't like it when trouble comes knocking.

'A lot. I don't even know where to start, but I'll try to cover everything and see how that goes. Fair warning: the fact that they're even letting me talk to you means nobody plans on releasing you any time soon.'

Ad manages a nod.

'Fuck it, mate. I've been waiting for something interesting to happen.'

By the time Odi strides in from the kitchen, Azi has run through the basics – Anna, Odi, Munira, Berlin, Athens, Kabir, Gomorrah – while sporadically pausing for Ad to swear in disbelief, stand up, sit down again, and rant about the universe's shitty sense of humour.

Odi is carrying a large bowl of pasta, three plates and three spoons, all of which he deposits onto the large coffee table in the middle of the room – also a supreme example of massively ugly décor. Metal and porcelain clatter on tiles. Odi gestures towards the food and then speaks in an approximation of the genial tone Azi last heard in the Berlin flat.

'Eat. Relax. I'll get water in a moment. A little music?'

Before they can answer, Odi has placed his phone into a docking station. Daft Punk begin to play, echoing tinnily off the walls. Odi sits down and stuffs several spoonfuls of pasta into his mouth before continuing.

'Gentlemen. Help yourselves, fill your mouths. We are being watched and listened to, but if we can all look relaxed then the music and food will stop them being able to listen and lip-read. Dig in, please.'

Ad shoots Odi a look of naked hostility.

'Azi told me all about you, *Odi*. So, now you've got us right where you want us, how about you explain this whole kidnapping, unlawful detention and spy-games fuckup?'

Odi looks at Ad, then bursts out laughing. Aside from

bleeding, it's one of the most genuine things Azi has ever seen him do. Eventually, bringing himself under control, Odi takes an enormous mouthful of pasta and addresses Ad.

'Right where I want you! I only wish that were the case. I am not a guard, holding you prisoner. We are all being held, together. In about an hour's time, myself and Azi will be taken to plead our case. Then we will be returned. Then we will find out what they wish to do with us. They are . . . upset with all three of us. For a variety of reasons.'

Ad stares at Odi, then at Azi, then at the pasta clinging to the end of his fork, apparently equally bewildered by all three. Azi takes up the conversation.

'And who exactly are *they*, Odi?'

Shedding his amusement, Odi sighs. 'Mostly, they're the National Security Agency. People who like to know more than everyone else put together. Only we've spent the last year turning up stuff they haven't even heard of. Now, it turns out we have got ourselves infiltrated, lost one precious asset while letting another go freelance – that's Munira and yourself, respectively – necessitated not one but two intensive clean-ups, then declared on the basis of evidence provided by the Islamic Republic that America is where the real action is. Not to mention allowing you to access the world's most dangerous darknet marketplace. Have I left anything out?'

Azi can't help hamming it up for Ad's benefit. 'Hordes of terrorists at large in Europe under brilliantly faked identities?' Odi shakes his head.

'They are the least of our problems. European national intelligence services are all over them, although it's true that the Americans greatly dislike our approach. They can be very insistent about intervention.'

Odi turns to Ad, who has started looking around the room as if waiting for a hidden camera crew to emerge and say that it's all a joke.

'We are damaged goods, my friends,' Odi says. 'But we have two advantages. First, the Americans believe they are in complete control – and it is dangerous to assume that you know everything. Second, there is a connection we have not yet found between yourself . . .' he gestures at Ad, who flinches ' . . . and Gomorrah. If we can tease this out, I believe there are ways we can outstrip their expectations. I have some resources.'

For a moment, there's nothing but Daft Punk's sad robot disco murmuring through the docking station. Then Ad dumps his pasta on the table, lurches out of his seat and begins to pace up and down the room, his voice a wild half-whisper.

'Right, yeah, about all this . . . there's some stuff I need to get off my chest. I have this thing about physical danger, and, y'know, high levels of unspecified risk in the service of a cause I know nothing about. Then there's all this *I have some resources* talk which is, basically, what a sinister German might say to a sidekick before they get their head tragically blown off. How many times did you say they've tried to kill you, Azi? I'm pretty attached to my head and the whole not being dead thing.'

Azi makes mollifying gestures with both hands. 'I hear you, Ad. I've been through this. I know that none of it makes sense—'

'No. You don't. Not to put too fine a point on it, mate, but I haven't seen you for the best part of one point five decades, I know fuck all about these people, I've been kidnapped and threatened, and no one has given me any money. So why the shitting fuck should I sit here listening to any of this?'

Ad is now shaking as he looms over the table, knotting and unknotting his fingers. What's strange is just how familiar it all feels to Azi, like a blast of hot air blowing straight out of a shed in Croydon in the late 1990s.

Azi never knew how to handle it when they were teenagers. No matter what their disagreement, he could never muster a matching intensity. This time, though, Ad's anger makes him feel sad. There's so much Azi could say. Yet the words don't really matter, because there are no good reasons for them to be here, doing what they are doing, beyond the one that counts – the fact that circumstances have stolen their choices.

Everything Ad says is perfectly reasonable and perfectly irrelevant. His ordinary life is over, just like Azi's ended the moment Anna walked into his shed. What matters is how far they can cope with the consequences.

Odi, who has been nodding along while Ad speaks, seems in a similarly sympathetic frame of mind.

'You are quite right, Adam. Perhaps we can speak more once Azi and I return from our meeting. Until then, please finish eating, get some rest. It is late.'

Ad is not to be mollified. 'Don't patronize me. I want to go out. Get some air. I want to be out of this place.'

'There is nowhere to walk.' Odi's tone is bland. 'Nobody walks, here. Do you still notice that? It must seem normal to you, now, but it is one thing I find—'

'You're crazy. You're both crazy. Do you know how much work I put into finding you, Azi, after I got your message? How much money, how many favours? You're the one person in the world I would do that for. I had been waiting for years, in case of something like this, and now it's all, what, a trap? You're the only one I trusted. And look what you've done, you stupid *bastard*. Look what you've done.'

Ad's hands clasp his face, the anger in his body turned inwards. He steps towards the apartment door, pauses, then spins back and stamps across the living room's tiled floor, his feet echoing except where they strike a violently patterned rug.

'I can't be here, I can't listen to another word. I'm going to my room.'

Odi sighs as Ad leaves, before giving Azi a conspiratorial look.

'People adjust in different ways. Would it help if I hit him?'

Azi thinks for a moment. 'Based on experience, probably not.'

CHAPTER **38**

Odi and Azi are escorted out of the building an hour later, into the California night. The air is dry, and loud with vehicles. They're outside for less than a minute – just long enough for Azi to register the alien scale of the buildings and roads, as if he's dreaming an oversized world. With a brief gesture, Odi indicates they should stay silent.

The car they enter is identical to the one that picked them up from the airport, and of a piece with its setting: a jet-black, leather-seated, air-conditioned wagon vaster than anything Azi would previously have labelled a 'car'. It feels like an over-appointed London taxi. He and Odi sit side by side, the space between them filled by an armrest filled in turn with half a dozen tiny water bottles. Two anonymously suited men sit up front, fifty per cent larger in all dimensions than the pair who shepherded Azi in Athens. Nobody has said anything about where they are going, what they are doing, or which rules apply in this world of seamless transits – so Azi decides to sit back and soak it up.

They move off with effortless power. Beyond the curvature of the rear windows' tinted glass, the landscape is a hallucination of headlights snaked along six-lane highways. They must be about halfway along one side of the San Francisco Bay, but it's nothing like Azi imagined back home: the scale is too great, the tarmac an oceanic sprawl. Out of nowhere a huge yellow moon appears, casting its reflection in a pillar across the water. They join a chain of car lights hurtling over a low, endless-seeming bridge which stretches across the empty heart of the bay. There are no stars, but red lights wink at them in pairs from the shores.

Because this is the way things are done in America, the car

eventually parks in a concrete cavern beneath a concrete citadel islanded by freeways, a beacon of ugliness amid traffic. Presumably the air outside is still warm, but all Azi feels is a recycled coolness as they pass through a reinforced steel elevator door and, after ascending, along beige carpeted corridors for further than ought to be possible.

Odi and Ad walk behind their suited escorts. Still nobody speaks as they pass multiple automated layers of security: near-invisible keypads and sunken cameras, hidden from hostile eyes. It's a kind of Platonic Travelodge, Azi finds himself thinking; a building scrubbed of distinctiveness, inside and out, its purposes existing entirely in the realm of data. They haven't encountered a single other human being since their arrival and, Azi realizes, they probably won't.

After further checks, they're ushered into a long meeting room, where they loiter at the end of an immense wooden table with a pale metallic sphere resting on a spider-like stand at its middle. Azi tries not to picture a malevolent mage muttering incantations over its gleaming surface. While he's doing so, Odi moves close to him and speaks for the first time since they left the apartment.

'We're almost on. Not a word, unless I give the cue. Let me handle all the questions.'

There's a crackle and buzz from the sphere. They are gestured to sit down by their escorts, then a processed voice hovering disconcertingly between male and female starts to speak from everywhere in the room at once.

'Odi. That's what we're calling you today, right?'

Odi nods, his body unmoving. The voice booms louder.

'Don't nod. Out fucking loud, that's how we do this. You understand?'

Odi speaks very clearly. 'I understand.'

'Goddam right. We're the only ones who can do a thing, you know. Keep the world from blowing up. We backed you, we backed your boss. And you fucked us.'

Odi's voice becomes even clearer. 'You reviewed my analysis?'

The room seems to hold its breath. That's the only way Azi

can think about what's happening: he and Odi are trapped somewhere inside a living building, its mind immense and inhuman, its senses everywhere and nowhere. And the building is really, really pissed off. Its voice grates and rasps off the walls.

'We cannot use a single thing you've found. We cannot trust a word you've written. You know why? Because you're arrogant sons of bitches who think you know it all. Europe is a whirl-wind of shit. You're going to be kept well out of the way until it's over. This is your chance to affect what happens after. So, Azi Bello. Tell us about Gomorrah.'

Azi opens his mouth but, before he can speak, is cut off by Odi.

'It would be better if Azi reported later. He doesn't know the full situation.'

Odi by now seems to have achieved an incomprehensible depth of calm, which is more than can be said for the two men who escorted them into the room. Beneath their dark suits, Azi can sense them starting to tense and sweat. This is not how things are supposed to happen.

'You will let him speak for himself.'

'No.'

There's an incredulous pause. 'Do you have any idea how many people get to say "no" to me?'

Odi remains unruffled. 'Being able to refuse you is part of my job. My line manager—'

'Fuck you. Fuck your boss. You're in my house now. The European targets are on the move. We will be shutting them down, hard. You have been more than wrong, over a period of months, at a cost of tens of millions of dollars and half a dozen lives. Now you're asking for another blank cheque. Do you take me for a fool?'

'The girl is not who she claims to be. Her current messages are a distraction. What matters is the California connection.'

When the voice replies, it has cooled – as if rage has been discarded as an ineffective tool.

'You always were a cold one. I see no sense in prolonging

this meeting. I am initiating action as we speak. A proper investigation, good people – not a bunch of hunches and hackers. I have defended your existence in the past. I can handle you paying me back by making me look foolish. But I am not prepared to be paid back in blood.'

Now Odi is the one doing the interrupting. 'I would like to return to—'

'Enough. My people have been through everything you sent. It is our belief that you are not only reckless, but out of control. The extraordinary autonomy you enjoy is ending. Likewise, your protection of this man and his friend.'

And with that, they're escorted back into the night.

CHAPTER 39

As a matter of principle, she finds at least one fault every time room service is brought to her suite. This morning, she claimed the water was insufficiently hot to infuse her tea leaves, necessitating a new tray groaning with pewter accoutrements. Yesterday, her salad didn't have the correct dressing served on the side. Tonight, by way of variation, she plans to highlight a dirty piece of cutlery and some imperfectly bleached linen. After all, nobody expects an espionage and infiltration expert to be making a fuss about napkins.

After the white-coated room service boy departs for the second time, leaving behind a scalding teapot and a written apology from his supervisor, she extracts a burner phone from a concealed compartment deep in her luggage. It's reserved for one particular class of contact: the senior intelligence officers of the Islamic Republic.

So far as these fanatics are concerned, she is providing a premium service via the ultra-secure Gomorrah darknet, for which they have already paid tens of millions of dollars. This service entails circumventing every conventional security measure around travel and identity, and installing loyal agents of the aforementioned Islamic Republic throughout Europe alongside an equally secure procurement network for the tools of the terrorist trade.

So far as *she* is concerned, the particular version of the Gomorrah darknet client these users have installed is a snooping package that gifts her total access to their systems, and that allows her to subvert the private auction process at any point. Meaning she has been able to place the playing pieces on her board with great precision, betraying fifty of their locations – locations that have, naturally, been under constant surveillance since she revealed them – while keeping a few dozen others, upon whom her plans rely, well hidden. Now all she needs to do is light the fuse and take a step back.

She dials the required number, waits for the idiot on the other end to pick up – he always lets the phone ring for at least fifteen seconds, he must think it makes him seem busy – then listens as a brusque male voice puts her in her place.

'You're late.'

Amira exhales demurely. 'My apologies, sir. It will not happen again. My employers have been preoccupied.'

Throughout her dealings with senior members of the Islamic Republic, she has played the role of cowed subordinate, occasionally drafting in a male 'superior' to enhance the illusion. They see her as a harmless facilitator – while she gets to scrutinize them in all their transparent pomposity. The man on the phone is one of her favourites: a mid-ranking fanatic who can't imagine being outwitted by a woman any more than he can imagine his phone turning into a giant spider.

'Everything is in place?' he asks.

'Yes, good sir. The equipment, the necessary access, the adjustments to all the security systems and lists, everything. They will wave your men through.'

'If it is not so, our displeasure will cross the world to find you. I envy these men, who will soon reach Jannah, who will strike this blow against the *kufars*. There is no greater work.'

Amira musters her enthusiasm. 'It is the highest thing!'

The Islamists certainly practise what they preach. This man, with his guns and his minions and his conquered city, wouldn't hesitate to die for his beliefs. He genuinely envies the martyrs. Which, of course, is what makes him so useful. After a pause, he continues.

'There was one complication.'

'Oh? I am sorry to hear that.'

'It was nothing. A traitor, with some access to our networks. He is dead now.'

This time it's easy for her to sound pleased. 'I am glad to hear it, sir.'

Now that he's discussing murder, the man on the other end of the phone is positively loquacious. 'The faith of one of our best men burns brighter because of it. He killed the traitor with his bare hands, an act of great justice and bravery. We do not believe there was any major breach.'

'Is there anything we can do? Do you wish me to tell my superiors, sir?'

There's a self-satisfied chortle. 'I wish them to know that this traitor's corpse is on display. In several places. I wish them to know that we will not be betrayed, and this is the fate awaiting all who attempt to do so. We are guided by divine grace.'

Divine grace, my arse, she thinks. Some of the Islamic Republic's networks are so full of security holes it's a wonder the NSA aren't running them.

'I will convey your message, sir. Peace be upon you.'

He doesn't favour her with a formal farewell, perhaps because he believes she too is a *kufar*, who could do with a good Islamist, or five, taking turns to rape her into a meeker mindset.

The Islamic Republic's approach to gender politics makes the power of life and death she wields all the more satisfying. Its leaders truly believe that they came up with the plan she fed them through her discreet manipulations of their messages, through tailored offerings and opportunities regarding Gomorrah, and through the good old-fashioned impersonation of a small army of non-existent informants. And the European intelligence services' fondness for surveillance over action has only made the opportunity still more golden.

Replacing the phone in her case, she reaches for her tea before realizing that the pewter pot is too hot to touch, even through the several layers of napkins wrapped around its handle. That will be another thing to complain about later. This may be the Four Seasons, but she has ways of being subtly demanding, demeaning and generally objectionable that even they are finding hard to handle.

What she needs is for her current performance to be memorable in all the ways she intends, and thus for none of what's hidden to be remarked upon. You can never be too careful. On which note, she ought to check up on that traitor now decorating Raqqa in several pieces. Not to mention her follow-up messages for Azi and the Organization. Their replies so far have been less than satisfactory.

CHAPTER 40

It's 8 a.m. and they're sitting in the same armchairs as last night. In accordance with time-honoured British tradition, Azi presented a wordless morning peace offering to Ad in the form of a hot beverage. In similar accordance with time-honoured tradition, Ad sniffily accepted it without saying a word. Then he hunched back over the tablet, leaving Azi to talk to the air over his head.

'Last night's meeting was a disaster.'

This opener doesn't even merit a glance. But Azi has plenty more where it came from.

'Only I think Odi meant it to be disastrous. And now all of us are confined here waiting for, I guess, a transfer to less comfortable confinement. Odi's in touch with our hosts, but I don't think he's very popular. So . . .'

Azi pauses, letting the syllable dangle enticingly. Ad viciously swipes his screen, his gaze downturned, refusing to bite.

' . . . I figured we could talk about the Institute, where you used to work. That place where you fell for the dating scam. Remember? The scam you only worked out after you'd revealed enough details to guide half the world to my shed.'

Now Ad looks up. In the daylight filtering through tinted glass he seems gaunt, his eyes deeply shadowed. Azi feels bad, but there's no time for niceties. After a pause, Ad stabs the tablet several times with a single finger, then lobs it across the coffee table onto Azi's lap.

'Here you go, mate. Eat your heart out.'

Azi sees that Ad has opened up the Institute's website. Against a background of oceanic blue, the head of a luminously bald man hovers alongside a block of text. Across the top of the screen in slender letters is written 'The Existential Institute', with an italicized slogan underneath: *saving the human future*.

The block of text is a mission statement written by the bald man, beginning with the words 'I wake every day and worry about the future of humanity'. *Me too*, thinks Azi, although he suspects it's for different reasons. He smiles at Ad, endearingly.

'It's a nice website.'

Ad grunts. 'I know, I helped build it.'

Azi's charm doesn't have much of a recent track record – but that doesn't mean he's going to stop trying. 'It's stunning, Ad. Really. What was your bit?'

'Backend. Obviously.'

On second thoughts, perhaps the time for charm has passed. 'Fuck's sake, Ad. Grow up. Yes, everything is shit and I'm sorry about that. I really, truly, genuinely wish that we weren't here. But we are, and we don't have much time.' He pauses. 'Please. Tell me about the Institute.'

Ad takes a deep sip of coffee, then another, draining his mug. Then he casts Azi a look of pained self-pity. 'I'm usually halfway through my Bikram yoga class by now. Dammit, my life is totally fucked, isn't it? I mean, I'd fucked up a few things already, but this is . . . I don't even know what this is.' He stares at Azi, who stares blankly back. Ad looks away. 'Okay, fine, you win. What do you want to know?'

Azi points at the website. 'The bald guy with the cheekbones – that's Erasmus, right?'

'Of course it is. You've seen his TED talks. Erasmus *is* the Institute.'

'So, did you meet him? What was he like?'

Ad leans back. Despite himself, there are few things he enjoys more than lecturing Azi on a specialist subject that he knows much, much more about than Azi does.

'You don't meet him, it's not like that. He's the real deal, unlike some of the twats who work there: a certified genius. He's raised billions. And he believes every word he says. Saving the world from existential threats, from the stuff that could wipe us all out. Environmental collapse. Meteorite strikes. Nuclear war. Pandemic disease. My personal favourite, rogue AI. Mate, it was a dream job.'

'So why did you leave?'

'Oh come on, Azi, you know me. They were secretive as fuck and I don't like that. I snooped around, did a few things. Did something seriously fucking clever – not that they caught me. They couldn't prove anything, so they let me go on medical grounds.'

This catches Azi by surprise. 'Medical grounds? What, they sacked you because you were ill? They can't do that.'

Ad shrugs. 'It was bullshit. I'm better now, but . . . it made sense for me to go. Anyway, some of them are pretty weird. Everyone's obsessed with *the mission*, which gets creepy. Only ultimate questions deserve our attention, that's the theory.'

Azi shoots him a sidelong glance. 'Is that what you think, Ad?'

'Hell no. It was like . . . People used to play a kind of game, internally, where they came up with *scenarios*. Thought experiments about the future of humanity. One guy got obsessed with what he called a fertility attack: a way of making people have less children. Not some bullshit nudge – literally doing something to reduce global fertility. Chemicals in the water supply, radiation, targeted diseases. Because he calculated that what the world needs, more than anything, is massively fewer people.'

'Because he was a sociopath.'

'Obviously. But some of them thought that was a *good thing*. There were people who seriously believed that being a sociopath could help you see things more clearly – because, if you're physically unable to care about anyone else's rules or feelings, you're better at focusing on the truly long-term.' Ad's eyes flicker between memories. 'So, imagine if that guy actually did it: dropped a dirty bomb, released a chemical into the environment, sterilized a million people. He'd be called a criminal, a terrorist. Right?'

Azi is not comfortable with where this is going. 'Right.'

'Except, in a hundred years, two hundred, three hundred – what would people say then? What would history say if it turned out he succeeded in reversing population growth, saving the planet? He might be considered a hero.'

Azi has the sudden feeling that he's wandered into one of those Reddit threads where very angry people discuss books they've never read. 'It doesn't work like that, Ad. Pretending that you'll get a prize long after you're dead is just a way of saying you can do whatever you like. Your ends justify any means. It's delusional.'

Ad shrugs. 'Anyway, the data suggests he was full of shit. He quit to invest in blockchains. But the point is, what if you do know something that nobody else does, or you can see something that almost nobody else is willing to accept? There are people at the Institute who can only see the big picture. All this everyday stuff we worry about, they'd say it's irrelevant. That in the long run, almost everything is irrelevant.'

'Please tell me you don't believe that, Ad. Don't start telling me that extreme measures are necessary, then suggest we sterilize a few million people.'

'Mate, it freaked me out. I thought they were joking. Then I thought they were trying to shock me. Then I realized that there's just a different way of thinking out here, and they're at the forefront. Hacking reality, solving the world.' Ad looks thoughtful. 'Take some of the stuff you're dealing with. Europe and terrorism and Nazis and all that darknet bollocks. It sounds a bit like another *scenario* to me. An experiment, but for real. If someone at the Institute is involved, there'll be an angle from which everything makes sense. Perfect logical sense.'

Azi knows what he means. 'It's just that, if you follow any logic far enough, it takes you to a strange place.'

'Now you're getting it! And that place is called California.'

For a moment, it's as if they're just old friends catching up – as if Azi had finally decided to take a west coast vacation and sample the San Francisco air. Then there's the slam of a door and Odi walks in, glowing with health and enthusiasm, a small dark backpack dangling from one shoulder. With a fixed grin and only the faintest whiff of irony, he looks from Azi to Ad.

'Gentlemen, good morning. I am so glad to find you getting on. Come with me, please. I want us all to go for a ride.'

Their ride turns out to be a waiting Uber whose driver – Yacine, according to the app on Odi's phone – welcomes them with a pantomime of profound enthusiasm. Odi waves knowingly to a couple of guards at the front of the building, then signals Azi and Ad towards the vehicle: a large, battered blue people carrier. They bundle into the back. Still smiling, Odi joins them, tugs the sliding door shut and buckles up.

It's bright outside and getting brighter. Both Ad and Odi are wearing sunglasses, Azi belatedly notices, thinking of his lone pair languishing in a Croydon bedroom drawer. There is something about the heat and clarity of the Californian air that demands protection, its creeping intensity threatening headaches even through glass. Beyond the tarmac and water lies a wrinkled barrier of green hills, but these are clearly ornamental, especially designed for driving past on cruise control.

For the first few minutes, nobody says anything. Then Yacine presses a selection of buttons on his dashboard, reaches into the footwell of the front passenger seat, and fishes out a bag identical to Odi's backpack which he tosses into the rear of the car. Odi breaks the silence with a whisper.

'Are we all good?'

Yacine nods briskly. 'Yes, boss.'

'Okay,' Odi murmurs, more to himself than the others. 'Let's get this show on the road.'

Before they can say anything, Odi reaches down to the new bag, opens the zip of its main compartment and pulls out a 2012 MacBook layered with an impeccably fashionable blend of logos and transfers. He inspects it with satisfaction, places it on his knees, then reaches into the bag again and draws out a dangerous-looking pocket knife. This is inspected, sheathed, then placed in an outside trouser pocket. At about this point, Ad finds his way towards speech.

'What the actual fuck is going on?'

Odi briskly exhales. 'I mentioned having some access to

resources. Well, here they are: an old friend and a large favour.'
Up front, Yacine gestures self-deprecatingly – although, now
that he looks, Azi can't help noticing that their driver's arms
are the approximate size of his own legs, slab-like under a
yellow polo shirt. *Great, another incredibly dangerous human
being in my life.* Odi continues. 'The Americans can't hear us,
which will bother them immensely. They know we are up to
something and they will want to see what we do – especially
after my display last night. That's why they let us go in the
first place. For now, they will wait.'

The expression on Ad's face suggests he is soberly considering hurling himself out of the vehicle onto the freeway. Now
that Azi's initial shock has died down, however, he has started
to feel that this is all about par for the course – and that Odi
is enjoying his show-but-don't-tell rather too much.

'Okay, Odi. You've had your fun. It's time to do some actual
explaining.'

Odi chuckles. 'Look at you, all grown up. Yes, I owe you an
explanation. For now, we are just driving. I do not have a plan
so much as the conviction that our window of opportunity is
closing fast. Adam, I need you to take a very close look at
what is on this computer. Please.'

Ad looks at Azi, then at Odi, then out of the window at the
dashing landscape. Then he takes the computer and opens it.
Odi points a careful finger halfway down the screen.

'These, my friend, are a series of IP addresses for darknet
nodes. Azi compiled them from a leaked file from the Islamic
Republic. You can see that they are based in California, but
they are also impossible to pin down geographically. For us,
at least. I have a hunch that they may be more familiar to you.'

Ad peers into the screen, cracking the knuckles of each hand
in turn. Azi had forgotten until this moment just how much he
detests this habit, but he also knows that it signifies focus, so
he grits his teeth and waits. It's several minutes until Ad speaks.

'Haven't got a fucking clue. Sorry.'

Odi purses his lips, resting one hand on the pocket into which
he slipped the knife. 'This is disappointing. Are you sure?'

Ad nods, sulkily, but Azi is already thinking aloud. 'Is that thing online, Odi? Okay. Forget the IP addresses. We need to work out what connects the Existential Institute and everything else. We know that someone targeted you, Ad, as well as other employees – and that finding a Brit with my profile was the prize. Why?' Azi pauses, but neither of the others leaps in to answer. So he keeps going.

'What I think they needed was control. Zero margin for error: total surveillance of the employees they were targeting, plus the details of a perfect patsy in the UK. Whoever was running the operation knew *exactly* what they needed for it to work. Which means we're talking about someone freakishly smart, dazzling at long-term thinking, with a sideline in psychopathic indifference to human life.'

'You'll need to narrow it down,' Ad mutters. 'That describes half of Silicon Valley.'

Azi isn't amused. 'Ad, please. What I'm saying is that we need a way to look into this, right now – and that means a look *inside* the Institute's systems. Because I'm willing to bet anything there's a connection. Ad, I know you. There's something you can do, right? If you really wanted to, you could find us a way in.'

Up front, Yacine shares a look with Odi before turning them off the freeway in the direction they came. Ad takes a deep breath.

'You guys, you're killing me.' He takes an even deeper breath. 'There's one thing. It's kind of a huge, irreversible, career-ending hack that'll get me locked up for ever. But, you know, maybe that's already happened. Maybe this is it, the fat fucking lady singing her solo.'

Despite everything, there's a flicker of pride building in his voice.

'I told you they were secretive, right? It pissed me off. They had a protocol for installing a new machine – and it was *perfect*. They assembled a brand new terminal, fresh from the factory. They got a brand new custom USB key. They gave it to a trusted employee, who walked to a secret location. And there, behind locked doors, was their clean zone: totally air-gapped, no connections, no vulnerabilities. That was where the operating system lived.'

He pauses, playing his audience.

'Every computer in the clean zone was assembled and set up on location, every line of code scrutinized before and after compilation. Everything had a cryptographic key. And of course they installed a government-grade perimeter: metal detection, vehicle barriers, laser-based anti-intrusion. The trusted employee plugged his USB into a clean zone computer, downloaded a pristine copy of the operating system, then exited and installed it on the new computer. Perfect. Except...'

Ad is now nakedly delighted by his own cleverness.

'... I hacked it.'

Safe in the knowledge that narrative convention demands nothing less, Azi offers an awed interrogative. 'How?'

'I'm so glad you asked. There was a hard bit, an easier bit, then something ridiculous. First, the hard bit. I pocketed a custom USB key and introduced a vulnerability into the controller chips driving the firmware. Then the easier bit. I worked out the route walked by the trusted employee. Then the ridiculous bit. I bumped into him and swapped his USB for mine when he dropped it. Sleight of hand. And it worked.'

'Genius!' Azi says, for once meaning it. 'Just the right amount of stupidity to fool a bunch of smart people. So, wait... This is exactly what we need. It means you *own* them, Ad – that you can take total control of their core operating system, everything. Why didn't you tell us before?'

Ad looks down. 'Because it was a proof of concept. The moment I do anything – the moment I even think about activating the vulnerability – a hundred separate warnings get triggered. I get complete control of their systems. Then they find out, switch everything off, hunt me down and sue me for a billion dollars.'

He pauses, cracking his knuckles percussively.

'Of course, I don't give a shit about any of that now. So let's do it.'

CHAPTER 41

'I'll give you the good news first,' Ad says, licking his lips with a nervousness that suggests he's already preoccupied with the bad news. 'I can see the routing, and there's a high chance the IP addresses Azi plotted do originate in the Existential Institute.'

Azi tries to take this in, alongside the fact that he now lives in a world where it's good news that a vastly well-funded California institution is apparently operating its own atrocity-on-demand global service.

'Here's the bad news,' Ad continues. 'I've only managed to compromise peripheral networks. If you want any more details, we'll need access to their systems from the *inside*. Deep inside.'

Azi tries hard not to look appalled. 'Right . . . And how long have we got? Before they, you know, notice what you've just done, switch everything off and come looking.'

Ad closes his eyes. 'I'd say . . . between one and two hours. More like one.'

'Right.' This time, Azi decides that he might as well look appalled – and that, with luck, one of the other members of their posse will take the hint and introduce a staggeringly smart plan. Odi and Yacine, however, are deep in whispered conversation. Much gesturing takes place, then Yacine reaches backwards and clasps Odi's arm. Azi doesn't like the look of this.

'Hey, you guys! I hope this isn't some kind of intense, let's-go-die-in-a-blaze-of-glory thing. We're not done yet.'

Odi turns towards him. 'Of course not, my friend. We were discussing the best place to go for breakfast.'

Azi doesn't have an answer to this. After a few minutes, the people carrier lurches across several lanes of traffic into a huge parking lot. 'Diner,' Odi murmurs by way of explanation, gesturing to Ad to zip the laptop back into the substitute rucksack.

The word 'diner' conjures a quaint image in Azi's mind, of a dilapidated yet bustling building full of salt-of-the-earth locals. But what Odi has guided them towards is a sleekly characterless air-conditioned box in one corner of a massive car park surrounded by other box-shaped outlets.

Yacine parks next to the front awning and indicates he'll wait in the car. With infuriating nonchalance, Odi slings the rucksack over one shoulder and beckons them to follow him inside.

They enter, sit as far away from the window as possible, and watch Odi order a round of bottomless coffees and pancake specials. Ad looks like he's about to slide off the seat onto the floor. Azi is holding himself together, but has decided that Odi will require at least one slap in the face during the course of the next two minutes if he doesn't stop being so fucking enigmatic. At last, Odi hoists his rucksack onto the table and starts to speak.

'We have approximately one hour, Adam?'

Ad twitches in agreement.

'Then we must put our heads together. There is something in my bag that will continue to ensure our privacy, within this building at least. Adam, you may have the laptop again . . . Good. You have been to this diner before?'

Ad twitches, this time in disagreement.

'I didn't think so. It is directly opposite the Institute – but I doubt any of its employees would ever step into a place like this.'

This doesn't need Ad's affirmation. To paraphrase the well-being section of the Existential Institute's website, its extensive on-site catering facilities offer three meals a day based upon a predominantly vegan, low glycaemic index, gluten-free, paleo hybrid diet, aimed at enhancing health just short of emaciation. No employee would be seen dead dipping a rasher of crispy bacon into a tiny bowl of high-fructose corn syrup, as Azi is currently doing under Ad's disgusted gaze.

'Okay.' Odi has the manner of a man chairing an important but ultimately routine meeting. 'I have brought us here, I have provided some equipment, I have a few more useful items in this bag. I do not yet know how we are going to get inside the Institute, let alone obtain administrative access to their systems. But I am confident we can solve this problem between us in the space of, let us say, ten minutes.'

Azi takes a vehement bite of bacon. It may be the sugar rush, but he's starting to feel unfamiliarly gung-ho – as if this is the kind of problem-solving he does every day. 'Okay. Hell, yeah. I've done stranger shit in the last week. Ad, any chance of you sneaking in?'

Looking miserably at his untouched stack of pancakes, Ad shakes his head. 'Mate, there's no way. They know me, they keep tabs on everything. I've got some systems access from here,' he taps the laptop affectionately, 'but nothing that can make them forget me. Odi, what about you?'

Odi shakes his head. 'I have a vital part to play elsewhere. The Americans, they are watching our every move – giving us rope with which to hang ourselves. They know that something is wrong, that we should not be able to block their snooping. But they will keep on waiting, because they think they have anticipated everything. I look forward to proving them wrong.'

'Then I guess that leaves me,' Azi continues. 'But why would they let me even walk through the door? They wouldn't, not in a million years. Although,' he swallows, 'Ad, surely there must be someone the Existential Institute *would* welcome if they pitched up at random, asking for the personal attentions of senior management?'

Now that Azi is the one on the spot and Ad is the one behind the keyboard, Ad seems to be enjoying things a little more. 'You might be onto something there, mate. Give me a moment . . . here. Take a look at this.'

Ad brings up a website that makes the Institute's look self-effacing. Against a black background, two red words pulse like a heartbeat. *Total Knowledge*. Ad clicks, revealing a mission statement in the same eye-warping font: *achieving total under-standing of the human condition through data and applied AI.*

'These aresholes,' Ad grins knowingly, 'have been the Institute's biggest acquisition target for the last three years. They're a British firm, valued at a few hundred million, boasting deep learning techniques they say can make sense of yottabytes of unstructured data. I reckon it's bollocks, but Erasmus is horny as hell for them.'

Enlightenment dawns on Azi. 'And you want me to pretend I'm one of them?'

'Yes, mate. It's another seriously short-term hack, but with the access I've got here I should be able to redirect traffic from inside the Institute to a dummy bunch of websites and search results. You can be, let's see, the brand new Chief Technology Officer at Total Knowledge.'

'That might just work!' Azi is starting to get the hang of this collective scheming. 'We can say I'm in the area, had a meeting cancelled, want to chat about mutual interests. Urgent and discreet. They'll provide someone senior, right?'

Ad's typing fingers are a blur. 'They'll bend over backwards, and probably try to brainwash you at the same time. It's like Scientology with extra shiny knobs on. They genuinely think that they know best about the ultimate questions facing humanity. Only difference is, they might be right.'

'Okay, okay. I don't look the part, but I'm guessing you've thought about that, Odi?'

Odi smiles a diamond-edged smile. 'I have had several thoughts. Appropriate clothes were one of them. But I'm afraid you won't like the others.' He taps the pocket within which his knife lies waiting. 'If you follow me, we can get the most important one out of the way.'

While Ad continues to tap at the keyboard – readying his payload for delivery inside the Institute, he mutters – Azi follows Odi at a careful distance into a fortuitously large, lockable restroom containing disabled facilities and a baby-changing table.

'I'm not going to lie, Azi.' Odi folds down the plastic changing table from the wall and gestures to Azi to lay his left forearm across it. 'This is going to hurt a great deal. But I will be fast and, as long as you do not move, accurate. Here.'

From the bag, Odi produces a selection of small bottles, some rolled bandages and two leather straps. It's at this point that Azi works out what he's going to do.

'Holy crap! You're going to remove the tracker. You're going to cut open my fucking arm.' Odi nods. 'Oh sweet Jesus, you're really going to do it. I can't believe it. There's got to be another way, Odi, surely. Please.'

By way of an answer, Odi fastens one strap tightly around Azi's upper arm, sprays something from two of the bottles onto both the blade of the knife and Azi's skin, then points to the other strap. 'You bite it,' he explains. 'I have applied local anaesthetic and disinfectant. Once I go in, it will be bad. But you are strong enough. Sit, please.'

Azi sits awkwardly on the toilet's closed lid, his arm outstretched. Odi washes his hands, leaving the hand-dryer running as he takes up the knife. 'Bite hard,' he cautions. 'And try to send your mind elsewhere.'

Before Azi can protest, Odi offers him the strap. Azi takes it between his teeth. What choice does he have? Odi moves with inexorable care, removing the bandages covering the tracker's insertion point. The skin underneath is a bruised mess, a small slit livid at its heart. Odi smiles at Azi, grasps his arm, then brings up the blade. Before Azi has fully registered what's about to happen, the knife enters his body.

At first there's no pain: only a tugging sensation followed by pressure, then intense cold. Azi looks away, his teeth biting deep into the leather, his gaze locked on what he realizes is the cleaning schedule for this toilet: a laminated sheet of paper with a box for each hour of the day. The rows of neat ticks in felt pen suggest that whoever does the cleaning takes great pride in their work.

Then the pain arrives. It comes from next to the bone, with a scraping rawness that is almost instantly too much to bear.

There's a terrible moaning sound which, Azi realizes, is coming from his own mouth and can't be stopped. He thrashes his head from side to side, choking on the bitter leather. It's worse than being stabbed – far worse – and he can feel himself losing control. His arm trembles and flexes against Odi's grip; tears fill his eyes; his feet thump and lurch as everything except the present moment vanishes.

Then it's over. Something sticky from another bottle is being applied to his skin, followed by bandages. Azi is offered a pair of pills that he gulps without water as soon as he's able to prise his jaw open. Odi wipes the blade, slips it into his pocket, then gathers Azi into a quick embrace.

'I'm proud of you.'

Azi allows himself to be held, trembling. After a moment, Odi releases him and begins methodically to unpack items from his bag.

'Look, here. I have your new clothes; earpieces for both yourself and Adam; a burner phone you can use to deliver the hack; even some sunglasses. And a few extras for me – for the extremely sophisticated diversionary method I am poised to deploy.'

As he has on several previous occasions, Azi gets the sense that Odi finds all this somehow amusing. But this time he doesn't mind. Bracing himself against the wall, Azi massages his jaw, adopts what he hopes is a courageous intonation and tries to talk his future into being.

'Okay, let me see if I get it. Ad stays here, running the tech, ready to find out the exact source of the Gomorrah IPs and scrape all their data – provided I can get in and give him access. Meanwhile, you ensure we're not violently intercepted. One, two, three, profit.'

'Precisely.' Odi ties off the bandage on Azi's forearm and passes him a pristine shirt. With difficulty, Ad wriggles into his new clothes.

'One last thing, Odi. Is there anything I ought to know about your diversion before, you know, you start diverting?'

Odi looks almost childishly eager.

'Only that I'm joking about the sophistication. Your tracker is in my pocket; I have already located and pocketed the two attached to your friend; Yacine and his car will now meet me at the back entrance. I will make it look as though all of us are fleeing at great speed. It will be immensely distracting, I promise.'

With unexpected formality, Odi offers Azi his hand and then shakes it, firmly, before offering his farewell.

'You will be bought as much time as possible. I am resting my hopes on you. And . . .' Odi hesitates ' . . . we must both hope that your friend doesn't utterly fuck everything up.'

CHAPTER 42

Five minutes later, entirely unmolested, Azi crosses a sun-baked eight-lane road and walks onto the Existential Institute campus.

Odi is gone as promised, amid squealing tyres. Ad silently inspected Azi's new look – sunglasses, baseball cap, skinny jeans, Superdry shirt, old-school Reebok tennis shoes – then pronounced him an immaculate douchebag CTO.

As well as his new threads and an aching arm, Azi is sporting a hidden earpiece, a burner phone loaded with malware, and the name Douglas Dingwall.

It's all so ridiculous he hasn't yet managed to become terrified.

Contrary to Azi's expectations, the campus is low-rise and almost invisible from the outside, sprawling between the highway and the bay on land that hosted nothing but mud and seabirds until the Institute landed like a terraforming spaceship. A footpath shaded by the ribs of a wooden pergola creeps alongside private roads, car parks and lush vegetation. It's more like a botanical garden than a corporate headquarters. There's not a single other person to be seen – which, given Azi's extreme time restrictions, makes it an immense relief when a man riding what looks like a minimalist golf buggy hurtles down the path towards him.

'Hey, Doug, welcome! Man, this is a buzz. To have you here, to be able to do this – I'm so excited. We are so excited. I'm Chuck, and I'm all yours. Hop on!'

Chuck is dressed with uncanny similarity to Azi – sunglasses, baseball cap, skinny jeans, Lanvin shirt, Common Project sneakers – and manages to inject his greeting with radiant sincerity. Health, ease and enthusiasm being the tech industry's primary status markers, Azi assumes he must be important. Then Ad starts to speak from somewhere deep in his ear.

We're up and running, mate. This is Charles Bartlett, Director of Digital Evangelism. Most senior guy I could get hold of. You're meeting him for some super-hasty ideation-cum-inspiration. There's a pause. *He's a total psycho. But he's not stupid, so watch out.*

Azi hops on. Building Number One, their destination, is the same size and shape as two aircraft hangars bolted together, and it seems everything else has been made to match. The walkway they're on would qualify as a minor road in England. The unhelpfully abstract map at its entrance is thirty feet high, etched into a glinting sheet of matt metal. The flower beds, irregularly strewn between secondary buildings, boast boulders, waterfalls and trees of a magnitude usually associated with national parks. It's almost as if the architect were making a joke about corporate gigantism.

There's a Disneyland feel to their journey: wooden beams flash overhead, the electric motor buzzes under their seats. The entire site, Azi's escort tells him in ecstatic tones, is a garden city, its water constantly recycled, much of its food grown in the vast garden on Building One's roof. For good measure, a series of giant robots can reshape large parts of the architecture at will. Azi can't help interrupting at this.

'Excuse me, did you say giant robots?'

'Oh yeah! They're super sweet. Giant robot cranes, hidden in the ground. Erasmus is a god when it comes to future-proofing. His vision for this place, his breadth of mind . . .' Chuck tails off into wistfulness. *I told you they were insane,* mutters Ad's ghost.

According to Ad, the Institute enjoys a steadily increasing endowment of over ten billion dollars, drawn from the pockets of multi-billionaire donors who watch TED talks in search of causes adequate to their ambitions. Causes don't come larger than the future of humanity and thus, it seems, neither do endowments.

The buggy glides to a halt next to a totem pole fashioned from recycled metal, where Azi is ushered under a veranda of angular wooden beams, girders and beaten metal panels. A ten-foot-high door glides open as they approach, leading into a soaring reception area where one dark-shirted employee eyes Azi sullenly from behind a standing desk. Douglas Dingwall, Azi has decided, is a grumpily taciturn Brit – and he's delighted to have found someone offering a truly British nadir of customer service on whom he can try out his new personality.

'Name,' the receptionist morosely intones.

'Douglas Dingwall,' Azi intones right back.

'Title.'

'Chief Technology Officer, Total Knowledge.'

'Passport or driving licence.'

This is the point at which his ersatz outrage needs to be perfect. Azi looks at the man as if he has just been asked to supply a vellum parchment. 'Physical identification? You're still using a *physical* identification system?' This produces an apologetic cough, so Azi keeps going. 'I find that amusing. I *am* my identification: my face, my eyes, my body, my data. That's all I carry, so don't waste my time. Just fucking Google me.'

After a frantic gesture from Chuck, the man at the reception desk does exactly that – bringing up, Azi hopes, Ad's redirect of the Total Knowledge website and matching search results. Azi glowers, switching his gaze pointedly between Chuck, the receptionist and an abstract metallic sculpture that might be either two penguins or a fantastically inept nude.

Under Chuck's watchful eye, the receptionist toils through several screens of results, rolls his eyes at the breach of protocol, then prints a pass and hands it over. Chuck twitches like a marionette and affixes it to Azi's shirt.

'I'll have to escort your personally! Very unorthodox, but that's what we love about you guys . . . you live data, you breathe data, you *are* data. It's beautiful. So, you're my very special guest. And given you haven't been here before, you'll want to pay attention. This is the good bit!'

Oh wow, Ad's voice murmurs mockingly, *you're about to get the stupid door treatment. Chuck must be in love.*

Azi has no idea why Ad is talking about doors, but the blunt force of Chuck's charisma is difficult to question at close quarters. Before Azi can do any more glowering, Chuck touches his ID card to a dark panel. A thirty-foot section of glass wall in front of them begins to ripple, shimmer and then break, its surface splitting into a dozen shards. Azi flinches as each shard commences a leisurely journey towards a hidden niche in the walls. Chuck beams like a preacher at the promise of salvation.

'Pretty mind-blowing, right? We don't open it for everyone, there's a regular door round the side. Special visitors only! Erasmus commissioned it. He came up with the concept, there's a patent in his name. *Where the Ocean Meets the Sky.* That's what he called it. Erasmus loves the ocean. It's where we glimpse eternity. Where all life began.'

Azi mulls this for a moment. 'Rod Stewart,' he says.

'What?'

'Rod Stewart. Where the line comes from. It's a song, right? "Rhythm of My Heart", with bagpipes at the start. Kind of a Scottish country rock vibe.'

'No, no. It's not that.'

'Erasmus isn't into British rock?'

'He is not, no.'

'Shame. I love a bit of early nineties Rod Stewart.'

As the shards of glass finish their miraculous journeys, Azi is pleased to see that Chuck has stopped smiling.

'So, hey! What do you think?'

Chuck taps Azi on the shoulder, then lifts the headset away from Azi's face. For a moment, the room they're in takes on a kind of hyper-reality. Azi's eyes cannot believe real life's flawless responsiveness to his gaze, its depth of colours and textures. He feels an urge to run his fingers through the dark, carpet-like padding that covers most of the walls and ceiling, then remembers that his mission is to keep Chuck on the back foot.

'I feel sick.'

'Right, yeah. Some people get that. But hey, not many people have seen what you've seen. The synergies with what you do, the possibilities . . .'

Once again, Chuck's voice tails off in wonder. They're in what the Institute calls its Virtual Reality Empathy Suite, which Chuck claims is the cutting edge of human–machine interactions. Azi has thus spent a few precious minutes drifting through a series of interactive representations of the Earth's most vulnerable ecosystems in the guise of a somewhat misshapen panda.

Chuck is being very, very nice to Azi, with a professionalism it's impossible not to admire. So far as Chuck is concerned, Doug Dingwall is a man being brought face to face with destiny: a future colleague glimpsing the end point of every conceivable good.

So far as Azi is concerned, he and Ad have got one chance to perform a very special trick near a centrally networked system that someone senior – namely, Chuck – is using. To maximize his chances of pulling this off, he needs Chuck to be as cognitively depleted as possible – because, experience and research suggest, this is how you fool someone who ought to know better.

Chuck's assimilationist bonhomie, however, seems alarmingly immune to fatigue. 'We're in the middle of a major pivot towards VR,' he says, guiding Azi towards another asymmetrically gleaming interior vista. 'Strategic investments, acquisitions. Seeing is believing!'

'Won't it be a problem if people start believing they're pandas?'

Azi is being perverse, but he also genuinely dislikes Virtual Reality. Almost every breathless VR pitch paints a picture of infinite freedom. You put on the magic headgear and you're released into a realm of pure imagination: you can walk on the surface of the moon, fly above the pinnacles of alien cities, hang out with friends around a Platonic campfire. Whenever Azi has actually tried it or thought about what it means, however, he has found himself faced with a technology not of escape but imprisonment.

In VR, your *body* is the interface. Clumsily virtualized versions of your hands manipulate unreal objects; everything must be seen and experienced within the rules of embodiment. In VR, there is no escaping your physicality, no typing or deft mouse manipulation, no multitasking or leaping between frames of reference. You're at the mercy of flesh in a way that ordinary life rarely achieves. And your virtual prison is entirely subject to somebody else's control. It's the opposite of everything Azi has ever hoped to achieve online.

No wonder, he thinks, so many tech firms are so excited about this most coercive of tools. Why bother changing the world if you can build a virtual one, pixel by pixel, that's pre-adjusted to corporate settings? Why let people gather in public spaces when you can build a proprietary communal experience?

Handing the headgear back to Chuck with a nod, Azi decides to take his cue from Ad's escalatingly urgent updates. *Time to make your move, mate. Stick with what I told you. You may be able to talk tech, but Silicon Valley bollocks is a whole other ball-game.* Azi turns to Chuck with a meaningful look.

'I admit, I'm impressed. By the tech – but also by you, Chuck. It's all about the people, right?' Chuck indicates a non-verbal approval so wholehearted Azi worries he might fall over. 'So, Chuck, I would like to talk – frankly – about the kind of proposals you guys have put on the table in the past. The legal situation, a sketch of the finances. How we might move things forwards. Can you do that for me?'

This is a big ask. But then again, if Ad's right, Total Knowledge is a hell of a big deal around these parts – and everyone knows that informal conversations between emotionally stunted ideologues are the backbone of innovation.

'Of course.' Chuck grins. 'It would be my very great pleasure. Informally, you understand. A couple of our best guys work near my office. They can scramble, dig out some stuff. You won't believe how fast they work! So many great kids want to work here, they're just amazing, really. This way.'

Azi starts to follow, only for Ad to halt him mid-step. *Wait! Not yet, mate. Sorry. One thing I need to sort. Two minutes.* Azi looks at Chuck, at the swoop of the long pale corridor, then barks out a single word. 'Coffee.'

'Excuse me?'

'I could really do with a coffee.' Always keep your lies as close to the truth as possible.

'Of course! Lordy, you must forgive me, I'm not doing caffeine this month. How do you take it?'

'Strong as you can make it.'

For the first time, Chuck seems less than confident. Who would have thought that requests for a hot drink would deposit him outside his comfort zone? Azi presses his advantage.

'And can I take a private moment in your office, please, before the others arrive? Just the two of us.'

'Sure, sure. Hey,' Chuck seems to have found something to smile about again, 'have you tried nitro coffee? So smooth you wouldn't believe. It's like drinking cream! It'll change your life.'

Azi acquiesces, follows Chuck to a kitchen around the corner, then watches in silence as Chuck deploys what look like horror movie props – a glass-and-steel liquid nitrogen injection system, apparently – to produce a mud-brown, freezing brew. Azi sips. The liquid is soapily soft. It may be the most hatefully unnecessary thing he has ever seen done to an innocent coffee bean.

With Chuck's equanimity restored, they walk past rows of aspirationally labelled meeting rooms – *Eternity*, *Resilience*, *Pathos* – deeper into the heart of the building. Eventually Chuck arrives at his office. It's nearly thirty feet long, fifteen feet wide and has no corners: half of its bubble-like exterior is glass, and half is concrete. Like everything else in this section of the building, it appears to have been scooped out of a concrete cliff, which rises dizzyingly to the roof garden through a maze of walkways, lightwells and suspended staircases. Chuck gestures with approval at its immensity.

'The heart of the action! Beyond the wall, that's our next-generation research. It's mind-blowing. The battle over inner space, that's where Erasmus believes the twenty-first century will be won or lost. Hearts and minds, beliefs and experiences, machines that know us better than we know ourselves . . . but all that's beyond even my pay grade. So, come in. We can have our minute, the guys are round the corner.'

Azi readies the phrases Ad has muttered into his ear. 'There are a few things we're working on. Integrated systems. Cloud, Big Data, ML, AI, IoT – a hybrid approach. Some really smart stuff with our data lakes, high-velocity aggregation and analysis, all blockchain-powered. We'll be starting an investment round soon. Unless, of course—' Azi breaks off, tantalizingly, before giving Chuck what he hopes is a conspiratorial glance. 'Chuck, I just remembered speaking to someone who worked here. They said you have voice-activated systems in all your offices?'

'That's correct, yes. Keyed to our voice signatures. You know the Star Trek computer—'

'I need you to turn off your system, please. I want everything to be private. Completely private, before I can tell you what's on my mind.'

Chuck leans forwards, his demeanour shifting as if he has smelled something unexpectedly delicious. Azi has his full attention, which is precisely what he was waiting for. As Chuck nods vigorously, Azi hovers his fingers above two buttons on the side of the phone in his pocket.

If he and Ad have set everything up correctly, this phone will do one thing when Azi presses both buttons: transmit a nugget of code through the medium of sound in the ultrasonic range. It's known in the trade as a dolphin hack. Because computers can detect a far wider range of sounds than humans, it's possible to issue secret instructions to a voice-activated system in the presence of countless witnesses. Azi has never had a hope of getting his hands on a networked computer inside the Institute – but, he and Ad reasoned, it should be possible for him to deploy a dolphin hack at the precise moment someone with high-level clearance speaks to unlock their system. If his timing is perfect. If Ad's software works.

Chuck, fortunately, is far too busy emoting to be suspicious. 'I get the idea, I understand completely! Consider me a friend, it's done. Computer, username Charles Bartlett,' *Go, go, go!* Ad bellows unhelpfully in Azi's ear, 'verify and engage full privacy mode.'

Azi activates his phone.

And nothing happens. There's no word from Ad, and – given that inaudibility is one of the hack's main advantages – no way Azi himself can tell if activating the phone did anything.

Glancing at the two very earnest, very young men now loitering outside Chuck's office, Azi sips his atrocity of a coffee and tries to look innocent. At a table in a nearby diner, Ad should right now be receiving the crucial notification: confirmation that the backdoor in the Institute's core operating system has opened wide.

Casually, Azi taps his earpiece. Half a minute has elapsed and, he realizes, Chuck is waiting with vulpine eagerness for the commencement of his revelations. Which is a problem because, without Ad's input, Azi doesn't have anything to say.

If the hack worked – Azi tells himself – Ad should be back in his ear any moment, freshly armed with master administrative access to every single network and device in the entire campus.

Azi tries to stay calm. Now that he thinks about it, this last prospect is deeply alarming. How far can Ad be relied upon to play his part with any modicum of sense?

As if in answer, alarm bells start to sound.

CHAPTER 43

You can tell when things are about to go wrong, if you know how to watch for the signs. First, the coincidences start to accumulate. Second, you start reassuring yourself that everything is fine. Third, you start ignoring the evidence that it's not.

Amira is focused on stopping the rot at step one – because the coincidences she's contemplating are, when taken together, anything but coincidental.

It turns out that the man the Islamic Republic enthusiastically strangled and dismembered for treachery was Munira Khan's surviving cousin – and that he may have managed to access some files that she really, really doesn't want the world to see. This is vexing in the extreme.

It also turns out that Azi and chums aren't replying to the lovely Munira's messages with either the ingenuity or the enthusiasm she expected. Her first pitiful missive was designed to let them know roughly where she was, followed by sufficient clues to sketch a tragic tale: the fair maiden trussed up in the back of a dark vehicle, transported between dens of iniquity into the Middle East, typing heroic dispatches in the dark.

By Amira's calculations, at least a few people ought to be en route to the locations she designated. Instead, although several promises of rescue have been sent, these have been muted to the point of indifference. Amira's access to the Organization's internal systems was finally shut down after Athens, but that was to be expected. What she can't understand is why they no longer seem to care whether Munira Khan lives or dies.

She has barely enough time and attention to make new arrangements – but adaptation is required. They may know about Munira. And if they've somehow found out about her, there's no end to what else they may think they know.

It's doubly enraging because, after so long and so much planning, she is close. Across Europe, the Islamists whose locations she betrayed to Azi are under constant observation. She has been watching the Americans and Europeans watching them. These sacrificial idiots will be isolated and captured within hours.

Around Görlitz, however, the second piece of her puzzle is slipping perfectly into place. Two dozen more jihadis are converging on the Defiance rally site with enough explosives in their very special vans to massacre the crowd ten times over. These are the ones who will sear today into the world's consciousness – and will precipitate the chaotic repercussions her employers have so carefully anticipated. This will be her masterpiece. It's too late for anything to change it.

And yet. *There are tigers on the bank, crocodiles in the water.* This affectionate tip, courtesy of her maternal grandmother, remains one of the few fragments of childhood worth remembering. Danger is everywhere – as are morons like Michael. Lifting herself regretfully out of the vast marble bathtub that commands one of her suite's bathrooms, she slips into a robe and disinters a variety of dedicated devices from her luggage: one for each distinct identity or facet of her operations.

There's an update from the Islamic Republic, which she ignores: they're ripping apart the hotel in which the traitor was killed, most likely because they can't find enough actual people to execute. There's an update from her sources in Defiance that suggests everything is proceeding smoothly ahead of this afternoon's rally: they're moaning about the fact that Tomi has banned the beating-up of anti-fascist protestors. Finally, there's an update from the Institute campus telling her that something unusual in the core operating system is under urgent investigation.

She idly plucks one eyebrow, letting the pain sharpen her discomfort. This last coincidence means she can no longer even contemplate inaction. With a wince, she unearths the most secure and least-used of all her devices, switches it on and confirms her fingerprints, passcode, facial features and hardware key. It looks like every other generic phone in her possession, yet it can make and receive calls only to one secure number.

Suppressing any hint of a tremor in her hand or voice, she dials and waits. It's a full minute until he picks up, but she knows this is nothing to do with status. This man has no need to play games. His voice, when he answers, is pure self-assurance.

'My dear. I have just been on the line to Michael.'

She smiles softly. 'And how is my colleague?'

'Not so good. I hope you said your farewells. He is not a man for detail. He lied, then he allowed me to find out that he lied. Then he denied it. Triply disappointing.'

This is heartening, even if it's irrelevant to her current concerns. 'I am pleased to report that the plan is unaffected, despite his incompetence. If anything the presence of protestors will enhance its impact.'

There's a thoughtful pause. 'You are right, of course. I mistrust unnecessary complexity – but some anti-fascist corpses will make the mess more piquant. Not that Michael will know.'

She allows herself to sound wistful. 'It's a shame, I would have liked to be there. To deal with him personally.'

He chuckles. 'If you wish, I will delay. You can kill him yourself.'

'I would love to, thank you.' Enough chat, she regretfully thinks. Time to get down to business. 'I am afraid I have serious news.'

The play vanishes from his voice. 'What do I need to know?'

'Three things. The surviving cousin in Syria has been executed. The Organization are not pursuing Munira as expected. And, as you must be aware, the core operating system is reporting urgent errors.'

'What do you propose?'

She hardens herself, focusing her anger. 'That I investigate in person. That I keep you apprised of all developments. And that all contingencies are active.'

'I agree. Nobody enters the research area apart from you, nobody but you leaves. No witnesses. You have discretion to handle everything. If there are points of failure, we may not speak again . . .'

'I understand.'

' . . . but I have every confidence.'

She touches one hand to the smooth skin of her cheek.

'Thank you, Erasmus.'

CHAPTER 44

'You've got to admit, mate, the alarm was a nice touch.'

'No. It wasn't.'

'How else was I going to get onto the campus? How else was I going to get you out, come to that? And I saved you from making a tit of yourself on the bullshitting front. Greater love hath no—'

Azi has to stop himself grabbing Ad by the shoulders and shaking him. 'This wasn't the plan, Ad. We agreed you'd investigate from the diner, feed me info through the earpiece, keep it low key. Alarms are literally designed to alarm everyone. They attract attention. This was meant to be a subtle infiltration. Instead, what you've done—'

Ad is fast approaching full self-righteous mode. 'I mixed things up. My exploit, my call. You were out of time, they were about to pull the plug. And this,' Ad gestures expansively at the scene of chaos and devastation surrounding them, 'is the only way we can access those IP addresses.'

Azi looks his friend up and down, then at the screaming hellscape of the campus. He has to admit, Ad has a point – although simultaneously setting off every fire *and* earthquake evacuation alarm while deactivating the entire internal security system still seems excessive. And that's before taking into account whatever Ad has done to the Institute's public-facing autonomous systems, which have developed a chaotic life of their own.

Hot off the back of the technical meltdown that sent Azi, Chuck and five thousand other employees hurtling towards emergency evacuation zones, four robotic cranes have appeared from their silos and are now busy demolishing the landscaping chunk by chunk. Meanwhile, electric buggies of varied sizes are screeching like anarchic arthropods up and down their pathways, herding phalanxes of evacuees onto manicured flower beds and lawns.

All of this provided enough of a diversion for Azi to obey the directions Ad was screaming through the earpiece, and to slip off the edge of a densely landscaped path towards the immense metallic sculpture – an angel, perhaps, or a melted Airbus – behind which they are both currently lurking. The sight of a fifty-foot tree being splintered effortlessly into fragments by a one-hundred-foot metal arm is not something Azi will forget in a hurry. But he isn't in the mood for forgiveness.

'If I didn't know better, I'd say this is a prank you've been wanting to pull ever since they chucked you out. Is this your revenge, your big laugh? Well, it's fucked up. You've fucked up. How are we going to get in and out? Now everyone involved knows something is happening. We're fucked, fucked, *fucked*.'

When did Azi last get this angry? He already knows the answer: half a lifetime ago, in a shed in Croydon. After all he's been through, there's something ludicrous and shameful about standing in this car park watching disaster unfold; about the stupidity of coming this close, working so hard, then blowing it all up into a giant practical joke. But Ad isn't giving any ground. Gesturing towards the rear of Building One's gigantic bulk, he shudders with fury.

'*That's* where we need to go. And this is the *only way*, mate. You need to get your head around that. Because, as it turns out, the origin of those Gomorrah IP addresses you're so desperate to track down is off the master grid in a top secret fucking research facility: a triple-secured bunker with rings of automated lockdown bollocks. And the only way into that facility is a full-on natural disaster evacuation shit-hits-fan scenario. Which is what I've delivered, for you. It's a wonder of the fucking world, mate, and we're standing here, together, and . . .' Ad has started to choke on his intensity of feeling ' . . . you're the same ungrateful goody-goody prick you always were. Taking my charity then throwing it back in my face. You dumb *fuck*.'

Azi stares at his friend, raging amid the chaos, hunched in blinding sunshine under a vast abstract statue in a billion-dollar campus, tanned and lean, five thousand miles and fifteen years distant from their childhood – yet still their past surrounds them. His fear, Ad's anger. They're drowning in who they used to be.

'I'm sorry,' Azi says. 'I'm sorry, Ad. You're right. It is the only way. I just . . . I've been through a lot. And this . . .'

He gestures towards the maelstrom.

' . . . is not how I pictured our reunion.'

Azi drops his arm and grins. Ad scowls, throws both his arms wide, then grins too.

'Is this the bit where we hug?' asks Azi, innocently.

'No fucking way. This is the bit where we kick ass.'

'Right. And how long do we have?'

Ad glances at the computer tucked under his arm, then at the mayhem still unfolding behind them, then shrugs. 'If we start running now, if we make it in through all the airlocks, about half an hour. Depending on how fast the military get here.'

Azi inspects their route – a simple enough scramble through the deep cover of ornamental beds, so long as crazed robot gardeners don't mow them down. It ends in a zone of inscrutable shadow.

They start running.

What does it look like when you invest more than a billion dollars in the future of virtual, augmented and mixed reality technologies? This is not a question Azi has ever thought about. Even if he had, however, he would never have guessed that it involved so much empty space.

Via a series of gaping airlocks – immense steel-and-concrete chambers, mercifully open to the air in the aftermath of the Institute's tech meltdown – Azi and Ad have finally arrived in the research area beyond the cliff where Chuck's office nestled. Azi had expected it to hold something similar to the corridors, mezzanines and meeting spaces through which Chuck guided him. Instead, as he and Ad step back from the final soundlessly pivoting door, they enter a space so cavernous that its ceiling and far walls are invisible.

'Bloody hell, Ad. Have you been here before?'

'Of course not. Nobody comes here, ever. It's fully automated, locked down . . . we're only here because they never dreamed someone could compromise everything at the same time.'

'While pretending there's an earthquake going on.'

'Yeah. Total evacuation protocols are a bitch.'

There are no echoes, Azi notices, their resonance damped by the carpet-like coating on every surface. It's like the Empathy Suite, expanded to monstrous proportions.

It's also, despite their bravado, dauntingly bizarre. There are no obvious sources for the dusky light to which their eyes are gradually adjusting, and no paths or compartments dividing up the interior, save for a few boxlike structures. It takes a while for Azi to place what they remind him of: the mock rooms used to display IKEA goods. Ad points towards a lighting rig suspended above the nearest one.

'They're projection boxes. Next-generation shit. You stand inside, the machinery tracks your movements, you wear a pair of special glasses. It's just like being in a fully furnished virtual room. Or whatever else they want you to see.'

The boxes are each the size of a respectable garden shed, yet they look like children's toys against the scale of this building: blocks casually strewn across a giant's playground.

'Why is it so huge?' Azi asks, his good arm testing the bandages under his shirt. They're hot and damp, with more than sweat. Rapid movement is very much not what his body needs at the moment.

'No idea, mate.' Ad squints into the dusk. 'The power drain is ridiculous, but I couldn't pick up any details from outside. That's why we're here.'

Azi gathers himself. They have a plan, they have a purpose. 'Right. You've narrowed down the IP addresses to somewhere inside this zone. So we're looking for a hub, anything you can network with. And we've got less than half an hour to find it, and then to use your hack and gather evidence. If we're lucky, we'll get inside access to everything in Gomorrah. If we're unlucky . . .'

Azi's determination tails off as the soft semi-darkness swallows his words. Beyond the farthest projection boxes, he can make out something skeletal stretching high into the air. It's hard to assess distances. The invisible ceiling can't be less than three hundred feet away, while the far wall might be as much as a thousand. After what's outside, the desertion is uncanny. The twilight seems to shimmer and pulse.

'Why are there no people, Ad? I mean, not even any evidence of people. It's like a mausoleum.'

Clutching the laptop, Ad steps briskly ahead. 'Now there's an image. Come on, mate, keep up. All the mixed reality stuff, even the light boxes, is old news. Their research is all about automation, now. Isolated systems, self-monitoring. Like whatever the fuck this monstrosity is.'

They approach the skeletal outline, which has resolved into a massively jointed arm supporting a sphere perhaps a hundred feet above them, the arm's base cantilevered with jet-black metal beams. It's like the chitinous limb of an impossible insect. Azi shivers.

'What in God's name has this got to do with saving humanity?'

Ad opens the laptop, types for a frantic few moments, then whistles. 'Sod all, so far as I can tell. Odi's beautiful machine has got a lot of non-standard sensors, and it's telling me that this *thing* is crazy with electromagnetic activity.'

'Meaning?' Azi has no idea where this is going, but he's sure the destination will be unpleasant.

'It's analysing us. Right now. It has its own network, so I can't break in unless there's some kind of access and – oh shit, oh holy shit.'

'Oh shit what?'

Before Ad can reply, the universe provides an answer in the form of a shrieking metallic nightmare rising above them. The sphere at the arm's summit is rippling with light, the arm beneath it flexing with alien precision. Ad and Azi look at each other, look at the awakened beast, then start to run.

They don't get far. After thirty feet, Ad – unencumbered by weeping wounds, he's leading the way – comes to a sudden halt and starts bellowing in fresh terror.

'Azi. Shit! Help me, what's this on my face? It's sticking to me, I can't get it off—'

Azi is just behind. 'What is it? Jesus, what's happening, are you okay?'

Ad claws at his face, yet there appears to be nothing there – until Azi steps forwards and feels some kind of sticky, twisting worm curl across his upper body. Ad is flailing both arms now, wielding the laptop like a weapon.

'What the fuck, Azi? I can't get these things off, they're trying to choke me! Help—'

'Ad.' Azi forces himself to stand perfectly still. 'Ad! Stop moving. Stop. I can feel it. Holy crap, holy crap, I think they're cables, wires, something like that. Just try to stop moving.'

Using his body weight, Azi manages to drop away from whatever was grasping him and tumbles onto the eerily textured ground. He looks up, then wishes he hadn't. Numberless fine tendrils hang from the glowing sphere, falling to within two feet of the ground. Ad is well and truly tangled, the writhing array snaring him as if by instinct.

We're under attack by a robot jellyfish, a small voice mutters in Azi's head. *We're about to be murdered by an absolutely massive evil autonomous fuck-knows-what and, to be honest, I haven't got anything in my repertoire adequate to stuff like this.* Ad is still screaming, the sound sucked away to nothing after each breath. Azi looks at him for a moment.

'Ad! Ad, drop the laptop. If you can, drop it on the floor. Now!'

Ad manages to excavate some rage from inside his horror. 'Fuck the laptop, I'm being eaten by Cthulhu!'

Trying not to think about what may happen if he fails, Azi raises himself onto his elbows and lunges for the laptop. For a moment, it hangs in the tendrils' grasp, their tips curling towards him. Then he and the computer tumble down.

Azi opens it. Weakly, the screen-light illuminates a cloud of writhing filaments. Ad is no longer screaming. Azi activates a sniffer protocol across as much of the electromagnetic spectrum as the machine can handle, trying to identify any readable packets of data. He needs something, anything, that will let him access the system. If it's a prototype, if it's designed to be controlled, there may be something – a chink in its digital armour.

There's no sound whatsoever now. Ad twitches, obscenely, like a fish on a hook. The distant sphere is riddled with light and seems to be descending, the tentacles' clearance above Azi's head shrinking inch by inch. The thing is near the limit of its motion, he realizes, straining against the cantilevers – hungry to escape.

Then he sees it. A simple routine surrounding the complexity, like a restraining pulse; a coordinate system for the arm's supporting motion. Thirty seconds and he's inside, overriding the sphere's autonomy. The arm jerks upwards, the tendrils stiffen, Ad twitches one last time and falls to the floor. There's silence, until . . .

'Ha!' For someone who looked near-deceased a minute ago, Ad is remarkably chipper. 'Take that, robot fuckface.'

'What the hell? I thought you were being digested,' Azi exclaims.

'Evolutionary biology, mate. I was playing dead. Also, I had a mouth full of tentacles. But it was my executive decision to pretend I was no longer living or breathing. And it worked.'

'Well.' Azi decides not to quibble. 'That was horrifying.'

Ad nods, staggers to his feet and helps Azi do the same. They're both shaking. Above them, the sphere continues to rise on the end of its arm, glistening like a false moon. The fine threads hung beneath it are almost beautiful: swaying between shadow and light, shifting each other's reflections. Next to Azi, Ad has taken the laptop and started to explore the jellyfish's systems, his eyes widening as he does.

'The sensors on this monster are crazy, Azi. Evil-fucking-genius crazy. They're taking in trace chemicals from the air, movements, sounds, magnetic fields. It's like a deep sea predator. Like a weapon. Fuck knows what else they've got in here.'

Azi doesn't retort, because he doesn't need to, that they now have fifteen minutes to find the source of the IP addresses – and that the likelihood of them achieving this and managing to escape with their lives is trending towards zero. They're in a huge, hostile, inhuman environment. No-one knows they're there, no-one is coming to save them – and Ad's campus-wide meltdown clearly hasn't affected the Institute's tame atrocities. What can they possibly accomplish?

'Ad,' Azi says, trying to focus. 'How can a place like this be hosting a global darknet? They hadn't even finished building this place when you were at the Institute, right?'

Ad looks up from the laptop. 'That's right. All kinds of freaky construction was going on the whole time. Massive machinery, in and out.'

'Right. Right.' An idea is coalescing inside Azi. It's sufficiently ridiculous that he doesn't want to think about it too hard before speaking. 'Okay, I've got a . . . I guess you'd call it a plan. We are going to run several hundred feet away from this spot, back to the light boxes. We are going to take control of this thing's movement. Then we are going to tell it to repeatedly smash itself against the floor.'

Ad stares. 'Not that I disapprove of killing the machine abomination, but we're going to do this because—'

'Because what we're looking for isn't in this room. It's underneath.'

By Azi's reckoning, his logic is impeccable. At least, he has taken a selection of insights to their logical extreme, California-style. Ad says the IP addresses originate from this specific site. Yet this building was only finished last year. If the Institute has been operating a private darknet for years, it must thus be both very well hidden and older than this building. And the only super-secure site that fits the bill is directly underneath them.

With a nervous grin, Ad sets a short time delay while they're still in sensor range of the jellyfish, then he and Azi manage something between a sprint and a hobble towards the projection boxes. After a hundred feet, they pause. Azi is breathing hard and raggedly, pain coursing up his side and arm. Despite his tentacular encounter, Ad seems barely to have noticed the exertion.

'What do you think,' Azi pants, eying the distant orb. 'Is it going to have enough momentum to exceed its structural limits?'

Before Ad can answer this attractively technical question, the orb descends at massive speed and vanishes. Then a wave of force hits them. The hangar's cladding absorbs most of the sound, but its resonance arrives directly in their bones, hammering the air out of their lungs and sending them clawing towards shelter in one of the projection boxes. Dimly, Azi registers concrete and metal grinding, squealing and sundering as the immense arm strikes again and again.

Even at this distance, the floor trembles with each shockwave. Lights flash across the edges of Azi's vision. Azi tries to speak but he can't make himself heard. That's when he notices Ad soundlessly shouting in his face, gesturing them further from the impact zone. Without warning, a hunk of machinery the size and shape of a grand piano appears a foot to their left, demolishing half of the projection box.

Azi gets up to run, stumbles and falls. Ad has already done the same. The world is nothing beyond the regular, ferocious percussion of a machine obliterating itself. Is that blood trickling down the side of his face, Azi wonders as he clings to the floor, or sweat, or tears?

Not for the first time, it's most likely to be all three.

CHAPTER 45

Scrabbling around the ruins of a house-sized metal jellyfish that has hammered its way through a reinforced concrete floor is even less fun than it sounds. Partly because the light level is so low it's a constant struggle not to trip over fragments of wire, concrete and fractured metal, but mainly because it's unclear until the very last minute whether Azi's plan has worked, or just created a hundred-million-dollar crater in the heart of someone else's sinister research facility.

Finally, with a triumphant shout, Azi summons Ad towards the trench that the body of the jellyfish gouged before reaching its final resting place. Light is emanating from a spot beneath its base, casting shadows through shards of machinery. A thick fluid stains the ground, which both men do their best to ignore.

'Ad, look. Here!'

They pick their way down and together heft a bent metal plate aside. The light streaming out of the trench becomes so bright that it takes a minute before they're sure what they're seeing.

'There's something down there.' Ad's tone is pure wonder.

They're peering through a hole in the floor into a spotless, spartan concrete bunker. As Azi moves closer, he sees a heap of dust and rubble resting upon a perfectly smooth floor perhaps a dozen feet below them, its shine reflecting bank after bank of lights. Towards its edges, the distinctive dark metal mesh of server cages is visible.

'It's a data centre! We've found it!' For the second time today, Azi considers hugging Ad, then thinks better of it.

'Okay. Okay! Let's do this,' Ad says.

'Ad, what are you doing?'

'Psyching myself up. It's only ten feet onto that rubble. No time to lose, remember? Making myself useful.'

'Wait! We need to talk about this. Wait, you—'

Ad vanishes. There's a crash and a scream, then a sheepish voice.

'Er, Azi . . . I may have slightly fucked my leg.'

Azi groans and peers down.

'Is that blood?'

'Maybe. A bit. Hang on, I'll try standing up. No, not good. Okay, I'll go for lurching. On the plus side, this is definitely a data centre.'

Eventually, Ad manages to lurch effectively enough to catch the laptop and clear a flattish area where Azi can drop down. The physical integrity of their expedition is not looking good. Azi's arm and chest are ticking incrementally towards agony. Ad has a gashed hand and a twisted ankle. He can still walk, with Azi's pained assistance, but their hopes of swift action and exit are becoming tenuous. Azi hasn't been keeping perfect track of time, but they can't have much of it left.

Around them, the room throbs with air conditioning. Caged servers are racked in dark ranks, their fans and wiring exposed to the air, thick ropes of cable running between them. It's a server farm, in all its brutal functionality: the apparatus behind what laughably tends to be called a 'cloud'. Clouds sound so fluffy and weightless, Azi thinks, like they're operated by angels in a realm of sunlight and harps. Yet most of the world's data resides in reinforced bunkers like this, where hundreds of miles of network cable connect thousands of motherboards, packed as densely as thermodynamics permit.

Despite the cooling ducts thronging the roof like the roots of a skyscraper-sized tree, the heat coming off the massed machinery is palpable. If everything they've found out is true, the information locked inside these wire-studded servers includes some of the most fiercely guarded secrets on the planet – and all that lies in their way is a few reinforced steel cages. At last, an obstacle that won't try to kill them.

With a businesslike nod, Azi presses the laptop back into Ad's grasp and fishes out of his pocket one of the last toys Odi entrusted them with: a lock-picking kit. No hacker should be without one. It's amazing, Azi reflects as he sets about opening the nearest cage, how much faith computer security types have in physical locks given how little use they are.

The lock on the cage door is open within moments.

Supporting Ad by the shoulder, Azi steps across the threshold.

'Time check, Ad.'

'Since you last asked me how long this was going to take, one entire minute. Until we run out of time, minus several fucking minutes and counting. So, you know, it's been great to have this little chat. Because they're coming for us, right now.'

As is often the case with hacking, even the most dramatic and dangerous of assaults soon starts to feel like a tricky homework assignment. It's just that, in this case, the best-case punishment for non-completion probably consists of death – while most other cases involve torture and mechanoid sea-monsters.

In other words, they've made it to the final hurdle – only for everything to go tits up in the most mundane way possible. The laptop is connected directly to the server farm, which is the gold standard for access. But the sheer scale and complexity of the system means that nothing is obvious, easy or quick.

'Ad, come on! Can you see anything that looks like a master list, a lookup table, database, systems map – anything at all?' Azi isn't panicking, he tells himself. He's just speaking very loudly and very fast in order to save time.

'Fucking hell, mate, I'm trying. It's all over the place. It's all customized: routers, protocols, switch chips. Crazy power, I've got no idea why they'd need it. How many people are using Gomorrah? How big can it be? This is an absolute shitting disaster, I'm not even sure what I'm looking for.'

'The name itself, you've searched for that?'

'Of course I have. Nothing. Just your ordinary massive, impenetrable server architecture hosting about a giga-ton of databases in parallel.'

Azi pauses, willing his thoughts into order. An idea bobs to the surface.

'Forget everything. See if you can find any reference to the name Jim Denison.'

Azi has just remembered the agreement he signed in the guise of his alter ego: the details of Jim's address and location and backers, alongside the elaborately unpleasant consequences he faced for abuse. What if this personalization went beyond the agreement into the fabric of the software itself? What if the darknet marketplace is tailored to each and every one of its users?

There's an agonizing delay, then Ad looks up. 'Mate . . . I've found something! Here, see.'

Azi peers at the screen.

'What am I looking at, Ad? What's all that data?'

'It's everything. Absolutely *everything* this guy Jim Denison did on his device, from the moment he logged into Gomorrah until the phone went dead. Plus a ton of metadata, references and messages. Facebook have got nothing on this. There's routines here for snooping on whatever someone does, every-where they go, anything else in their lives that Gomorrah even touches. It's like, like . . .'

'The world's biggest phishing scam. It's a trap.'

'This is fucked up. If you were an admin on here, the things you could do, the things you'd know, the people you'd own . . . so that's what we need. Right now. Details of an admin account. Then we can download its logs to the laptop, scarper the fuck out of whatever exit we can open. And not die.'

'I love it! And I have an idea.' Azi pauses, waiting for his brain to do its thing and follow through. This time, it doesn't oblige. He pinches himself, runs both hands over his shaven scalp, tries to massage his mind into motion. There's nothing.

'Shit, no. I don't have an idea.' Azi is desolate. 'I've gone blank. I need a moment. I need . . . What's that?'

Behind them, there's the sound of a distant heavy door opening. They shrink back in the server cage, towards the towering rack of machines, close enough to feel their heat. Ad is still crouched over the laptop, Azi kneeling beside him, when there's a nearer rattle of metal followed by footsteps. One person, walking fast. There's nowhere to hide in the bunker's caged light: just the humming machines, the ducts above, the polished concrete below.

Azi can't believe it. To have come so close, to have touched Gomorrah's heart. It's unbearable. Not knowing what else to do, tracking the footsteps as they come closer, Azi half-stands as if to shield his friend. Then a woman's voice echoes towards him, cold and clear.

'Stop what you're doing and show me your hands. I'm armed. Let me get a—'

It breaks off. There's an incredulous pause and then, its edges quivering with rage, the voice continues.

'I do not believe this. Of all the people. You are like a disease, Azi Bello. The damage you've done, the trouble you've made . . .'

Another pause.

'I'm going to enjoy this.'

Turning, Azi sees what a part of him already knew would be there: the woman he called Munira, a gun in her hand. The colour of her hair, her clothes, the amused contempt on her face – everything about her is different. Yet she is unmistakably the same. He knew that all that they had and did was a lie. But he wasn't prepared for this.

'Munira?'

She inclines her head. 'Not any more. Don't you remember, you left her to die?'

Ad looks wildly between Azi and the woman stood motionless in the open door of the server cage. Azi takes a breath, then tries to shape what's happening inside him into words.

'Who are you? Why are you doing this . . . How could you do this?'

'Azi, I don't have time for questions. You are about to tell me everything I need to know. Right now.'

'And then you're going to kill us.'

She flashes a faint smile 'I expect so. You've seen enough movies.' She taps the pistol against the cage's metal door. 'But I can hurt you an awful lot first.'

Something thickens in Azi's throat – a constriction between horror and nausea. His body still wants to hold her, to feel the heat and safety of her hands. From a place far away, his mouth keeps speaking.

'If . . . If we're already dead, why would we tell you anything?'

'Azi, come on. I've done this before. Everyone talks. It takes a while. But they always do.'

Hatred: that's what he has to draw upon. Enough hatred to make him brave, to keep her talking – to fill his blood with fire. 'Fuck you, Munira. Or whoever you are. Fuck you, fuck you, fuck you. It's over. We know everything, this place is surrounded. You're done.'

She laughs at this, as though delighted that he knows his lines so well.

'So tough, Azi, it's admirable. A lovely bluff! But I have a shortcut that always takes me to the truth. Adam . . . look at me. That's right, I know all about you. Give me a smile.'

Ad looks up, winces, then gives Munira the benefit of his middle finger. 'No thanks. You're not my type.'

'Oh, but I was. Remember? And I'm so glad I finally get the chance to do this.'

In one steady motion Munira angles her gun towards Ad and pulls the trigger. The bottom half of his left leg seems to burst. With a gurgling scream, Ad falls forwards. Blood drips between his clutching fingers, black under the fluorescent light. Munira adjusts her grip on the gun.

'I told you, I've done this before. He'll die, but not for a while. Plenty of time for the other leg. Then for the arms. Then it will be your turn, Azi.'

Azi has seen more violence in the last week than he feared or dreamed of seeing in a lifetime. Yet this is different. Here, the pain belongs to someone else. And he can end it. As if addressing a lazy student, Munira continues.

'Take a good look. I will hurt your friend until he begs for death. I will maim and mutilate him while you watch. It's all the same to me. But I don't think you're up to this.'

Azi looks at the cage walls, the polished floor, the dazzling lights. Ad is breathing fast and sobbing high in his chest, like a child.

'Munira . . . Please don't do this. Tell me what you want. There must be something. Just let me help him, he's going to bleed to death.'

She speaks fast, as if rattling off a list. 'How did you find out the Institute was involved?'

'IP addresses. From the Islamic Republic. I blackmailed your cousin . . . her cousin. Kabir. He sent files showing exit nodes for Gomorrah in this building.'

She nods. 'I see. And how, exactly, could you get in here?'

'Ad planted a vulnerability when he worked at the Institute. In the main operating system, the clean zone. It was everywhere. So we activated it, to create a diversion.'

'And you just decided to hammer your way through the floor?' She sounds impatient. 'I'm not an idiot. You had someone on the inside. Who was it?'

'Nobody, I swear it! We worked it out.'

At his words, Munira points her gun towards Ad's intact leg. 'You're lying. One last chance.'

Azi's vision has started to do strange things. Everything is out of focus apart from the small, dark gun.

With a shuddering breath, Ad turns to him. 'Fuck . . . her . . . mate. Don't tell her . . . anything.'

Ad has levered himself back into a sitting position and seems, somehow, to be bringing his pain under enough control to lean forwards. If he and Ad can both make a move at the same time, Azi thinks, if they can manufacture some kind of distraction, perhaps there is a slim chance. Perhaps there's hope.

The stink of blood is hot and bitter in the air. Raising his voice and trying to draw her attention, Azi looks Munira in the eye.

'It was just us! Just us, nobody else. But I—'

She sighs and pulls the trigger again. There's a crash and a wet thud. Ad's screams are those of an animal, without control. He falls onto his face, blood pooling thickly beneath him, his hands flailing towards the gore of his legs. Azi starts to move, but the gun has now turned in his direction. It gestures him into stillness, gliding in its owner's grasp.

'How is your memory now, Azi?'

'Oh my God, oh Jesus, please . . . There was nobody inside. Odi, he helped us. He came over with me. We came together, from Athens. After Ad got in touch, because I sent him a message. The Americans refused to help. It was just me, Odi and Ad, I swear it. Please, don't kill him. I'll tell you everything, anything. Please! Please.'

'Fine. What have you found out about Gomorrah?'

'Nothing! Not yet. We've just started. Nothing. Nothing! Oh Jesus, please—'

The wordless noise still coming from Ad fills Azi's head. It's the most appalling thing he has ever heard. The gun gestures, delicately.

'I'm aiming at his left arm. Last chance to tell me anything you've left out. Anything.'

'I swear it, I swear it, there's nothing . . . we used a dolphin hack, smashed the giant jellyfish, came through the floor, picked the lock, I . . . please, let me help him.'

Munira arrives at a decision, as if enough time has been allocated to this bothersome task.

'Well, this is getting boring, Azi. The damage you've done is unbelievable. Yet, I want you to know, it doesn't matter. Whatever you think you've found in here will die with you. I guess I should congratulate you. But this is goodbye.'

She points the gun at Ad's face. With furious concentration, Azi starts to speak, watching Munira, hunting for any flash of recognition or distraction as he throws words towards her.

'I'm begging you! Look. I'm on my hands and knees. Let me tell you something you don't know. About the Organization. And the Institute. And Erasmus. The director. There is something I know about him, something we found. Just let Ad live, please, just let me tell you. It's on the laptop, look, please, let me show you . . .'

The Organization, the Institute, Erasmus. It's a kind of cold reading, beloved of con men and spiritualists. But it's working. At this last name, her eyes widen involuntarily. *Erasmus.* There's something there that matters. Something that she fears, or loves, or needs to know.

Hauling himself into a kneeling position on the blood-slicked floor, Azi keeps begging and repeating Erasmus's name, gesturing towards the laptop. Then, the instant her eyes shift, he lunges and kicks with all his strength at the metal door of the server cage.

Munira turns, but it's too late. She's standing just outside and the gate's momentum slams it shut, clicking the lock into place. Its mesh – he hopes – is too finely woven for any bullet. Without looking around, Azi turns to Ad and rips the T-shirt off his own back. It's only as he's desperately trying to fasten the blood-soaked strips of fabric around Ad's ruined legs that he realizes Munira is chuckling.

'Very clever. Proper spy stuff, Azi. Great job. Now you get to die in a new and exciting way.'

Carefully, Munira holsters her gun, folds her arms and composes her voice into a monotone.

'Computer, username Amira Dewan, verify. Override all protocols. Lockdown all exits. Begin coolant dump. Confirm.'

A distant gushing sound floods the room at her words. Still tending to Ad, Azi glances at Munira one more time.

'Goodbye, Azi. This entire space will soon be full of water. It doesn't mix with electricity, or people. You'll be dead, the servers will be dead. And I will be relaxing in a giant marble bath, drinking something expensive, not giving a moment's thought to either this or you again. Ever. Sorry it didn't work out.'

She turns and walks away, her heels tracing ripples in the first few waves.

CHAPTER 47

It took her a long time to persuade Erasmus that hers was the way to go, to convince him that she could manage the timings, the expectations, the revelations. But she did it, and now, at last, her plan is unfolding.

On the outskirts of Paris, four heavily armed jihadis in an unmarked van are arrested in a raid that sees no loss of life. The men all bear French passports and have been under constant observation since the Organization first became aware of their existence.

In unrelated rural locations outside major German cities, four well-dressed groups of young men are arrested as they make their final preparations for what appear to be weekend trips in smart new camper vans. One of the vans explodes when a nineteen-year-old slipping back inside manages to trigger the explosives with which its seat cushions are packed. Four policemen and both remaining suspects are killed instantly, while a fifth policeman will die later that day in hospital.

In the southern outskirts of Berlin, six men gathered in a nondescript rented office are subdued by gas pumped through the ventilation system, before they can access the crate of automatic weapons that has been sitting in a delivery bay for the last week.

Twenty-four further individuals are tracked down across rural France, Germany and Italy with minimal incidental damage. It is the largest, most impressively coordinated and successful anti-terrorist operation the continent has ever known. Two men manage to kill themselves before they can be captured – one with the detonator from a larger device, one with a kitchen knife – but everything else is expertly anticipated.

Entire regions are on lockdown. Social media and news speculation is instant, intense and riddled with conspiracies. The French president, German chancellor and Italian prime minister announce a simultaneous press conference at the European Union headquarters in Brussels, where they will stand alongside fellow leaders and speak to the magnitude of the averted crisis. Behind the scenes, multiple security services rip up old rulebooks, abandon protocols and start wondering what the hell went wrong with every single system they own.

Munira is glad that she dispensed with Azi and his friend in time to witness this in real time. She needs to leave the hotel soon, but it's important both to savour and to learn from the execution of something so long planned. In its way, what is playing out is simple, ticking along with a clockwork inevitability. This is the nature of well-made plans. They become the only possible future, because you've stripped away every other path events might take.

Simplify, simplify, simplify. This is her own motto, with which she shed the wasteful, complicated misery of her childhood like a snake's skin. Who is more useless than a daughter born into wealth and tradition, a prize polished for someone else's aspirations? Defiance is the absence of regret. And, speaking of Defiance, the grand finale in Görlitz is at last about to begin.

Tomi's rally will go ahead, its security guaranteed by the imminent arrival of four vans' worth of elite troops from Interpol's Counter-Terrorism Centre. Other police and troops are being quietly stood down. A picturesque rabble of protestors will only add to the confusion.

Amid ferocious turbulence, nothing is simpler than men with the correct credentials arriving to take charge. The state lives and dies by its monopolies of violence, security, verification – and these are what she has pledged to dismantle and reshape.

Across Europe, the last hour of the old world begins.

CHAPTER **48**

For the first few minutes, Azi does nothing but struggle to staunch the flow of blood from Ad's legs. Miraculously, reducing his own and then Ad's T-shirts to rags seems to have some effect, once these rags have been knotted as tightly as slipping hands can manage above each knee. Azi clasps Ad, trying to soothe his friend's shaking and gasping, whispering that everything will be fine.

Only when he's sure that the flow has become a trickle does Azi dare turn to the laptop to see if what he was attempting has worked. He and Ad created the dolphin hack on this computer. It remained ready, in theory, to blast soundlessly out from its speakers at the push of a button. If Azi managed to time his button-press for the minute the woman he knew as Munira spoke her instructions, the computer should have access to her admin account.

In theory.

Ad is watching him, Azi realizes, with something like a gleam in his eyes – with the realization of what Azi was trying to do. Despite everything, Ad manages to summon a shadow of his voice.

'Mate . . . did it work?'

'Hang on in there!' Azi replies. 'I'm checking, I'm checking. Waiting for the system to talk to your routine. It's going to work.'

'If it doesn't, you get out. Try.'

'Bollocks to that, Ad. You're coming with me. Both of us. We did it, we're going to make it. We're good.'

'Don't forget . . .' Ad seems to be drifting out of consciousness now, unable to finish his sentence.

'Ad? Ad! Stay with me here. Look, it's coming! Access, Amira Dewan . . . it's lighting up!'

They're in. Azi can see it, onscreen: a log of actions under Amira Dewan's master account. It's definitely too late to stop the data centre from filling up with water – nothing about the coolant dump she initiated looks reversible – and nor does he have any hope they can climb back out through the ceiling. There is, however, a function labelled *exit nine* that she appears to be using for her own escape.

Azi watches it, onscreen. The exit flashes open for a few seconds, then closes. This must have been her departure. He waits, letting her get clear. Seconds pass like hours. Then he orders the exit to release. It flashes open once again – and, miraculously, stays that way.

If Azi can find a route across the data centre before the trickle of water thickens into a torrent, they should be able to make it. As long as he can drag Ad with him. As long as the woman he now needs to call Amira really has left and isn't waiting to finish them off. As long as whatever waits outside isn't as fatal as what's inside.

Grasping Ad by the waist, ignoring the screaming pain under what is left of his stitches, Azi releases the server cage door and prepares to move. Then he realizes that Ad is resisting him – gesturing back towards the laptop and the rope of cable still connecting it to the servers.

'Don't forget, Azi . . . The primary goal.'

'What are you talking about, Ad? This isn't a movie. You're going to die if we don't get out of here.'

'To win the game. Gomorrah.'

'Fuck that. Fuck all of that. You're dying.'

Ad pushes Azi feebly, gesturing towards the laptop.

'Then I'm not fucking . . . dying . . . for nothing.'

There's no way Azi can attempt any rescue without Ad's cooperation. Even half-dead, he's the world's most stubborn bastard.

Swearing, Azi lunges towards the laptop, lifting it just clear of a wave flooding the floor of the server cage. How long do they have before core systems start to shut down and the exit closes? Trying to block out everything apart from the keyboard and screen, Azi dives into Amira Dewan's account.

As his glimpse of Jim Denison's data suggested earlier, every single action taken by every single user of the Gomorrah darknet has been visible to her at all times. Even a glance at these records shows that she has constantly been creating messages and content, manipulating auctions, using Gomorrah to pull its users' strings.

Desperately, Azi starts copying files to the laptop, capturing the most recent logs first, the blocks of data coded by date and location. Ad is breathing faster and more shallowly on the floor behind him, the air catching in his throat.

Onscreen, Azi recognizes something. The locations in the Middle East, the timings, familiar from the document dump that Sigma – as he knew her then – shared when she first got in contact. These are the names of the jihadis she betrayed when she handed over their details to Azi: tens of millions of dollars poured into false European identities, their recipients betrayed by the very darknet that supplied them. What was her plan?

Then Azi sees it. Two dozen more names and locations, none of them familiar, complete with transactions and messages dating all the way to the present – the most recent originating just half an hour before she arrived here. A second, secret jihadi army. Azi sets the files to copy. There's a noise behind him. Turning, his knees now trailing through half an inch of water, he watches Ad slump forwards. Ad's skin is horribly pale against eddies of blood and dirt. There is no time left.

Ripping the laptop away from the cable and wedging it under one elbow, Azi reaches under Ad's shoulder with his free arm and tries to stand up. It's impossible. Ad is cold and limp, his eyes unfocused. The pain in Azi's body has spread and sharpened into a stabbing assault across his entire torso. Breathing through it, he leans down and slaps Ad across the face, once, twice, then rests his forehead against his friend's and speaks with all the force he can muster.

'Hold me, Ad. You need to hold on. Arms around my shoulders.'

Ad groans.

'Ad. This is it. End of the road. Win or lose. Don't let them win. Hold on.'

Somehow, Ad's cold hands fasten around his neck. Azi rises, leaning Ad's weight across his back, hunching out of the server cage through filthy water. There's nothing to differentiate one direction from another except the liquid flowing across the floor. They're underground, which means the way out is surely upwards.

Turning against the water's flow, Azi moves between the caged servers, his half-naked body slick with sweat and humidity. Ad is hanging on, but it's not clear how long he will last.

Then Azi sees it. A door on what might be an outside wall, a number illuminated above it. Eight. He looks left and right, slipping and skidding against a current that's now almost at his knees. One more number, one more door. Azi doesn't look at the blood, at the ruins of his friend's lower legs, at the server lights blinking and turning dark. There is another glow above a door, perhaps thirty feet away. He walks, he staggers, half-kneels and then rises, crawling against the slope and the spillage of the floor. Number nine. Open. And then . . .

. . . a concrete ramp, the dazzled intensity of daylight, a last staggering ascent, and a scene of unmitigated mayhem.

CHAPTER 49

The best thing about being met by a horde of armed, dangerous and extraordinarily efficient-looking Americans, plus their entourage of extraordinarily formidable-looking vehicles, is that Ad is instantly hefted into the back of a vaguely medical truck.

The worst thing is that, with similar rapidity, Azi is gestured at gunpoint towards a van with a strong about-to-be-imprisoned-for-ever vibe. Has anything of significance *not* happened to him at gunpoint during the last twenty-four hours?

The campus appears to be under military occupation. Everywhere Azi looks, uniformed men and women are dashing in knots, like soldier ants dismantling a rival nest. His own gun-toting escorts, wearing far beefier combat gear than anything he saw in Europe, push him forcefully onto a metal bench, then leap out and slam the door of the van behind them. Azi is within a high-tech tomb, its windowless inner surfaces grooved and bulging above two long benches. He breathes for what feels like the first time since he exited the data centre. Around him, the van shifts into motion.

It's only then that Azi notices a man sitting opposite him, staring mildly at the metal-plated ceiling. The man is Odi, and he is handcuffed to the floor by a thick chain. Azi hurtles into speech.

'Munira, she was here. I think her real name's Amira Dewan. She came out, just before us. Did they get her?'

'I think not. Breathe, Azi. Focus.' Odi's eyes are alight with urgency. 'Do you know where she is going? What did you find?'

'Shit, shit . . . they can hear me, right? Can you hear me?' Azi starts banging on the wall, his voice rising over the impacts.

'She shot us, tried to drown us. She was manipulating everything, behind the scenes. She must have been based close to here, within half an hour's drive. She mentioned a giant marble bathtub. A hotel? She was dressed expensively. She looked like . . . someone else.'

Azi looks at Odi, taking in both the handcuffs and some extensive bruises masking half of his face. With an effort, he shifts gears.

'It looks like you and Yacine enjoyed your diversion.'

Odi flashes a smile, showing a missing front tooth. 'Oh, the Americans relished our surprises. Hence these new bracelets. Was it worth it?'

Azi nods. 'I found proof.' He raises his voice. 'Do you hear me? On this laptop, proof of everything we were trying to tell you. And you need to pay attention, because the news isn't good.'

He waits an instant, then turns to Odi with a whisper. 'So what the hell is this, the van, everything?'

'This?' Odi whispers back. 'It's a mobile office, enhanced interrogation centre and rendition facilitator. In Europe, we'd be in a Portakabin handcuffed to a radiator. Now, you have their attention. Look.'

Azi looks. To his astonishment, the wall at the front of the van is splitting in two, exposing a screen stretching almost from floor to ceiling. At the same time, a panel in front of him glides open, revealing a shallow tray and network cable.

Azi wakes the laptop, connects it, and starts talking.

'Okay, here. These are logs for the woman you knew as Munira: every recent thing she's done via Gomorrah. She was running the show. And the private darknet was a trap all along. All the amazing, irresistible bad shit that's on the marketplace – it's there to pull in the users. Then someone behind the scenes pulls the strings. Like she did for the Islamic Republic: delivered everything she promised, then betrayed them.'

He dashes through screen after screen of data.

'Here's what really matters. She gave up the names of most of the terrorists in Europe. But she kept some secret. *These* names, these identities. Whatever you think is happening right now, these people are the key to it.'

At this, the huge screen at the front of the van comes to life. It's divided into segments, mixing body camera and surveillance footage with status updates, showing fragmentary glimpses of European countryside, the inside of armoured cars and police vehicles, a series of bland-looking official rooms – and a selection of men in civilian clothes, trussed and captured, alongside labelled caches of weapons and crated equipment.

Odi gestures in explanation. 'These are feeds, from across Europe. The jihadis we already knew about, the takedowns.'

Azi consults the status feeds, cross-referencing with his screen, light-headed. What was Amira's plan? She deliberately betrayed fifty Islamists, knowing it would put half a continent on high alert, knowing it would expose Gomorrah's capabilities. Why tip off the world? The only possible reason, he thinks with a shudder, is that it was all a gambit – and that the true game is being won somewhere else. Where are the ones she didn't betray?

Azi keeps digging through the data. The names and addresses of this second, secret contingent are all German. Gradually, what he's looking at starts to tell its story.

'Odi, is anything big happening in the far east of Germany that a bunch of counter-terrorism experts might be asked to protect? Given that the biggest terrorist operation in living memory is apparently being foiled elsewhere at this very moment.'

Odi slowly nods. 'You remember our good friends from the Defiance party? Tomi's biggest ever speech is starting, very soon. In the city where he grew up, where he founded the party: Görlitz. Crowds, press, party elite.'

Azi sits up, electrified. 'That's it. There are four heavily armoured vans. They're in the possession of jihadis with all the documentation needed to identify themselves as members of Interpol's Counter-Terrorism Centre. That's her plan.' He clasps his hands together, as if applauding the apocalypse.

'She put the continent on high alert, she let us think we knew it all. Then she arranged extra security for the biggest political rally of the year – only this particular security contingent is about to do God knows what. Assassinate Tomi, destroy the city, blow several thousand people to pieces. All of the above.'

Azi stops speaking, as if he can't quite believe the words coming out of his mouth.

Then, across the width of the van's vast screen, camera after camera starts to turn blank.

CHAPTER 50

The van grinds to a halt. Azi remains hunched over the laptop as the double doors at the back creak open. Half the feeds within the screen at the front of the van are now blank, turning it into a chessboard of lost signals.

Three suited men step up, two of whom are escorting a black-clad woman. The third approaches Odi, gingerly releases his cuffs, then retreats. The woman is Anna, which may explain why the men beside her look as though they've been asked to handle Hannibal Lecter's grumpy older sister.

With a nod, the three men retreat into a featureless concrete bunker, heft in a crate of supplies, then close the van's doors behind them.

Odi rips open the supply crate and thrusts what turn out to be warm cans of Sprite into each of their hands. Then he and Anna squeeze onto the long metal bench beside Azi, granting them all a clear view of both the laptop and the giant screen's mosaic. It's almost blank now, its feeds riddled with static. Anna looks as though she hasn't slept in a long time, but her voice crackles with energy.

'I came from Europe under . . . unusual circumstances. I was relieved of operational oversight. But as of now they are relying upon us, largely because everything that we have learned – everything that has happened so far – is unprecedented. Take me through it, Azi.'

Azi gulps his warm, cloying drink, realizing as he does how much his body needs it – how close he is to the limit.

'You heard, in the van? The terrorists you've been tracking since Sigma's first leak, they were a diversion. The Interpol men heading to the continent's biggest political rally are the ones that matter. Paid-up, tooled-up, highly trained members of the Islamic Republic, sitting on a ton of explosives. I'm assuming you guys are poised to blow the living shit out of them. Right?'

Anna bows her head.

'We are trying to contact authorities in the area, but we are having little success. Almost all official communications are down, as are most local internet and cellphone services. None of which should be possible. Yet it's of a piece with the control Gomorrah has exerted elsewhere.'

She pauses. 'Which leaves us with the most important question of all. *Why?* Given that level of power, what possible advantage can this bring that they don't already have? What are they poised to achieve?'

Azi's mind hurtles through the turmoil, hunting for sense. Every angle shows only a system ripped to shreds: identity databases, policing and intelligence, terrorism and trafficking, Gomorrah itself. By the end of today, there'll be nothing left that those on either side of the law can trust. Then he sees it.

'Fear, chaos, entropy, that's what they want. Total loss of confidence in existing systems. Add a war of civilizations into the mix and it means opportunity. For someone, or something. Whoever is behind Gomorrah wants to step into the vacuum. The pattern is chaos.'

Odi is muttering under his breath.

'*The programme for the reconstruction is determined by the magnitude of the distress crippling our political, moral and economic life.* March 1933. A new law forged in the fires of crisis. *Gesetz zur Behebung der Not von Volk und Reich.* The Law to Remedy the Distress of People and Reich. Granting absolute power.'

'Who to?'

'A man who knew what can be bought with blood. The chancellor of Germany. Adolf Hitler.'

Azi has heard enough. 'It's not going to happen. We can stop this! Fight fire with fire, faith with faith. That's what you told me. If there's a Defiance party rally then there's also going to be a counter-demonstration, right?'

'Yes.' Odi turns to Azi. 'I believe someone tried to shut out the protestors, but they found a way. They always find a way.'

Azi is shouting now. 'Yes! They always find a way, because they're like me. Hacktivists, idealists, networked citizens. Fucking mentalists, some of them, but they know how to self-organize – to find their way through the cracks. They're our way in, don't you see? Thanks to them we have bodies on the ground, systems Gomorrah hasn't compromised. A human network. Where are the fake Interpol vans?'

On cue, a map appears on the big screen alongside a selection of still images. These show a crowd thronging through picturesque streets, placards and banners populating the air, gaggles of children at the edges. Defiance party members vastly outnumber the protestors. It looks ordered, almost idyllic. Anna gestures with uncharacteristic uneasiness.

'These are the last images we have. From half an hour ago. We have now lost most of our access. The vans were last seen approaching this street, Luisenstraße. Long, narrow, lined with shops and housing, granting vehicle access to the Untermarkt – which is the square in the middle. That's the heart of the rally, that's where everyone's headed for the big speech. It'll be starting any moment.'

Azi looks at the map, then at Odi and Anna. They're staring at him, expectantly. Waiting for him to speak. Taking a last sip of his drink, he gazes from the laptop to the large screen and back.

'I'm going to get the word out. AZ has contacts – people I've run protest hacks with, ethical mobs in chatrooms and forums. Some of them will have beaten the blackout, I know it. And they're a network of networks. Whatever I send, they can share it. Like a self-replicating swarm. Bringing some fucking ownage.'

Odi and Anna are motionless. Azi has their total attention. He has the lives of God knows how many thousand people at stake. He has no clue whether this will work, whether it's already too late, but that's not going to stop him. Pushing down a vision of Amira's sneer and Ad's bleeding body, he starts to type.

The Defiance rally is about to come under terrorist assault. Spread the word, tell the crowd. Block Luisenstraße! Four Interpol vans have been hijacked by terrorists and must be stopped. They are packed with weapons and explosives. It is an Islamist conspiracy. This is real, this is happening. The authorities are helpless. Block the streets, use anything, everything. Spread the word and flee. Be brave, be fast.

It's too long, Azi thinks – and it could definitely be more inspirational. But what matters is getting out the message, everywhere and anywhere, saturating every avenue of communication; every forum, feed, chatroom and hijacked device; every secure messaging account; every hashtag. This is real-time counter-terrorism. Logging in everywhere and anywhere he can, AZ spreads the word.

Mirroring the laptop display on the big screen, Azi waits. At first there's nothing. Then he starts to see it: a spark, then a flicker, then a conflagration of messages, responses, shares, denials, accusations. Whatever he has ignited, it's burning with fierce virality. God only knows what the wider world will make of this. Then again, God only knows what the world will look like once this is over. Suddenly, Azi recognizes one feed in particular.

'There! That's a hacker I know. I remember the username. Ursus. He's on the scene, he's managing to stream something on a dark site – look. Here.'

Azi clicks – and they're looking through the lurching, granular lens of a smartphone at the edge of the Untermarkt.

The idyll of the earlier images has shattered into chaos. Bodies scramble, grappling across each other in an effort to escape. Whoever is holding the phone is running, lunging and bellowing in German for others to follow. He sounds like a young man – little older than a teenager. Cobbles blur under his feet. He staggers over a woman who has been knocked to the ground, then an old man, their arms ineffectually shielding their faces. Shouting, screaming, beseeching voices blend together. Above the crush of bodies, a few banners still flutter at wild angles alongside what look like children, lofted by a sea of hands. It takes Azi a moment to realize what's going on. The crowd have heard his message. They're trying to send the youngest to safety.

Then, at one corner of the screen, something else appears: a television news van lurching forwards through pedestrians, smashing its way through bollards. In a detonation of broken glass, it comes to rest in the distant window of a souvenir shop. The driver staggers onto the street, his forehead laced with blood, waving frantic arms. Anna watches with an ashen face.

'It's anarchy. They're going to die. They're all going to fucking *die*.'

Azi isn't so sure. Something else is happening.

'Wait! Look. That's Luisenstraße. The television van's not the only thing there. I think that was . . . I think that was on purpose. The driver must have been on one of the protestor's networks, or had access. He meant to do it.'

The bearer of their viewpoint has forced his way to within a hundred feet of Luisenstraße now, pushing against the flow of runners on the street, shouting an incomprehensible commentary. Then, as the camera stops dancing for a second, they see it clearly for the first time. An astonishing mess of vehicles and other debris is accumulating where the TV news van crashed: scooters, a bronze statue toppled onto its side, café tables and chairs, two small cars, a street-cleaning lorry complete with still-whirling brushes, a drinking fountain.

'They're doing it! The street, it's impassable . . . it's working!'

Azi pauses, daring to look up for the first time – but then Odi sees something.

'Azi, wait. Look! They need to get out of there, now. The terrorists are armed, and I see a movement among the vans. They must realize they are trapped, and the moment they work out—'

Before he can finish the sentence, the image in the feed shakes and tumbles. An armoured Interpol truck has erupted through the improvised roadblock. The news van topples aside, chairs and ornaments splinter, as a metal-reinforced bonnet and windshield shudder into view. Dark, sleek and deeply stained, the truck's doors slide open and men in riot gear start to emerge, clambering over the wreckage – three, four, five of them facing the crowd. There are automatic weapons in their hands.

Odi and Anna watch in silence. The sound from the feed is muffled, but they can still hear the crowd's shouts and screams, escalating towards incoherence as more and more people realize what is happening. Odi opens his mouth. Azi's hands hammer a faint beat on the laptop. Onscreen, the men raise their weapons.

Then the phone drops onto the cobbled road. The screen becomes an unfocused blur, its view of dark stone and pale dust trembling in the shockwave. There are no voices, no detectable human sounds. A minute passes. Azi's lip is bleeding where he has bitten it. A spot of blood hits the keyboard.

Suddenly the camera lifts into air still thick with dust and the lens turns, approximating their previous view. It's impossible to see anything with clarity – but Luisenstraße is no longer there. All that remains is rubble between the barest bones of buildings.

A few feet in front of the camera lens lies an inverted TV news van with a bearded bronze head nestled deep in its panelling. People are running, screaming, waving their hands, staggering through rubble. Yet they're alive – which is more than can be said for the five armed men who were standing directly in front of an armoured truck that has just obliterated its vicinity. Azi is the first to speak.

'Munira . . . I mean, Amira Dewan. Her admin account – she was running the show. She had a direct line to these guys. So I told the ones at the back that it was now or never. That they should hit detonate, trigger their explosives, set off a chain reaction . . .'

He stops for a moment, trying to take in what's onscreen. 'And I thought . . . I thought the street would take the worst of it. And everyone was running away. And there was no time, and so . . . and so . . . and so . . .'

Words become impossible. Is he crying, or laughing, or abandoning his grip on sanity? To either side of him, the windowless van's steel walls rebound reflections in what look like rainbows. Surely the van can't be doing what it seems to be doing: melting, opening like a flower, its petals cracked apart in glinting light.

Anna moves for the first time in five minutes.

'You can take that look off your face. This really is happening.'

With a start, Azi realizes that the van has indeed unfurled itself, revealing the concrete chamber from his and Odi's meeting. Men and women in suits are dotted around, standing at terminals, holding phones, holstering weapons. They're all staring at the three figures sitting in the box's metal heart.

A booming, sexless voice fills the space, its noise rushing from all sides like the sea.

'Mr Azi Bello. Odi, Anna.'

A pause.

'Thank you.'

CHAPTER 51

They are coming for her. And, frustratingly, there appears to be little she can do about it, beyond the systematic destruction in which she is currently engaging. Wisps of dust and ash emerge from the largest of her suitcases as the devices within are incinerated. She has perhaps ten minutes. She will be ready.

Then, unexpectedly, the last of her phones rings. It's the only one yet to be destroyed. She answers. Contingencies are in place. Nothing at this stage can be changed.

'Erasmus.'

'My dear.'

She takes a deep breath. 'I am sorry.'

His voice is delicate, compassionate. 'It cannot be helped. You are ready?'

'Of course. It all points to me. Gomorrah is gone. I am looking forward to your public performance.'

'It will be hard. But it is necessary.'

'Yes.'

'We have a moment.' He hesitates, sounding almost wistful. 'Do you remember what I told you, when we first met?'

There is no need to answer. She remembers. He asked to meet her in person. A hotel in Paris, dripping with splendour. She expected one of those men who had groped and ogled their way through her adolescence: pride, libido and chemical-assisted potency in an Armani suit. Instead a slender man walked towards her and, without raising his voice or breaking her gaze, spoke about their place in history. What he said changed her life.

History isn't written by the victors. It is written by the survivors. Look at the Jews. Five thousand years of loss and exile. Yet they endured. The only judge is time, and it only knows one judgement: stay or cease. All that matters is for a species to go on carrying itself through eternity. The rest is detail.

There's a silence on both ends of the line. Not awkwardness but acknowledgement. Finally, Erasmus speaks.

'You will need to endure. They will try to break you.'

'I know.'

'We will not speak for a long time. But I will come for you. Remember that.'

She believes him. 'I will.'

'Now. There is something I wish you to hear. You are dear to me. Consider it a gift.'

Her microphone mutes, then she hears a phone ringing: a European tone. It rings for perhaps a minute until, eventually, a loud, deep voice sounds from the other end.

'*Hallo?*'

Erasmus replies in a voice she has not heard before. He sounds unsure, compliant.

'*Hallo, Tomi?* It is your friend, from across the water.'

'*Gut. Zwei Minuten.* You may speak.'

'I am checking in. To confirm that you are well.'

There's a mighty cough. 'You know that I am. This was not as we discussed.'

'I am sorry. Unforeseen complications arose.'

'No matter. It will be well. Enough blood to baptize me a hero. Enough fear to win me a nation.'

'I am proud to have been of service. And of course—'

'Yes?'

'This is only the beginning. Those facilities I can put at your disposal: have you reached a decision?'

'I will let you know what I decide. When I decide.'

'Of course, Herr Christian. I am at your service.'

Suddenly, the man speaking to Erasmus sounds self-conscious, as if there's something he needs to explain. 'This was necessary, you understand. If there had been another way . . . Every drop of German blood spilled pains me, as if it were my own.'

'I understand perfectly. *Die Deutschen immer vor dem Ausländer.*'

'*Und den Juden!* Not to mention the fucking Arabs. Yes. I must go now.'

'Your good health, Chancellor.'

A last, preening pause. 'Not yet. Soon.'

The phone clicks. Amira's microphone unmutes.

'Five minutes until they are with you. Goodbye, my dear. Endure.'

She hangs up, deposits the phone in the case, commits her final act of destruction. Nothing remains. Erasmus is untouchable. Glancing in the full-length mirror, she adjusts the hem of her dress, slips on her chosen pair of shoes, then pours a glass of wine.

Azi Bello is alive. This is a problem. Moreover, it's *personal* – the only problem she has ever failed to resolve.

Taking a sip of wine, Amira Dewan salutes her beautiful reflection. Even now, it all comes down to the story you tell; the mobilization of facts in a cause.

Every ending is also a beginning.

CHAPTER 52

Within a few minutes, after a sequence of events that may become clear at a later point in his life, Azi finds himself seated in a reassuringly anonymous and windowless office facing Anna across an IKEA desk. There is a cup of coffee in front of him. He doesn't precisely remember how he got here, or at what point Odi left them. But he does know that two things, above all, demand answers – and that this woman is firmly back in the role of Someone Who Knows More Than Him.

'So . . . Ad.'

'Alive. He should be fine. Eventually.'

'Munira . . . Amira, I mean.'

'I am told we'll have her within minutes. The Four Seasons, Silicon Valley.'

Azi pauses. The next question is more complicated.

'The rally. Görlitz. What happened? How many dead?'

'You saved thousands of lives.'

'Right. That's not what I'm asking.'

'It's what I'm telling you, because I'm not in a position to answer your other question.'

'Was it tens? Or hundreds? Or . . .'

Anna gives him a hard look across the table. Then, to his surprise, she looks away.

'Maybe a hundred, slightly more. Ballpark. It's . . . You wouldn't believe it. I have never seen, not since . . .'

She shrugs, pauses, then meets his eyes again.

'You need to rest, Azi. There are things you shouldn't think about until you have rested.'

Now it's his turn to shrug. For the first time since Anna stepped into his shed, the beat of peril has dulled. It's a strange feeling. Like a hangover that hasn't been preceded by anything remotely entertaining. The future lies ahead, imponderable. There are horrors out there, with greater horrors lurking behind them. Yet, for this moment at least, they can wait.

'So, Anna. What happens now?'

She looks at him evenly. 'I could ask what you want to happen. But that would be dishonest. You're not going back to your old life.'

Azi knew this already, which is why he's surprised to find the information catching in his throat. 'Sure.'

'What interests me,' Anna continues, choosing to ignore his emotion, 'are people's motives. Most of the people in our trade – Homeland, NSA, black bag, special ops – care a great deal about *what* people do. They are obsessed with *what* is happening. But they're not so interested in the *why*. That's my department.'

'Right.' Azi has no idea where this is going, but that's hardly new.

'*Why* is a dangerous word. It picks things apart, ruins the best conspiracies. Given what you know, and where we'd have to lock you up to ensure you didn't repeat it, perhaps you would be interested in an extension of our current contractual relationship. Assuming our hosts release us into daylight at some point.'

This was not what Azi expected. 'You're offering me a job.'

'I'm quite specifically not doing that. I'm offering not to put you in prison and throw away the key.'

'With pay?'

Anna smiles. 'Think of it as a very, very exclusive freelance gig. We've recently contracted a Greek doctor on a similar basis. I'd say you'll like her, but I think she plans to rip off your head next time you meet.'

'Jesus. Eleni? Are you being serious?'

'We are open to talent. And I am extremely persuasive.'

'I can believe that. One question. Does this mean you can tell me who I'll be not-working for – what your operation is actually called?'

'We have a dull designation. Global Operations. It could be anything. Deliberately so.'

'I see. Well, that's pretty rubbish. If we're going to be working together, I'll need to make up something cooler.'

Anna reaches out and offers Azi a handshake that lasts just long enough for him to flinch at the coiled force in her grasp.

'To be clear, Azi. I reserve the right to destroy you if you ever, ever betray my trust. Or start giving my organization nicknames.'

Azi raises an eyebrow.

'Oh, I'd expect nothing less.'

THANKS AND ACKNOWLEDGEMENTS

In the popular imagination, writing a novel often looks like this: an author locks themselves away with only inspiration for company; months or years pass until, eventually, they emerge clutching the finished object, ready to meet the world. Some novels may get written this way – but mine didn't. From the beginning, I have owed an extraordinary amount to the acuity of my agent, Jon Elek, and to the expertise and passion of my editor, Melissa Cox. This book could never have happened without them, or become anything like the text in front of you. I owe them an immense debt, together with everyone at United Agents and Hachette who has poured expertise into it – not least my US editor, Josh Kendall, and UK assistant editor, Lily Cooper, my copy-editor, Susan Opie, and proofreader, Charlotte Webb. Thank you. It has been a privilege and an astonishment.

This novel was also written from within the maelstrom of family life, where my wife, Cat, has managed to juggle her career, our two young children and in excess of a dozen readings of the evolving manuscript – in addition to putting up with me. I simply couldn't have done it without her, or without the collective support and belief of our wider family. They've been among my first and most generous readers, together with friends who have helped me keep faith: Anton Irvine, Ziyad Marar, Susha Ireland, Jamie Bartlett.

Jamie occupies a double place on this list, because his non-fiction books *The Dark Net* and *Radicals* are among those that drove me towards this topic – and provided factual fuel for the fiction. The real world is much, much stranger than anything I can come up with, and those who wish to know more should seek out his books, together with the writings of

Carl Miller, Evgeny Morozov, Jaron Lanier, Kevin Mitnick, Mikko Hyppönen, Thomas Rid, and countless other researchers grappling with technology's darker sides.

I'm not going to provide a bibliography, because this is avowedly a work of fiction – and one I have relished writing slantwise to reality, mixing the plausible and fantastical, the historical and the things that simply amuse me. Unlike reality, fiction has an obligation to make sense. But it's allowed to do so on its own terms, and I hope these have here included some wit, hope and illumination. God knows we're in need of all three.

Do you wish this wasn't the end?

Join us at www.hodder.co.uk, or follow us on
Twitter @hodderbooks to be a part of our community
of people who love the very best in books and reading.

Whether you want to discover more about a book
or an author, watch trailers and interviews, have the
chance to win early limited editions, or simply browse
our expert readers' selection of the very best books,
we think you'll find what you're looking for.

And if you don't,
that's the place to tell us what's missing.

We love what we do, and we'd love you to be part of it.

www.hodder.co.uk

@hodderbooks

HodderBooks

HodderBooks